THROUGH THE BREACH

THROUGH THE BREACH

THE

BREACH

DAVID DRAKE

ACE BOOKS, NEW YORK

THROUGH THE BREACH

An Ace Book
Published by The Berkley Publishing Group
200 Madison Avenue, New York, NY 10016

First Edition: April 1995

Library of Congress Cataloging-in-Publication Data

Drake, David.
  Through the breach / David Drake.—1st ed.
    p.   cm.
  ISBN 0-441-00171-8 : $19.95
  I. Title.
PS3554.R196T47 1995   94-25744
813´.54—dc20   CIP

Printed in the United States of America

10   9   8   7   6   5   4   3   2   1

To Allyn Vogel

Most of my friends are smart, competent,
and unfailingly helpful to me when
I need it. Allyn is all those things.
She is also a gentle and genuinely good person,
which puts her in a much smaller category.

THROUGH THE
THE
BREACH

BETAPORT, VENUS

7 Days Before Sailing

"Mister Jeremy Moore," announced the alien slave as he ushered me into the private chamber of the Blue Rose Tavern. The public bar served as a waiting room and hiring hall for the Venus Asteroid Expedition, while General Commander Piet Ricimer used the back room as an office.

I'd heard that the aide now with Ricimer, Stephen Gregg, was a conscienceless killer. My first glimpse of the man was both a relief and a disappointment. Gregg was big, true; but he looked empty, no more dangerous than a suit of ceramic armor waiting for someone to put it on. Blond and pale, Gregg could have been handsome if his features were more animated.

Whereas General Commander Ricimer wasn't . . . *pretty,* say, the way women enough have found me, but the fire in the man's soul gleamed through every atom of his physical person. Ricimer's glance and quick smile were genuinely friendly, while Gregg's more lingering appraisal was . . .

Maybe Stephen Gregg wasn't as empty as I'd first thought.

"Thank you, Guillermo," said Ricimer. "Has Captain Macquerie arrived?"

"Not yet," the slave replied. "I'll alert you when he does." Guillermo's diction was excellent, though his tongueless mouth clipped the sibilant. He closed the door behind him, shutting out the bustle of the public bar.

1

Guillermo was a chitinous biped with a triangular face and a pink sash-of-office worn bandolier fashion over one shoulder. I'd never been so close to a Molt slave before. There weren't many in the Solar System and fewer still on Venus. Their planet of origin was unknown, but their present province was the entire region of space mankind had colonized before the Collapse.

Molts remained and prospered on worlds from which men had vanished. Now, with man's return to the stars, the aliens' racial memory made them additionally valuable: Molts could operate the pre-Collapse machinery which survived on some outworlds.

"Well, Mister Moore," Ricimer said. "What are your qualifications for the Asteroid Expedition?"

"Well, I've not myself been involved in off-planet trade, sir," I said, trying to look earnest and superior, "but I'm a gentleman, you see, and thus an asset to any proposal. My father—may he continue well—is Moore of Rhadicund. Ah—"

The two spacemen watched me: Ricimer with amusement, Gregg with no amusement at all. I didn't understand their coolness. I'd thought this was the way to build rapport, since Gregg was a gentleman also, member of a factorial family, and Ricimer at least claimed the status.

"Ah . . ." I repeated. Carefully, because the subject could easily become a can of worms, I went on, "I've been a member of the household of Councilor Duneen—chief advisor to the Governor of the Free State of Venus."

"We know who Councilor Duneen is, Mister Moore," Ricimer said dryly. "We'd probably know of him even if he weren't a major backer of the expedition."

The walls of the room were covered to shoulder height in tilework. The color blurred upward from near black at floor level to smoky gray shot with wisps of silver. The ceiling and upper walls were coated with beige sealant that might well date from the tavern's construction.

The table behind which Ricimer and Gregg sat—they hadn't offered me a chair—was probably part of the tavern furnishings. The communications console in a back corner was brand-new. The ceramic chassis marked the console as of Venerian manufacture, since an off-planet unit would have been made of metal or organic resin instead, but its electronics were built from chips stockpiled on distant worlds where automated factories continued to produce even after the human colonies perished.

Very probably, Piet Ricimer himself had brought those chips to Venus on an earlier voyage. Earth, with a population of twenty millions after the Collapse, had returned to space earlier than tiny Venus. Now that all planets outside the Solar System were claimed by the largest pair of ramshackle Terran states, the North American Federation and the Southern Cross, other men traded beyond Pluto only with one hand on their guns.

Piet Ricimer and his cohorts had kept both hands on their guns, and they traded very well indeed. Whatever the cover story—Venus and the Federation weren't technically at war—the present expedition wasn't headed for the Asteroid Belt to bring back metals that Venus had learned to do without during the Collapse.

I changed tack. I'd prepared for this interview by trading my floridly expensive best suit for clothing of more sober cut and material, though I'd have stayed with the former's purple silk plush and gold lace if the garments had fit my spare frame just a little better. The suit had been a gift from a friend whose husband was much more portly, and there's a limit to what alterations can accomplish.

"I believe it's the duty of every man on Venus," I said loudly, "to expand our planet's trade beyond the orbit of Pluto. We owe this to Venus and to God. The duty is particularly upon those like the three of us who are members of factorial families."

I struck the defiant pose of a man ashamed of the strength of his principles. I'd polished the expression over years of explaining—to women—why honor forbade me to accept money from my father, the factor. In truth, the little factory of Rhadicund in Beta Regio had been abandoned three generations before, and the family certainly hadn't prospered in the governor's court the way my grandfather had hoped.

Piet Ricimer's face stilled. It took me a moment to realize how serious a mistake I'd made in falsely claiming an opinion which Ricimer felt as strongly as he hoped for salvation.

Stephen Gregg stretched his arm out on the table before Ricimer, interposing himself between his friend and a problem that the friend needn't deal with. Gregg wasn't angry. Perhaps Gregg no longer had the capacity for anger or any other human emotion.

"About the manner of your leaving Councilor Duneen's service, Moore," Gregg said. He spoke quietly, his voice cat-playful. "A problem with the accounts, was there?"

I met the bigger man's eyes. What I saw there shocked me out of all my poses, my calculations. "My worst enemies have never denied that their purse would be safe in my keeping," I said flatly. "There was a misunderstanding about a woman of the household. As a gentleman—"

My normal attitudes were reasserting themselves. I couldn't help it.

"—I can say no more."

The Molt's three-fingered hand tapped on the door. "Captain Macquerie has arrived, sir."

"You have no business here, Mister Jeremy Moore," Gregg said. He rose to his feet. Gregg moved with a slight stiffness which suggested that more than his soul had been scarred beyond Pluto; but surely his soul as well. "There'll be no women where we're going. While there may be opportunities for wealth, it won't be what one would call easy money."

"Good luck in your further occupations, Mister Moore," Ricimer said. "Guillermo, please show in Captain Macquerie."

Ricimer and his aide were no more than my own age, 27 Earth years. In this moment they seemed to be from a different generation.

"Good day, gentlemen," I said. I bowed and stepped quickly from the room as a squat fellow wearing coveralls and a striped neckerchief entered. Macquerie moved with the gimballed grace of a spacer who expects the deck to shift beneath him at any moment.

I knew that arguing with Ricimer and Gregg wouldn't have gained me anything. I knew also that Mister Stephen Gregg would *literally* just as soon kill me as look at me.

There were more than thirty men in the tavern's public room—and one woman, a spacer's wife engaged in a low-voiced but obviously acrimonious attempt to drag her husband away. The noise of the crowd blurred whenever the outer door opened onto Dock Street and its heavy traffic.

I pushed my way to one corner of the bar, my progress aided somewhat by the fact I was a gentleman— but only somewhat. Betaport was more egalitarian than Ishtar City, the capital; and spacers are a rough lot anywhere.

The tapster drew beer and took payment with an efficiency that seemed more fluid than mechanical. His eyes were sleepy, but the fashion in which he chalked a tab or held out his free hand in a silent demand for scrip before he offered the glass showed he was fully aware of his surroundings.

I opened my purse and took out the 10-Mapleleaf coin. That left me only twenty Venerian consols to live on for the next week, but I'd find a way. Eloise, I supposed. I hadn't planned to see her again after the problem with her maid, but she'd come around.

"Barman," I said crisply. "I want the unrestricted use of your phone, immediately and for the whole of the afternoon."

I rang the coin on the rippling blue translucence of the bar's ceramic surface.

The barman's expression sharpened into focus. He took the edges of the coin between the thumb and index fingers of his right hand, turning it to view both sides. "Where'd *you* get Fed money?" he demanded.

"Gambling with an in-system trader on the New Troy run," I said truthfully. "Now, if you don't want the coin . . ."

That was a bluff—I needed this particular phone for what I intended to do.

The tapster shrugged. He had neither cause nor intention to refuse, merely a general distaste for strangers; and perhaps for gentlemen as well. He flipped up the gate in the bar so that I could slip through to the one-piece phone against the wall.

"It's local net only," the tapster warned. "I'm not connected to the planetary grid."

"Local's what I want," I said.

Very local indeed. The tool kit on my belt looked like a merchant's papersafe. I took from it a device of my own design and construction.

The poker game three weeks before had been with a merchant/captain and three of his officers, in a sailors' tavern in Ishtar City. The four spacers were using a marked deck. If I'd complained or even tried to leave the game, they would have beaten me within an inch of my life.

The would-be sharpers had thought I was wealthy and a fool; and were wrong on both counts. They let me win for the first two hours. The money I'd lived on since the game came from that pump priming. Much of it was in Federation coin.

The captain and his henchmen ran the betting up and cold-decked me, their pigeon. I weepingly threw down a huge roll of Venerian scrip and staggered out of the tavern. I'd left Ishtar City for Betaport before the spacers realized that I'd paid them in counterfeit—and except for the top bill, very poor counterfeit.

I attached to the phone module's speaker a contact transducer which fed a separate keypad and an earpiece. The tapster looked at me and said, "Hey! What d'ye think you're doing?"

"What I paid you for the right to do," I said. I pivoted deliberately so that my body blocked the tapster's view of what I was typing on the keypad—not that it would have meant anything to the fellow.

On my third attempt at the combination, the plug in my ear said in Piet Ricimer's voice, " . . . not just as a Venerian patriot, Captain Macquerie. All *mankind* needs you."

The communications console in the private room was patched into the tavern's existing phone line. The commands I sent through the line converted Ricimer's own electronics into a listening device. I could have accessed the console from anywhere in Betaport, but not as quickly as I needed to hear the interview with Macquerie.

"Look, Captain Ricimer," said an unfamiliar voice that must by elimination be Macquerie, "I'm flattered that you'd call for me the way you have, but I gave up voyaging to the Reaches when I married the daughter of my supplier on Os Sertoes. Long runs are no life for a married man. From here on out, I'm shuttling my *Bahía* between Betaport and Buenos Aires."

"We mean no harm to the Southern Cross," said Stephen Gregg. "Your wife's family won't be affected."

With Macquerie, there was obviously no pretense that the expedition had anything to do with asteroids. Os Sertoes was little more than a name to me. I vaguely thought that it was one of the most distant Southern colonies, uninteresting and without exports of any particular value.

"Look," said Macquerie, "you gentlemen've been to the Reaches yourself. You don't need me to pilot you—except to Os Sertoes, and who'd want to go there? It's stuffed right in the neck of the Breach, so the transit gradients won't let you go anywhere but back."

"Captain," said Ricimer, "I wouldn't ask you if I didn't believe I needed you. Venus *must* take her place in the greater universe. If most of the wealth of the outworlds continues to funnel into the Federation, President Pleyal will use it to impose his will on all men. Whether Pleyal succeeds or fails, the attempt will lead to a second Collapse—one from which there'll be no returning. The Lord can't want that, nor can any man who fears Him."

A chair scraped. "I'm sorry, gentlemen," Macquerie said. His voice was subdued, but firm. Ricimer's enthusiasm had touched but not won the man. "If you really need a pilot for the Reaches, well—you can pick one up on Punta Verde or Decades. But not me."

The door opened at the corner of my eye. The Molt standing there stepped aside as noise from the public bar boomed through the pickup on my earpiece. Captain Macquerie strode past, his face forming into a scowl of concern as he left the Blue Rose.

"No one just yet, Guillermo," called Piet Ricimer, his words slightly out of synchrony as they reached my ears through different media.

The door closed.

"I could bring him along, you know," Gregg said calmly in the relative silence.

"No," said Ricimer. "We won't use force against our own citizens, Stephen."

"Then you'll have to feel your way into the Breach without help," Gregg said. "You know we won't find a pilot for Os Sertoes at any of the probable stopovers. There's not that much trade to the place."

"Captain Macquerie may change his mind, Stephen," Ricimer replied. "There's still a week before we lift."

"He won't," snapped Gregg. "He feels guilty, sure; but he's not going to give up all he has on a mad risk. And if he doesn't—what? The Lord will provide?"

"Yes, Stephen," said Piet Ricimer. "I rather think He will. Though perhaps not for us as individuals, I'll admit."

In a brighter, apparently careless voice, Ricimer went on, "Now, Guillermo has the three bidders for dried rations waiting outside. Shall we—"

I quickly disconnected my listening device and slipped from behind the bar, keeping low. If Ricimer—or worse, Gregg—saw me through the open door, they might wonder why I'd stayed in the tavern after they dismissed me.

"Hey!" called the barman to my back. "What is it you think you're doing, anyway?"

I only wished I knew the answer myself.

BETAPORT, VENUS

6 Days Before Sailing

The brimstone smell of Venus's atmosphere clung to the starships' ceramic hulls.

Betaport's storage dock held over a hundred vessels, ranging in size from featherboats of under 20 tonnes to a bulk freighter of nearly 150. The latter vessel was as large as Betaport's domed transfer docks on the surface could accommodate for landings and launches.

Many of the ships were laid up, awaiting parts or consignment to the breakers' yard, but four vessels at one end of the cavernous dock bustled with the imminence of departure. The cylindrical hulls of two were already on roller-equipped cradles so that tractors could drag them to the transfer docks.

I eyed the vessels morosely, knowing there was nothing in the sight to help me make up my mind. I'd familiarized myself with the vessels' statistics, but I wasn't a spacer whose technical expertise could judge the risks of an expedition by viewing the ships detailed for it.

I supposed as much as anything I was forcing myself to think about what I intended to do. I rubbed my palms together with the fingers splayed and out of contact.

A lowboy rumbled slowly past. It was carrying cannon to the expedition's flagship, the 100-tonne *Porcelain*. The hull of Ricimer's vessel gleamed white, unstained by the sulphur compounds which would bake on at first exposure to the Venerian atmosphere. She was brand-new, purpose-built for distant exploration. Her frames and hull plating were of unusual thickness for her burden.

9

The four 15-cm plasma cannon on the lowboy were heavy guns for a 100-tonne vessel, and the Long Tom which pivoted to fire through any of five ports in the bow was a still-larger 17-cm weapon. The *Porcelain*'s hull could take the shock of the cannons' powerful thermonuclear explosions, but the guns' bulk filled much of the ship's internal volume. The most casual observer could see that the *Porcelain* wasn't fitting out for a normal trading voyage.

I ambled along the quay. Pillars of living rock supported the ceiling of the storage dock, but the huge volume wasn't subdivided by bulkheads. The sounds of men, machinery, and the working of the planetary mantle merged as a low-frequency hum that buffered me from my surroundings.

The *Absalom 231* was a cargo hulk: a ceramic box with a carrying capacity as great as that of the flagship. She was already in a transport cradle. Food and drink for the expedition filled the vessel's single cavernous hold. Lightly and cheaply built, the *Absalom 231* could be stripped and abandoned when the supplies aboard her were exhausted.

The expedition's personnel complement was set at a hundred and eighty men. I wondered how many of them, like the hulk, would be used up on the voyage.

A bowser circled on the quay, heading back to the water point. Its huge tank had filled the *Porcelain* with reaction mass. I moved closer to the vessels to avoid the big ground vehicle. I walked on.

The *Kinsolving* was a sharp-looking vessel of 80 tonnes. A combination of sailors and ground crew were loading sections of three knocked-down featherboats into her central bay. Though equipped with star drive, a 15-tonne featherboat's cramped quarters made it a hellish prison on a long voyage. The little vessels were ideal for short-range exploration from a central base, and they were far handier in an atmosphere than ships of greater size.

What would it be like to stand on a world other than Venus? The open volume of the Betaport storage dock made me uncomfortable. What would it be like to walk under an open sky?

Why in God's name was I thinking of doing this?

The last of the expedition's four vessels was the 80-tonne *Mizpah,* also in a transport cradle. She was much older than the *Porcelain* and the *Kinsolving.* Clearly—even to a layman like me—the *Mizpah* wasn't in peak condition.

The *Mizpah*'s main lock and boarding ramp amidships couldn't be used because of the transport cradle, but her personnel hatch forward stood open. On the hatch's inner surface, safe from reentry friction and corrosive atmospheres, were the painted blazons of her co-owners: the pearl roundel of Governor Halys, and the bright orange banderol—the oriflamme—of Councilor Frederic Duneen.

The *Mizpah* wasn't an impressive ship in many ways, but she brought with her the overt support of the two most important investors on the planet. If nothing else, the *Mizpah*'s participation meant the survivors wouldn't be hanged as pirates when they returned to Venus.

If anyone survived. When I eavesdropped on the private discussion between Ricimer and Gregg, I'd heard enough to frighten off anyone sane.

Thomas Hawtry—Factor Hawtry of Hawtry—stepped from the *Mizpah*'s personnel hatch. Two generations before, Hawtry had been a name to reckon with. Thomas, active and ambitious to a fault, had mortgaged what remained of the estate in an attempt to recoup his family's influence by attaching himself to the great of the present day.

He was a man I wanted to meet as little as I did any human being on Venus.

Hawtry was large and floridly handsome, dressed now in a tunic of electric blue with silver lamé trousers and calf-high boots to match the tunic. On his collar was a tiny oriflamme to indicate his membership in Councilor Duneen's household.

Hawtry's belt and holster were plated. The pistol was for show, but I didn't doubt that it was functional nonetheless.

"Moore!" Hawtry cried, framed by the hatch coaming two paces away. Hawtry's face was blank for an instant as the brain worked behind it. The Factor of Hawtry was a thorough politician; though not, in my opinion, subtle enough to be a very effective one.

"Jeremy!" Hawtry decided aloud, reforming his visage in a smile. "Say, I haven't had an opportunity to thank you for the way you covered me in the little awkwardness with Lady Melinda."

He stepped close and punched me playfully on the shoulder, a pair of ladies' men sharing a risque memory. "Could have been *ve*-ry difficult for me. Say, I told my steward to pass you a little something to take the sting out. Did he . . . ?"

Lady Melinda was an attractive widow of 29 who lived with her brother—Councilor Duneen. Hawtry'd thought to use me as his go-between in the lady's seduction. I, on the other hand—

I would never have claimed I was perfect, but I liked women too much to lure one into the clutches of Thomas Hawtry. And as it turned out, I liked the Lady Melinda a great deal more than was sensible for a destitute member of the lesser gentry.

"Regrettably, I *didn't* hear from your steward, Thom," I said. No point in missing a target of opportunity. "And you know, I'm feeling a bit of a pinch right now. If—"

Not much of a target. "Aren't we all, Jeremy, aren't we all!" Hawtry boomed. "After I bring my expedition back, though, *all* my friends will live like kings! Say, you know about the so-called 'asteroids expedition,' don't you?"

He waved an arm toward the docked ships. A hydraulic pump began to squeal as it shifted the *Absalom 231* in its cradle.

"Captain Ricimer's . . ." I said, hiding my puzzlement.

"*And* mine," said Hawtry, tapping himself on the breast significantly. "I'm co-leader, though we're keeping it quiet for the time being. A very political matter, someone of my stature in charge of a voyage like this."

Hawtry linked his arm familiarly with mine and began pacing back along the line of expedition vessels. His friendliness wasn't sincere. In the ten months I knew Hawtry intimately in the Duneen household, the man had

never been sincere about anything except his ambition and
his self-love.

But neither did Hawtry seem to be dissembling the hatred
I'd expected. Irritated at his go-between's lack of progress
and very drunk, Hawtry had forced the Lady Melinda's
door on a night when her brother was out of the house.
The racket brought the servants to the scene in numbers.

I, the gentleman who *was* sharing the lady's bed that
night, escaped in the confusion—but my presence hadn't
gone unremarked. The greater scandal saved Hawtry from
the consequences of his brutal folly, but I scarcely expected
the fellow to feel grateful. Apparently Hawtry's embarrassment was so great that he'd recast the incident completely
in his own mind.

"I'm going to take the war to the Federation," Hawtry
said, speaking loudly to be heard over the noise in the storage dock. He accompanied the words with broad gestures
of his free hand. "And it *is* a war, you know. Nothing less
than that!"

A dozen common sailors examined the *Porcelain*'s hull
and thruster nozzles, shouting comments to one another.
The men weren't on duty; several of them carried liquor
bottles in pockets of their loose garments. They might
simply be spectators. Ricimer's flagship was an unusual
vessel, and the expedition had been the only subject of
conversation in Betaport for a standard month.

"Asteroids!" Hawtry snorted. "The Feds bring their
microchips and pre-Collapse artifacts into the system in
powerful convoys, Jeremy . . . but *I'm* going to hit them
where they aren't prepared for it. They don't defend the
ports on the other side of the Mirror where the wealth
is gathered. I'll go through the Breach and take them
unawares!"

Hawtry wasn't drunk, and he didn't have a hidden reason to blurt this secret plan. Because I was a gentleman
of sorts and an acquaintance, I was someone for Hawtry
to brag to; it was as simple as that.

Of course, the proposal was so unlikely that I would
have discounted it completely if I hadn't heard Ricimer
and Gregg discussing the same thing.

"I didn't think it was practical to transit the Breach," I said truthfully. "Landolph got through with only one ship of seven, and nobody has succeeded again in the past eighty years. It's simpler to voyage the long way, even though that's a year and a half either way."

Interstellar travel involved slipping from the sidereal universe into other bubbles of sponge space where the constants for matter and energy differed. Because a vessel which crossed a dimensional membrane retained its relative motion, acceleration under varied constants translated into great changes in speed and distance when the vessel returned to the human universe.

No other bubble universe was habitable or even contained matter as humans understood the term. The sidereal universe itself had partially mitosed during the process of creation, however, and it was along that boundary—the Mirror—that the most valuable pre-Collapse remains were to be found.

Populations across the Mirror had still been small when the Revolt smashed the delicate fabric of civilization. Often a colony's death throes weren't massive enough to complete the destruction of the automated factories, as had happened on the larger outworlds and in the Solar System itself.

For the most part the Mirror was permeable only to objects of less than about a hundred kilograms. Three generations before, Landolph had found a point at which it was possible to transit the Mirror through sponge space.

Landolph's Breach wasn't of practical value, since energy gradients between the bubble universes were higher than ships could easily withstand. Perhaps it had been different for navigators of the civilization before the Collapse.

"Oh, the Breach," Hawtry said dismissively. "Say, that's a matter for sailors. Our Venus lads can do things that cowards from Earth never dreamed of. If they were real men, they wouldn't kiss the feet of a tyrant like Pleyal!"

"I see," I said in a neutral voice.

I supposed there was truth in what Hawtry said. The ships of today were more rugged than Landolph's, and if half of Captain Ricimer's reputation was founded on fact, he was a sailor like no one born to woman before him. But the notion that a snap of the fingers would send a squadron through the Breach was—

Well, Hawtry's reality testing had always been notable for its absence. His notion of using the Lady Melinda as a shortcut to power, for example . . .

The *Porcelain*'s crew was shifting the first of the plasma cannon from the lowboy. A crane lifted the gun tube onto a trolley in the hold, but from there on the weapon would be manhandled into position.

The *Porcelain*'s ceramic hull was pierced with more than a score of shuttered gunports, but like most vessels she carried only one gun for every four or more ports. The crew would shift the weapons according to need.

"They'll get their use soon!" Hawtry said, eyeing the guns with smirking enthusiasm. "And when I come back, well—it'll be Councilor Hawtry, see if it isn't, Moore. Say, there'll be nothing too good for the leader of the Breach Expedition!"

I felt the way I had the night I let the spacers inveigle me into the crooked card game, where there was a great deal to gain and my life to lose. I said, "I can see that you and Captain Ricimer—"

"Ricimer!" Hawtry snorted. "That man, that artisan's son? Surely you don't think that a project of this magnitude wouldn't have a gentleman as its real head!"

"There's Mister Stephen Gregg, of course," I said judiciously.

"The younger son of a smallholder in the Atalanta Plains!" Hawtry said. "Good God, man! As well have you commander of the expedition as that yokel!"

"I take your point," I said. "Well, I have to get back now, Thom. Need to dress for dinner, you see."

"Yes, say, look me up when I return, Moore," Hawtry said. "I'll be expanding my household, and I shouldn't wonder that I'd have a place for a clever bugger like you."

Hawtry turned and stared at the ships which he claimed to command. He stood arms akimbo and with his feet spread wide, a bold and possessive posture.

I walked on quickly, more to escape Hawtry than for any need of haste. Dinner was part of Eloise's agenda, though dressing was not. Quite the contrary.

In an odd way, the conversation had helped settle my mind. I wasn't a spacer: I couldn't judge the risks of this expedition.

But I could judge men.

Hawtry was a fool if he thought he could brush aside Piet Ricimer. And if Hawtry thought he could ride rough-shod over Stephen Gregg, he was a dead man.

BETAPORT, VENUS

The Night Before Sailing

Three sailors guarded the city side of Dock 22. Two of the men carried powered cutting bars. The third had stuck forty centimeters of high-pressure tubing under his belt, and a double-barreled shotgun leaned against the wall behind him.

On the other side of the airlock, a tubular personnel bridge stretched to the *Porcelain*'s hatch. Though Dock 22 was closed and the interior had been purged, too much of the hellish Venerian atmosphere leaked past the domed clamshell doors for the dock to be open onto the city proper.

Traffic on Dock Street was sparse at this hour. The airlock guards watched me with mild interest. That turned to sharp concern when they realized that I was guiding directly toward them the drunk I supported. The sailor with the length of tubing closed the pocket Bible he'd been reading and threw his shoulders back twice to loosen the muscles.

"My name doesn't matter," I said. "But I've an important message for Mister Gregg. I need to see him in person."

"Piss off," said one of the sailors. He touched the trigger of his cutting bar. The ceramic teeth whined a bitter sneer.

"This the *Bahía*?" mumbled the drunk.

I held a flask to the lips of the man draped against me. "Here you go, my friend," I said reassuringly. "We'll be aboard shortly."

17

"Gotta lift ship . . ." the drunk said. He began to cough rackingly.

"I wouldn't mind a sip of that," said one of the guards.

"Shut up, Pinter," said the man with the tubing. "You know better than that."

He turned his attention to me and my charge. "No one boards the *Porcelain* now, sir," he said. "Why don't you and your friend go about your business?"

"This is our business," I said. "Call Mister Gregg. Tell him there's a man here with information necessary to the success of the expedition."

Pinter frowned, leaned forward, and sniffed at the neck of the open flask. "*Hey,* buddy," he said. "What d'ye have in that bottle, anyhow?"

"You wouldn't like the vintage," I said. "Call Mister Gregg now. We need to get this gentleman in a bunk as soon as possible."

The sailor who'd initially ordered me away looked uncertain. "What's going on, Lightbody?" he asked the man with the tubing. "He's a gentleman, isn't he?"

"All right, Pinter," Lightbody said in sudden decision. He gestured to the wired communicator which was built into the personnel bridge. "Call him."

He smiled with a grim sort of humor. "Nobody asks for Mister Gregg because they want to waste his time."

Gregg arrived less than two minutes after the summons. His blue trousers and blue-gray tunic were old and worn. Both garments were of heavy cloth and fitted with many pockets.

Gregg didn't wear a protective suit, though the air that puffed out when he opened the lock was hot and stank of hellfire. He didn't carry a weapon, either; but Stephen Gregg was a weapon.

Sulphurous gases leaking into the personnel bridge had brought tears to Gregg's eyes. He blinked to control them. "Mister Jeremy Moore," he said softly. The catch in his voice might also have been a result of the corrosive atmosphere.

I lifted the face of the man I supported so that the light

fell fully on it. "I'm bringing Captain Macquerie aboard,"
I said. "We're together. I, ah, thought it would be wise
not to trouble the general commander."

"Where's 'a *Bahía*?" Macquerie mumbled. "Gotta lift
tonight . . ."

"Ah," said Gregg. I couldn't see any change in his
expression; the three common sailors, who knew Gregg
better, visibly relaxed. "Yes, that was good of you. Piet's
resting now. The two of us can get our pilot aboard quietly,
I think."

He lifted the shanghaied captain out of my grip. "Piet's
too good a man for this existence, I sometimes think. But
he's got friends."

Gregg cycled the airlock open. The inner chamber was
large enough to hold six men in hard suits. He paused.
"Lightbody? Pinter and Davies, all of you. You did well
here, but don't report the—arrival—until after we've lifted
in the morning. Do you understand?"

"Whatever you say, Mister Gregg," Lightbody replied;
the other two sailors nodded agreement. The men treated
Gregg with respect due to affection, but they were also
quite clearly afraid of him.

As the airlock's outer door closed behind us, Gregg
looked over the head of the slumping Macquerie and said,
"You say you want to come with us, Moore. I'd rather
pay you. I've got more money than I know what to do
with, now."

The inner door undogged and began to open even as
the outer panel latched. The atmosphere of the personnel
bridge struck me like the heart of a furnace.

The bridge was a 3-meter tube of flexible material,
stiffened by a helix of glass fiber which also acted as a
light guide. The reinforcement was a green spiral spinning dizzily outward until the arc of the sagging bridge
began to rise again. A meter-wide floor provided a flat
walkway.

I sneezed violently. My nose began to run. I rubbed it
angrily with the back of my hand.

"I'll come, thank you," I said. My voice was already
hoarse from the harshness of the air. "I'll find my own

wealth in the Reaches, where you found yours."

"Oh, you're a smart one, aren't you?" Gregg said harshly. "You think you know where we're really going . . . and
perhaps you do, Mister Moore, perhaps you do. But you
don't know what it is that the Reaches cost. Take the
money. I'll give you three hundred Mapleleaf dollars for
this night's work."

The big man paced himself to walk along the bridge
beside me. The walkway was barely wide enough for two,
but Gregg held Macquerie out to the side where the tube's
bulge provided room.

"I'm not afraid," I said. I was terribly afraid. The personnel bridge quivered sickeningly underfoot, and the air
that filled it was a foretaste of Hell. "I'm a gentleman of
Venus. I'll willing to take risks to liberate the outworlds
from President Pleyal's tyranny!"

The effect of my words was like triggering a detonator.
Stephen Gregg turned *fast* and gripped me by the throat
with his free left hand. He lifted me and slammed me
against the side of the bridge.

"I wasn't much for social graces even before I shipped
out to the Reaches for the first time," Gregg said softly.
"And I never liked worms taking me for a fool."

The wall of the bridge seared my back through the
clothing. The spiral of reinforcing fiber felt like a white
slash against the general scarlet pain.

Macquerie, somnolent from the drugged liquor, dangled
limply from Gregg's right arm. "Now," Gregg said in the
same quiet, terrible voice. "This expedition is important
to my friend Piet, do you understand? Perhaps to Venus,
perhaps to mankind, perhaps to God—but certainly to my
friend."

I nodded. I wasn't sure I could speak. Gregg wasn't
deliberately choking me, but the grip required to keep my
feet above the walkway also cut off most of my air.

"I don't especially want to kill you right now," Gregg
continued. "But I certainly feel no need to let you live.
Why do you insist on coming with us, Mister Moore?"

"You can let me down now," I croaked.

The words were an inaudible rasp. Gregg either read my

lips or took the meaning from my expression. He lowered me to the walkway and released me.

I shrugged my shoulders. I didn't reach up to rub my throat. I am a gentleman!

"I—" I said. I paused, not because I was afraid to go on, but because I'd never articulated the reason driving me. Not even to myself, in the dead of night.

"I have a talent for electronics," I continued. I fought the need to blink, lest Gregg think I was afraid to meet his gaze. "I couldn't work at that, of course. Only artisans work with their hands. And there was no money; the Moores have never really had money."

"Go on," Gregg said. He wiped the palm of his left hand on the breast of his tunic.

"So I've had to find ways to live," I continued, "and I've done so. Mostly women. And the problem with that is that when I found a woman I really cared about—there was no place the relationship could go except the way they've all gone, to bed and then nowhere. Because there's no me! Doesn't that make you want to laugh, Mister Gregg?"

"I'm not judging you, Moore," Gregg said. He shifted Macquerie, not for his own comfort but for that of the snoring captain. Gregg's effortless strength would have been the most striking thing about him, were it not for his eyes.

"I'm twenty-seven," I said. My bitterness surprised me. "I want to put myself in a place where I *have* to play the man. I pretended it was the money that was pulling me, but that was a lie. A lie for myself."

"Let's walk on," Gregg said, suiting his action to his words. "The air in this tube isn't the worst I've breathed, but that's not a reason to hang around out here either."

I managed a half smile as I fell into step beside the bigger man. Now I massaged the bruises on my throat.

"You don't have to play the man when you're out beyond Pluto, Moore," Gregg said reflectively. "You can become a beast—or die. Plenty do. But if you're determined to come, I won't stop you."

He looked over his shoulder at me. His expression could be called a smile. "Besides, you might be useful."

The *Porcelain*'s airlock was directly ahead of us. I dropped back a step to let Gregg open the hatch.

I thought about the cold emptiness of Stephen Gregg's eyes. I had an idea now what Gregg meant when he spoke of what the Reaches cost.

VENUS ORBIT

Day 1

I'd never been weightless before. My stomach was already queasy from the shaking the *Porcelain* took from the 500 kph winds of the upper Venerian atmosphere. I hadn't eaten since early the night before, but I wasn't sure that would keep me from spewing yellow bile across the men working nonchalantly around me.

I clung to the tubular railing around the attitude-control console. The starship's three navigational consoles were in the extreme bow; the heavy plasma cannon was shipped in traveling position between the consoles and the attitude controls.

Guillermo was at the right-hand console. Ricimer, Hawtry, and the vessel's navigator, Salomon, stood behind the Molt, discussing the course.

"We need to blood the force, *blood* it," Hawtry said. He was the only member of the group speaking loudly enough for me to hear.

Hawtry wore a rubidium-plated revolver and the silver brassard which identified him as an officer in the Governor's Squadron. He had at least enough naval experience to keep his place without clutching desperately at a support the way I did.

A sailor carrying a tool kit slid along the axis of the ship, dabbing effortlessly at stanchions for control. "Careful, sir!" he warned in a bored voice before he batted my legs—which had drifted upward—out of his way.

Because the sailor balanced his motion by swinging the heavy tools, his course didn't change. My feet hit the shell locker and rebounded in a wild arc.

Stephen Gregg stood in the center of the three-faced attitude-control console. He reached out a long arm over Lightbody, reading placidly in one of the bays, caught my ankle, and tugged. I released my own grip and thumped to the deck beside Gregg.

Gregg's right boot was thrust under one of three 20-cm staples in the deck. I hooked my toes through both of the others. My hands hurt from the force with which I'd been holding on since liftoff.

"Want to go home now, Moore?" Gregg asked dryly.

"Would it matter if I did?" I said. The spacer who'd pushed past me was working on the Long Tom's traversing mechanism. A hydraulic fitting spit tiny iridescent drops which would shortly settle and spread over the *Porcelain*'s inner bulkheads.

"Not in the least," said Gregg. His voice was calm, but his head turned as he spoke and his gaze rippled across everything, *every*thing in his field of view.

"Then I'm happy where I am," I said. I glanced, then stared, at the controls around me. "These are fully automated units," I said in surprise. "Is that normal?"

"It will be," Gregg said, "if Piet has his way—and if we start bringing back enough chips from the outworlds to make the price more attractive than paying sailors to do the work."

"What we *should* be doing," I said bitterly, "is setting up large-scale microchip production ourselves."

Gregg looked at me. "Perhaps," he said. "But that's a long-term proposition. For now it's cheaper to use the stockpiles—and the operating factories, there are some— on the outworlds. And it's important that men return to the stars, too, Piet thinks."

In a normal starship installation, there was a three-man console for each band of attitude jets—up to six bands in a particularly large vessel. The crewmen fired the jets on command to change the ship's heading and attitude, while the main thrusters, plasma motors, supplied power for propulsion.

On the *Porcelain,* a separate artificial intelligence controlled the jets. The AI's direction was both faster and more subtle than that of even the best-trained crew—but spacers are conservative men, those who survive, and they tend to confuse purpose-built attitude AIs with attitude control through the main navigational unit.

The latter could be rough because the equipment wasn't configured for the purpose. Even so, I believed machine control was better nine times out of ten than anything humans could manage.

"You do know something about electronics, then," Gregg said, though he wasn't looking at me when he spoke.

"Do people often lie to you?" I snapped.

"Not often, no," the bigger man agreed, unperturbed.

"Usually there's an officer to command each control bank," Gregg continued mildly. "Here, I'm just to keep the crew from being bothered by—gentlemen who feel a need to give orders. Lightbody, Jeude, Dole."

The sailors looked up as Gregg called their names.

"Dole's our bosun," Gregg said. "These three have been with Piet since before I met him, when he had a little intrasystem trader. He put them on the controls because they can be trusted not to get in the way of the electronics."

Jeude, a baby-faced man (and he certainly wasn't very old to begin with), wore a blue-and-white striped stocking cap. He doffed it in an ironic salute.

"Boys, meet Mister Jeremy Moore," Gregg went on. "I think you'll find him a resourceful gentleman."

"A friend of yours, Mister Gregg?" Jeude asked.

Gregg snorted. Instead of answering the question, he said, "Do you have any friends, Moore?"

"A few women, I suppose," I said. "Not like he means, no."

My guts no longer roiled, but they'd knotted themselves tightly in my lower abdomen. I focused my eyes on the viewscreen above the navigational console. Half the field was bright with stars, two of which were circled with blue overlays. A three-quarter view of Venus, opalescent with the dense, bubbling atmosphere, filled the rest of the screen.

"That's a very high resolution unit," I said aloud. "I'm amazed at the clarity."

"Piet doesn't skimp on the tools he needs," Gregg said. "It's a perfect view of the hell that wraps the world that bore us, that's certainly true."

He paused, staring at the lustrous, lethal surface of gas. "Does your family have records from the Collapse, Moore?" he asked.

"No," I said, "no. My grandfather sold the factory ninety years ago and moved to Ishtar City. If there were any records, they were lost then."

"My family does," Gregg said. "The histories say it was the atmosphere that protected Venus during the Revolt, you know. Outworld raiders knew that our defenses wouldn't stop them, but they couldn't escape our winds. The Hadley Cells take control from any unfamiliar pilot and fling his ship as apt as not into the ground. The raiders learned to hit softer targets that only *men* protected."

"Isn't it true, then?" I said, responding to the bitterness in Gregg's voice. "That's how I'd already heard it."

"Oh, the atmosphere saved us from the rebels, that much was true," Gregg said. "But when the histories go on, 'Many died because off-planet trade was disrupted . . . ' *That's* not the same as reading your own ancestors' chronicle of those days. Venus produced twenty percent of its own food before the Collapse. Afterwards, well, the food supply couldn't expand that fast, so the population dropped. Since the distribution system was disrupted also, the drop was closer to nine in ten than eight in ten."

"We're past that now," I said. "That was a thousand years ago. A thousand *Earth* years."

A third spark in a blue highlight snapped into place on the star chart. "The *Kinsolving,*" said Dole, ostensibly to the sailors to either side of him at the console. "And about fucking time."

Lightbody sniffed.

Piet Ricimer raised a handset and began speaking into it, his eyes fixed on a separate navigational tank beneath the viewscreen.

"Bet they just now got around to turning on their locator

beacon," Jeude said. "Though they'll claim it was equipment failure."

"Right," said Gregg, his eyes so fixedly on the pearly orb of Venus that they drew my gaze with them. "At Eryx, that's the family seat, there was a pilot hydroponics farm. They figured what the yield would support and drew lots for those who could enter the section of the factory where the farm was."

Gregg's face lost all expression. "The others . . ." he continued. "Some of the others tried to break into the farm and get their share of the food. My ancestor's younger brother led a team of volunteers that held off the mob as long as they could. When they were out of ammunition, they checked the door seals and then blew the roof of their own tunnel open to the surface. That's what the atmosphere of Venus means to me."

"It was worse on Earth," I said. "When the centralized production plants were disrupted, only one person in a thousand survived. There were billions of people on Earth before the Revolt, but they almost all died."

Gregg rubbed his face hard with both hands, as if he were massaging life back into his features. He looked at me and smiled. "As you say, a thousand years," he said. "But in all that time, the Greggs of Eryx have always named the second son Stephen. In memory of the brother who didn't leave descendants."

"That was the past," I said. "There's enough in the future to worry about."

"You'll get along well with Piet," Gregg said. His voice was half-mocking, but only half. "You're right, of course. I shouldn't think about the past the way I do."

It occurred to me that Gregg wasn't only referring to the early history of Eryx Hold.

The bisected viewscreen above Ricimer shivered into three parts, each the face of a ship's captain: Blakey of the *Mizpah;* Winter of the *Kinsolving;* and Moschelitz, the bovine man who oversaw *Absalom 231*'s six crewmen and automated systems.

Blakey's features had a glassy, simplified sheen which I diagnosed as a result of the *Mizpah*'s transmission being

static-laden to the point of unintelligibility. The AI controlling the *Porcelain*'s first-rate electronics processed both
the audio and visual portions of the signal into a false
clarity. The image of Blakey's black-mustached face was
in effect the icon of a virtual reality.

Ricimer raised the handset again. Guillermo switched a
setting on the control console. The Molt's wrists couldn't
rotate, but each limb had two more offset joints than a
human's, permitting the alien the same range of movement.

"Gentlemen," Ricimer said. "Fellow venturers. You're
all brave men, or you wouldn't have joined me, and all
God-fearing and patriots or I wouldn't have chosen you."

The general commander's words boomed through the
tannoy in the ceiling above the attitude-control console;
muted echoes rustled through the open hatchways to compartments farther aft. No doubt the transmission was being
piped through the other vessels as well, though I wondered
whether anybody aboard the *Mizpah* would be able to
understand the words over the static.

"I regret," Ricimer continued, "that I could not tell you
all our real destination before we lifted off, though I don't
suppose many of you—or many of President Pleyal's
spies—will have thought we were setting out for the
asteroids. The first stop on our mission to free Venus
and mankind from Federation tyranny will be Decades."

"We'll make men out of you there!" Hawtry said in
guttural glee. The pickup on Ricimer's handset was either
highly directional or keyed to his voice alone. Not a whisper of Hawtry's words was broadcast.

"A Fed watering station six days out," Jeude said, speaking to me. As an obvious landsman, I was a perfect recipi-
ent for the sort of information that every specialist loves
to retail.

"They wouldn't need a landfall so close if their ships
were better found," Dole put in. "Fed ships leak like
sieves."

On the screen, Captain Winter's lips formed an angry
protest which I thought contained the word " . . . piracy?"

This was Ricimer's moment; the equipment Guillermo controlled brooked no interruption. Blakey tugged at his mustache worriedly—he looked to be a man who would worry about the color of his socks in the morning—while Moschelitz couldn't have been more stolid in his sleep.

"Our endeavors, with the help of the Lord," Ricimer continued, "will decide the fate of Venus and of mankind." He seemed to grow as he spoke, or—it was as if Piet Ricimer were the only spot of color in existence. His enthusiasm, his *belief,* turned everything around him gray.

"We must be resolute," he said. His eyes swept those of us watching him in the flagship's bow compartment, but the faces on the viewscreen also stiffened. Though his back was toward the images, Ricimer was looking straight into the camera feeding his transmission.

"I expect the company of every vessel in the expedition to serve God once a day with its prayers," Ricimer said. "Love one another: we are few against the might of tyranny. Preserve your supplies, and make all efforts to keep the squadron together throughout the voyage."

The general commander stared out at his dream for a future in which mankind populated all the universe under God. Even Thomas Hawtry looked muted by the blazing personality of the man beside whom he stood.

"In the name of God, sirs, do your duty!"

ABOVE DECADES

Day 7

The *Porcelain* made nineteen individual transits in the final approach series; that is, she slipped nineteen times in rapid succession from the sidereal universe to another bubble of sponge space and back.

At each transit, as during every transit of the past seven days, my stomach knotted and flapped inside out. I clung to the staple in the attitude-control station, holding a sponge across my open mouth and wishing I were dead. Or perhaps I *was* dead, and this was the Hell to which so many people over the years had consigned me . . .

"Oh, God," I moaned into the sponge. My eyes were shut. "Oh, God, please save me." I hadn't prayed in real earnest since the night I found myself trapped in Melinda's room.

The transit series ended. Only the vibration of the vessel's plasma motors maintaining a normal 1-g acceleration indicated that I wasn't standing on solid ground. I opened my eyes.

A planet, gray beneath a cloud-streaked atmosphere, filled the forward viewscreen. "Most times the Feds've got women on the staff," Jeude was saying as he and his fellows at the console eyed Decades for the first time. "And they aren't all of them *that* hostile."

I released the staple I was holding and rose to my feet. I smiled ruefully at Gregg and said, "I'll get used to it, I suppose."

Gregg's mouth quirked. "For your sake I hope so," he said. "But I haven't, and I've been doing this for some years now."

Besides the ship's officers, the forward compartment was crowded by Hawtry and the nine gentlemen-adventurers who, like him, stood fully equipped with firearms and body armor.

The ceramic chestplates added considerably to the men's bulk and awkwardness. Many of them had personal blazons painted on their armor. Hawtry's own chestplate bore a gryphon, the marking of his house, and on the upper right clamp the oriflamme of the Duneens.

"Now that's navigation!" said Captain—former captain—Macquerie with enthusiasm. "We can orbit without needing to transit again."

It had taken Macquerie a few days to come to terms with his situation, but since then he'd been an asset to the project. Macquerie was too good a sailor not to be pleased with a ship as fine as the *Porcelain* and a commander as famous as Piet Ricimer.

"The *Kinsolving*'s nowhere to be seen," said Salomon as he leaned toward the three-dimensional navigation tank. "As usual. The *Mizpah* can keep station, the *cargo* hulk can keep station, more or less. Winter couldn't find his ass with both hands."

"There they are," Ricimer said mildly. He pointed to something in the tank that I couldn't see from where I stood. It probably wouldn't have meant anything to me anyway. "One, maybe two transits out. It's my fault for not making sure the *Kinsolving*'s equipment was calibrated to the same standards as the rest of ours."

"If the *Absalom* can keep station," Salomon muttered, "so could the *Kinsolving*—if she had a navigator aboard."

"Enough of this nonsense," said Thomas Hawtry. Several of the gentlemen about him looked as green as I felt, but Hawtry was clearly unaffected by the multiple eversions of transit. "We don't need a third vessel anyway. Lay us alongside the *Mizpah*, Ricimer, so that I can go aboard and take charge."

Guillermo looked up from his console. "The cutter should be launched in the next three minutes," he said to Ricimer in his mechanically perfect speech. "Otherwise we'll need to brake now rather than proceeding directly into planetary orbit."

"You'd best get aft to Hold Two, Mister Hawtry," Ricimer said. If he'd reacted to the gentleman's peremptory tone, there was no sign of it in his voice. "The cutter is standing by with two men to ferry you."

Hawtry grunted. "Come along, men," he ordered as he led his fellows shuffling sternward. Watching the sicker-looking of the gentlemen helped to settle my stomach.

"Sure you don't want to go with them?" Gregg said archly. "When they transfer to the *Mizpah,* there won't be any proper gentlemen aboard. Just spacers."

"I'm a proper gentleman," I snapped. "I just have little interest in weapons and no training whatever with them. If you please, I'll stay close to you and Mister Ricimer and do what you direct me."

"Mister Hawtry?" Ricimer called as the last of Hawtry's contingent were ducking through the hatchway to the central compartment. "Please remember: there'll be no fighting if things go as they should. We'll simply march on the base from opposite directions and summon them to surrender."

Hawtry's response was a muted grunt.

Salomon and Macquerie lowered their heads over the navigation tank and murmured to one another. The Molt Guillermo touched a control. His viewscreen split again: the right half retaining the orb of Decades, three-quarters in sunlight, while the left jumped by logarithmic magnifications down onto the planetary surface.

A fenced rectangle enclosed a mixture of green foliage and soil baked to brick by the exhaust of starships landing. In close-up, the natural vegetation beyond the perimeter had the iridescence of oil on water.

There were two ships with bright metal hulls in the landing area, and a scatter of buildings against the opposite fence. The morning sun slanted across the Federation base. Obvious gun towers threw stark, black shadows from the corners and from the center of both long sides.

I licked my lips. I didn't know what I was supposed to do. The *Porcelain* shuddered like a dog drying itself. Lights on the attitude-control panels pulsed in near unison, balancing the shock. The three sailors looked alert but not concerned.

"That's the cutter with Hawtry aboard casting off," Gregg said. He glanced at the bosun. "How long before we begin atmospheric braking, Dole?" he asked.

Dole, a stocky, dark man with a beard trimmed to three centimeters, pursed his lips as he considered the images on the viewscreen. "About two hours, sir," he said.

Jeude, beside him, nodded agreement. "We could go into orbit quicker," he said, "but it'll take them that long to transfer the fine gentlemen to the *Mizpah*—good riddance to them."

"Watch your tongue, Aaron Jeude," the bosun said.

Jeude's smile flashed toward Gregg, taking in me beside the bigger man as well.

"What do we do, Gregg?" I asked. My voice was colorless because of my effort to conceal my fear of the unfamiliar.

"We wait," Gregg said. "Ten minutes before landing, we'll put our equipment on. And then we'll march a klick through what Macquerie says is swamp, even on the relative highlands where the Feds built their base."

"I don't have any equipment," I said. "If you mean weapons."

"We'll find you something," Gregg said. "Never fear." He spoke quietly, but there was a disconcerting lilt to his tone.

Six sailors under Stampfer, the *Porcelain*'s master gunner, bustled around the Long Tom, opening hydraulic valves and locking down the seats attached to the carriage. They were readying the big weapon for action.

"Will there be fighting, then, Gregg?" I asked, sounding even to myself as cool as the sweat trickling down the middle of my back.

"At Decades, I don't know," Gregg said. "Not if they have any sense. But before this voyage is over—yes, Mister Moore. There will be war."

The *Porcelain*'s two cargo holds were on the underside of the vessel, bracketed between the pairs of plasma motors

fore and aft, and the quartet of similar thrusters amidships.
Number Two, the after hold, had been half-emptied when
the cutter launched. Now it was filled by a party of twenty
men waiting for action, and it stank.

"You bloody toad, Easton!" a sailor said to the man
beside him. "That warn't no fart. You've shit yourself!"

My nose agreed. Several of the men had vomited from
tension and atmospheric buffeting as the ship descended,
and we were all of us pretty ripe after a week on shipboard.
I clutched the cutting bar Gregg had handed me from the
arms locker and hoped that I wouldn't be the next to spew
my guts up.

The *Porcelain*'s descent slowed to a near-hover. The
rapid pulsing of her motors doubled into a roar. "Surface
effect!" Gregg said. "Thrust reflected from the ground.
We'll be touching down—"

The big gentleman wore back-and-breast armor—the
torso of a hard suit that doubled as protection from vacuum
and lethal atmospheres—with the helmet locked in place,
though his visor was raised for the moment. In his arms
was a flashgun, a cassegrain laser which would pulse the
entire wattage of the battery in its stock out through a
stubby ceramic barrel. Gregg was shouting, but I needed
cues from his mouth to make out the words.

The last word was probably "soon," but it was lost
in still greater cacophony. The starship touched its port
outrigger, hesitated, and settled fully to the ground with
a crash of parts reaching equilibrium with gravity instead
of thrust.

I relaxed. "Now what?" I asked.

"We wait a few minutes for the ground to cool," Gregg
explained. "There was standing water, so the heat ought
to dissipate pretty quickly. Sufficient heat."

It seemed like ten minutes but was probably two before
a sailor spun the undogging controls at a nod from Gregg.
The hatch, a section of hull the full length of Hold Two,
cammed downward to form a ramp. Through the opening
rushed wan sunshine and a gush of steam evaporated from
the soil by the plasma motors.

It was the first time I'd been on a planet besides Venus.

"Let's go!" boomed Stephen Gregg in the sudden dampening of the hold's echoes. He strode down the ramp, a massive figure in his armor. "Keep close, but form a cordon at the edge of the cleared area."

I tried to stay near Gregg, but a dozen sailors elbowed me aside to exit from the center of the ramp. I realized why when I followed them. Though the hatchway was a full ten meters wide, the starship's plasma motors had raised the ground beneath to oven heat. The center of the ramp, farthest from where the exhaust of stripped ions struck, was the least uncomfortable place to depart the recently-landed vessel.

I stumbled on the lip at the end of the ramp. The surroundings steamed like a suburb of Sheol, and the seared native vegetation gave off a bitter reek.

The foliage beyond the exhaust-burned area was tissue-thin and stiffened with vesicles of gas rather than cellulose. The veins were of saturated color, with reds, blues, and purples predominating. Those hues merged with the general pale yellow of leaf surfaces to create the appearance of gray when viewed from a distance.

I wore a neck scarf. I put it to my mouth and breathed through it. It probably didn't filter any of the sharp poisons from the air, but at least it gave me the illusion that I was doing something useful.

Sailors clumped together at the margin of the ravaged zone instead of spreading out. The forward ramp was lowered also, but men were filtering slowly down it because Hold One was still packed with supplies and equipment.

"Stephen," called the man stepping from the forward ramp. "I'll take the lead, if you'll make sure that no one straggles from the rear of the line."

The speaker wore brilliant, gilded body armor over a tunic with puffed magenta sleeves. The receiver of his repeating rifle was also gold-washed. Because the garb was unfamiliar and the man's face was in shadow, it was by his voice that I identified him as Piet Ricimer.

Gregg broke off in the middle of an order to a pair of grizzled sailors. "Piet, you're not to do this!" he said. "We talked—"

"You talked, Stephen," Ricimer interrupted with the crisp tone of the man who *was* general commander of the expedition. "I said I'd decide when the time came. Shall we proceed?"

Forty-odd men of the *Porcelain*'s complement of eighty now milled in the burned-off area. About seventy-five percent of us had firearms. Most of the rest carried cutting bars like mine, but there were two flashguns besides Gregg's own. Flashguns were heavy, unpleasant to shoot because they scattered actinics, and were certain to attract enemy fire. I found it instructive that Stephen Gregg would carry such a weapon.

The sky over the Federation base to the south suddenly rippled with spaced rainbow flashes. Four seconds later, the rumble of plasma cannon discharging shook the swamp about the *Porcelain*.

A ship that must have been the *Mizpah* dropped out of the sky. The sun-hot blaze of her thrusters was veiled by the ionized glow of their exhaust. Plasma drifted up and back from the vessel like the train of a lady in court dress.

"The stupid *whore*son!" said Stephen Gregg. "They were to land together with us, not five minutes later!"

Ricimer jumped quickly to the ground and trotted toward Gregg. "Stephen," he said, "you'd best join me in the lead. I think it's more important that we reach the base as quickly as possible than that the whole body arrives together. I'm very much afraid that Blakey is trying to land directly on the objective."

As the *Mizpah* lurched downward at a rate much faster than that of the *Porcelain* before her, a throbbing pulse of yellow light from the ground licked her lower hull. From where I jogged along a step behind Ricimer and Gregg, the starship was barely in sight above the low vegetation, but she must have been fifty or more meters above the ground.

The plume of exhaust dissipated in a shock wave. Seconds later, we could hear a report duller than that of the *Mizpah*'s cannon but equally loud.

Ricimer held a gyro compass in his left hand. "This way," he directed. Twenty meters into the forest, the *Porcelain* was out of sight.

"The bloody whoreson!" Gregg repeated as he jogged along beside his friend and leader.

"How . . ." I said. My voice was a croaking whisper. I couldn't see for sweat between the angry passes I made across my eyes with my sopping kerchief.

" . . . do you stand this?" I finished, concluding on a rising note that suggested panic even to me. I deliberately lowered my voice to add, "You're wearing armor, I mean."

Piet Ricimer squeezed my shoulder. Ricimer's face was red, and the sleeves of his gorgeous tunic were as wet as my kerchief. "You'll harden to it, Moore," he said. He spoke in gasps. "A kilometer isn't far. Once you're used to, you know. It."

"The men won't follow . . ." Gregg said. He was a pace ahead of us, setting the trail through the flimsy, clinging vegetation. He didn't look back over his shoulder as he spoke. "Unless the leaders lead. So we have to."

"A little to the right, Stephen," Ricimer wheezed. "I think we're drifting." Then in near anger he added, "Macquerie says the base was set on the firmest ground of the continent. What must the rest be like?"

Each of my boots carried what felt like ten kilos of mud. The hilt of the cutting bar had a textured surface, but despite that the weapon kept trying to slide out of my grip. I was sure that if I had to use the bar, it would squirt into the hands of my opponent.

The assault force straggled behind the three of us. How far behind was anybody's guess. About a dozen crewmen, laden with weapons and bandoliers of ammunition, slogged along immediately in back of me. They were making heavy going of it. The mud had stilled their initial chatter, but they were obviously determined to keep up or die.

Three of the spacers were the regular watch from the attitude-control consoles. I suspected the others were among Ricimer's long-time followers also. With their share of the wealth from previous voyages, why in *God's* name were they undergoing this punishment and danger?

And why had Jeremy Moore made the same choice? The day before sailing, Eloise had made it clear that there was a permanent place for me. On her terms, of course, but they weren't such terrible terms.

The only thing that kept me up with the leaders was that I *was* with the leaders. I was with two undeniable heroes; staggering along, but present.

"If she'd really crashed," Ricimer said, "we'd have— she'd shake the ground. The *Mizpah.*"

"Fired off all ten guns descending," Gregg muttered. There was a streak of blood on his right hand and forearm, and his sleeve was ripped. "Means they landed with them empty. Feds may be cutting all their throats before we come up. Stupid whoresons."

Then, in a coldly calm voice, he added, "Stop here. We've reached it."

I knelt at the base of a spray of huge, rubbery leaves. My knees sank into the muck, but I didn't think I could've remained upright without the effort of walking to steady me. Ricimer halted with his left hand on Gregg's shoulder blade. Sailors, puffing and blowing as though they were coming up after deep dives, spread out to either side of the trail we had blazed.

The native vegetation had been burned away from a hundred-meter band surrounding the Federation base. Water gleamed in pools and sluggish rivulets across the scabrous wasteland. The natural landscape was inhuman and oppressive; this defensive barrier was as ugly as a cinder.

The perimeter fence was of loose mesh four meters high. Judging from the insulators the fence was electrified, but it didn't provide visual screening. Trees heavy with citrus fruit grew within the enclosure.

In the center of the fenceline were a gate and a guard tower, at present unoccupied. Two men were strolling toward the tower up a lane through the trees. They were laughing; one carried a bottle. Both had rifles slung.

Gregg aimed his flashgun from the concealment of a plantainlike growth with blue leaves the size of blankets.

"Wait, Stephen," Ricimer ordered. He took off his gilt-braided beret, wiped his face in the crook of his arm, and put the beret on again. "Mister Sahagun!" he called, stepping out into the cleared area. "Mister Coos!"

At the words, I recognized the pair as two of the gentlemen who'd transferred to the *Mizpah*. They'd taken off their heavy armor. I'd thought they were Federation soldiers whose bullets might kill me in the next seconds.

Sahagun groped in startlement for his slung weapon before he recognized the speaker. "Ricimer, is that you?" he called. "Say, we're supposed to bring you in, but I just see that this bloody gate is locked. We'll—"

Gregg had shifted infinitesimally when Sahagun touched his rifle. Now he moved an equally slight amount. His flashgun fired, a pulse of light so intense that the native foliage wilted from the side-scatter. Great leaves sagged away, fluttering in the echoes of the laser's miniature thunder.

I tried to jump to my feet. I slipped and would have fallen except that a sailor I didn't know by name caught my arm.

The bolt hit the crossbar where it intersected the left gatepost. Metal exploded in radiant fireballs which trailed smoke as they arced away. Coos and Sahagun fell flat on ground as wet as that through which we'd been tramping.

"That's all right," Gregg called as he switched the battery in his weapon's stock for a fresh one. As with his friend and leader, there was no hint of exhaustion in his voice now. "We'll open it ourselves."

"I think," said Piet Ricimer softly, "that we'll wait till our whole force has come up before any of us enter the base."

There was nothing menacing in his words or tone, but I felt myself shiver.

"Ah, glad you've made it, Ricimer," said Thomas Hawtry as he rose from the porch of the operations building. A score of men stood about him. Many of them were frightened-looking and dressed in tags of white Federation uniforms. "I've got some very valuable information here, *very* valuable!"

Hawtry spoke with an enthusiasm that showed he understood how chancy the next moments were likely to be. Like the others of the *Mizpah*'s gentlemen, he'd put aside his breastplate and rifle.

"In a moment, Mister Hawtry," said Piet Ricimer. He wiped his face again with his sleeve. "Captain Blakey. Present yourself at once!"

The *Mizpah* had come down within a hundred and fifty meters of the administration buildings and base housing, blowing sod and shrubbery out in a shallow crater. The multitube laser that slashed the descending vessel from a guard tower had shattered a port thruster nozzle.

Yawing into the start of a tumble, the *Mizpah* had struck hard. The port outrigger fractured, though the vessel's hull appeared undamaged. Our men and Molts from the base labor force now surveyed the damage.

I bubbled with relief at having gotten this far. Clouds scudded across the pale sky. It felt odd to know that there was no solid roof above, but it didn't bother me the way I'd been warned it might.

I wondered where I could find a hose to clean my boots. I glanced down. My legs. They were covered in mud from mid-thigh.

Blakey broke away from the group beside the *Mizpah* and trotted toward Ricimer. The *Mizpah*'s plasma cannon were still run out through the horizontal bank of gunports. To fire paired broadsides into the Federation base as the ship descended, Blakey must have rolled the *Mizpah* on her axis, then counter-rolled.

"There's a treasure right here on Decades," Hawtry said, pretending that he didn't realize he was being ignored, "and I've located it. The Feds here are too cowardly to grab it up themselves!"

A freighter was docked at the far edge of the perimeter, nearly a kilometer from the administration building. That ship had taken much of the *Mizpah* gunners' attention. One blast of charged particles had struck her squarely, vaporizing a huge hole. The shock of exploding metal dished in the light-metal hull for half its length and set fire to the vessel's interior. Dirty smoke billowed from the wreck and drifted through the nearby fenceline.

I couldn't imagine any purpose in shooting at the freighter beyond a general desire to terrorize the defenders. In all likelihood, the Feds stationed here wouldn't have been aroused *to* defense except for the sudden blaze of cannonfire.

Blakey whipped off the broad-brimmed hat which he, like many experienced Venerian travelers, wore under an open sky. "Mister Ricimer," he blurted, "I didn't have any choice. It was Mister Hawtry who—"

"May I remind you that I gave you specific direction to land a kilometer north of the Federation compound, Captain Blakey?" Ricimer said in a knife-edged voice. "No one but the Lord God Almighty takes precedence to the orders I give on this expedition!"

"No sir, no sir," Blakey mumbled, wringing his hat up in a tight double roll. The spacer's hair was solidly dark, but there was a salting of white hair in his beard and mustache.

"Now, wait a minute, Ricimer," Hawtry said. He remained on the porch, ten meters away. The Federation personnel about him were easing away, leaving the gentlemen exposed like spines of basalt weathered out of softer stone.

"The *Mizpah*'s condition?" Ricimer snapped.

"We'll jack up the port side to repair the outrigger," Blakey said. He grimaced at his crumpled hat. "Then we'll switch the thruster nozzle, we've spares aboard, it's no—"

"You lost only one thruster?" Ricimer demanded, his tongue sharp as the blade of a microtome.

"Well, maybe shock cooling from the soil took another," Blakey admitted miserably. "We won't know till we get her up, but it's no more than three days' work with the locals to help."

I noticed that one of the Federation personnel was a petite woman who'd cropped her brunette hair short. She nervously watched the byplay among her captors, gripping her opposite shoulders with her well-formed hands.

I wondered if we'd be on Decades longer than three days. Although a great deal could happen in three days.

"Look here, Ricimer!" boomed Hawtry as he stepped off the porch in a determination to use bluster where camaraderie had failed. "The Molts that have escaped from here, they loot the ships that crash into the swamps. There've been *hundreds,* over the years, and the Molts have all the treasure cached in one place. That's the real value of Decades!"

Ricimer turned his head to look at Hawtry. I couldn't see his eyes, but the six gentlemen stepping from the porch to follow lurched to a halt.

"The real value of Decades, Mister Hawtry," Ricimer said in a tone without overt emotion, "was to be the training it gave our personnel in discipline and obedience to orders."

Ricimer turned to the men who'd accompanied him from the flagship. "Dole," he said mildly, "find the communications center here and inform the *Absalom* and *Kinsolving* to land within the perimeter. Oh—and see if you can raise Guillermo aboard the *Porcelain* to tell them that we're in control of the base."

"I'll go with him," I volunteered in a light voice. "I, I'm good with electronics."

"Yes," Ricimer said. "Do it."

Dole didn't move. I started toward the administration building as an obvious place to look for the radios. Stephen Gregg laid a hand on the top of my shoulder without looking away from Ricimer and the gentlemen beyond. I stopped and swallowed.

Ricimer swiveled back to the *Mizpah*'s captain. "Mister Blakey," he said. "You'll leave repairs to the *Mizpah* in the charge of your navigator. You'll proceed immediately to the *Porcelain,* in company with Mister Hawtry and the other gentlemen adventurers who were aboard the *Mizpah* when you decided to ignore my orders."

"Lord take you for a fool, Ricimer!" Hawtry said. "If you think I'm going to rot in a swamp when—"

Gregg locked down his helmet visor with a sharp *clack.* The flashgun's discharge was liable to blind anyone using it without filters to protect his eyes. Dole snicked the bolt of his rifle back far enough to check the load, then closed it again. Others of Ricimer's longtime crewmen stood braced with ready weapons. A cutting bar whined as somebody made sure it was in good order.

"There'll be no blasphemy in a force under my command, Mister Hawtry," Ricimer said. Though his voice seemed calm, his face was pale with anger. "This time I will overlook it; and we'll hope the Lord, Who is our only hope for the success of these endeavors, will overlook it as well."

Hawtry stepped backward, chewing on his lower lip. He wasn't a coward, but the muzzle of Gregg's weapon was only two meters from his chest. A bolt at that range would spray his torso over hectares of swamp.

Ricimer's posture eased slightly. He reached into his belt pouch, handed Blakey the compass from it, and resumed. "You will find the *Porcelain* on a reciprocal of this course. Tell Mister Salomon that your party will guard the vessel until we're ready to depart. The crew will be more comfortable here at the base, I'm sure."

Hawtry let out a long, shuddering breath. "We'll need men to deal with the menial work," he said.

Ricimer nodded. "If you care to pay sailors extra to act as servants," he said, "that's between you and them."

Hawtry glanced over his shoulder at the accompanying gentlemen. Without speaking further, the group sidled away in the direction of the *Mizpah* and the gear they'd left aboard her.

Gregg opened his visor. His face had no expression.

Dole plucked at my sleeve. "Let's get along and find the radio room, sir," the bosun said. "You know, I thought things were going to get interesting for a moment there."

I tried to smile but couldn't. I supposed I should be thankful that I could walk normally.

DECADES

Day 8

I turned at the console to look out the window of the commo room. Halfway across the compound, male prisoners from the Decades garrison and the damaged freighter were unloading spoiled stores from the *Absalom 231*. With my left hand I picked a section from the half orange while my right fingers typed code into the numeric keypad.

"That's it!" said Lavonne. She'd been Officer III (Communications) Cartier when Decades Station was under Federation control. "You've got the signal, Jeremy!"

"Thanks to you and this wonderful equipment," I added warmly, patting my hand toward Lavonne without quite touching her. I pursed my lips as I looked over the console display. "Now if only the *Mizpah*'s hardware weren't a generation past the time it should've been scrapped . . ."

The console showed the crew emptying the hulk, from the viewpoint of the port-side optical sensors in the *Mizpah*'s hull. Occasionally some of the Venerians and Molts replacing the *Mizpah*'s damaged thrusters came in sight at the lower edge of the display, oblivious of the fact they were being electronically observed. Because the *Mizpah*'s sensors only updated the image six times a second, the picture was grainy and figures moved in jerks.

Lavonne stripped the fascia from one of the orange sections I'd handed her, using her fingers and the tip of a small screwdriver. "Why, we could connect all the tower optics with this!" she said in pleased wonder. "Superintendent Burr keeps worrying that one day the Molts on guard will decide to let in the wild tribes from the swamp.

But someone could watch what's going on in the towers from here."

Several people came up the stairs from the lower level of the admin building, talking among themselves. I'd left the commo room's door ajar, though I'd made sure the panel could be locked if matters with Lavonne proceeded faster than I expected.

"Ah—it's Molts that you're afraid of," I said, "and you use Molts for *guards?*"

"Well, the ones who've been trained to work for humans are trustworthy, I suppose," the woman said defensively. "Freshly caught ones used to escape from the holding pens while the ships carrying them laid over here."

She bent past me to tap the screen where a corner of the inner compound was visible past the cargo hulk. Electrified wire surrounded thatch-roofed wooden racks. If it hadn't been for the voices in the hallway, I'd have taken up the offer implicit in Lavonne's posture.

"That was years ago," she added, straightening. "They can't get out of the station now that the perimeter's fenced too."

The door opened. Piet Ricimer stepped in, his head turned to catch Gregg's voice: " . . . who on Duneen's staff was paid to load us with *garbage* in place of the first-quality stores we were charged for."

I jumped to my feet, knocking my knees on the console. Macquerie and Guillermo entered behind Ricimer and his aide. I'd learned to recognize Guillermo from the yellowish highlights of his chitin and his comparatively narrow face. It was odd to think of the aliens as having personalities, though.

"I've, ah, been connecting the squadron's optics through the console, here, Ricimer," I said. "Ah—save for the *Porcelain;* I'd have to be aboard her to set the handshake."

I was nervous. What I'd done here had been at my own whim; and there was the matter of Lavonne, not that things there had come to fruition. Birth in a factorial family made me the social superior of the general commander, but I hadn't needed Hawtry's humiliation to teach me that the reality here was something else again.

Ricimer glanced at the display. "From the *Mizpah*?" he said. "I'm delighted, Moore."

Gregg offered me a bleak grin over the general commander's shoulder. Lavonne, who'd moved toward a corner when the command group entered, eyed the big man speculatively. There were things about women that I would *never* understand.

"I was surprised to find you aboard after we lifted off," Ricimer commented. "Stephen explained, though; and I can see that you'd be an asset in any case."

"I, ah, regret the inconvenience I've caused," I said. I nodded to the pilot. I'd tried to avoid Macquerie thus far during the voyage, but a starship was close confinement for all those aboard her. If there was going to be trouble between us, best it happen under the eyes of Ricimer—and more particularly Gregg.

Macquerie smiled wryly. "My own fault not to wonder why somebody was buying me drinks, Mister Moore," he said. Unlike the others, Macquerie respected me for my birth. "Anyway, Captain Ricimer says he'll put me down on Os Sertoes with my in-laws."

A white asterisk pulsed at the upper corner of the screen as Macquerie spoke. I noticed it from the corner of my eye. The icon might have been there for some while, and I didn't have any notion of what it meant.

I opened my mouth to call a question to Lavonne. Before I spoke, Guillermo reached an oddly-jointed arm past me and touched a sequence of keys. Captain Blakey, his image streaked by static, snarled, "Come *in,* somebody, isn't there anybody on watch on this God *damned* planet?"

Piet Ricimer put his left hand on my shoulder, guiding me out of the way so that he could take over the console. The general commander's grip was like iron. If I'd hesitated, he would have flung me across the radio room.

"I'm here, Captain Blakey," Ricimer said.

The static thinned visibly with each passing moment. I recognized the pattern. Thrusters expelled plasma, atoms stripped of part or all of their electron charge. The exhaust radiated across the entire radio frequency spectrum, with harmonics as it reabsorbed electrons from the surrounding atmosphere. A thruster was firing in the vicinity of the *Porcelain* . . .

"Mister Hawtry's taken the cutter!" Blakey said. "He and the others, they're sure they know where Molt treasure is and they've gone off to get it. They have a map!"

"Do you know where—" Ricimer began.

Blakey cut him off. "I don't know where they're going," he blurted. "I wouldn't go, sir, I refused! But they got two of the sailors to fly the cutter for them, and now there's nobody aboard the ship but me and the other four sailors they brought. I tried to stop them, but they wouldn't even let me to the radio to warn you, sir."

"We can't call the cutter while its thruster's operating," Gregg said. "Not that the damned fools would listen to us."

"Outside of the plateau the station's on . . ." Captain Macquerie said grimly. "I know, you think it's a swamp, but it's the only solid ground on the continent. Five klicks in any direction from the station, it's soup. It maybe won't swallow them, but they'll play hell unclogging their nozzles to lift off again."

My face grew still as glass; my mind considered the capabilities of the console built to the standards of the chip-rich North American Federation. The cutter's motor created RF hash that would smother normal attempts at communication, but that meant the thruster itself was a signal generator.

"The superintendent got the map years ago from an old drunk in the maintenance section," Lavonne volunteered. "He really believes it, Burr does. But even if it was real, it'd be suicide to go so far outside the base."

I changed displays to a menu, then changed screens again. A jagged line drew itself across a display gridded with kilometer squares and compass points. "There's a range and vector," I said to the room in general. "I don't have terrain data to underlay."

The track quivered into a tight half-circle and stopped. The thruster had been shut off. The terminus was a little over ten kilometers from the screen's reference point—the console itself.

Ricimer nodded and said crisply to Guillermo, "Alarm?"

The Molt entered a four-stroke command without bothering to call up a menu. One of Guillermo's ancestors, perhaps more than a thousand years before, had been trained to use a console of similar design. That experience, genetically imbedded, permitted the Molt to use equipment that he himself had never seen before. A four-throated horn in the roof of the admin building began to whoop *Hoo-Hee! Hoo-Hee!*

So long as men depended on Molts and pre-Collapse factories to provide their electronics, there would be no advance on the standards of that distant past. I was one of the few people—even on Venus—who believed there *could* be improvement on the designs of those bygone demigods.

I reached between Ricimer and Guillermo to key a series of commands through the link I had added to the system. The *Kinsolving*'s siren and the klaxon on the *Mizpah* added their tones to the Fed hooter. *Absalom 231* didn't have an alarm, or much of anything else.

Ricimer flashed me a smile of appreciation and amusement. Stephen Gregg's mouth quirked slightly also, but the big gentleman's face was settling into planes of muscle over bone, and his eyes—

I looked away.

When Ricimer nodded to Guillermo, the Molt entered fresh commands into the console. The hooter and klaxon shut off, and the *Kinsolving*'s siren began to wind down.

"This is the general commander," Ricimer said. His voice boomed from the alarm horns; the tannoys of the three Venerian ships should be repeating the words as well. "All Porcelains report armed to the cargo hulk. Captain Winter, march your Kinsolvings at once to the flagship. Other personnel, guard the station here and await further orders."

Ricimer rose from the console in a smooth motion and swept me with him toward the door. Gregg was in the lead, Guillermo and Macquerie bringing up the rear. Lavonne gaped at us. Her confusion was no greater than my own.

"But the *Absalom,* Captain?" Macquerie said. "Sure-ly . . ."

"The *Mizpah* can't lift, the *Kinsolving* with the feath-erboats aboard won't hold but thirty or forty men," said Stephen Gregg in a voice as high and thin as a contrail in the stratosphere. His boots crashed on the stair treads. "The hulk's half empty. This is a job for troops, not can-non. If it's a job for anyone at all."

"We can't abandon them, Stephen," Piet Ricimer said, snatching up his breastplate from the array in the build-ing's entrance hall.

The others, all but the Molt, were grabbing their own arms and equipment. I supposed my cutting bar was some-where in the hardware, but I didn't have any recollection of putting it in a particular place. Guillermo wore a holstered pistol on his pink sash, but the weapon was merely a symbol.

"Can't we, Piet?" Gregg said as he settled the visored helmet over his head. "Well, it doesn't matter to me."

I thought I understood the implications of Gregg's words; and if I did, they were as bleak and terrible as the big gunman's eyes.

"Stand by!" Piet Ricimer called from the control bench of the *Absalom 231.*

"Stand by!" Dole shouted through a bullhorn as he stood at the hatch in the cockpit/hold bulkhead. The bosun braced his boots and his free hand against the hatch coaming. A short rifle was slung across his back.

Most of the eighty-odd spacers aboard the hulk were packed into the hold, standing beside or on the pallets of stores that hadn't yet been dumped. At least half the food we'd loaded at Betaport was moldy or contaminated. Fortunately, the warehouses at Decades were stocked in quantities to supply fleets of the 500-tonne vessels which carried the Federation's cargoes.

I was crowded into the small crew cabin with about a dozen other men. I gripped the frame of the bunk folded against the bulkhead behind me. I had to hold the cutting bar between my knees, because its belt clip was broken.

The hulk's thrusters lit at half throttle, three nozzles and then all four together. The moment of unbalanced thrust made the shoddy vessel lurch into a violent yaw which corrected as Ricimer's fingers moved on the controls.

"If he hadn't shut off the autopilot," Jeude grumbled to my right, "the jets'd have switched on about quick enough to flip us like a pancake. Which is what we'd all be when this pig hit."

"If he hadn't shut off the autopilot," said Lightbody to my left, "he wouldn't be our Mister Ricimer. He'll get us out of this."

The tone of the final sentence was more pious than optimistic.

The *Absalom 231* lifted from its bobbling hover to become fully airborne. The roar of the motors within the single-hulled vessel deafened me, but flight was much smoother than the liftoff had been.

"Say, sir," Jeude said to me, "wouldn't you like a rifle, sir? Or maybe a flashgun like your friend Mister Gregg?"

"I've never fired a gun," I shouted in reply to the solici- tous spacer. *Your friend Mister Gregg.* Did Gregg and I have friends, either one of us?

"I thought all you gentlemen trained for the militia," Lightbody said with a doubtful frown. He held a double- barreled shotgun, perhaps the one he'd had when guarding access to the *Porcelain.* Bandoliers of shells in individual loops crossed his chest.

"Well, don't worry about it, Mister Moore," Jeude said cheerfully. "A bar's really better for a close-in dustup anyway."

Someone in the hold—most of them, it must be to be heard in the cabin—was singing. " . . . *is our God, a bul- wark never failing.*"

Macquerie and Guillermo peered from either side over Ricimer's shoulders to see the hulk's rudimentary naviga- tional display. The Molt had downloaded data from the base unit to the *Absalom 231* before leaving the commo room. I couldn't guess how fast we were traveling. The hulk wallowed around its long axis. No starship was meant for atmospheric flight, and this flimsy can less than most.

Gregg stood behind the general commander, but he didn't appear interested in the display. He glanced back, his face framed by helmet, and noticed me. Gregg bent down and touched the sliding switch on the hilt of my cutting bar.

"That's the power switch," Gregg said, speaking with exaggerated lip movements instead of bellowing the words. "Click it forward to arm the trigger."

I laid my thumb on the switch. "Thank you," I said. My mouth was dry.

Gregg shrugged and straightened again.

"There it is!" Macquerie shouted. "There it is, a pentagon, and there's the cutter!"

"Stand by!" Dole cried, his amplified voice a dim shadow as thruster noise doubled by reflection from the ground. The men in the hold couldn't hear the bosun's warning, but the changed exhaust note was as much notice as veteran spacers needed.

The *Absalom 231* lurched, wobbled, and swung an unexpected 30° on its vertical axis. Jeude grabbed me as centrifugal force threw me forward.

The hulk hit with a sucking crash. My shoulders banged into the bed frame behind me, but I didn't knock my head.

More people than me had trouble with the landing. Two of the sailors in the cockpit lost their footing, and the clangor of equipment flying in the hold sounded like someone was flinging garbage cans.

"Move! Move! Move!" Dole shouted. Gregg was at the cockpit's external hatch, spinning the manual undogging wheel more powerfully than a hydraulic pump could have done the job.

My bar had spun away at the landing. Lightbody retrieved the weapon as Jeude hustled me forward with a hand on my elbow. "Think that was bad," Jeude remarked, "you'll appreciate it when you ride in a hulk with anybody else piloting."

Gregg jumped out the hatch, his shoulders hunched and the flashgun cradled in both hands. Piet Ricimer followed, wearing a beret and carrying a repeating carbine. "For God and Venus!" he cried. Guillermo leaped clumsily next, half pushed by a sailor named Easton who followed him.

Lightbody cleared the hatchway, his shotgun at high port. The opening was before me. The ground was meters below; I couldn't tell precisely how far. The vegetation was similar to what we'd seen on the trek from the *Porcelain* to the Federation base, but it seemed lusher. Huge leaves waved in the near distance, hiding the figures who brushed their supporting trunks.

I jumped with my eyes closed. A leaf slapped my face and tore like wet paper.

I landed and fell over when my right leg sank to the knee in soupy mud. I could see for five meters or so between the stems in most directions, though the broad leaves were a low ceiling overhead. The trees rose from pads of surface roots. Between the roots, standing water alternated with patches of algae as colorful as an oil slick.

I struggled upright. My left boot was on firmer ground than the right, though I couldn't tell the difference visually. I saw a group of figures ahead and struggled toward them. Jeude hit with a muddy splash and a curse.

"Easton, what's the line?" Piet Ricimer demanded. The pudgy sailor bent over an inertial compass the size of his hand.

The swamp was alive with chirps and whooping. I hadn't noticed anything like the volume of sound nearer the base. I sank into a pool hidden by orange weed floating in a mat on its surface. Lightbody reached back and grabbed me.

A lid lifted from the ground at Easton's feet. The underside of the lid had a soft, pearly sheen like the inner membrane of an egg; the hole beyond was covered with a similar coating to keep the wet soil from collapsing. The Molt in the spiderhole rammed a spear up into Easton's abdomen.

The fat Venerian screamed and dropped the compass. Gregg shot the Molt at point-blank range with his flashgun. The alien's plastron disintegrated in a white glare and a shock wave that jolted me a step backward. Shards of chitin stripped surrounding leaves to the bare veins.

Easton lurched three steps forward until the spear protruding from his belly tripped him. He fell on his face, his legs thrashing against the soft dirt.

Jeude turned and fired. I couldn't see his target, if there was one. Screams and shots came from the direction of the hulk's rear loading ramp.

Piet Ricimer picked up the compass, wiped its face on his sleeve, and checked a line.

Gregg slung his flashgun. He hadn't had time to lower the filtering visor, so he must have closed his eyes to avoid being blinded by his own bolt. Easton carried a rifle. Gregg pulled it and the bandolier of ammunition from the body which still trembled with a semblance of life.

"Guillermo," Ricimer ordered coolly as he dropped the compass in his purse, "go back to the ship and sound recall with the bullhorn. The rest of you, follow me to the cutter!"

He swung the barrel of his carbine forward, pointing the way for his rush. Another spiderhole gaped beside him. Lightbody and Gregg fired simultaneously, ripping the Molt with buckshot and a bullet before the creature was halfway into its upward lunge.

Ricimer vanished beyond a veil of dropping leaves. The others were following him. I stumbled forward, terrified of being left behind. The only thing I was conscious of was Gregg's back, two meters in front of me. Guns fired and I heard the whine of a cutting bar, but the foliage baffled sound into a directionless ambience.

I burst out of the trees. A swath of bare soil bubbled and stank where the cutter's motor had cleared it while landing.

The boat itself lay at a skew angle five meters away. A human, one of the sailors who'd accompanied the gentlemen exiled to the *Porcelain,* lay beside the vessel. A Molt of olive coloration leaned from the cutter's dorsal hatch, pointing a rifle.

Ricimer shot the Molt and worked the underlever of his repeater. Ten more aliens with spears and metal clubs rushed us from the opposite side of the clearing. I was the man closest to them.

"Watch it!" somebody shouted. A rifle slammed, but none of the Molts went down.

I swept my bar around in the desperation of a man trying to bat away a stinging insect. I tugged at the trigger but the blade didn't spin. The ceramic edge clinked on the shaft of a mace hammered from the alloy hull of a starship. Another Molt thrust a metal-tipped spear at my crotch.

"The power switch, you whore's cunt!" Stephen Gregg bellowed as he butt-stroked the Molt spearman, then thrust the blunt muzzle of his rifle into the wedge-shaped skull of the alien with the mace. A ruptured cartridge gleamed partway out of the rifle's chamber, jamming Gregg's weapon until there was time to pick the case out with a knifepoint.

Lightbody fired. Jeude was reloading his rifle; Ricimer had dropped to one knee, pumping rounds into Molts who were too close to miss.

I found the power switch and thumbed it violently. My index finger still tugged on the trigger. The torque of the live blade almost snatched the weapon from my grasp.

One of the aliens was twice the size of the others. He shambled forward with an axe in either hand. Bullets smashed two, then three dribbling holes in his chest.

Gregg clubbed another spearman. He held his rifle by one hand on the barrel while he tried to untangle the flashgun's sling with the other. The big Molt lunged close to Gregg and brought an axe down.

I stepped forward, focused on what I was doing and suddenly oblivious of the chaos around me. My cutting bar screamed through the steel axe-helve in a shower of sparks.

Somebody fired so close that the muzzle flash scorched my sleeve. I ignored it, continuing the stroke. The blade's spin carried it through the Molt's triangular head and into the torso. Brownish ichor sprayed from the wound.

Motion, more Molts beyond the toppling body of the giant. I couldn't see out of my left eye. I stepped over the Molt thrashing in front of me and cut at the next without letting up on the bar's trigger. The Molt tried to club me, but I was within the stroke. The shaft, not the studded tip, of the club gashed my forehead.

The Molt's head and club arm fell to one side while the remainder of the corpse toppled the other way. I followed the cutting bar's edge toward another alien, but that one was already flailing, its plastron shattered by a charge of buckshot.

I turned, looking for Molts. They were all down. I hacked at the alien giant, tearing a wide gouge down his carapace. Nerve trauma sent the creature into another series of convulsions.

Somebody grabbed me from behind. I twisted to bring my howling bar back over my head. A hand closed over mine. Gregg's thumb switched off the cutting bar.

"I've got him!" Gregg said. "It's all right, Moore."

Ricimer wiped my face with a swatch torn from the tail of his own red plush tunic. I could see again; I'd been blinded by fluids from the Molt I'd cut apart.

Jeude looked all right. Lightbody was breathing hard. He'd opened the breeches of his shotgun, but he hadn't inserted the reloads ready between the fingers of his left hand. There was a bloody tear in his tunic.

"Into the cutter, *now!*" Ricimer ordered as he jogged drunkenly toward the small vessel.

"All personnel return to the ship!" crackled an amplified voice. Through the bullhorn, Guillermo's mechanically precise tones were indistinguishable from the voice of a human speaker. "All Porcelains return to the ship!"

"Piet, watch—" Gregg shouted as Ricimer gripped the coaming of the cutter's dorsal hatch with his left hand and leaped upward. Ricimer held the repeater like a pistol in his right hand, aiming it ahead of him as he swung into the hatchway. The *wham* of the rifleshot within the cabin was duller but hugely amplified compared to the blast it made in the open air. Ricimer dropped into the vessel.

"Get him!" Gregg ordered as he bent to pick up the rifle dropped by the Molt shot in the cutter.

I didn't realize I was "him" until Dole and Jeude gripped me by opposite arms and half hoisted, half heaved me into the cutter's roof hatch. I grabbed the coaming as I went over so that at least I didn't hit like a sack of grain.

Ricimer was in the seat forward. Two Molts and a human lay dead in the cabin. The human had been gutted like a trout.

Jeude, Lightbody, and Dole leaped into the cabin in quick succession. Three of the attitude jets snarled, rocking the cutter to starboard. Lightbody sprawled against the side of the cabin. His eyes were open but not animated. I wondered if the spacer's wound was more serious than the surface gash it appeared to be.

Ricimer glanced over his shoulder as Gregg boarded, his breastplate crashing against the coaming. The cutter's single plasma motor lighted with a bang and a spray of mud in all directions from the hull.

The vessel hopped forward from the initial pulse, then lifted in true flight as Ricimer relit the thruster. The initial cough of plasma had cleared mud from the nozzle so that the motor could develop full power without exploding.

Stephen Gregg braced his legs wide, leaning outward from the dorsal hatch. His rifle's muzzle lifted in a puff of white propellant gases. The blast was lost in the roar of the thruster.

Gregg dropped the rifle back into the cabin behind him without looking; Dole slapped the grip of his own weapon into Gregg's open hand. The big gunman aimed again. Jeude reached forward to take Ricimer's repeater and five cartridges from a pocket of the bandolier the general commander wore over his body armor.

I stood beside Gregg, gripping the coaming with my free hand to keep from being flung away by the cutter's violent maneuvering. I still held the cutting bar. The ichor sliming the blade had dried to a saffron hue.

Gregg fired. A Molt twisting through shrubbery forty meters away toppled on its face.

The Molt was visible because Ricimer reined the cutter in tight circles only five meters above the soggy ground. The thruster's plasma exhaust devoured plants directly below the nozzle and wilted the foliage of those ten meters to either side.

Ricimer dropped the little vessel almost to the soil. A dozen puffs of vapor fountained from the surrounding vegetation, some of them forty meters away. The nearer plumes were iridescent plasma, the more distant ones steam. Piet had set down directly on a spiderhole. The exhaust blasted through all the passages connected with the initial target. Molts anywhere in that portion of the tunnel system were incinerated.

Gregg shot, using Ricimer's repeater. He shifted as he worked the lever action, never taking the butt from his shoulder, and fired again.

The cutter rotated vertiginously as well as porpoising up and down. I couldn't *see* the Molts in the foliage until Gregg's bullets slapped them into their death throes, but the gunman didn't appear to waste a shot.

A gray streak splashed itself on the yellowed ceramic hull near where I stood. I gaped at it for a moment before I realized a bullet had struck and ricocheted harmlessly.

The goal that drew Hawtry and his fellows was a stone platform less than five meters across. Foliage curtained all but the center of the structure. Macquerie must have been looking at a radar image to tell that it was a pentagon.

Ricimer swept the cutter at a walking pace along the side away from the *Absalom 231,* fifty meters distant. He was avoiding men from the group in the hold who might have fought their way toward the target. Searing exhaust wilted enough vegetation to show a doorway in one face of the building. A Molt flopped in tetanic convulsions nearby, its carapace the deep red of a boiled lobster.

Ricimer set the cutter down on ground which plasma had baked on an earlier pass. He jumped up from the controls, shouting, "Dole, radio the hulk and bring the men back!"

Ricimer snatched a rifle the bosun had just reloaded. Gregg hoisted his buttocks onto the hatch coaming, swung his legs over and dropped, ignoring the steps and hand-holds formed into the outer hull.

I tried to follow and instead tumbled sideways. The ground was still spongy enough to cushion my landing.

Thomas Hawtry stepped out of the stone structure, holding a rifle. He'd lost his helmet, and a powerful blow had crazed the surface of his breastplate.

"We've found the treasure, Ricimer!" Hawtry called in attempted triumph. His face was white and his voice cracked in mid-sentence. "And an idol that we'll destroy in the Lord's name!"

"You others, keep guard," Ricimer ordered curtly as he strode toward the Molt temple. Coos came through the doorway behind Hawtry. Ricimer pushed him aside and went within.

Gregg followed Ricimer; I followed Gregg. I walked almost without volition, drifting after the leaders as thistle-down trails a moving body.

The temple's floor was set three steps below the ground surface. The walls were corbeled inward, enclosing a great-er volume than I'd expected from the size of the roof.

A Venerian battery lamp illuminated the interior. A spindle of meteoritic iron, twenty kilos or so in weight, rested on a stone pedestal in the center. Microchips—sacked, boxed, and loose—were piled in profusion on low benches along the walls. A silver starburst marked some of the containers, indicating the chips within were purpose-built: new production from pre-Collapse factories operating under Federation control.

Six gentlemen stared at us, their saviors. Sahagun clasped his hands together in prayer; Delray's face was as pale as ivory. Four were seriously wounded. The three missing men must be dead, unless they'd had sense enough to stay aboard the *Porcelain*.

A Molt in a loose caftan lay face-up on the stone floor. I didn't remember having previously seen a Molt wearing more than a sash. The alien had been shot at least a dozen times. Judging from the smell, someone had then urinated on the body.

Salomon appeared at the door to the temple, holding a cutting bar. "I left Macquerie in charge aboard the ship," he said. "Say, there *is* a fortune here!"

"We'll need stretchers," said Piet Ricimer. His voice was colorless.

"I've got blankets coming," the navigator said. "We can use rifles for poles. Any Molts left are keeping out of the way for now."

Salomon's bright tones grated on my consciousness. I suddenly realized that I wasn't the man I'd been ten minutes before. Ten minutes . . .

Piet Ricimer lurched toward the doorway without speaking further. Gregg jumped up the steps to precede his commander. He'd unslung the flashgun and held it ready for use. Salomon backpedaled quickly to get out of their way. I followed the others, swaying slightly.

"Mister Salomon," Ricimer said in a cold, clear voice in the daylight. "See to it that the chips are loaded as quickly as possible. If the *Absalom*'s hoses will stretch, we'll refill the cutter's tank. I ran her out of reaction mass. If they won't reach, we'll blow the cutter in place. I'm not staying in a place so dangerous any longer than necessary. We'd best call the *Porcelain* into the fenced perimeter as well."

"We'll take the idol," Hawtry said. "We can't leave the bugs to their idol. It's an affront to the Lord!"

Men from the *Absalom*'s hold stared about the steaming devastation, holding their weapons ready. Many of them had fresh wounds. Dole was already organizing carrying parties to load the captured chips.

"Yes, Mister Hawtry," Ricimer said in a voice as bleak as the ravaged surface of Venus. "It is an affront to the Lord."

DECADES

Day 11

The garrison of Decades Station had mobile floodlights to illuminate threatened portions of the perimeter if the wild Molts should attack. Two banks of them threw a white glare over the *Porcelain*'s gathered crew. I stood at the rear of the assembly, feeling dissociated from my body.

"By the grace of God, we have come this far," Piet Ricimer said. He spoke without amplification from the flagship's ramp. His clear, vibrant voice carried through the soft breeze and the chugging of the prime movers that powered the lights. "The coordinates of our next layover have been distributed to every captain and navigator. We won't have settled facilities there, so be sure to complete any maintenance requiring equipment we don't carry."

The next layover would be Mocha, one of the Breach worlds. The Southerns occasionally laid over on Mocha, but there was no colony. Mocha's only permanent inhabitants were a handful of so-called Rabbits: hunter-gatherers descended from pre-Collapse settlers. Though remnant populations like Mocha's were scattered across the former human sphere, none of them had risen to the level of barbarism.

"We've gained a small success," Ricimer said. Stephen Gregg was a bulky shadow in the hold behind the general commander, out of the light. Dole and other of Ricimer's longtime followers stood at the foot of the ramp. Not a bodyguard, precisely, but—there.

"We have also had losses," Ricimer said, "some of them unnecessary. Remember that success is with the Lord, but that we owe to Him and to our fellows discipline as well as courage."

Federation prisoners listened to the general commander's address from beyond the pool of light. We'd left them unguarded since the day we landed. When we lifted off in the morning, the Feds could carry on as they had before.

I wondered if Lavonne was listening. After the hulk returned to the base, she'd been very . . . "understanding" would be the wrong word; Lavonne hadn't in the least understood my desperate need to return to *life*. But she'd done what she could, as much as anyone could who hadn't been there, and I thought it had been enough.

I prayed it had been enough.

"There'll be one personnel change on the next stage of the voyage," Ricimer said. "I'm transferring Mister Hawtry to the *Absalom*—"

"You'll do *what,* you little clown?" Thomas Hawtry bellowed as he pushed his way onto the loading ramp. He'd been standing in the middle of his coterie of gentlemen. He stepped forward alone.

"Mister Hawtry—" Ricimer said. Behind him, Stephen Gregg moved into the light, tall and as straight as a knifeblade.

"If you were a gentleman and not a potter's whelp," Hawtry cried, "I'd call you out!"

I slid forward through the crowd. My hands were flexing.

Gregg stepped in front of the general commander. He held a rifle muzzle-down along his right thigh. His face had no expression at all. "I'm a gentleman, Mister Hawtry," he said.

Hawtry stopped, his right foot resting on the ramp.

Gregg pointed his left index finger at Hawtry. "And take your hat off when you address the general commander," Gregg said. His voice had a fluting lightness, terrible to hear. "As a mark of respect."

"Stephen," Ricimer said. He lifted a hand toward Gregg's shoulder but didn't touch the bigger man. "I'll handle this."

"Mister Hawtry," Gregg said. He didn't shout, but his tone pierced the night like an awl. "I won't warn you again."

I reached the front of the assembly. Easy to do, since men were edging back and to either side. Ricimer's veterans formed a tight block in the center.

Hawtry wasn't a coward, I knew that. Hawtry stared at Gregg, and at Ricimer's tense face beyond that of the gunman. Hawtry could obey or die. It was as simple as that. As well argue with an avalanche as Gregg in this mood.

Hawtry snatched off his cap, an affair of scarlet and gold lacework. He crushed it in his hands. "Your pardon, Mister Ricimer," he said. The words rubbed each other like gravel tumbling.

Gregg stepped aside. He looked bored, but there was a sheen of sweat on his forehead.

"There will be no duels during this expedition," Piet Ricimer said. His tone was fiery, but his eyes were focused on the far distance rather than the assembly before him. "We are on the Lord's business, reopening the stars to His service. If anyone fights a duel—"

Ricimer put his hand on Gregg's shoulder and turned the bigger man to face him. Gregg was the dull wax of a candle, and his friend was a flame.

"If anyone fights a duel," Ricimer said. "Is that understood?"

Gregg dropped to one knee before the general commander. He rotated his right wrist so that the rifle was behind him, pointing harmlessly into the flagship's hold.

Ricimer lifted him. Gregg stepped back into the shadows again. "If anyone fights a duel," Ricimer repeated, but the fierceness was gone from his voice, "then the surviving parties will be left at the landfall where the offense against the Lord occurred. There will be no exceptions."

He looked out over us. The assembly gave a collective sigh.

Ricimer knelt down. "Let us pray," he said, tenting his hands before him.

• • •

Decades Station had barracks to accommodate more transients than the whole of the Venerian force. One of the blocks was brightly illuminated. In it, spacers with a flute, a tambourine, and some kind of plucked string instrument were playing to a crowd.

I sat on the porch of the administration building across the way, wondering if any of the Federation women were inside with our men.

Lavonne would be waiting for me in her quarters. I'd go to her soon. As soon as I calmed down.

" . . . could stick them all in the hulk," said a voice from the darkness. Footsteps crunched along the path. Two sailors were sauntering toward the party. "None of them gentlemen's worth a flying fuck."

"Well, they're not much good for real work," said a second voice, which I thought might be Jeude's. "Get into a fight, though, they can be something else again."

"Gregg?" said the first voice. "I give you that."

"I swear the new fellow, Moore, he's as bad," replied might-be-Jeude. The pair were past the porch now, continuing up the path. "Straight into a dozen Molts, *no* armor, nothing but a bar."

"Likes to get close, huh?"

"He didn't even stop when they were dead!" the second man said, his voice growing fainter with increasing distance. "I swear, Dorsey, you never saw anything like it in your life."

My eyes were closed and I was shivering. After a time, I'm not sure how long, I stood shakily and began to walk toward the station's staff quarters.

MOCHA

Day 37

The mid-afternoon sun was so wan that stars were already out on the western horizon. At night they formed a sky-filling haze, too dense to be called constellations. The wind that swept across the ankle-high tundra was dank and chill.

"There's one of them," I said. I started to raise my hand to point at the Rabbit sidling down the slope a kilometer away.

The native didn't seem to be walking directly toward the ships on the shallow valley's floor. His track would bring him there nonetheless, as a moth spirals in on a flame.

Piet Ricimer caught my arm before it lifted. "He'll think you're trying to shoot him," Ricimer said.

"Yeah," Macquerie agreed. "No point in putting the wind up the little beasts. They can fling stones farther than you'd believe."

A pump chuffed as it filled the *Kinsolving* with reaction mass from a Southern well we'd reopened the night before. The Southerns had also left a score of low shelters whose walls were made of the turf lifted when the interior was cut into the soil. The dwellings crawled with lice, so today some of our people were building similar huts at a distance from the originals.

"There were a dozen Rabbits in the old Southern camp when we landed," Gregg muttered. "Where did they go?"

Macquerie shrugged. "Mostly they sleep in little trenches without top cover," he said. "Hard to see unless you step

64

in one. Anyway, if they're gone, they aren't pilfering from us."

"They can't take enough to harm us seriously," Ricimer said. "They're men like us. I won't have them treated as animals."

Macquerie sniffed and said, softly enough to be ignored, "Hard to tell the difference, *I'd* say."

Ricimer resumed walking toward the top of the slope. Distances were deceptively great on Mocha's treeless landscape. The surface rippled in shallow valleys separated by low ridges. Rare but violent storms cut raw gullies before the torrents drained to impermeable rock layers from which the vegetation would in time lift the water again.

"There's nothing on the other side different from here, you know," Macquerie said. He was breathing harshly by now.

"I need the exercise," Ricimer said. He paused again and looked back. "Was this where Landolph landed, then?" he asked.

Macquerie and the general commander were unarmed. Gregg cradled his flashgun; the weight of the weapon and its satchel of spare batteries wasn't excessive to a man as strong as he was.

I carried a cutting bar. I'd known to pick one with a belt clip this time.

"Yes, that's right," Macquerie agreed. "Since then, nobody touches down on Mocha unless there's a problem with the gradients into Os Sertoes. Once or twice a year, that can happen."

The *Kinsolving*'s crew had off-loaded a featherboat and were assembling it. Ricimer planned to use the light craft to probe the Breach without stressing one of the expedition's larger vessels.

"Three more of them," I said. "Rabbits, I mean." I lifted my chin in a quick nod toward mid-slope in the direction of the camp.

The four of us must have passed within a few meters of where the natives had appeared. The Rabbits slouched along, apparently oblivious of the starships scattered in line for half a kilometer across the valley floor. One Rabbit wore a belt twisted from the hides of burrowing animals; another carried a throwing stick. Mocha's winds limited the growth of plants above ground, but the vegetation had sizable root systems.

"Some of them know Trade English," Macquerie said.

"From before the Collapse?" Gregg asked. I noticed that the big man continued to scan the ridgeline above us while we others were focused on the Rabbits.

Macquerie shrugged. "I don't have any idea," he said.

Piet Ricimer wore a cape of naturally-patterned wool. He threw the wings back over his shoulders. The wind was behind him now, though it was still cold enough for me. "That's why what we're doing is important," Ricimer said. "Those people."

"You're risking your life for the Rabbits?" Macquerie said in amazement.

"For mankind, Captain," Ricimer said. His voice was rich, his face exalted. "If man is to survive, as I believe the Lord means him to, then we have to settle a thousand Earths, a hundred thousand. There'll always be wars and disasters. If we're confined to one star, to one planet really—when the next Collapse comes, it'll be for all mankind, and forever."

"Earth has returned to the stars," I said. "The Feds and the Southerns are out on hundreds of worlds between them. They have no right to bar Venus from space—"

"Nor will they," Gregg said. His voice was as gray and hard as an iron casting.

"—but they're *there,*" I continued. "Mankind is."

"No," said Ricimer, speaking with the certainty of one to whom the truth has been revealed. "What they're doing is mining the stars and the past to feed the present whims of tyrants. None of the settlements founded by the Federation and the Southern Cross is as solid as the colony on Mocha was before the Collapse. The destiny of mankind isn't to scuttle and starve in a ditch on a hillside!"

Captain Macquerie cleared his throat doubtfully. "Do you want to go on up the hill?" he asked.

Ricimer laughed. "I suppose we've seen what we needed to see here," he said. The power informing his tones of a moment before had vanished, replaced with a light cheerfulness. "And had our exercise."

The distance back to the *Porcelain* looked farther than the ridge—still above them—had seemed from the vessel's ramp. "We're not here to found colonies," I said.

"Ah, we're here to bait the whole of mankind out to the stars by bringing back treasure," Ricimer said.

He strung his laughter across the breeze like quicksilver on a glass table. "To break Earth's monopoly, so that there won't be another revolt of outworlds against the home system, another Collapse . . . And quite incidentally, my friends, to make ourselves very wealthy indeed."

The trio of Rabbits glanced around, their attention drawn by the chime of distant laughter.

MOCHA

Day 38

I lounged at the flagship's main display, watching an image of the floodlit featherboat transmitted from the *Kinsolving*'s optics. A six-man crew had finished fitting the featherboat's single thruster. Guillermo was still inside the little vessel, setting up the electronics suite. Ricimer intended to take the vessel off exploring tomorrow or the next day.

Trench-and-wall barracks had sprouted beside each of our ships. Plastic sheeting weighted with rocks formed the roofs and sealed walls against the wind. The turf-and-stone dwellings weren't much roomier than the ships, but they were a change after a long transit.

I was alone aboard the *Porcelain*. I'd volunteered for communications watch, and I hoped to tie the featherboat— Ricimer had named it the *Nathan*—into the remote viewing net I'd created. No reason, really. Something to do that only Jeremy Moore could do. The audio link was complete, but the Molt was still enabling the featherboat's external optics.

I had one orange left from the bags of citrus fruit we'd loaded on Decades. It'd taste good now, and oranges don't keep forever . . .

Boots scuffed in the amidships section. Somebody— several somebodies, from the sound of it—had entered via the loading ramp to the hold.

Crewmen returning for personal items, I supposed. I was bored, but I didn't particularly want to chat with spacers who'd never read a book or a circuit diagram.

The hatch between the midships section and me in the

bow was closed but not dogged. It opened for Thomas Hawtry, followed by Delray and Sahagun. I got up from the console.

"We brought you some cheer, Jeremy," Hawtry said as he walked past the 17-cm cannon, locked in traveling position on its cradle. He was smiling brightly.

Sahagun carried a square green bottle without a label. Delray held a repeating carbine; uncharacteristic for him to be armed, but perhaps they were worried about Rabbits in the starlit night.

Hawtry held out his hand for me to shake. Holding— not quite seizing—my hand, Hawtry guided me away from the console. Delray stepped between me and the controls. The other four surviving gentlemen of Hawtry's coterie entered the bow section.

Hawtry patted the back of my hand with his left finger-tips, then released me. "Sorry for the little deception, Jeremy," he said. His tone was full and greasy. "Didn't want to have an accident with you bumping the alarm button, because then something awkward would happen. That's it there, isn't it?"

Hawtry nodded toward the console.

"Yes," I said. "The red button at the top center."

Coos wiggled the cage over the large button to make sure it was clipped in place. He and Farquhar carried rifles also. Levenger and Teague wore holstered pistols like Hawtry's own, but those could pass simply as items of dress for a gentleman.

When I came back to the *Porcelain* from our hike, I'd returned my cutting bar to the arms locker in the main hold. *A bar's really better for a close-in dustup,* Jeude had said on Decades, but there were seven of them here . . .

"We're here to save the expedition, Jeremy," Hawtry said. "And our lives as well, I shouldn't wonder. You've seen how that potter's whelp Ricimer hates gentlemen? You've been spared the worst of the insults, but that will change."

He lowered himself into the seat I'd vacated. Coos and Sahagun stepped to either side so that Hawtry could still view me directly.

"So you're planning to kill the general commander and replace him?" I said baldly. I crossed my hands behind my back.

Delray and Teague looked uncomfortable. "Say, now, fellow," Hawtry said with a frown. "Nobody spoke of killing, not in the least. But if we—the better class of men—don't act quickly, Ricimer will abandon us here on Mocha. He as good as stated his plans when he put me, *me,* aboard the *Absalom.* A hulk can't transit the Breach, anyone can see that!"

"Go on, then," I said. My voice was calm. I watched the unfolding scene from outside my body, quietly amazed at the tableau. "If you're not going to kill General Commander Ricimer, what?"

Sahagun glanced at Hawtry and held the bottle forward a few centimeters to call attention to it.

"Say, I'm the real commander of the expedition anyway," Hawtry said. He looked away and rubbed the side of his nose. "By Councilor Duneen's orders, and I shouldn't wonder the governor's directly. If it should be necessary to take over, and it is."

"Thomas, what are you going to do?" I said, with gentle emphasis on the final word.

"A drink so that that psychotic bastard Gregg goes to sleep," Hawtry said, rubbing his nose. "That—that one, he won't listen to reason, that's obvious."

Sahagun lifted the green bottle again. The liquor sloshed. The container was full, but the wax seal around the stopper had been broken. Delray grimaced and turned his back on the proceedings.

"Ricimer, he's not a problem without Gregg," Hawtry continued. "We'll put them on the *Absalom*—and a few sailors for crew, I suppose. There won't be any problem with the men. They'll follow their natural leaders, be *glad* to follow real leaders!"

"But you want me to give Gregg the bottle," I said. I sounded as though I was checking the cargo manifest. "Because he'd wonder if any of you offered it."

"Well, drink with him, jolly him along," Hawtry said.

"It won't do you any harm. You'll wake up in the morning without even a headache."

He rubbed his nose again.

"That Gregg's got a hut of his own," Levenger said in a bitter voice. "While the rest of us sleep with common sailors!"

"Gregg doesn't sleep well when he's on the ground," I said. I felt the corners of my mouth lift. Maybe I was smiling. "He doesn't want to distress other people. And there's the embarrassment, I suppose."

Hawtry lifted himself angrily from the seat in which he'd been pretending to relax. "Listen, Moore," he said. "Either you can do this and things'll go peacefully—or I'll *personally* shoot you outside Gregg's door, and when he comes out we'll gun *him* down. He won't have a chance against seven of us."

Not a proposition I'd care to bet my life on, Thomas, I thought. My lips tingled, but I didn't speak aloud.

"We'll kill you as a traitor, and him because he's too damned dangerous to live!" Hawtry said. "So which way will it be?"

"Well, I wouldn't want anyone to think I was a traitor," I said. "But you'll have to wait—"

Hawtry raised his arm to slap me, then caught himself and lowered his hand again. His face was mottled with rage. "There'll be no delays, Moore," he said savagely. "Not if you know what's good for you."

"Gregg knows I'm on watch," I explained in a neutral voice. "If I appear before I've been relieved, he'll be suspicious."

"Oh," said Hawtry. "Oh. How long are you . . ."

I looked at the chronometer on the navigation console set to ship's time. "Oh," I said, "I think ten minutes should do it."

The midships hatch banged violently open. "No time at all, gentlemen," said Stephen Gregg as he stepped through behind the muzzle of his flashgun. His helmet's lowered visor muffled his voice, but the words were as clear as the threat.

Gregg wore body armor. So did Piet Ricimer, who followed with a short-barreled shotgun. Dole and Lightbody were behind the commander with cutting bars. Stampfer, the gunner, carried a heavy single-shot rifle, and Salomon had a repeater. There were more sailors as well, shoving their way into the bow section.

Hawtry dived for the compartment's exterior hatch, an airlock. Perhaps he felt that no one would shoot in a room so crowded.

"Steady," Ricimer murmured.

Hawtry tugged the hatch open. No one tried to stop him. Jeude waited in the airlock with his cutting bar ready. He twitched the blade forward, severing Hawtry's pistol belt and enough flesh to fling the gentleman back screaming.

"Take their weapons," Ricimer said calmly.

"It may interest you *gentlemen* to know," I said, my voice rising an octave as my soul flooded back into my body, "that there was a channel open to Guillermo in the featherboat all the time we were talking. And if there hadn't been, I assure you I would have found another way to stop you traitors!"

"It wasn't me!" Coos cried. He was a tall man, willowy and supercilious at normal times. "It wasn't—"

Lightbody punched Coos in the stomach with the butt of his cutting bar, doubling him up on the deck. Coos began to vomit.

"I'll expect you to have that cleaned up by end of watch, Lightbody," Ricimer said as he uncaged the alarm button.

"Aye-aye, *sir!*" Lightbody said.

The flagship's siren howled a strident summons.

"Listen, Moore," snarled Hawtry's voice through loudspeakers mounted to either side of the main hatch. A spotlight on the *Kinsolving* two hundred meters away was focused on the flagship's hold. "I'll *personally* shoot you outside Gregg's door, and when he comes out we'll gun *him* down."

Wind sighed across the valley, bearing away the murmur of the gathered spacers. Someone called, "Bastard!" in a tone of loud amazement.

"Ricimer, he's not a problem without Gregg," said Hawtry's voice. Guillermo was working the board, mixing the gentleman's words for greatest effect from the recording the Molt had made in the *Nathan*.

Hawtry struggled against his bonds in the center of the hold. Dole had cinched Hawtry's ankles to a staple. The gentleman's wrists were tied in front of him and he was gagged besides. Hawtry's six followers stood at the base of the ramp—disarmed and discreetly guarded by trusted sailors, but not shackled.

"We'll kill you and him!" said Hawtry's voice. You'd have had to hear the original words to realize the speech was edited. At that, Guillermo hadn't distorted the thrust of the gentleman's harangue.

Piet Ricimer stepped forward. "Thomas Hawtry," he said. "You knew that this expedition could succeed only if we all kept our oaths to strive together in brotherhood. Your own words convict you of treason to the state, and of sacrilege against God."

Stephen Gregg, a statue in half armor, stood at the opposite side of the hatch from Ricimer. He hadn't moved since Dole and Jeude fastened the prisoner in front of the assembly.

A kerchief was tied behind Hawtry's head. Ricimer tugged up the knot so that the gentleman could spit out the gag.

Hawtry shook himself violently. "You have no right to try me!" he shouted. "I'm a factor, a *factor!* I need answer to no judge but the Governor's Council."

Unlike Ricimer's, Hawtry's voice wasn't amplified. He sounded thin and desperate to me.

"Under God and Governor Halys," Ricimer said, "I am general commander of this expedition. I and your shipmates will judge you, Thomas Hawtry. How do you plead?"

"It was a joke!" cried Hawtry. He turned from side to side in the glare of lights focused on him. "There was no plot, just a joke, and that whorechaser Moore knew it!"

The crowd buzzed, men talking to their closest companions. Hawtry's coterie stood silent, with gray faces and stiff smiles. Gregg's eyes, the only part of the gunman that moved, drifted from them to the prisoner and back.

Contorting his body, Hawtry rubbed his eyes with his shoulder. He caught sight of me at the front of the assembly. "There he is!" Hawtry shouted, pointing with his bound hands. "There's the Judas Jeremy Moore! He lied me into these bonds!"

I climbed the ramp in three crashing strides. The cutting bar batted against my legs, threatening to trip me. Hawtry straightened as he saw me coming; his eyes grew wary.

A tiny smile played at the corners of Stephen Gregg's mouth.

"Aye, strike a fettered man, Moore," Hawtry said shrilly.

I pulled the square-faced bottle from the pocket of the insulated vest I wore over my tunic. Hawtry's face was hard and pale in the spotlights.

"Here you are, Thomas," I said. A part of my mind noted in surprise that a directional microphone picked up my voice and boomed my words out through the loudspeakers so that everyone in the crowd could hear. "Here's the bottle that you ordered me to drink with Mister Gregg."

Hawtry's chin lifted. He shuffled his boots, but Dole had shackled him straitly.

I twisted out the glass stopper. "Take a good drink of this, Thomas," I said. "And if it only puts you to sleep, then I swear I'll defend your life with my own!"

Hawtry's face suffused with red hatred. He swung his bound arms and swatted the container away. It clanked twice on the ramp and skidded the rest of the way down without breaking. Snowy gray liquor splashed from the bottle's throat.

"Yes," I said as I backed away. I was centered within myself again. For a moment I'd been . . . "I rather thought that would be your response."

I'd watched in my mind as the bar howled in the hands of my own puppet figure below. It swung in an arc that continued through the spray of blood and the shocked face of Thomas Hawtry sailing free of his body.

Piet Ricimer stepped forward. He took Hawtry's joined hands in his own and said, "Thomas, in the name of the Lord, won't you repent? There's still—"

"No!" said Stephen Gregg thunderously as he strode into the center of the hatchway. The ceramic armor added bulk to the rangy power of his form. "There's been forgiveness aplenty. The next time it'll be your life, Piet, and I'll not have that."

Gregg laid his great left hand over Hawtry's wrists and lifted them away from Ricimer. Gregg raised Hawtry's arms, ignoring the prisoner's attempt to pull free, and shouted to the assembly, "Is this man guilty of treason? Shall he be marooned here as a traitor?"

"Yes!" I screamed. Around me I heard, "Aye!" and "Guilty!" and "Yes!" A murmur of, "No," a man crying, "You have no right!" But those latter were the exceptions to a tide of anger tinged with bloodlust. The sailors were Betaport men, and in Betaport Piet Ricimer sat just below the throne of God.

"No, you can't do this!" Delray shouted angrily. The other gentlemen stood silent, afraid to speak lest Gregg turn the mob on them as well.

Gregg dropped the prisoner's arms. "You didn't want to obey the general commander, Hawtry," he said. "Now you can rule a whole planet by yourself."

Officers of the *Mizpah* and *Kinsolving* stood in a clump at the back of the assembly, muttering and looking concerned. They knew better than the common sailors how much trouble could come from punishing a powerful noble. Blakey was Councilor Duneen's man, while Captain Winter trimmed his behavior to the prevailing winds.

"You can't *do* this!" Delray repeated. The wind toyed with his voice. Perhaps a third of the assembly could make out his words, while the rest heard only faint desperation. "The Rabbits will kill him!"

The other gentlemen moved away as though Delray was thrashing in a pool of his own vomit. A sailor behind Delray patted a baton of steel tubing against the calluses of the opposite palm, but the gentleman took no notice.

"They'll flay him with sharp stones!" Delray shouted. "You can't do this!"

I didn't know Delray well and hadn't liked what I did know: the third son of Delray of Sunrise, a huge hold in the Aphrodisian Hills. Very rich, very haughty, and even younger than his 19 Earth years.

It struck me that there was a person under Delray's callow exterior who might have been worth knowing after all.

"He's right," Gregg said abruptly. The amplified boom of his voice startled me after an interval of straining to hear Delray's cries. "Dole, cut his feet loose. Hawtry, we'll find a gully out beyond the ships."

I blinked, shocked by a sudden reality that I'd avoided until that moment. It was one thing to eat meat, another to watch the butcher. Dole stepped up the ramp, his bar humming.

"No!" said Ricimer, placing the flat of his hand on Gregg's breastplate. He directed the bigger man back. *Piet's too good a man for this existence,* Gregg had said the last night on Venus.

"Give me a ship!" Hawtry blurted. His face was as white as a bone that dogs were scuffling over. "Give me a featherboat, C-cap-com*man*der Ricimer!"

"Mister Hawtry," Ricimer said, "you cannot pilot a starship, and I will not diminish a force devoted to the Lord's work for the sake of a traitor. But the judgment on your treason was that of the expedition as a whole. Therefore the expedition will carry out the necessary sentence."

Ricimer turned to face the assembly. He didn't squint, though the spotlight was full on his face. He pointed to the front of the crowd, his arm as straight as a gun barrel.

"Coos, Levenger, Teague," he said, clipping out syllables like cartridges shucked from a repeater's magazine. "Farquhar, Sahagun. And Delray. Under the direction of Mister Gregg, you will form a firing party to execute sentence of death on the traitor Thomas Hawtry. Tomorrow at dawn. Do you understand?"

None of the gentlemen spoke. Farquhar covered his face with his hands.

Hawtry shuddered as though the first bullet had struck him. He closed his eyes for a moment. When he reopened them, his expression was calm.

"This assembly is dismissed," the general commander said in a voice without triumph or pity. "And may God have mercy on our souls."

MOCHA

Day 39

Mocha's sun laid a track of yellow light from the eastern horizon. Ricimer and Hawtry stood at the edge of the shallow mere, talking in voices too low to carry twenty meters to where the nearest of the other men waited.

The air was still, for the first time that I could remember since we landed here. I shivered anyway.

A group of sailors commanded by the *Porcelain*'s bosun held single-shot rifles. The men were chatting companionably. Jeude punctuated his comment by raising his left hand in the air and wriggling the fingers. He and the others laughed.

About half the expedition's complement had trekked to the north end of the valley to watch the execution. The remainder stayed with the ships, pretending this was a normal day. Occasionally someone might pause and glance northward, but there would be nothing to see. The irregularity of the valley's floor seemed slight, but it was enough to swallow a man-height figure in half a kilometer.

I didn't know why I was here. I rubbed my hands together and wondered if I should have brought gloves.

The gentlemen of the firing party faced one another in a close circle, shoulders together and their heads bowed. A spacer cried out, "Pretty little chickens got their feathers plucked, didn't they?"

The remark didn't have to be a gibe directed against the gentlemen . . . but it probably was. Delray spun to identify the speaker. The gentleman remembered his present place and subsided in impotent anger.

Stephen Gregg, standing alone as if contemplating the sunrise, turned his head. "Roosen?" he called to the spacer who'd flung the comment. "I'm glad to know you have spirit. I often need a man of spirit to accompany me."

Roosen shrank into himself. His companions of a moment before edged away from him.

I chuckled.

Gregg strolled toward me, holding the flashgun in the crook of his left arm. Gregg wore his helmet and a satchel of batteries, but he didn't have body armor on for the morning's duties.

The big man nodded toward the mere thirty meters away, where Hawtry and the general commander still talked. "So you would have protected Mister Hawtry from me if he'd been willing to drink from your bottle, Moore?" Gregg said in a low, bantering tone.

Sometimes Ricimer's aide looked like an empty sack. Now—there was nothing overtly tense about Gregg, but a black power filled his frame and dominated the world about him.

I shrugged. "Thomas isn't the sort for half measures," I said evenly. "Sleep where death would do, for example. Besides . . . I rather think he resented my—closeness. With Councilor Duneen's sister."

My mouth smiled. "Though to listen to him, he wasn't aware of that. Closeness."

Gregg turned again to face the sunrise. "I was mistaken in my opinion of the man I brought aboard in Betaport, wasn't I? Just who are you, Moore?"

I shrugged again. "I'm damned if I know," I said. Then I said, "I could use a woman right now. The Lord *knows* I could."

Ricimer and Hawtry clasped hands, then embraced. Ricimer walked back to the company. His face was still. The crowd hushed.

Gregg's visage became cold and remote. "Distribute the rifles," he ordered as he strode toward the gentlemen and the sailors waiting to equip them for their task.

Dole muttered a command. He gave a single cartridge and a rifle, its action open, to Sahagun. That gentleman and the other members of the firing party accepted the weapons with grimaces.

"Take your stand!" Gregg ordered. He placed himself beside and a pace behind the gentlemen. His flashgun was ready but not presented.

"I'll give the commands if you please, Mister Gregg," Thomas Hawtry called in a clear voice. He stood at apparent ease, his limbs free.

Gregg looked at Ricimer. Ricimer nodded agreement.

"May God and you, my fellows, forgive my sins!" Hawtry said. "Gentlemen, load your pieces."

The men of the firing party were mostly experienced marksmen, but they fumbled the cartridges. Coos dropped his. He had to brush grit off the case against his trouser leg. Breeches closed with a variety of clicks and shucking sounds.

Hawtry stood as straight as a sunbeam. His eyes were open. "Aim!" he said.

The gentlemen lifted their rifles to their shoulders. Farquhar jerked his trigger. The shot slammed out toward the horizon. Farquhar shouted in surprise at the accidental discharge.

"Fire!" Hawtry cried. The rest of the party fired. Two bullets punched Hawtry's white tunic, and the bridge of his nose vanished in a splash of blood.

Hawtry crumpled to his knees, then flopped onto his face. There was a hole the size of a fist in the back of his skull. The surface of the water behind him danced as if with rain.

Delray opened the bolt of his rifle to extract the spent case, then flung the weapon itself toward the mere. The rifle landed halfway between him and the corpse twitching spastically on the ground.

Delray stalked away. The remainder of the firing party stood numbly as Dole's team collected the rifles.

Gregg turned and walked back to me. He looked drawn and gray.

"I'm impressed with the way you handled yourself the other night," he said quietly. "And on Decades, of course;

but courage in a brawl is more common than the ability to stay calm in a crisis."

I hugged myself and shivered. A spacer had tossed a tarp over Hawtry's body. Two other men were digging a grave nearby.

Piet Ricimer knelt in prayer, his back to the dead man. *Brains and bits of bone, splashing the mere in a wide arc.*

"How do you sleep at all, Mister Gregg?" I whispered.

Gregg sniffed. "You can get used to anything, you know," he said. "I suppose that's the worst of it. Even the dreams."

He put a hand on my shoulder and turned me away from the past. "Let's go back to the ship," he said. "I have a bottle. And you may as well call me Stephen, Jeremy."

MOCHA

Day 51

When the alert signal throbbed on the upper right corner of the main screen, I slapped the sidebar control that I'd preselected for potential alarm situations. Salomon dumped the transit solutions he'd been running at the navigation console and echoed all my data on his display.

A grid of dots and numbers replaced the 360° visual panorama I'd been watching for want of anything better to do. Presumably some of the Rabbits were female, but it hadn't come to that yet.

I didn't understand the new display. A pink highlight surrounded one of the dots.

I held the siren switch down briefly to rouse the men sleeping, gambling, or wandering across Mocha's barren landscape. A few seconds could be important, and even a false alarm would give the day some life it otherwise lacked.

"It's the passive optical display," Salomon explained. "An object just dropped into orbit. If it's not a flaw in the scanner, something came out of trans—"

"*Nathan* to squadron," said Piet Ricimer's voice, flattened by the program by which the *Porcelain*'s AI took the static out of the featherboat's transmission. "Respond, squadron. Over."

I switched the transceiver to voice operation while my left hand entered the commands that relayed the conversation through the loudspeakers—tannoys I'd taken from Federation stores on Decades—on poles outside the temporary shelters. It'd been something to do, and the disor-

82

ganized communications among the ships scattered here had offended my soul.

"Go ahead, Commander," I said before I remembered that Salomon was on watch this morning. "We're on voice."

Handover procedures were cumbersome and basically needless between two parties who knew one another. Without visuals—the featherboat's commo was rudimentary—there was a chance that one speaker's transmission would step on the other's, but that wasn't a serious concern.

"Moore?" Ricimer said. His words blared through the external speakers to the men alerted by the siren. "We've got to leave immediately. Get essential stores out of the *Absalom;* we're leaving her. We'll be abandoning the *Nathan* here too, so that frees up space on the *Kinsolving* for the Decades loot. We'll be coming in on the next orbit—"

The featherboat couldn't communicate through her thruster's discharged ions.

"—and I want to lift off within an hour of when we land. Is that understood?"

"We understand, Commander," I said. I rose from the console. Officers and senior men would be gathering work crews from men more concerned with getting their personal gear back aboard the ships.

"I'll address the squadron when we reach orbit," Ricimer said. The transmission was beginning to break up beyond the AI's capacity to restore it. The caret on the main screen that was the *Nathan* had already slipped beneath the horizon of the display. "Before we negotiate the Breach . . ."

His words died in a burst of static.

"I've got takeoff and initial transit programs loaded," Salomon said to me with a wry smile. Perhaps it was a comment on the way the gentleman had hijacked communications with the general commander.

Men were already crashing aboard the *Porcelain,* shouting to one another in a skein of tangled conversations. I strode for the midships hatch to get through it before the crush arrived in the other direction.

"I'm going to pull the AI from the hulk," I called back to the navigator. "It's not worth much, but it's something . . . and it's the only thing *I* can do now."

MOCHA ORBIT

Day 51

Because of the adrenaline rush of the hastened liftoff, weightlessness didn't make me as queasy as it had on every previous occasion.

"Men of Venus," Piet Ricimer said, standing before the video pickups of the main console.

The general commander's tone and pose were consciously theatrical, but not phony. An unshakable belief in his mission was the core of Ricimer's being. "My fellows. While I was on Os Sertoes, a Southern colony three days transit from here, six Federation warships landed. Their admiral announced that they'd arrived to protect the Breach from Venerian pirates under the command of the notorious Ricimer."

He allowed himself a smile.

The interior of the *Porcelain* looked as if a mob had torn through the vessel. Belongings seemed to expand in the course of a voyage. Objects were never repacked as tightly as they'd been stowed before initial liftoff. Loot, even from a near-wasteland like Mocha, added to the bulk, and the crew's hurried reboarding would at best have created chaos.

The interior of the *Kinsolving,* visible on the split screen past the set face of Captain Winter, was an even more complete image of wreckage. The quality of the *Mizpah*'s transmission was so poor that the flagship's AI painted the field behind Blakey as a blur of color. On all the vessels, items that hadn't been properly stowed before liftoff drifted as the ships hung above Mocha.

"The Feds will be patrolling all the landing sites in the region, I have no doubt," Ricimer said. I could hear the words echoing from tannoys in the compartments sternward. On the *Kinsolving,* sailors listened in the background as tense, dim shapes. "We aren't here to fight the Federation. We're here to take the wealth on which President Pleyal builds his tyranny and turn that wealth to the use of all mankind."

Another small smile. "Ourselves included."

Stephen Gregg stood between a pair of stanchions, doing isometric exercises with his arms. He was too big to be comfortable for any length of time on a featherboat, but not even Piet Ricimer had dared suggest Stephen remain on Mocha during the exploratory run.

"I've set an initial course," Ricimer continued. "The *Nathan* tested the gradients within the throat of the Breach. I won't disguise the fact that the stresses are severe; but not too severe, I believe, for us to achieve our goal."

"It was rough as a cob," Jeude muttered, trying to emasculate his fear by articulating it. "The boat nigh shook herself apart. Mister Ricimer, he kept pushing the gradients and she couldn't *take* it."

I put a hand on the eyebolt which Jeude held. I didn't quite touch the young sailor's hand, but I hoped the near-contact would provide comfort.

Part of my mind was amused that I was trying to reassure someone who understood far better than I did the risks we were about to undergo. There were times that the risks couldn't be allowed to matter. At those times, it was a gentleman's duty to be an example.

"There is one further matter to attend before we proceed," Ricimer continued. "Our flagship has been named the *Porcelain*. I am taking this moment, as we enter a new phase of our endeavors, to rechristen her *Oriflamme*. May she symbolize the banner of the Lord which we are carrying through the Breach!"

He swept off his cap and cried, "In the name of God, gentlemen, let us do our duty!"

"Hurrah!" Salomon cried, so smoothly that I remembered Ricimer's whispered conversation with his navigator before he began his address. Throughout the flagship—the *Oriflamme*—and aboard the other vessels, men were shouting, "Hurrah!"

I shouted as well, buoyed by hope and the splendor of the moment. For the first time in my memory, Jeremy Moore was part of a group.

Ricimer shut off the transmission and slipped into his couch to prepare for transit. Guillermo and Salomon watched from the flanking consoles.

I let go my grip and thrust myself across the compartment toward Stephen. My control in weightlessness was getting better—at least I didn't push off with all my strength anymore—but it was short of perfect. Stephen caught me by the hand and pulled me down to share a stanchion.

"You may think you dislike transit now," Stephen said, "but you'll know you do shortly."

"Yes, well, I was going to suggest that I'd get out and walk instead," I said. "Ah—it occurs to me, Stephen, that the oriflamme is the charge of Councilor Duneen's arms."

Stephen nodded. "Yeah," he said. "Piet thinks it may take the Councilor's mind off the fact that we've executed one of his chief clients. Not that Hawtry was any loss, not really; but the Councilor might feel that he needed to . . . react."

"Ah," I said. "It was the general commander's idea?"

"Prepare for transit!" Salomon warned over the PA system.

"Oh, yes," Stephen agreed. "Piet thinks ahead."

I followed Stephen's glance toward the general commander. It struck me that Ricimer was, in his way, just as ruthless as Stephen Gregg.

IN TRANSIT

Day 64

The leg of the attitude-control console nearest me began to quiver with a harmonic as the *Oriflamme*'s thrusters strained. The vessel flip-flopped in and out of transit, again, *again*. The surface of the leg dulled as tiny cracks spread across the surface, metastasizing with each successive vibration.

Life was a gray lump that crushed Jeremy Moore against the decking. My vision was monochrome. Images shifted from positive to negative as the *Oriflamme* left and reentered the sidereal universe, but I was no longer sure which state was which.

The sequence ended. Bits of ceramic crazed from the leg lay on the deck beneath the attitude controls.

Salomon got up from his console. His face looked like a skin of latex stretched over an armature of thin wires. "The charts are wrong!" he shouted. "Landolph lied about coming here, or if he did, it's closed since then. There *is* no Breach!"

Pink light careted a dot on the starscape above Guillermo's console. Either the *Kinsolving* or the *Mizpah* was still in company with the flagship. I didn't care. All that mattered now was the realization that if I was dead, the nausea would be over.

"I'm going to add one transit to the sequence without changing the constants," Piet Ricimer said from the central couch. Above him, the main screen was a mass of skewed lines. "From the tendency of the gradients, I believe we're very close to a gap."

Guillermo's three-fingered hands clicked across his keyboard, transmitting the solution to the accompanying vessel.

Stephen Gregg was curled into a ball on the deck. He'd started out leaning against the attitude-control console, but lateral acceleration during a previous series of transits had toppled him over. He either hadn't wished or hadn't been able to sit up again.

The sailors without immediate duties during transit were comatose or praying under their breath. Perhaps I should have been pleased that experienced spacers were affected as badly as I was.

"The gradients are rising too fast!" Salomon shouted. "The levels are already higher than I've ever seen them, and—"

Lightbody came off his seat at the attitude-control console. The sailor didn't have a weapon, but his long arms were spread like the claws of an assassin bug. Salomon started to turn, shocked from his panic by the palpable destruction lunging toward his throat.

Stephen caught Lightbody's ankle and jerked the sailor to the deck. I leaped onto the man's shoulders.

Lightbody's face was blank. The wild light went out of his eyes, leaving the sailor with a confused expression. "What?" he said. "Wha . . ."

"Sorry, sir," Salomon muttered. He sat down on his couch again.

I rolled away. I had to use both hands to lever myself back to a squat and then rise. The jolting action had settled my mind, but my limbs were terribly weak. I could stand upright, so long as I gripped a stanchion as though the *Oriflamme* was in free fall rather than proceeding under 1-g acceleration.

Lightbody stood, then helped Stephen up as well. Lightbody returned to his seat. I held out a hand to bring Stephen to his stanchion.

"Prepare for transit," Piet Ricimer said. He hadn't risen from his couch or looked back during the altercation.

Light and color. Blankness, blackness, body ripped

inside out, soul scraped in a million separate Hells.
    Light and color again.
    "There," said Piet Ricimer. "As I thought, a star . . .
and she has a planet. We will name the planet Respite."

RESPITE

Day 68

The plateau on which the *Oriflamme* and *Mizpah* rested above the jungle was basalt. The fresh ceramic with which teams resealed the vessels' stress-cracked hulls was black, and the sound of grinders processing the dense rock into raw material for the glazing kilns was nerve-wracking and omnipresent.

Stephen checked the weld which belayed the glass-fiber line around a vertical toe of basalt near the plateau's rim. He nodded. I let myself drop over the edge.

The mass of the plateau dulled the bone-jarring sound. My chest muscles relaxed for the first time in the three days since the grinders had started work.

The basalt had formed hexagonal pillars as it cooled from magma in the depths of the earth. Cycles of upthrust and weathering left this mass as a tower hundreds of meters above the surrounding jungle. As the outermost columns crumbled, they created a giant staircase down into the green canopy.

Forty meters below the top of the plateau, my boots touched the layer of dirt covering the sloping top of a broken pillar. I released my harness from the line and stepped away, waving Stephen down in turn.

A pair of arm-long flying creatures paused curiously near Stephen, hovering in the updraft along the plateau's flank. The "birds" were hard-shelled, with four wings and sideways-hung jaws. They were harmless to anything the size of a man and hadn't learned to be wary.

The forest far below was a choir of varied calls. Mist

trailed among the treetops, and a plume hectares in area rose a few kilometers away like a stationary cloud. I wondered if a hot spring or a lake of boiling mud broke surface there in the jungle.

Respite's atmosphere had a golden hue. I found I actually liked being under an open sky, unlike most men raised in the tunnels and impervious domes of Venus. It made me tingle with uncertainty, much the way I felt when making my initial approaches to a woman.

The feeling of peace below the rim was relative. The rock vibrated from the teeth of the grinders, felt if not heard. The terrace was a nesting site for a colony of the flying creatures. Hundreds of them stood at the mouths of burrows excavated in the soil, goggling at us with octuple eyes. They clacked the edges of their front and rear pairs of wings together querulously.

Opinions of the flyers' taste among our crew ranged from adequate to delicious: Salomon swore he'd never before eaten anything as good as the sausage of smoked lung tissue and organ meat he'd made from the creatures. In any event, the expedition would leave Respite well stocked with food.

Stephen landed with a grunt. His fingers massaged his opposite shoulders. For this excursion he'd slung a short rifle across his back, rather than the flashgun he favored. "I don't know about you," he said, "but I'm not looking forward to the climb back, ascenders or no. I'm not in shape for this."

"I'm not looking forward to going back to the noise," I said. I felt the strain in my arms and thigh muscles also, but I thought I'd be physically ready before I was mentally ready to return. "I suppose it's better than falling apart in transit, though."

Stephen sniffed. "Worried about the *Kinsolving*?" he said. "Don't be. Winter just didn't have the stomach for this. He's headed back to Venus with the rest of Hawtry's node of vipers. That lot'd make me ashamed to be a gentleman—if I gave a damn myself."

The hexagonal terrace sloped at 30°, enough to tumble a man over the edge if he lost his footing. Each of the basalt columns was about ten meters wide across the flats. I stepped forward carefully. "With the Decades loot besides," I noted.

As I passed close to nesting sites, the creatures drew themselves down as far as they could into their burrows. Because the soil was so shallow, their heads remained above the surface but the clicking of the wings was muted.

"Commander Ricimer," I went on, "thinks they've just missed this landfall and gone on through the Breach. The *Kinsolving*."

"Piet likes to think the best of people," Stephen said. He walked over to me without apparent caution. The wind from the forest ruffled our cuffs and tunics upward and bathed us in earthy, alien odors.

"And you?" I asked without looking at my companion. Something moved across the distant forest, perhaps a shadow. If the motion had been made by a living creature, it was a huge one.

"Oh, I'd *like* to, sure," Stephen said, adjusting his rifle's sling.

"The loot's the reason I'm not angry," Stephen added. "There's enough value aboard the *Kinsolving* to arouse attention, but not nearly enough to buy Winter's way out of trouble for attacking the colony of a state with whom Venus is at peace. That lot has punished themselves."

I looked at my companion. "Technically at peace," I said.

"Politicians are *very* technical, Jeremy," Stephen said. "Until it's worth the time of somebody in court to cut corners. And the Decades loot won't interest the likes of Councilor Duneen, which is what it'd take to square this one."

I peered over the edge of the terrace. The next step down was within five meters of the outer lip of the one we were on. A pattern of parallel semicircular waves marked the surface of the step, springing out like ripples in a frozen pond from the side of the column on which we stood.

Pits weathered into the rock offered toeholds. I turned and swung my legs over.

"It's a long way down," Stephen warned. "And it's

likely to be a longer way back up."

"I want to check something," I said. "You don't have to come."

I clambered my own height down the rock face, then pushed off and landed with my knees flexed. Perhaps Stephen could pull me up with our belts paired into a rope, or—

Stephen slammed down beside me. He'd jumped with the rifle held out so that it didn't batter him in the side when he hit the ground. He grinned at me.

I shrugged. "It's the pattern here," I said, walking toward the ripples in stone.

Conical nests built up from the surface indicated that flyers of a different species had colonized this step. These were hand-sized and bright yellow in contrast to the dull colors of the larger creatures. Hundreds of them lifted into the air simultaneously, screeching and emitting sprays of mauve feces over the two of us.

I ducked and swore. Stephen began to laugh rackingly. The cloud of flyers sailed away from the plateau, then dived abruptly toward the jungle.

Stephen untied his kerchief, checked for a clean portion of the fabric, and used that to wipe down the rifle's receiver. "I was the smart-ass who decided if you thought you could make it back, I sure could," he explained. "Nobody's choice but mine—which is why I let Piet make the decisions, mostly."

I stepped to the point from which ripples spread from the rock face. As I'd expected, the basalt had been melted away. Because the rock was already fully oxidized, it splashed into waves like those of metal welded in a vacuum.

The cavity so formed was circular and nearly two meters in diameter. It was sealed by a substance as transparent as air—not glass, for it responded with a soft *thock* when I tapped it with my signet ring.

The creature mummified within was the height and shape of a man, but it was covered with fine scales, and its limbs were jointed in the wrong places. At one time the mummy had been clothed, but only shreds of fabric and fittings remained in a litter around the four-toed feet.

"Piet said it looked from the way the rocks were glazed that ships had landed on the plateau in the past," Stephen remarked. "Landolph, he thought. But after he looked closer at the weather cracking, he decided that it must have been millennia ago."

"What does it mean?" I asked.

"To us?" said Stephen. "Nothing. Because our business is with the Federation; and whoever this fellow was, he wasn't from the Federation."

IN TRANSIT

Day 92

The *Oriflamme* came out of transit—out of a universe which had no place for man or even for what man thought were natural laws. This series had been of eighteen insertions. The energy differential, the gradient, between the sidereal universe and the bubbles of variant space-time had risen each time.

I stood with one hand on the attitude-control console, the other poised to steady Dole if the bosun slipped out of his seat again. I hadn't eaten in . . . days, I wasn't sure how long. I hadn't kept anything down for longer yet. Every time the *Oriflamme* switched universes, pain as dull as the back of an axe crushed through my skull and nausea tried to empty my stomach.

Dole had nothing to do unless Piet Ricimer ordered him to override the AI—which would be suicide, given the stresses wracking the *Oriflamme* now. Helping the bosun hold his station, however pointless, gave me reason to live.

Stephen Gregg stood with a hand on Lightbody's shoulder and the other on Jeude's. Stephen was smiling, in a manner of speaking. His face was as gray and lifeless as a bust chipped out of concrete, but he was standing nonetheless.

During insertions, the *Oriflamme*'s thrusters roared at very nearly their maximum output. Winger, the chief of the motor crew, bent over Guillermo's couch. He spoke about the condition of the sternmost nozzles in tones clipped just this side of panic.

A few festoons of meat cured on Respite still hung from wires stretched across the vessel's open areas. We'd been eating the "birds" in preference to stores loaded on Decades, for fear that the flesh—smoked, for the most part—would spoil. There was no assurance we'd reach another food source any time soon.

Salomon's screen was a mass of numbers, Ricimer's a tapestry of shaded colors occasionally spiking into a saturated primary. The two consoles displayed the same data in different forms, digital and analogue: craft and art side by side, and only God to know if either showed a way out of the morass of crushing energies.

The *Mizpah* in close-up filled Guillermo's screen. The gradients themselves threw our two vessels onto congruent courses: the navigational AIs both attempted with electronic desperation to find solutions that would not exceed the starships' moduli of rupture. The range of possibilities was an increasingly narrow one.

"Stand by for transit," Piet Ricimer croaked. "There will be a sequence of f-f-four insertions."

He paused, breathing hard with the exertion. Guillermo compiled the data in a packet and transferred it to the *Mizpah* by laser.

Winger swore and stumbled aft again to his station. He would have walked into the Long Tom in the center of the compartment if I hadn't tugged him into a safer trajectory.

The *Mizpah*'s hull was zebra-striped. The reglazing done on Respite had flaked from the old ship's hull along the lines of maximum stress, leaving streaks of creamy original hull material alternated with broader patches of the black, basalt-based sealant. Leakage of air from the *Mizpah* must be even worse than it was for us, and it was very serious for us.

More pain would come. More pain than anything human could survive and remain human. *Oh God our help in ages past, our hope in years to come . . .*

"We need to get into suits," Salomon said. He lay at the side console like a cadaver on a slab. "They're in suits already on the *Mizpah*." The navigator's eyes were on the screen before him, but he didn't appear to be strong enough to touch the keypad at his fingertips.

A sailor sobbed uncontrollably in his hammock. Stephen's eyes turned toward the sound, only his eyes.

"This sequence will commence in one minute forty seconds," Ricimer said. His words clacked as if spoken by a wood-jawed marionette. "The gradients have ceased to rise. We're. We're . . ."

Stephen didn't turn his head to look at Ricimer, but he said, "You're supposed to tell us that we've seen worse, and we'll come through this too, Piet."

Watching Stephen was like watching a corpse speak.

Ricimer coughed. After a moment, I realized that he was laughing. "If we do come through this, Stephen," Ricimer said, "be assured that I will say that the next time."

"Prepare for t-trans—" Salomon said. He couldn't get the final word out before the fact made it redundant.

My head split in bright skyrockets curving to either side. Guillermo's screen, fed by the external optics, became hash as the *Oriflamme* entered a region alien to the very concept of light as the sidereal universe knew it.

Back a heartbeat later, another blow crushing me into a boneless jelly which throbbed with pain. The gasp that started with the initial insertion was tightening my throat and ribs, or I might have tried to scream.

Half the *Mizpah* hung on the right-hand display. A streak of centimeter-thick black ceramic ringed the stern. Where the bow should have been, I saw only a mass as confused as gravel pouring from a hopper.

Transit. There was a God and He hated mankind with a fury as dense as the heart of a Black Hole. The mills of His wrath ground Jeremy Moore like—

Back, only gravel on Guillermo's screen, dancing with light, and then *nothing* because the *Oriflamme* had cycled into another bubble universe and I wished that I'd been aboard the *Mizpah* because—

The *Oriflamme* crashed into the sidereal universe again and stayed there while I swayed at Dole's station and Stephen Gregg held Jeude's slumping form against the back of his seat. There must have been a fourth insertion and return, but I hadn't felt it. Perhaps I'd blacked out, but I was still standing . . .

"The gradients have dropped to levels normal for intrasystem transits," Ricimer said. He sounded as though he had just been awakened from centuries of sleep. The muscles operating his vocal cords were stiff. "We'll make a further series of seven insertions, and I believe we'll find Landolph's landfall of Pesaltra at the end of them. Gentlemen, we have transited the Breach."

I tried to cheer. I could only manage a gabbling sound. Dole put up a hand to steady me; we clutched one another for a moment.

"We made it," Jeude whispered.

Guillermo's display showed a blank starscape, and there was no pulsing highlight on the main screen to indicate the *Mizpah*.

PESALTRA

Day 94

The ramp lowered with squealing hesitation, further sign that the stress of transiting the Breach had warped the *Oriflamme*'s sturdy hull. Air with the consistency of hot gelatin surged into the hold. I was the only man in the front rank who wasn't wearing body armor. Sweat slicked my palm on the grip of the cutting bar.

"Welcome to the asshole of the universe," muttered a spacer. He spoke for all of us in the assault party.

"Well," said Piet Ricimer as he raised the visor of his helmet. "At least nobody's shooting at us."

Steam still rose from the mudflat that served Pesaltra as a landing field. Nine of the local humans were picking their way toward the *Oriflamme*. Molts—several score and perhaps a hundred of them—stood near the low buildings and the boats drawn up on the shore of the surrounding lagoons. The aliens formed small groups which stared at but didn't approach the vessel.

There were no weapons in sight among the Feds or their slaves.

Finger-length creatures with many legs and no obvious eyes feasted on a blob of protoplasm at the foot of the ramp. They must have risen from burrows deep in the mud, or the thruster exhaust would have broiled them. The creatures were the only example of local animal life that I could see.

"No shooting unless I do," Stephen Gregg said, "and *don't* expect that. Let's go."

He cradled his flashgun and strode forward. Stephen's

boots squelched to the ankles when he stepped off the end of the ramp. I sank almost as deep, even though I didn't have the weight of armor and equipment Stephen carried.

The front rank, ten abreast, stamped and sloshed forward. The second rank spread out behind us. The locals wore thigh-length waders of waterproofed fabric. In this heat and saturated humidity, their garments must have been nearly as uncomfortable as our back-and-breast armor.

There were mountains in the western distance, but the Pesaltran terrain here and for kilometers in every direction was of shallow lagoons and mud banks with ribbons and spikes of vegetation. None of the plants were as much as a meter high; many of them sprawled like brush strokes of bright green across the mud.

A bubble burst flatulently in the middle of the nearest channel. I guessed it was the result of bacterial decay, not a larger life-form.

I felt silly holding a cutting bar as a threat against people so obviously crushed by life as the Fed personnel here. How the rest of the assault party must feel with their guns, armor, and bandoliers of ammunition!

Though Stephen Gregg wouldn't care . . . and maybe not the others either. Overwhelming force meant you were ready to overwhelm your enemy. What could possibly be embarrassing about that?

"Ah, sirs?" said one of the locals, a white-haired man with a false eye. "You'd be from the Superintendency of the Outer Ways, I guess?"

He stared at the *Oriflamme* and its heavily-armed crew as if we were monsters belched forth from the quavering earth.

It wasn't practical to carry building materials between stars. The colony's structures were nickel steel processed from local asteroids or concrete fixed with shell lime. Three large barracks housed the Molt labor force; a fourth similar building was subdivided internally for the human staff.

A middle-aged woman stood on the porch with the aid of crutches and leg braces. The door to the room behind her was open. Its furnishings were shoddy extrusions of light metal, neither attractive nor comfortable-looking.

The same could be said for the woman, I thought with a sigh.

Sheet-metal sheds held tools and equipment in obvious disorder. A windowless concrete building looked like a blockhouse, but the sliding door was open, showing the interior to be empty except for a few shimmering bales.

Garbage, including Molt and human excrement, stank in the lagoon at the back of the barracks. The hulls of at least two crashed spaceships and other larger junk had been dragged to the opposite side of the landing site.

Ricimer halted us with a wave of his hand and took another step to make his primacy clear. "I'm Captain Ricimer of the Free State of Venus," he said to the one-eyed man. "We've come through the Breach. We'll expect the full cooperation of everyone here. If we get it, then there'll be no difficulties for yourselves."

The Fed official looked puzzled. The men approaching with him had halted a few paces behind. "No, really," the man said. "I'm Assistant Treasurer Taenia; I'm in charge here. If anyone is. Who are you?"

Dole stepped forward. The butt of his rifle prodded Taenia hard in the stomach. "When Captain Ricimer's present," he said loudly, "nobody else is in charge—and especially not some dog of a Fed! Take your hats off, you lot!"

Only two of the locals wore headgear, a cloth cap on a red-haired man and another fellow with a checked bandanna tied over his scalp. Dole pointed his rifle in the face of the latter. The Fed snatched off the bandanna. He was bald as an egg.

Dole shifted his aim. "No, put that up!" Piet Ricimer snapped, but the second Fed was removing his cap and a third man knelt in the mud with a look of terror on his face.

Taenia straightened up slowly. He blinked, though the lid covering his false eye closed only halfway. "I don't . . ." he said. "I don't . . ."

Ricimer stepped up to the man and took his right hand.

"You won't be hurt so long as you and your fellows cooperate fully with us. Are you willing to do that?"

"We'll do anything you say," Taenia said. "Anything at all, of course we will, your excellency!"

Ricimer looked over his shoulder. "Mister Moore," he said. "When we lift off, I'll want to put a transponder in orbit to inform Captains Winter and Blakey of our course should they pass this way. Can you build such a device with what we have on hand?"

I nodded, flushing with silent pleasure. Ricimer had noticed my facility with electronics and was willing to use it. "Yes, yes, of course," I said. "But I suspect I can use local hardware."

Ricimer smiled at me. "I can understand a man being interested in a challenge," he said. "Though I'm surprised at a man who doesn't find this voyage enough of a challenge already."

Ricimer's face set again; grim, though not angry. There was no headquarters building, so he indicated the human barracks with a nod of his carbine's muzzle. "Let's proceed to the shelter," he said.

"But why in God's name would you want to come *here*?" blurted the Fed wringing his bandanna between his hands.

"That," remarked Stephen Gregg as we twenty Venerians swept past the flabbergasted locals, "is a fair question."

"Well, we don't have anybody to communicate *with*," Schatz, Pesaltra's radio operator, said defensively to me. "They were supposed to send a new set from Osomi with the last ferry, but they must've forgot it. Besides, the ferry comes every six months or a year, and nobody else comes at all. It's not like we've got a lot of landing traffic to control."

Across the double-sized room that served the station's administrative needs, Salomon rose from a desk covered with unfiled invoices. "What do you *mean* you don't have any charts?" he snarled at Taenia. "You've got to have some charts!"

The floor was covered with tracked-in mud so thick that a half-liter liquor bottle was almost submerged in a corner. Paper and general trash were mixed with the dirt, creating a surface similar to wattle-and-daub. I'd dropped a spring fastener when I pulled the back from the non-functioning radio. I'd searched the floor vainly for almost a minute, before I realized that the task was vain as well as pointless.

"We're not going anywhere," Taenia said in near echo of Schatz's words a moment before. "What do we need navigational data for?"

"If we were going anyplace," Schatz added with a variation of meaning, "they wouldn't have stuck us on Pesaltra."

"We'll search the files," Piet Ricimer said calmly. He gestured his navigator to the chair at the desk and dragged another over to the opposite side. "Sometimes a routing slip will give coordinates."

"But not *values*," Salomon moaned. He organized a thatch of hard copy to begin checking nonetheless.

"But how do you communicate across the planet?" I said to Schatz. The sealed board was still warm when I pulled it from the radio, though the Fed claimed it had failed three months before. Schatz hadn't bothered to unplug the set—which had a dead short in its microcircuitry.

Venerians stood in the shade of buildings, staring at a landscape that seemed only marginally more interesting than hard vacuum. The low haze the sun burned off the water blurred the horizon. The glimpse I'd gotten through the *Oriflamme*'s optics during the landing approach convinced me that better viewing conditions wouldn't mean a better view.

"There's nobody . . ." Schatz said. "I mean, there's just us here and the collecting boats, and nobody goes out in the boats but the bugs. So we don't need a radio, I'm telling you."

Three Venerians had boarded one of the light-alloy boats on the lagoon. It was a broad-beamed craft, blunt-ended and about four meters long. A pole rather than oars or a motor propelled the craft. From the raucous struggle the men were having, the water was less than knee-deep.

"Bugs?" I repeated in puzzlement.

"He means the Molts, Jeremy," Stephen Gregg said dryly. "It's a term many of the folk on outworld stations use, so that they can pretend they're better than somebody. Which these scuts obviously are not."

I unhooked my cutting bar. The tool's length made it clumsy for delicate work, but it would open the module.

"There's no call to be insulting," Schatz muttered. He was afraid to look at Stephen. His hand rose reflexively to shield his mouth halfway through the comment.

"Is he helping you, Jeremy?" Stephen asked.

I looked up from the incipient operation with a scowl. "What?" I snapped, then remembered I owed Stephen . . . Well, owed him the chance to be whatever it was I'd become. "Sorry, Stephen. No, he's useless to me."

"Get a shovel and a broom," Stephen ordered Schatz crisply, "and get to work. I expect to see the entire floor of this room in one standard hour."

I triggered my bar and let it settle after the start-up torque. I held the electronics module against the blade with my left hand, rotating the work piece while holding the cutting bar steady.

"But there's bugs—" Schatz said, raising his voice over the keen of the bar's ceramic teeth.

Stephen's face went as blank as a concrete wall. His eyes seemed to sink a little deeper into his skull, and his lips parted minusculely.

Schatz backed a step, backed another—hit the door-jamb, and ducked out into the open air.

I shut off the power switch for safety's sake before I hung the bar back on my belt. I parted the sawn casing with a quick twist.

"Useless," Stephen said in a hoarse voice. "But he *will* clean this room."

"And so's this," I said. "Useless, I mean—fried like an egg."

I dropped the pieces of module back onto the radio's chassis and shook my head. "I'm going out to check the wrecked ships," I said. "Could be something there will help. I doubt this lot is any better at salvage than at anything else."

Stephen's eyes focused again. "Yes, well," he said. "I'll come with you, Jeremy."

He gestured me out the door ahead of him. Schatz stood halfway along the porch, holding a mattock in one hand and arguing with the woman on crutches.

"To keep from doing something you'll regret, you mean," I said over my shoulder to Stephen.

"Not quite," Stephen said. "But I don't want to do something that Piet would regret."

The high scream of my cutting bar ground down into a moan as the battery reached the limits of its charge. I backed away from the twisted nickel-steel pedestal I'd sawn most of the way through. Federation salvagers at the time of the crash had removed the navigational AI from the pedestal's top.

I gasped for breath. My gray tunic and the thighs of my trousers were black with sweat.

Stephen looked down into the freighter's cockpit. The wreck lay on its side, so a rope ladder now dangled from the hatch in the ceiling. The force of the crash had twisted the hatchway into a lozenge shape.

"I repeat," Stephen said. "I could take a shift."

"I know what I'm doing," I snarled, "and you bloody well wouldn't! I haven't put in this much work to have somebody saw through the middle of the board."

I was trembling with fatigue and the heat. I hadn't recovered from the strains my mind had transmitted to my body during the weeks of brutal transit. Maybe I'd never recover. Maybe—

"Come on up and have some water," Stephen said mildly, reaching a hand out to me. "The distillation plant here works, at least."

Stephen's touch settled my flailing mind so that I could climb the ladder. As Stephen lifted, the muscles of my right forearm twisted in a cramp and pulled my hand into a hook. I flopped onto the crumpled hull, cursing under my breath in frustration.

Salomon trudged toward us across the seared mud of the landing field, holding a curved plate of shimmering gray. The object was as large as his chest. Hydraulic fluid from the infrequent ships had painted swatches of ground with a hard iridescence.

Stephen's flashgun was equipped with a folding solar panel to recharge the weapon when time permitted. He had spread the panel as a parasol while I worked in the cabin below.

Stephen had brought a 10-liter waist jug from the *Oriflamme* when I got my tool kit. The curved glass container was cast with a carrying handle and four broad loops for harness attachment. I lifted it with care, letting my left hand support most of the weight.

Stephen took my cutting bar and opened the battery compartment in its grip. He swapped the discharged battery for the one in the flashgun's butt. The charging mechanism whined like a peevish mosquito when the flashgun's prongs made contact.

The jug's contents were flavored with lemon juice, enough to cut the deadness of distilled water. Micropores in the glass lifted water by osmosis to the outer surface, cooling the remaining contents by convection. The drink was startlingly refreshing.

"Thought I'd join you," Salomon said. He lifted the object he held, the headshield of some large creature, to Stephen to free his hands.

The Federation freighter was a flimsy construction built mostly of light alloys on this side of the Mirror. It had touched down too hard, ramming a thruster nozzle deep into the mud as the motors were shutting down. The final pulse of plasma blew the vessel into a cartwheel and ripped its belly open.

The crew may have survived with no worse than bruises, but the ship itself was a total loss. The hull had crumpled into a useful series of steps, though you had to watch the places where metal bent beyond its strength had ripped jaggedly.

"There's no information at all," the navigator complained bitterly. I offered him the heavy jug, but he waved it away. "We'll have to coast the gradients, looking for the next landfall, and there's no guarantee that'll have navigational control either. Osomi sounds like another cesspool, sure, maybe a bit shallower."

"If Landolph could do it, Piet can," Stephen said calmly. He tapped the plate of chitin. "What's this?"

"The values aren't even the same on this side of the Mirror!" Salomon said. "The people here live like animals, drinking piss they brew for a couple months after the ferry from Osomi drops off supplies. Then they run out of dried fruit and don't even have that!"

"It's from a local animal, not a Molt, I suppose?" I asked. By helping Stephen break the navigator's mind out of its tail-chasing cycle of frustration, I found I was calming myself. I smiled internally.

Salomon shrugged. "It's a sea scorpion," he said. "They live in the lagoons. The head armor fluoresces, so it's used for jewelry this side of the Mirror. That's the only reason anybody lives here—if you call this living!"

Stephen looked at his arm through the chitin. The shield was nearly transparent, but sunlight gave it a rich luster that was more than a color.

"Pretty," I said. I liked it. "How big is the whole animal?"

"Three, four meters," Salomon said. He reached for the jug, then grimaced and withdrew his hand. "I've got a bottle back on the ship," he said. "I was going to celebrate when we transited the Breach, but when the time came, I didn't feel much like it."

He glared at the surrounding terrain. "We've come through the Breach, we've lost most of the squadron—"

His head snapped toward Stephen and me. "You know that the *Kinsolving* and *Mizpah* aren't going to show up, don't you?" Salomon demanded.

"Yes," said Stephen evenly. "But we're going to leave a transponder here anyway."

Salomon shuddered. "And what we've got for it is a mud bank—and a bale of crab shells that wouldn't be worth a three-day voyage, much less what *we've* gone through!"

"They'll be trading material," Stephen said. "We'll need

food as we go on, and sticking a gun in somebody's face isn't always the best way to bargain."

I grinned at him. "Though it works," I said.

"It's not a magic wand, Jeremy," Stephen said. "It depends on the people at either end of the gun, you see."

Stephen's voice dropped and he rasped the last few syllables quietly. I felt sobered by the results of my quip. I put my hand over his and drew the gunman back to the present.

"You know," Stephen resumed with a dreamy softness, "Pesaltra is actually a pretty place in its way. Water and land stitched together by the plants, and the mist to soften the lines."

Salomon knew Stephen well enough to fear him in a killing mood. He nodded with approval that we'd stepped back from an unexpected precipice. "They catch the scorpions in traps, Taenia says," he said. "It's dangerous. Every year they lose a few boats and half a dozen Molts running the trapline."

"We're not doing it for the shell," Stephen said. He wasn't angry, any more than a storm is angry, but his tone brooked as little argument as a thunderbolt does. "We're not doing it for the wealth, either, though we'll have that by and by."

In a way, it wasn't Stephen Gregg speaking, but rather Piet Ricimer wearing Stephen's hollow soul. There was fiery power in the words, but they were spoken by someone who knew he had nothing of his own except the Hell of his dreams. "We're doing it for all men, on Venus and Earth and the Rabbits, bringing them a universe they can *be* men in!"

Stephen's big frame shuddered. After a moment, in a changed voice, he added, "Not that we'll live to see it. But we'll have the wealth."

I flexed my hands and found they worked again, though my right arm had twinges. "I'm going to finish down below," I said.

"Let me take a look," Stephen said. He furled the charging panel and collapsed its support wand so that he could bring the flashgun with him into the wreck.

Inside the cockpit, we stood on what had been the outer bulkhead. The freighter was a single-hulled vessel, shoddier by far than the hulk we'd abandoned on Mocha. The navigational pedestal stuck out horizontally from the nearly vertical deck. I'd sawn more than three-quarters of the way around its base.

"You know," said Salomon reflectively from the hatchway, "we might do best to wait for the Osomi ferry to come for the shell. They'll have at least local charts. Though it may be ten months, from what Taenia says, and I'm not sure I'd last four."

"We'll last if we have to," Stephen said calmly. His fingertips explored the pedestal and ran the edges of my careful cut. He unslung the flashgun and handed it to me. "Though I doubt that's what Piet has in mind."

"Give me a little room, Jeremy," he said as he gripped the flanges which once held the AI module. Even as Stephen spoke, the huge muscles in his back rippled. The unsawn portion of the base sheared with a sharp crack.

Stephen had twisted the pedestal rather than simply levering it down with his weight. He set it before me, fractured end forward. "Satisfactory?"

I wiggled the data module which the Feds hadn't bothered to remove after the crash. They couldn't lift it from the top because the pedestal was warped. The bayonet contacts were corroded, but they released on the third tug and the unit slid out.

"Lord Jesus Christ," Salomon said in startled hope. "Do you suppose . . ."

I touched the probes of my testing device to the bank's contacts. Numbers scrolled across the miniature screen. The data couldn't be decoded without a proper AI, and they wouldn't have meant anything to me anyway; but the data were present.

"I think," I said as I folded the probes back into my testing device, "that we've got a course for Osomi."

TEMPLETON

Day 101

The planet's visible hemisphere was half water, half land covered by green vegetation. A single large moon peeked from beyond the daylit side of the disk.

"That's not Osomi," Salomon said. He'd pitched his voice to suggest he was willing to be proven wrong.

"No, that's Templeton," Piet Ricimer agreed with obvious relish. "Mister Moore? Is Jeremy here forward?"

"Shutting off power in forty-three seconds," Guillermo warned over the tannoys.

"I'm here," I said as I tried to get to the bow.

The *Oriflamme* was at action stations, so we were all wearing hard suits. That made me clumsier than usual after transit. Besides, each crewman took up significantly more room than he would under normal conditions.

I knocked the attitude controls with my right knee, then my hip bumped Stampfer at the sights mounted on the turntable with the Long Tom. I was in a hurry because for the next few seconds, the thrusters were braking the *Oriflamme* into orbit. I knew I wouldn't be able to control my movements at all without that semblance of gravity.

The only thing we'd known about the destination in the salvaged module was that we were headed for a Federation planet—*if* scrambled data hadn't sent the *Oriflamme* to the back of beyond. Our five plasma cannon were manned, but the gunports were still sealed. We'd have to lock our helmet visors if the guns were run out.

I caught the side of the general commander's couch just as the thrusters shut off. An attitude control fired briefly.

111

My legs started to drift out from under me. I managed to clamp them hard against the deck. "Yes, sir?" I said.

Piet Ricimer turned from adjustments he was making in the external optics. The lower quadrant of the main screen held an expanded view of a settlement of some size on the margins of a lake. It was after nightfall on the ground, but a program in the display turned the faint glimmers which charge-coupled devices drew from the scene into a full schematic.

"You did better than you knew, Jeremy," Ricimer said. "Templeton is the center for the entire district. This may be exactly where we needed to be."

I smiled mechanically. I was glad the general commander was pleased, but it didn't seem to me that arriving at a Federation center was good luck.

"How do you know—" Salomon said from the side couch. He remembered where he was and smoothed the stressed brittleness of his voice. He resumed, "Captain, how do you know it's—any particular place? Our charts don't . . ."

Templeton's dayside flared under the *Oriflamme*'s orbit, though the screen insert continued to show the settlement. The Feds had graded a peninsula for use as a spaceport. Forty-odd ships stood on the lakeshore where they could draw reaction mass directly. The number surprised me, but not all the vessels were necessarily starships.

"I talked to the personnel on Pesaltra," Ricimer explained. "They weren't a prepossessing lot or they wouldn't have been shipped to such a dead end. But they'd all been at other ports in the past, and they were glad to have somebody to talk to. They weren't navigators, but they knew other things. Taenia was a paymaster on Templeton until his accounts came up short last year."

Ricimer manipulated his display into a plot of the planet/satellite system. "The district superintendent is on the moon," he continued, nodding to include me. "Rabbits have attacked the Templeton settlement several times, so there's a strong garrison—but the garrison has mutinied twice as well. The superintendent feels safer on the moon, where he's got plasma cannon to protect him. The chips are

warehoused there too until the arrival of the ship detailed
to carry them to Umber."

Men in the forward section craned their necks to hear
Ricimer's explanation. He noticed them and switched on
the vessel's public address system.

"What about the garrison?" Stephen Gregg asked. His
voice was strong and his face had some color. The prospect
of action had brought Stephen through in better condition
than I'd seen him after most transit sequences.

"We need air and reaction mass," Ricimer said through
the shivering echo of the tannoys. "Our hull was seriously
weakened when we crossed the Breach, and the rate of
loss will be a problem until we're able to effect dockyard
repairs."

I frowned. *Surely we wouldn't see a dockyard until
we'd returned to Venus? And that meant a second passage
through the Breach . . .*

Salomon noticed my expression. He lifted his eyebrows
in the equivalent of a shrug—his shoulders were hidden
beneath the rigid ceramic of his suit.

"We have to land somewhere soon to restock," Ricimer
continued, "but we need to gather intelligence and navigational data also. Templeton is the place to do that. We'll
go in quietly, get what we need, and leave at once. We
won't have to fight."

"I've plotted a descent to the port," Salomon said. "Will
you want to go in on the next orbit or wait, sir?"

Piet Ricimer's smile swept the nearest of the men who
followed him. "I think we'll go in now, Mister Salomon,"
he said. "I think now."

We'd been down for twenty minutes.

Trusted sailors watched panoramas of the *Oriflamme*'s
surroundings on the upper half of the three bow displays.
On the lower half, Guillermo planned liftoff curves while
Salomon ran transit solutions. We didn't have another plotted destination, but if necessary the officers could coast the
energy gradients between bubble universes until a radical
change in values indicated the presence of a star in the
sidereal universe.

Piet Ricimer was considering other ships in port with us. I watched him expand images one at a time, letting the AI program fill in details which were a few pixels of real data. Some of the ships were tugs and orbital ferries, obvious even to my untrained eyes. None of them seemed to be warships.

Our hull pinged as it continued to cool from the friction of its descent. I unlatched the back-and-breast armor, the last remaining portion of my hard suit. Stripping the ceramic armor had been a ten-minute job for fingers unfamiliar with the process. It would take me longer yet to put the suit back on if I had to.

Most of us had doffed only the arm and leg pieces. To me armor was crushing, psychologically crushing. I felt as though I was drowning every time I put the suit on.

Stephen grinned harshly at me. "You'll wish you hadn't done that if we lift under fire in the next ten seconds," he observed.

Piet Ricimer turned his head. "If that happens," he said, "*I'll* certainly regret it, Stephen. There don't appear to be plasma cannon protecting the port, but there are at least a dozen multitube lasers on the settlement's perimeter. I suspect they'd do nearly as well against us as they would a Rabbit assault."

"There's a car coming!" called Fahey, watching the sector northward, toward the port buildings. "Straight to us!"

Ricimer stood up. All eyes were on him.

"I think we'll admit them by the cockpit hatch," he said calmly, "since the assault squad's drawn up in the hold. Remember, if we're to succeed, we'll do it without trouble."

Stephen took a cutting bar from the forward arms locker. "Without noise, at any rate," he said.

The forward hatch was a chambered airlock; Ricimer cycled the inner and outer valves together. I felt heat from the plasma-cooked ground radiate through the opening in pulses.

Piet stepped to one side of the hatchway with Guillermo beside him. I hesitated a moment, but Stephen guided me to stand across from the general commander. My body was a screen of sorts for Stephen's threatening bulk.

The Federation car pulled up before the cockpit stairs. The lightly built vehicle had four open seats and rode on flotation tires; the port area flooded on a regular basis.

The driver was a Molt wearing a red sash. Two more Molts were in back, and a small man with a high forehead and a gray pencil mustache rode in the forward passenger seat.

The human got out and straightened his white uniform as if he didn't see us watching him from the ship. A Molt handed him a briefcase. He tucked the case under his arm, took three brisk strides to the steps, and climbed them with a *click-whisk* sound of his soles on the nonskid surface. The driver remained in the vehicle, but the other Molts followed. The aliens walked with a sway because of their cross-jointed limbs.

The little man glared from me to Ricimer. Close up, the Fed's uniform was threadbare, and the one and a half blue bars on the collar implied no high rank. "I'm Collector Heimond," he said, "and I want to know why you landed without authorization! I'm the officer in charge, you know!"

"If you're in charge," Ricimer snapped in return, "then maybe you can tell me why our request for landing instructions was ignored for two orbits! We need to replenish our air tanks after a run from Riel, and I wasn't about to wait till tomorrow noon when some of you dirtside clowns decided to switch on your radios!"

"Oh!" said Heimond. "Ah. From Riel . . ."

We hadn't—of course—signaled the port control before braking in, but Federation standards were such that nobody on the ground was going to be sure of that. Even if the radio watch happened to be awake, the set might have failed—again—for lack of proper care.

Heimond's eyes took in the 17-cm plasma cannon which dominated the *Oriflamme*'s forward section. "Oh!" he said in a brighter tone. He glared at Ricimer, sure this time he held the high ground. "You're the escort, then? Where have you been? She's already left a week ago without you!"

"*She* left?" Ricimer said. He sounded puzzled but nonchalant. Maybe he was.

"*Our Lady of Montreal!*" Heimond snapped. "The treasure ship! You're the *Parliament,* aren't you? You should have been here weeks ago!"

"Yes, that's right, but we were delayed," Ricimer agreed easily. "We'll just catch up with her. You'll have her course plan on file at port control?"

"Yes, yes," Heimond said, "but I don't see why nobody's able to do anything when it's supposed to be—"

One of the Molts flanking Heimond said, "This ship isn't made of metal."

The cockpit stairs were four steps high. I jumped straight to the ground. Though the surface was originally gravel, repeated baths in plasma had pulverized it and glazed the silica. I felt the residual heat from our landing through my bootsoles, but the breeze off the lake was refreshingly cool.

I got into the vehicle and thumbed the power switch of my cutting bar. "Please wait here quietly," I said to the driver.

"Or you will kill me?" the driver asked in a rusty voice. His chitin had a dark, almost purple cast in the light above the hatchway. The Molts who'd gone aboard with Heimond were lighter and tinged with olive, complexions rather like Guillermo's.

"I think my friend aiming a laser from the hatchway will kill you," I said. I didn't bother to look at Stephen. I *knew* what he would be doing. "I'm here to warn you so that he doesn't have to do that."

"All right," the Molt said. His belly segments began to rub together in alternate pairs. The sound had three distinct tones, all of them gratingly unpleasant.

"What are you doing?" I snapped, raising the cutting bar.

"I am laughing, master," the Molt said. "Collector Heimond will not be pleased."

My subconscious had been aware of the light of a new star. Distance-muffled thrusters began to whisper from the night sky. Another ship was on its landing approach.

The *Oriflamme*'s main ramp shrieked and jolted its way open. Stephen swung from the hatch with Piet behind him. Following them, protesting desperately, was Collector Heimond in the arms of Jeude and Lightbody.

Stephen gestured to the Molt and ordered, "Get aboard the ship for now. We'll release you when we lift."

"Yes, master," the Molt said. He got out of the vehicle and climbed the stairs. Dole watched from the hatchway with a rifle. The Molt was slowed by spasms of grating laughter.

Ricimer slid into the driver's seat. "We're going to the port office," he said to me. He had to shout to be heard over the roar of the starship landing. "Heimond's going to find the *Montreal*'s course for us. She took on board six months' accumulation of chips, most of them purpose-built in the factory still working on Vaughan."

The four others, one of them Stephen in his half armor, clambered into the back. It was really a storage compartment with a pair of jump seats. The car sagged till the frame and axles touched.

"Let me bring my kit and I can get more than the one course," I said. I lifted my leg out of the car. "I'll dump all the core memory!"

Stephen's big arm blocked me like an I-beam. "I have your kit, Jeremy," he shouted as Ricimer put the overloaded vehicle in gear. Behind us, the *Oriflamme*'s crewmen were dragging hoses to the lake to top off our reaction mass.

The incoming ship set down at a slip on the other side of the peninsula, much closer to the buildings on the mainland. Silence crashed over the night, followed by a final burp of plasma.

"Tell us about the *Montreal*, Heimond," Ricimer ordered. He drove at the speed of a man jogging. Faster would have been brutal punishment. The surface of the quay was rough, and the weight the car carried had collapsed the springs.

"Last year President Pleyal ordered that only armed ships could carry more than a hundred kilos of chips," the Fed official said. "We'd never worried about that before.

It makes routing much more difficult, you see—and then an escort vessel besides!"

He sounded shell-shocked. It didn't seem to occur to him that present events proved that Pleyal had been right to worry about treasure shipments even among the Back Worlds.

Some of the ships we passed had exterior lights on. Occasional human sailors watched our car out of boredom. Most of the crews were Molts who continued shambling along at whatever task had been set them. If I hadn't heard the driver laugh, I might have thought the aliens were unemotional automata.

"How many guns does the *Montreal* carry?" Ricimer asked calmly. His eyes flicked in short arcs that covered everything to our front; the men behind him would be watching the rear. Despite the rough road, Piet's hands made only minuscule corrections on the steering yoke.

"How would I know?" Heimond snapped. "It's none of my business, and it's a damned waste of capacity if you ask me!"

He drew in a breath that ended with a sob. I looked back at Heimond as we passed a ship whose thruster nozzles were being replaced under a bank of floodlights. The port official's cheeks glistened with tears. He was looking straight ahead, but I didn't think he was really seeing anything.

"*Our Lady of Montreal* is rated at five hundred tonnes," Heimond said softly. "I think she has about a dozen guns. I don't think they're very big, but I don't know for sure. I don't know even if you kill me!"

A wave of dry heat washed us. The ship that landed after ours had baked the ground we were crossing. She was a largish vessel, several hundred tonnes. Her exterior lights were on, but she hadn't opened her hatches yet.

"We're not going to kill anybody, Mister Heimond," Piet Ricimer said. "You're going to get us the information we need, and then we'll leave peacefully. Don't worry at all."

Port control was a one-story, five-by-twenty-meter building of rough-cast concrete at the head of the peninsula.

A man sat on a corner of the roof with his legs crossed and his back to an antenna tower, playing an ocarina. He ignored us as we pulled up in front.

"Here," Stephen said in a husky voice, handing my electronics kit forward. Stephen's face was still, his soul withdrawn behind walls of preparation that armored him from humanity. He took Heimond's collar in his free hand.

The control building, a line of repair shops, and a three-story barracks that stank of Molt excrement separated the peninsula from the rest of Templeton City, though there was no fenced reservation. The dives fronting the port were brilliantly illuminated.

I could see at least a dozen lighted compounds on the hills overlooking the main part of the city. That's where the wealthy would live.

Woven-wire screens instead of glass covered the front windows of the port control building. Lights were on above the doorway and within. A Molt stood behind the counter that ran the length of the anteroom.

Stephen pushed Heimond ahead of him into the building; the rest of us followed as we could. I was clumsy. My kit and the cutting bar in my other hand split my mind with competing reflexes.

"Don't do anything, Pierrot!" Heimond called desperately to the Molt. "Don't!"

Only the Molt's eyes had moved since the car pulled up anyway. The creature looked as placid as a tree.

"The data bank is in back?" Ricimer said, striding toward the gate in the counter.

A truck returning from the city with a leave party drove past port control. The diesel engine was unmuffled. The sudden *Blat!Blat!Blat!* as the vehicle came around the corner of the building spun us all.

Heimond cried out in fear. A drunken Fed flung a bottle. It bounced off the screen and shattered in front of the building. Lightbody raised his carbine to his shoulder.

"No!" Ricimer shouted. Stephen lifted the carbine's muzzle toward the ceiling.

"Let's get into the back," Stephen ordered. He gestured the Molt to join us.

Heimond found the switch for the lights in the rear of the building. The data bank stood in the center of a bullpen. There were six screen-and-keyboard positions on either side, with long benches for Molt clerks. The human staff had three separate desks and a private office in the back, but I didn't care about those.

I sat on a bench and opened my kit beside me. The bank had both plug and induction ports. I preferred the hard connection. The plug was one of the three varieties standard before the Collapse.

Jeude bent to look into my kit. "What—" he said.

"No!" ordered Piet, placing his left hand under the young sailor's chin and lifting him away from me. I appreciated the thought, but Jeude wouldn't have bothered me. I lose all track of my surroundings when I'm working on something complex.

I attached the partner to the data port and matched parameters. The five-by-five-by-ten-centimeter box hummed as it started to copy all the information within the Fed data bank.

The job would have taken a man months or years. I'd designed the partner to emulate the internal data transfer operations of whatever unit I attached it to. It was an extremely simple piece of hardware—but as with the larva of an insect, that simplicity made it wonderfully efficient at its single task of swallowing.

The partner couldn't do anything with data except absorb it. Sorting the glut of information would be an enormous job, but one the *Oriflamme*'s AI could handle with the same ease that it processed transit calculations.

Plasma motors coughed, shaking the ground and casting rainbow flickers through the bullpen's grimy side windows. Heimond sat at a desk with his head in his hands. Stephen and Piet interrogated him, pulling out responses with the relentless efficiency of a mill grinding corn. I couldn't hear either side of the conversation.

The partner clucked. A pathway query replaced the activity graph on the little screen. So far as I could tell, neither supplemental cache was terribly important. One held the operating system, while the other was probably either backup files or mere ash and trash. I cued the second option, though maybe we ought to—

I rose, drawing the others' eyes. The thruster snarled again, raggedly. Some ship was testing its propulsion system.

"I think I've got everything important," I said. I'd been hunched over the partner for long enough to become stiff, though it hadn't seemed more than a minute or two. "This is—"

A Fed in a blue uniform with a gold fourragère from the left shoulder strode through the door from the anteroom. "Hey!" he shouted. Jeude shot him in the chest, knocking him back against the jamb.

There were half a dozen other Feds in the anteroom. They wore flat caps with PARLIAMENT in gold letters above the brim. One of them grabbed at his holstered pistol. Stephen shot him with the flashgun from less than five meters away.

The laser sent dazzling reflections from the room's brightwork as it heated the air into a thunderclap. The Fed's chest exploded in a gout of steam and blood, knocking down the men to either side of him.

I keyed shutdown instructions into the partner's miniature pad. If I disconnected the unit mechanically first, the surge might cost us the data we'd risked our lives for.

I glanced over my shoulder. Jeude fired the other barrel of his shotgun at a woman running for the outside door. He missed low and chewed a palm-sized hole in the counter instead. Ricimer hit the running woman. She slammed full tilt against the window screen and bounced back onto the floor. A pair of Fed sailors made it out the door despite Lightbody's shot and two more rounds from the commander's carbine.

The partner chirped to me. I jerked it free and slammed the lid of the kit down over it. "I'm coming!" I shouted, because by now I was the last Venerian left in the building.

Heimond was hiding under his desk and the Molt clerk stood like a grotesque statue in one corner. The first Fed victim sat upright in the doorway. His legs were splayed and his face wore a dazed expression. Jeude's buckshot had hit him squarely at the top of the breastbone, but he was still—for the moment—alive.

Which is all any of us can say, I thought as I jumped his legs. My boots skidded on the remains of the man Stephen's bolt had eviscerated. I caught the counter with my free hand and swung myself through the gate. I'd left my cutting bar behind. There was more shooting outside the building.

The room stank worse than a slaughterhouse. Ozone, powder smoke, and cooked meat added their distinctive smells to the pong of fresh-ripped human guts. The woman Ricimer shot was huddled beside the outer door. She'd smeared a trail of blood across the floor to where she lay.

Heimond's car pulled a hard turn as I ran out the front door. Ricimer was driving again. Stephen stood on the passenger seat. He'd slung the flashgun and instead held Piet's repeating carbine.

The man on the roof now lay full length on his back. I don't know if he'd been killed or had passed out from drink.

I jumped into the back with Lightbody and Jeude. The car hadn't slowed, and I'm not sure anybody realized I wasn't already on board. Jeude fired again. The flash from the shotgun's muzzle was red and bottle-shaped.

"Shut that popgun down until there's a target in range, you whore's turd!" Stephen snarled in a voice with more hatred than you'd find in a regiment of Inquisitors.

Stephen swayed as the car jounced. I grabbed his belt so that if he fell he wouldn't be thrown out. He poised the butt of the carbine to crush my skull, but his conscious mind overrode reflex at the last moment.

I sucked breaths through my mouth. I was dizzy, and nothing around me seemed real.

The car had a quartet of headlights above the hood, but only the pair in the center worked. They threw a long shadow past a bareheaded man in blue running down the track a hundred meters ahead of us.

Stephen fired once. The man pitched forward with one arm flung out and the other covering his eyes. We jolted past the body at the car's best speed, 50 kph or so. There was no sign of the other Feds who'd escaped from port control with that one.

"Stephen, sit down!" Piet Ricimer ordered. Gregg ignored him.

The boarding ramps of the ship that landed after ours were down, and the vessel was lighted like a Christmas star. Molts and humans in blue uniforms stood on the ramps and at a distance from the vessel: the ground directly underneath would still be at close to 100°C from the ship's exhaust.

A man on the vessel's forward ramp pointed toward our swaying vehicle and shouted orders through a bullhorn. "The fucking *Parliament*!" Jeude snarled. "The real fucking escort, and why she couldn't have showed up tomor—"

A uniformed woman ran into our path, waving her arms over her head. Piet swerved violently. Stephen fired, a quick stab of yellow flame. The Fed toppled under our right front wheel.

We lurched but the wheels were mounted on half-axles and had a wide track. Stephen flailed, completely off balance. The car didn't go over. By bracing my leg against the side of the compartment I kept Stephen from falling out as well.

Lightbody cried, "Lord God of hosts!" as he fired toward the *Parliament,* and Jeude's shotgun boomed again despite the fact that I was sprawled half across him as I clung desperately to Stephen. The car's frame swayed upward as the heavy front wheel slammed down. The rear wheel hit the woman's body, and Stephen shot the blue-sashed Molt who tried to leap over the hood at Ricimer.

A ship down the line lit her thrusters. A bubble of rainbow fire lifted and cooled to a ghostly skeleton of itself before vanishing entirely. The *Parliament* was a dedicated warship. I'd seen three rectangular gunports gape open in succession in my last glimpse of her, but now we were past.

Stephen got his legs straight and sat down. His carbine's bolt was open. He opened a pocket of Piet's bandolier and took out a handful of cartridges. The *Parliament*'s siren howled and a bell on the Molt barracks clanged a twice-a-second tocsin.

A ship tested her thrusters again. This time the vessel lifted slightly from her berth and settled again ten meters out in the roadway. She was the *Oriflamme*. The 20-cm hoses with which she'd been drawing reaction mass dangled from her open holds.

Glowing exhaust backlit us. I stared stupidly at the spray of dust ahead of our right front wheel. "There's a truck following—" Jeude shouted.

Maybe he meant to say more, but three violent hammer blows shook our vehicle. Stephen pitched forward, the severed tags of his flashgun's sling flapping. A palm-sized asterisk of lead smeared his backplate; the ceramic was cracked in a pattern of radial lines. My face stung, my hands bled where bits of bullet jacket had splashed them, and I still didn't realize the Feds were shooting at us.

I twisted to look back the way we'd come. A slope-fronted truck bounced down the road in a huge plume of dust. It was moving twice as fast as we could. Red flame winked from the framework on top of the vehicle. The Feds had welded dozens of rifle barrels together like an array of organ pipes.

Bits of rubber flew off our left rear tire, though it didn't go flat. Because of Rabbit attacks, the garrison of Templeton had a mobile reaction force. It was too mobile for us.

Stephen leaned across the back of his seat and rested his left elbow on my shoulder. It was like having a building fall on me. I had just enough awareness of what was happening to close my eyes. The flashgun drove its dazzling light through the tight-clenched eyelids, shocking the retinas into multiple afterimages when I looked up again.

The laser mechanism keened as it cooled beside my ear. Stephen tilted the weapon and slapped a fresh battery into the butt compartment. The flashgun wasn't going to do any good; even I could see that.

The truck was armored. The metal shutter over the windshield glowed white, but the driver behind it was unharmed.

Flashgun bolts delivered enormous amounts of energy, but a monopulse laser has virtually no penetration. Even a hit on the driver's periscope might be useless, since properly designed optics would shatter instead of transmitting a dangerous amount of energy.

"Bail out!" I shouted. I squirmed to the side of the compartment. Jeude wasn't moving; Lightbody thumbed a cartridge into the breech of his rifle.

"Jump!" I shouted, but as I poised Lightbody fired again and Stephen leaned forward against the butt of his squat laser.

A bullet hit our right rear wheel and this time the tire did blow. The car fishtailed, flinging me against the seats. The sky ripped in a star-hot flare. Concussion pushed the car's suspension down to the stops, then lifted us off the ground when the pressure wave passed.

The *Oriflamme* had fired one of her 15-cm broadside guns. The truck was a geyser of flame. Fuel, ammunition, and the metal armor burned when the slug of ions hit the vehicle.

Ricimer crossed his wrists on the yoke, countersteering to bring us straight. The wheel rim dragged a trail of sparks across the gravel.

"Salomon shouldn't have risked running out—" Ricimer cried.

Another of the *Oriflamme*'s cannon recoiled into its gunport behind a raging hell of stripped atomic nuclei.

The facade of the Molt barracks caved in. The interior of the three-story building erupted into flame as everything that could burn ignited simultaneously.

Wreckage spewed outward like the evanescent fabric of a bubble popping. Shattered concrete and viscous flame wrapped port control and the maintenance shop on the barracks' other side.

Ricimer stood on the car's brakes. Because of the blown tire we spun 180° and nearly hopped broadside into the lip of the *Oriflamme*'s stern ramp. Stephen rose in his seat and poised like a statue aiming the flashgun. I tried to raise Jeude one-handed—I'd clung to my electronics kit since the moment I slammed it over the data we'd come to get. Lightbody bent to help me.

Stephen fired. A secondary explosion erupted with red flame.

Piet grabbed Jeude's legs. He and I and Lightbody lifted Jeude out. The smooth surface of Jeude's body armor slipped out of my hand, but Lightbody's arms were spread beneath the wounded man's torso.

Beneath the torso of the dead man. A bullet had struck Jeude under the right eye socket and exited through the back of his neck. Strands of his blond hair were plastered to the wounds, but his heart no longer pumped blood.

A thumping shock wave followed several seconds after Stephen fired. He'd managed to do effective damage with the flashgun instead of leaving the fight to the thunderous clamor of plasma cannon.

We ran up the ramp, carrying Jeude among us. The air shimmered from the hop that had lifted the *Oriflamme* into firing position. Salomon poured full power through the thrusters. Heat battered me from all sides. I would have screamed but my lips and eyelids were squeezed tight against the ions that flayed them like an acid bath.

I fell down, feeling the shock as the third of our big guns fired. Acceleration squeezed me to the deck as the jets hammered at maximum output. I was blind and suffocating and at last I did scream but the fire didn't scour my lungs.

I thrashed upright. The crewman spraying me with a hose shut it off when he saw I was choking for breath. I was wrapped in a soaking blanket. So were the others who'd staggered aboard with me.

Dole knelt and held Piet's hands with a look of fear for his commander on his face. Stephen checked the bore of his flashgun and Lightbody was trying to unlatch his body armor. The fifth blanket must cover Jeude, because it didn't move.

Our ramp was still rising. Through the crack I could see waves on the lake fifty meters below, quivering in the icteric light of a laser aimed at us from the Templeton defenses. Something hit the hull with a sound more like a scream than a crash. Our last broadside gun slammed as the ramp closed against its jamb.

Piet got to his feet. Dole tried to hold him. Piet pushed past and staggered toward the companionway to the *Oriflamme*'s working deck. His face was fiery red under the lights of the hold. Stephen walked behind Piet like a giant shadow.

I stood up. Pain stabbed from my knuckles when I tried to push off with my free hand. My face was swelling, so that I seemed to be looking through tubes of flesh. Soon I wouldn't be able to see at all.

I stumbled to the companionway, swinging my arm to clear startled crewmen from my path.

I had to get to the bridge. *My* partner held the course we would follow until we won free or died.

INTERSTELLAR SPACE

Day 102

"Sir, *please* leave the dressing in place," begged Rakoscy, the ship's surgeon. "I can't answer for what will happen to your eyes if you don't keep them covered for the next twenty-four hours at least."

"It's under control, Piet," Stephen said, taking Piet's hands in his own. He pulled them down from Piet's eye bandage with as much gentle force as was necessary. "There's nothing to see anyway. Salomon'll tell us when the data's been analyzed."

Dressings muffled both men's hands into mittens. The visored helmet Stephen wore because of the flashgun's glare had protected his face.

Lightbody moaned in a hammock against the cross-bulkhead, drugged comatose but not at peace. He'd come through the night better than the rest of us physically, but I was worried about his state of mind.

I hadn't thought of Lightbody and Jeude as being close friends. I don't suppose they were friends in the usual sense, a deeply religious man and an irreverent fellow who talked of little but the women and brawls he'd been involved with between voyages. But they'd been together for many years and much danger.

I could see again. Shots had shrunk the tissues of my face enough for me to look out of my eye sockets, and Rakoscy had left openings in the swaths of medicated dressings that covered the skin exposed to the plasma exhaust. I felt as though a crew had been pounding on my body with mauls, but Rakoscy assured me there'd be no permanent injury.

It was good to worry about Lightbody's state of mind, because then I didn't have to consider my own.

Salomon turned his couch and said, "Sir, Guillermo and I have a course to propose."

Rakoscy led Piet by the hands to the center console. I suppose it would have made better sense for Salomon to use Piet's couch under these circumstances. The same AI drove all three consoles, but the main screen was capable of more discriminating display because it had four times the area of the others.

Salomon hadn't suggested he take over, much less make the decision without asking. Logic wasn't the governing factor here. It rarely is in human affairs.

Stephen moved nearer to me and hesitated. I'm not sure whether or not he knew I could see.

"That seemed close," I said quietly. "Or is it something I'll get used to after the fiftieth time?"

Stephen gave a minuscule smile. "No," he said, "that was pretty near-run, all right. If it hadn't been for Salomon taking the initiative, it would've been a lot too close."

He coughed. "You're all right?"

"Yeah," I said. "I don't have much color vision at the moment, that's all."

He looked hard at me, but he didn't push for answers to the real questions. *Why had God saved me and taken Jeude beside me?*

If there was a God.

Piet settled onto his couch and sighed audibly. Fans, thrusters, and the noise of the ship herself working filled the *Oriflamme* with a constant rumble. With time, that drifted below the consciousness.

There were no human sounds aboard now. The crew in the forward section had fallen tensely and completely silent.

Piet switched on the public address system by feel. "Go ahead," he said.

"Trehinga is about six days transit from Templeton," Salomon said. "Seven, according to Federation charts, but I'm sure we can do it in six."

The navigator had shown himself to be able and quick-thinking. As Stephen said, he'd saved us on Templeton. Salomon ran out the big guns against orders when he heard the landed *Parliament* identify herself as a presidential vessel—a dedicated warship—over the radio. The Feds we met were a party sent by the *Parliament*'s captain to port control when nobody replied to the radio.

Despite his proven ability, Salomon licked his lips from nervousness as he proposed a solution based on information that the general commander couldn't see. Alone of us aboard the *Oriflamme,* Salomon was afraid that his responsibilities were beyond him.

"It has dock facilities," he continued. "We've lost two attitude jets, and the upper stern quarter of the hull was crazed by laser fire as we escaped. But there shouldn't be much traffic."

"Trehinga grows grain for the region," Guillermo put in from the opposite console. "There are no pre-Collapse vestiges, and therefore little traffic or defenses."

Salomon nodded, gaining animation as he spoke. "The port's supposed to have a company of human soldiers," he said, "but Mister Gregg says he doubts that." He looked up at Stephen.

Piet nodded agreement. "A few dozen militia, counting Molts with spears and cutting bars," he said. "Unless the Back Worlds are much better staffed than the Reaches in general."

"Of course, Templeton was no joke," Stephen said. The lack of concern in his voice wasn't as reassuring as it might have been if a less fatalistic man were speaking.

"Templeton was a treasure port," Piet said briskly. "Go on, Mister Salomon. What about the risk of pursuit from Templeton?"

"The bloody *Parliament* isn't pursuing anybody till they build her a new bow, sir," Stampfer said. "Since me and the boys on Gun Three blew the old one fucking off as we lifted."

The satisfaction in the master gunner's voice was as obvious as it was deserved.

Piet nodded again in approval. "And there wasn't anything docked on Templeton when we arrived that would be a threat," he said. "Nevertheless, we'll need to take some precautions if we're going to do extensive repairs."

Piet turned his head—"looked," but of course he couldn't see—from Salomon to Guillermo and back. "Are we ready to go, then?" he asked. The infectious enthusiasm of his tone helped me forget how much I hurt. Piet had been burned at least as badly.

"The first sequence of the course is loaded," Guillermo said. Salomon glanced up in surprise, but the Molt knew Piet Ricimer.

"Then let's go," Piet said. "Gentlemen, prepare for transit!"

TREHINGA

Day 109

The cutter touched bow-high. Piet cut the motor and we skipped forward on momentum, crashing down on the skids about the boat's own length ahead of its thruster's final pulse. It was a jolting landing compared to Piet's usual, but I understood why he wouldn't take chances with plasma for a while.

Lightbody and Kiley had undogged the dorsal hatch when we dropped below three thousand meters. They and the four other sailors packed beneath the hatch slid it open, but Stephen was first out of the vessel and I managed not to be far behind. I was more mobile than the men in half armor and bandoliers of ammunition.

A featherboat with room for twenty men and a small plasma cannon would have been better for this assault, but that option had gone missing with the *Kinsolving*. Twelve of us were squeezed into the cutter. Four spacers would cover the pair of grain freighters on the landing field, while we others "captured" the settlement of New Troy: a two-story Commandatura with bay windows and a copper-sheathed front door, and fifty squalid commercial and residential buildings.

The landing field was adobe clay, flat and featureless. Dust puffed under my boots. The sun was near zenith, but the air felt pleasantly cool.

The *Oriflamme* roared down from orbit above us. Salomon would be on the ground in three minutes, but it would be at least five minutes more before anyone left the ship safely except wearing a full hard suit. The flagship could dominate the community by her presence and the threat of her heavy guns, but a quick assault required a lighter vessel.

The Commandatura was fifty meters from where we'd landed. People watched us from its windows and the doorways of other buildings.

According to the database I'd copied on Templeton, Trehinga was fairly well populated, but most of that population lived on latifundia placed along the great river systems of the north continent. New Troy was the planet's administrative capital and starport, but it was in no sense a cultural center.

Still, some of the people watching were women.

A pair of men in white tunics, one of them wearing a saucer hat with gold braid on the brim, walked out of the Commandatura. Stephen and I started toward them. Dole was beside me, carrying a rifle as well as a cutting bar, and the other sailors fanned out to the sides. Piet ran to join us, last out of the cutter because he'd been piloting it.

The Fed officials paused at the base of the three steps to the Commandatura's front door. They stared at us, all armed and most of us wearing body armor.

"Raiders!" the older man shouted.

Stephen pointed his flashgun.

"Don't anyone shoot!" Piet cried as he aimed his own carbine toward the Feds. "And you, wait where you are!"

"Raiders!" the Fed repeated. He turned and took the four steps in two strides. His companion raised his hands and closed his eyes. The onlookers of a moment before vanished, though eyes still peeked from the corners of windows.

I ran toward the Commandatura, holding my cutting bar in both hands to keep it from flailing. The others followed me as quickly as their equipment allowed.

"You won't be harmed!" Piet said.

The Fed official grabbed the long vertical handhold and started to pull the door open. Piet fired. His bullet whacked the door near the transom, jolting the panel out of the Fed's hand. The Fed ran into the edge of the door instead of slipping between it and the jamb. The impact knocked him back down the steps, scattering blood from a pressure cut over his right eye.

I ran past the man. He moaned and squeezed his forehead with his palms stacked one on the other. I tugged at the door with my left hand. Piet's bullet had split the wood of the heavy panel, wedging it tighter against the jamb. Stephen jerked the door open but I eeled into the reception area ahead of him.

There were offices to right and left behind latticework partitions. Either half held a dozen Molts and a few humans among the counters and desks. A man in his fifties had crawled under his desk. The opening faced the front door, so he was perfectly visible.

Two rifles lay on the wooden floor of the anteroom. Men in white Federation military tunics stood in the office to the left, with the lattice between them and their weapons. Their hands were raised, but from the looks on their faces they expected to be killed anyway.

I started up the central staircase to the second story, taking the steps two at a time. Behind me Piet ordered, "Get them all in the left room. Loomis and Baer to guard them!"

Heavier boots crashed on the stairs behind me. Stephen breathed in gasps. Dole whuffed, "Christ's *blood*!" as his boot slipped. Armor and equipment slammed down loudly on the hardwood treads. *I could be shot from behind by accident,* I realized, but the thought didn't touch the part of me that was in control.

As fast as we'd arrived, the personnel of New Troy had found time to respond. The folk downstairs reacted by hiding and dissociating themselves from their weapons, but that might not be everyone's choice.

To the right of the stair head was an openwork gate of cast bronze. The workmanship was excellent. The pattern was based on pentacles, like that of the Molts' own architecture. The gate was locked. Somebody inside had tried to draw a curtain for visual privacy, but he/she had torn the fabric in panic. The room beyond had thick rugs and a good deal of plush furniture, though I couldn't see any people in the glance I spared it.

The door to the left was thick, ajar, and carried the legend in letters cut from copper sheet-stock GUARDS OF THE REPUBLIC. I rammed it fully open with my shoulder.

The interior was dim because the space was partitioned into smaller rectangular chambers. A man stood at the end of the central hallway, trying to step into his trousers one-handed. He saw me and straightened, aiming his rifle.

I lunged toward him. He flung away the rifle and screamed, "No, don't shoot!" He crossed his arms in front of his face.

"Watch the other doors!" Stephen ordered behind me, the fat muzzle of his flashgun pointed at the Fed soldier. The partition walls didn't reach the high ceiling. Dole, Lightbody, and I kicked open doors.

Two men came out with their hands raised. One of them snarled, "Traitor!" He must have thought we were mutineers from a Back Worlds garrison. Dole knocked the man down with his rifle butt, then gave him a boot in the stomach.

There were ten cubicles in all, each with a bunk, a table, and a freestanding wardrobe. Others had been occupied recently, but the three men who'd surrendered were the only ones present now.

"Maher, take them down with the rest," said Piet. He'd waited at the stair head until he was sure there'd been no trouble in the guards' dormitory.

"I'll—" Stephen said.

Piet turned and smashed the gate open with the heel of his right boot. He strode into the room beyond with his carbine slanted across his body—ready for trouble but not expecting it. I was the last man to follow him.

Four Molt servants huddled at the rear corner of the room, out of sight from the doorway. French windows opened onto a balcony overlooking the walled garden behind the Commandatura. A narrow staircase led from the balcony to the garden.

A Molt was pruning Terran roses, apparently oblivious of the commotion going on around him. There was a shed against the back wall, and a small but ornate residential outbuilding at the end of the pathway through the center of the garden. The outbuilding's door closed as I watched.

"Where's the commander?" Piet said, pointing his left hand imperiously at the cowering Molts. Piet held his carbine muzzle-up in his right hand; the butt rested in the crook of his elbow.

One of the Molts gestured toward a heap of large, embroidered pillows along the sidewall. "Masters," the Molt said, "none of us know where Secretary Duquesne might be."

Dole groped in the pile of pillows, found something, and jerked a fat man in loose trousers and an open-throated shirt into view. "Wakey, wakey," the bosun said, laying the muzzle of his rifle on the bridge of Secretary Duquesne's nose.

"Please!" Duquesne squealed. "Please!"

"Let him up," Piet said, obviously relaxing. "I don't think he'll be any difficulty."

"Piet, there's somebody in the building behind this," I said, nodding toward the French windows.

The *Oriflamme* touched down. While the thrusters' roar reflected from the ground, the doubled noise rattling the window casements made further speech impossible. Piet gestured first to me, then to Lightbody, and last toward the outside stairway. Stephen nodded the ceramic barrel of his flashgun and stepped to a window from which he could command the whole back of the garden.

I'd reached the midway landing when Salomon shut off the *Oriflamme*'s motors. The sudden silence released a vise the noise had clamped around my chest. I wasn't aware of the pressure until it stopped.

"Sir?" said Lightbody. I glanced over my shoulder. "Will there be treasure in there?" He nodded down the path ahead of us.

"In a manner of speaking," I said, because I had a notion as to just who might be housed in the cottage. "Not that'll make us rich, though."

I wondered if Piet had the same suspicions I did; and if so, what he'd meant by sending me to investigate.

The gardener continued spraying his roses with a can designed for a Molt's three-fingered hands. He crooned in a grating voice as we passed, but it wasn't us he was speaking to.

The *Oriflamme*'s ramp began to lower with a loud squeal. The ship was going to need a lot of work. I didn't believe she could ever be reconditioned to the point she could pass the Breach a second time.

The curtain on the window to the left of the door fluttered as we approached. I paused to hang the cutting bar from my belt . . . though of course, she could be guarded, probably *would* be guarded. The place had blue trim and white stucco walls, though both were flaking to a degree.

"Open in the name of the Free State of Venus," I said, pitching my voice to command rather than threaten.

Nothing happened. I tried the latch. It was locked.

"This is absurd," I muttered.

Lightbody stuck the muzzle of his shotgun into the six-pane window casement and swept the barrel sideways, shattering half the glass and snatching the curtain aside. There were two women within. I'd expected only one, and these were both tough-looking. They wore the white jackets of the Federation military.

"Open the door, then!" Lightbody said. His face grew red and his voice sank into a growl. "You whores!"

"We're not armed!" snarled the 40-year-old woman with light brown hair. The name tag over her left pocket read VANTINE. She might have been handsome at one time, but not since the scar drew up the left side of her mouth.

Lightbody kicked the center panel out of the bottom of the doorframe. He was furious. "Easy . . ." I warned, but his bootheel smashed the central crossbrace from the door, flinging jagged fragments into the room. Vantine jumped back from the latch when she realized that we were in no mood to play games.

"Lightbody!" I said, but I might as well have been in Betaport for the effect I had. He half turned, then lunged against the remnants of the door. The back of his armored shoulder hit the top panel. It splintered also as Lightbody spun into the small living room. The furniture—a couch, two chairs, and an end table—was of local wood with lacework coverings. The oval area rug was patterned in small pentagons of gray, pink, and white thread.

The two women backed toward the couch, keeping their hands plainly in sight.

I stepped between them and Lightbody. "Where's the person who lives here?" I asked. The cottage had two more rooms, a kitchen and—through a bead curtain—a bedroom.

"We live here," said the second woman, whose black hair was shot with gray. Her name tag read PATTEN and her face was less attractive than Dole's. "We're not billeted with the other soldiers because we're women, can't you see?"

"You're whores!" Lightbody shouted. "Soldiers of Hell, most like! Prancing about as if you was men!"

He swung his shotgun toward Patten. I grabbed it with both hands. He was bigger than me and stronger for his size. He forced me back.

I snatched the cutting bar from my belt. "Lightbody!" I shouted. I thumbed on the power and triggered the bar. "If you won't obey me, then by God you'll obey this!"

I don't think it was the threat that brought Lightbody to his senses so much as having my face pressed into his above the crossways shotgun. He slumped back.

"Sorry, sir," he muttered. He turned his face aside and wiped it with his callused right palm. "It's against God and nature to see women pretending to be men."

I let go of him. I was trembling. The bar shook as much with my finger off the trigger as it had the moment before. "We're not here for that," I said. My voice shivered too.

I turned. The women watched with a mixture of anger and loathing. Patten wore a crucifix around her neck. I jerked it with my left hand, breaking the thin silver chain. "We're not mutineers," I said, "we're from Venus. And we're Christians."

I'd spent more time in the Governor's Palace than I had in a church, and I'd only been to the palace twice.

I slapped the crucifix into Patten's hand. "Keep your idols out of sight, or I won't answer for the consequences."

The bead curtain rattled as I walked into the bedroom. The chance that either Patten or Vantine was the secretary's mistress was less than that of Piet swearing allegiance to President Pleyal.

I opened the large freestanding wardrobe beside the door. The clothes within were gauzy and many-layered, decorated with lace and ribbons. Shades of blue predominated. The bottom of the wardrobe held shoes in ranks; no one was hiding there.

The wood above me thumped. I backed a step and looked up. A flaring cornice ornamented the wardrobe's top. The hollow behind the cornice was about twenty centimeters deep. A blonde woman, gagged and with furious blue eyes, peered over the edge at me.

I tossed my cutting bar onto the bed to free both hands. "Lightbody, watch that pair of yours!" I warned.

I got extra height by hopping onto the wardrobe's bottom shelf, scattering delicate shoes. The woman squirmed completely over the cornice, trusting me to take her. Her weight was no problem.

Her wrists were tied, first behind her back, then to her ankles. Patten and Vantine had been busy in the minutes they'd had since we landed. They'd used filmy stockings for the bonds; not Terran silk, but something at least as strong. I ripped my bar's ceramic teeth across the fabric with the power off.

The captive pulled the gag out of her mouth when I'd freed her hands. She was in her mid-twenties and far, far too supple and beautiful to be wasted on a pig like Secretary Duquesne . . .

Well, that was true of a lot of women, and no few men.

"Thank you, sir," she said as she got to her feet in a motion as smooth as that of smoke rising. "My name is Alicia."

She walked into the living room without looking back at me. I suppose she was used to having men follow her without question.

Alicia's dress was pale orange. The soft fabric fit loosely and had no particular shape of its own. She moved like a puff of flame.

Lightbody faced the two soldiers, holding his shotgun at low port. His eyelids flicked in surprise when he saw Alicia. Patten and Vantine glared at her with molten hatred. My thumb slid the bar's power switch forward.

"Sergeant Vantine here . . ." Alicia said coldly. She stepped to the soldier's side without coming between Vantine and Lightbody's shotgun, then reached under the tail of Vantine's tunic.

" . . . has a gun," Alicia continued. Vantine moved minusculely. I reached over Alicia's shoulder and touched the tip of the bar to Vantine's right ear.

Alicia pulled a small revolver from Vantine's waistband. "I know about it," she went on in the same distant voice, "because the sergeant—"

Her face suddenly broke into planes like those of an ice carving, inhuman and terrible though still beautiful. Alicia backhanded Vantine across the jaw with the butt of the revolver. Vantine staggered.

Alicia hit her again, this time on the forehead. Vantine's head jerked back. There was an oval red splotch above her left eye.

I closed my left hand over Alicia's on the gun. She relaxed with a great shudder, leaning against me and closing her eyes. "Because the sergeant put it *into* me," Alicia said softly. "And she told me to be a good girl and stay quiet like Ducky wanted, or she'd shovel hot coals there instead."

I dropped the revolver into my pocket. It was surprisingly heavy for something so small. Patten held Vantine by the shoulder and elbow, helping her stay upright. Alicia straightened and stepped to the side. She watched the proceedings regally.

"Strip," I said to the soldiers. Lightbody looked at me oddly, Patten with fear.

"Oh, don't worry about your virtue, ladies, not from me," I said. "You'll strip to make sure you've no more toys hidden. We'll tie your hands with our belts, and then Lightbody'll march you to the Molt pen where you and your friends will stay until we lift."

My voice caught repeatedly on images my mind threw up; Vantine and Patten, and the bound girl between them. Secretary Duquesne had acted quickly to keep his mistress safe when raiders landed. Safe in his terms, safe from other *men*.

The Fed soldiers only stared at me. I touched Vantine's tunic with the tip of my cutting bar, then triggered it. White fluff spun up from the whine.

"Don't worry about your virtue, ladies," I repeated. My voice quivered like the cutting bar's blade. "But your lives, now, that could very easily be a different matter."

TREHINGA

Day 111

The Federation freighter *C**, renamed the *Iola* after Salomon's mother and for the next few days a Venerian warship, lifted thunderously from New Troy. The freshly-cut gunports in her hold gaped like tooth cavities when the rest of the bare metal hull reflected sunlight. The *Iola* was 15° nose-down; she rotated slowly around her vertical axis because the thrusters weren't aligned squarely.

"I thought you said automated ships were safer on liftoff than landing?" I said to Piet, moderating my voice as the *Iola* climbed high enough to muffle her exhaust roar.

Piet quirked a smile at me. "The concept of automation isn't a problem," he said. "Just the cheap execution. Besides, it's safe enough."

"Or you'd be taking her up yourself," Stephen said in a tone of mild reproof. Alicia heard enough in the gunman's voice to look sharply at him. She'd known a lot of men in her 25 standard years, but none like Piet or Stephen Gregg.

She'd known men like me. I didn't doubt that.

The *Iola* had risen to a dot of brilliant light in the stratosphere. The sound of saws and the rock crusher became loudly audible again, now that the thrusters were gone.

The Federation laser battery that hit us as we escaped from Templeton had crazed several hull laminations as well as taking out two attitude jets. The shock of repeated transits flaked the damaged sheathing off in a five-meter gouge.

The crew was sandblasting the fractured edges just as

142

a surgeon would debride a wound in flesh before closing it. When they finished the prep, they'd flux the boundaries and layer on ceramic again. I suspected Piet would oversee that final process himself. Hawtry was right when he claimed Piet's father was a craftsman rather than a gentleman.

Another team removed attitude jets from the second Federation freighter, the *Penobscot*. We carried spare jets in the *Oriflamme,* but all the original nozzles were badly worn from the long voyage. Jets from the ships and stores here would replace our spares.

Dole had muttered to me that he'd rather use burntout ceramic than trust Fed metalwork, but Piet seemed to think the tungsten nozzles would be adequate. Sailors as a class were conservative: "unfamiliar" was too often a synonym for "lethal." The general commander of an expedition through the Breach had to be able to assess options on the basis of fact, though, not tradition.

Alicia raised a slim hand toward where the *Iola* had vanished. "But *where* are you sending the ship?" she asked.

It didn't seem to occur to her that anybody might think she was asking out of more than curiosity. Stephen and I exchanged glances: mine concerned, his clearly amused.

Piet, with an innocence as complete as I'm sure Alicia's was, answered, "We're just putting her in orbit with two guns, Mistress Leeman. The *Oriflamme* can't lift while we're working on her hull, and there's the risk that a Federation warship will arrive while we're disabled."

As he spoke, Piet began walking down Water Street. New Troy stretched along a broad estuary. It had a surfaced road along the water and a parallel road separating the buildings from the field where starships landed. A dozen barges were moored to quays behind the grain elevators.

"Warships here?" Alicia said. "Don't worry about that. I haven't seen one in . . ." She shivered. "Nine months, I've been here. Earth months. I was born in Montreal."

There was more to the last statement than information. I wasn't sure whether she meant it as a challenge or an admission, though.

"Still, it's better not to run a risk," Piet said mildly. "We'll reship the guns to the *Oriflamme* in orbit, I think. Since, as Jeremy points out, the *C** is worse maintained than I'd thought from viewing her."

He tipped me a nod.

"Dole takes a crew up in the cutter to replace Salomon tomorrow?" Stephen asked.

Piet shook his head. "Guillermo tomorrow, Dole the following day. Stampfer asked for a watch, but I don't trust his shiphandling, even with automated systems."

He glanced at me. "I wouldn't put it so bluntly to Stampfer, you know, Jeremy," he said.

I shrugged. "He's a gunner," I said. "One man can't do everything."

Though maybe Piet could. Being around him gave you the feeling that he walked on water when nobody was watching.

The pen for Molts being transshipped was adjacent to the Commandatura. There'd been a dozen aliens behind the strands of electrified razor ribbon when we landed. Neither the *C** nor the *Penobscot* was a dedicated slaver, but both vessels carried a handful of Molts as part of their general cargo.

We'd turned the Molts loose. Half of them still wandered about New Troy, looking bewildered and clustering when we distributed rations from the Fed warehouse. Secretary Duquesne, his seven soldiers, and three of the officials who'd been cheeky enough to sound dangerous had replaced the slaves in the pen.

For the most part, the humans—residents as well as transients from the barges and two starships—seemed willing to do business on normal terms and otherwise keep out of our way. The local Molts were no problem without human leaders. Stephen, Piet, and a sailor who'd been to the Reaches with them had separately warned me that Molts *would* fight for human masters, even masters who treated them as badly as the Feds generally did. It was a matter of clan identification among the aliens.

Duquesne trembled with anger as he watched the four of us saunter by the pen. He touched the razor ribbon, forgetting that the metal was charged. A blue spark popped and threw him back. Patten and a male soldier heard the secretary bellow and ran to help.

"Run toward the wire," I ordered Alicia in a low voice.

"Ducky!" she cried.

I let her go two steps and grabbed her roughly around the neck. "Get back here or you'll be in there with him!" I shouted as I swung her between me and Piet.

Stephen faced the pen and raised the flashgun's butt toward—not quite to—his shoulder in warning. Duquesne and his henchmen scurried out of sight within the wooden shed meant to shelter slaves.

We walked on. "That was a good thought, Jeremy," Piet said.

I shrugged. "Maybe it'll help," I said. I didn't suggest we hang Duquesne and the two women who'd been so enthusiastic to carry out his orders. Piet wouldn't go along with the idea, and I've got better things to do than waste my breath.

We passed one of the hotels/boardinghouses for human transients. Men watched from chairs on the lower-level stoop. Stephen eyed them, shifting slightly the way he carried the flashgun. The captain of the *Penobscot* banged his chair's front legs back down on the deck and threw us a salute.

Piet had addressed the population of New Troy the night we arrived, promising that we would deal fairly with them as individuals, paying for whatever merchandise or services we required. Our quarrel was with President Pleyal and his attempt to dictate to all mankind.

When Piet was done, Stephen added a few words: if there was trouble, the colony would pay for it. If one of our men was killed, there would be no colony when we left. The next visitors would find the bones of the present inhabitants in the ashes of their buildings.

There was a line of men—our men—reaching out the door of the next building, a brothel. There were three girls, though Dole said the fiftyish madame had turned tricks as well during the crush the night before.

The waiting spacers grew silent and looked away. Piet

turned his head in the direction of the river and said to Alicia, "Do the landowners have guards on their estates, Mistress Leeman?"

Alicia sniffed. "They arm trusties to track Molts who run away," she said. "None of the landowners are going to risk their life or property to help the secretary, though."

We were past the brothel. Piet didn't approve of whoring or drunkenness, but he didn't order his crew to remain chaste and sober while on leave. A cynic would say Piet was too smart to give orders he knew would be ignored . . . but I'm not sure most of this crew would ignore an order of his, even an order that went so clearly against their view of nature.

Sunset painted clouds in the eastern sky, while veils of heat lightning shimmered behind them. We might have a storm before morning. I doubted the shed in the Molt pen was waterproof.

The combination saloon and general merchandise store next to the brothel was owned by Federation Associates— President Pleyal himself, in his private capacity. The facade sagged, and I could see through the grime of the display windows that the roof leaked badly. The store had twenty meters of frontage, but the shelves within were dingy and almost empty. A Molt clerk stared back at us, as motionless as a display mannequin.

Boards filled the lower three-quarters of the saloon's window frames, leaving only a single row of glass panes for illumination. A drunk lay in the street. Two men arguing in front of the door stepped inside when they saw who we were.

"This is why we have to bring Venus to the stars," Piet said. "New Troy, a thousand New Troys—this can't be allowed to continue as man's face to the universe."

"Commander," I said, "it's a frontier. You can't expect polish on a frontier."

Piet stood arms akimbo in the middle of the street. Tracked-on clay covered the plasticized surface. The adobe would be slick as grease in a rainstorm.

Three grain elevators marked the boundary of the human community of New Troy. Beyond were pentagonal towers the Molt labor force had built for itself. Their upper floors were served by outside staircases. Though constructed from scrap material by slaves, the towers had a neat unity that the human buildings lacked.

"Let's go back," Piet said. He turned up the broad passage beside the saloon and the nearest elevator. After a moment, he went on, "It's not a frontier, Jeremy. It's a dumping ground, a midden. Pleyal is mining the universe for his personal benefit, not mankind's."

His voice was rising. The louvered shutters of most of the windows on this side of the saloon were swung back from unglazed casements. A barge crewman at a table followed us with his eyes as we passed.

"The only kind of men who'll come to the stars to serve a tyrant are the trash, or men as grasping and shortsighted as their master is," Piet said. "The few of a better sort sink into the mire because they're almost alone. This isn't a frontier where hardship makes men hard, it's a cesspool where filth makes men filthy! And it will *not* change until the claim of Pleyal to own the universe beyond Pluto is disproved. At the point of a gun if necessary!"

The fronts of commercial buildings on the starport side duplicated those on Water Street. The saloon's facade had one fully-glazed sash window. The bartender was a Molt. A dozen men sat inside, drinking from 100-ml metal tumblers.

None of the clientele was from the *Oriflamme*. Our men had taken over a saloon at the other end of town by arrangement between Dole and local businessmen. Nobody wanted the sort of trouble that could explode when violent enemies got drunk together.

"One ship won't bring down the North American Federation," Alicia said. This evening she wore a frock of translucent layers. The undermost was patterned with Terran roses which seemed to climb through a dense fog of overlying fabric.

"Our success will bring other ships, Mistress Leeman," Piet said. "Raids on the Federation Reaches have already increased twentyfold in the two years since, since *we*—"

He gripped Stephen's right hand, though he continued

to look toward Alicia on his other side.

"—came back with more microchips than had been seen on Venus since the Collapse."

"It's not just the wealth for Venus," Stephen said. "It's the wealth that doesn't go to Earth to help President Pleyal strangle everyone but Pleyal."

There was no line on the starport side of the brothel. A lone Federation spacer glanced at us from the doorway. A pink-shaded lamp inside was lighted. I stepped into a pothole that the sky's afterglow hadn't shown me.

Alicia lifted her chin in a taut nod. "So you'll replace bums with pirates? That's your plan?" She paused. "Bums and whores!"

"We'll break the present system, mistress," Piet said, "because it can't be reformed. With the help of God we'll do that. Then there'll be room for men—from Earth, from Venus, from the Moon colony and Mars, perhaps—to expand in however many ways they find. Rather than as a tyrant demands, in a fashion that will come crashing down when the tyranny does—as it must!—in a second Collapse that would be forever."

The last words were a trumpet call, not a shout. Another man would have blazed them out with anger, but Piet's transfiguring vision was a joyous thing. Though even I'd seen how harsh the execution would be.

"I went to the Reaches to trade," Stephen said in the thin, lilting voice I'd heard him use before. "I wonder what would have happened if we'd been left to trade in peace, hey?"

He laughed. Alicia shut her eyes and missed a step. She squeezed against me instinctively.

"Maybe I'd sleep at night, do you think?" Stephen went on in the same terrible voice. Piet took his friend's hand again.

The slave pen was unlighted. Figures moved around a lantern at the Water Street end. It was about time for the prisoners to get their rations.

Floodlights gleamed on the *Oriflamme.* Half a dozen crewmen continued to work on the hull. "If I thought we had time," Piet said, "I'd grind off the repairs we made on Respite and reglaze from the original. I don't think the basalt bonded well, despite the surface crazing."

"There'll be time for that after we've taken the *Montreal*," Stephen said. "Or it won't matter."

Piet gave a nonchalant shrug. "We'll take her," he said. "And return home, with the help of God."

He looked at Alicia, smiled, and bowed slightly. "I think I'll go aboard and see how the repairs are coming," he said. "Mistress Leeman, I've appreciated your company."

"I'll go along with you, Piet," Stephen said. "Maybe I'll bunk in the ship tonight."

He gave me a wan smile. The two of them walked in step toward the *Oriflamme,* though I'm sure neither was attempting to match strides. They were as different as an oyster and its shell; and as much akin.

I opened the wicket into the Commandatura garden for Alicia.

"Captain Ricimer really believes in what you're doing," she said softly. Roses perfumed the air. There were lights in the far wing of the building, but the garden seemed to be empty. "But Mister Gregg doesn't."

"I think Stephen believes the same things as Piet does," I said. "I just don't think he cares very much."

"He frightens me," she said.

Stephen would never kill anyone by accident, I thought; but Alicia understood too much for that to sound reassuring to her. "He's a good friend to Commander Ricimer," I said. "Not a very good friend to himself, though."

I paused to twist off a rose. Its deep pink glowed like a diamond's heart with the last of the sunset. I broke the thorns off sideways with the tip of my thumb, then handed the flower to Alicia.

She giggled and put the stem behind her ear. Flying creatures as big as gulls swooped and climbed over the river. Their calls were surprisingly musical.

Alicia turned at her cottage's new door—a panel of raw wood that Molt workmen had fitted the evening before. "You're a very gentlemanly pirate, aren't you?" she said. "You could easily have forced me to—whatever you chose."

I shrugged. My skin was tingling. "I respect you too much for that," I said. *I respect myself too much.* Again, though I don't lie when I can avoid it, one chooses the particular truth he speaks aloud.

"A girl doesn't always want to be respected quite so much," Alicia said. My arms were around her by the middle of the sentence, and my lips muffled the final word.

Near morning, as I was starting to dress to be gone before dawn, Alicia told me about Secretary Duquesne's personal cache of chips in a pit beneath the floor of the garden shed.

TREHINGA

Day 114

"Here's the whores you wanted, Mister Moore," Lightbody said in a tone that could have been forged on an anvil. He gestured Patten and Vantine into the walled office I'd taken for this interview. Baer stood behind the women with a cutting bar.

Because the Federation soldiers wore trousers and had hired on to fight, Lightbody called them whores, *thought* of them as whores. He treated Alicia with the deference due a lady; and she was a lady, as surely as I was a gentleman, but the twists of Lightbody's mind disturbed me at a basic level nonetheless.

The *Oriflamme* fired a matched pair of attitude jets in the field outside. The hull repairs were complete. Piet and Guillermo were doing the final workup. We'd lift by evening, so it was time for me to act.

"You can take their hands loose, Lightbody," I said. The women were filthy. Facilities in the slave pen were limited to a trough, buckets, and mud. Twice so far we'd had rain before dawn, and the yellow adobe clay was everything I'd expected it to be.

Were conditions reversed, Secretary Duquesne would have us hanged out of hand—unless he directed Patten and Vantine to torture us to death instead. I didn't think of this pair as whores. More like vicious dogs, to be trusted only in their malice.

Lightbody looked doubtful, but he opened the knots on the women's wrists with the spike of his clasp knife. He held his shotgun out to the side where the prisoners

151

couldn't easily grab it. "You'll want us to stay in here with you then, sir?" he suggested.

I shook my head. "No," I said, "I want to have a friendly talk in private. Close the door and wait outside."

The two sailors obeyed, but I could tell they didn't think much of the idea. To reassure them, I laid my cutting bar on top of the desk I was using, with its grip ready for my hand.

I'd chosen the office of the Clerk of Customs because the room was private and it had a large window. I wanted the light behind me for this interview. The clerk—the older of the pair who'd come out to the cutter initially—had decorated the walls with wood carvings. Molt workmanship, I supposed. The pieces were intricate, but I didn't find them attractive.

The women glared at me with caged fury. Their white tunics were sallow with dried mud, and their faces weren't much cleaner.

I waited for the next pair of jets to finish their screaming test, then said, "You can sit down." I gestured to the chairs against the wall behind the women.

"What do you want from us?" Vantine demanded in a voice which broke with anger.

"Help," I said. "For which I'm willing to pay."

They were making it easy for me, though I'd have carried through in any case. I'd seen this pair in action the morning we arrived. No amount of feigned contrition now would have changed the decision I'd made.

"And if we don't agree, you're going to threaten us with that toy?" Patten said, nodding toward my cutting bar. "I ought to feed it to you!"

"No threat," I said. I picked up the bar and waited a moment. If Lightbody and Baer heard the blade whine, they'd burst in on us.

The *Oriflamme* fired two more attitude jets. I triggered the bar and shaved the corner off the desk. I laid the weapon down again.

"This is so that you won't make the mistake of attacking me," I said. "If you did, I'd—"

Another part of my mind started to fog my conscious

intelligence. My voice was husky and very soft.

"—cut you into so many pieces that they'd have to fill your coffins by weight." I swallowed. "And I don't want that, I want a friendly conversation, that's all."

The part of me that hid behind the red fog, the part that had been in control at the Molt temple and was almost in control just a moment before—that part very much wanted another chance to kill.

The women had straightened as I spoke. Their faces were expressionless, and the earlier bluster was gone.

"What do you want?" Vantine repeated quietly.

"We'll be lifting for Quincy soon," I said. I was all right again, though my hands still trembled. "We're hoping to meet *Our Lady of Montreal* there." I smiled. "If not there, then we'll catch her farther on. It depends on how long she lays over on Fleur de Lys. But before we leave Trehinga, I'd like to find the treasure stored here."

The women looked at one another cautiously, then back to me. Patten massaged her right thigh through her dirty trousers.

"There's no chips, no artifacts here," Vantine said. She was more afraid of keeping silent than of speaking. "Trehinga wasn't settled before the Collapse. There's nothing but wheat."

"I can't imagine that a man like Secretary Duquesne doesn't have a private hoard," I said. "I don't know what sort of favors he's trading to the ships' captains who land here, but there'll be something. He'll be building up a store so that when he retires to Earth he has something better than a Federation pension to support him. Chips are the most likely, but maybe pre-Collapse artifacts smuggled from other planets, sure."

"We don't," Vantine said very carefully, "know anything about that." She watched me the way a rabbit watches a snake.

Attitude jets—the last pair of the morning, unless Piet saw a need to retest—fired. The sound wasn't so loud that I couldn't have talked over it, but the three-second pause was useful.

"I'd pay you each a hundred Mapleleafs if you showed

me where the cache was," I said. I held up a pair of twelve-sided coins bearing President Pleyal's face toward the women.

The paymaster's safe on the opposite side of the Commandatura contained a fair amount of currency. As Piet had promised, we weren't robbing the businessfolk of Trehinga, but the Federation government was another matter.

The women stared at me. Patten began to laugh. "Are you crazy?" she said. She regained her composure. "Do you think *we're* crazy? We lead you to Duquesne's personal stash, and then you go off and leave us here? Do you have any idea what he'd do to us then?"

I shrugged. "I've got a notion, yeah," I said. "Open the door, would you please?"

Vantine obeyed. Her companion's laughter was half bravado, but Vantine was clearly terrified. She'd sensed . . . not, I think, what was about to happen, but that *something* was about to happen.

Lightbody raised his shotgun's muzzles when he saw everything was calm. "Baer," I said, "go out and gather as many of our off-duty people as you can in five minutes. Into the garden. And tell the locals to come, too. There'll be some entertainment."

"What are you doing, sir?" Lightbody said as Baer ran down the corridor shouting.

"For the moment," I said, "you and I wait here with the ladies. Then we'll go out to the garden too."

I put my hand on the cutting bar. I was shaking so badly that the blade rattled on the desk and I had to put it down. Patten was silent, and Vantine was as gray as if someone was nailing her wrists to a cross.

There were easily a hundred people in the garden when we came out—me in front, the prisoners behind, and last of all Lightbody with the shotgun. I'd had him tie Patten's right wrist to Vantine's left while we waited. They couldn't escape, but it was important that they not be seen to try.

"Hey, Mister Moore!" Kiley called from the crowd. "Do they take their clothes off now?"

I waved with a grin; but the joke made me think of Jeude, and the grin congealed.

The Molt gardener stood on one leg, rasping the other one nervously against his carapace as he watched people brush his precious roses. Because of the thorns, the bushes weren't likely to be trampled; but sure, some sailor might clear more room with his cutting bar.

Funny to think of a Molt worrying about Terran roses on one of the Back Worlds. In those terms, most of life seemed pretty silly, though. I suppose that's where religion comes in, for those who can believe in a god.

I waved my bar ahead of me to make a path. A lot of those present were locals, as I'd hoped, but they kept to the edges of the courtyard. The central walkway and an arc facing the back of the Commandatura were filled with Venerians. More spectators streamed in through the wickets beside the building and the larger gate onto Water Street.

Baer had done a good job, though I wasn't quite sure how he'd managed it so quickly. I'd wanted a big enough gathering that word would spread at once throughout the community, but this was ideal.

Alicia's jalousies were lowered; she would be watching from behind them. I'd told her she should at all costs stay hidden this morning.

"What are we doing?" Vantine asked over the chatter of the crowd.

"Keep moving, whore!" Lightbody snapped. I suspected he prodded Vantine with the gun as he spoke.

"None of that!" I ordered. "The ladies are helping us."

As I turned my head to speak, I saw that Piet and Stephen had come out the back of the Commandatura. They were following us.

The storage shed was padlocked. I sheared the hasp off in twinkling sparks. A bit remained hanging from the staple. I flicked it away with the tip of the cutting bar: the steel would be just below red heat from friction.

Stephen reached past and slid the door open. He grinned in a way that was becoming familiar, but he didn't ask any questions.

The shed's floor was wooden and raised a few centimeters from the ground. Tools optimized for Molt hands, crates, a coil of fencing, and other impedimenta were stacked around the walls, but the two square meters in the center of the shed were clear.

There'd be a catch hidden somewhere, but I wasn't going to hunt for it. I swept my bar in an arc through the flooring. Nails *ping*ed bitterly within the cloud of sawdust; the head of one bounced from my shin.

I stepped forward, turned, and drew the reverse arc. The crowd outside was pushing for a better view, but Stephen planted himself in the doorway to keep people out of my blade's way. Patten and Vantine watched in dawning awareness.

Stringers gave. The rough circle of floor fell with a crackle under my weight. I kicked the fragments of lumber aside.

A rectangular steel door measuring a meter by eighty centimeters was set in concrete where there should have been bare soil. I gripped my bar with both hands.

"Jeremy?" Piet Ricimer called.

I looked up. Piet handed Stephen the white silk kerchief he'd worn around his neck. "Cover Jeremy's eyes," he said.

Stephen knotted the silk behind my head. I saw through a white haze. The doorplate had no keyhole, but the hinges were external.

"We didn't—" Patten shouted at the top of her voice, but the scream of my bar cutting metal drowned her out.

A rooster tail of white sparks cascaded to either side of the bar's tip, pricking my bare hands and charring trails of smoke from the wood they landed on. A chip of steel flicked my forehead. Momentary pain, gone almost as soon as I jerked my head.

"Step back, Jeremy," Stephen ordered. His arm kept me from stumbling on the wood floor that I'd forgotten.

I was shaking with effort and my tunic was soaked. I'd been holding the cutting bar as though it supported me over a chasm. I pulled the kerchief off so that I could breathe freely, then mopped my face with it.

There were three black-edged holes in the silk. *I* wouldn't have thought of covering my eyes.

Stephen kicked the door with his bootheel, aiming for the concealed lock. The plate rang. This wasn't a real safe, just a protected hiding place. The second time Stephen stamped down, the back of the lid where I'd sheared the hinges sprang up.

The lid was more than two centimeters thick. Stephen lifted it by the edges with his fingertips. He tossed it past me into a corner of the shed.

"We didn't have anything to do with this!" Patten cried. Vantine hugged herself, shaking as if in a cold wind.

Stephen reached into the opened stash. He came up with a mesh bag of microchips in one hand and what looked like the core of a navigational AI in the other.

He walked out into the sunlight. "There's fifty kilos of chips here!" he shouted to the crowd. There were shouts of awe and surprise, some of them from the local spectators.

I came out with Stephen. "Lightbody," I called loudly, "release these women at once."

Patten tried to hit me. I stepped close and embraced her. I caught a handful of her short hair to keep her from biting my ear in the moment before I backed clear again. Lightbody still didn't understand, but Piet held both women's free elbows from behind so that they couldn't move.

I waved the hundred-Mapleleaf coins so that they caught the sunlight. Vantine was numb. Patten spat at me, but nobody at any distance could see that. Certainly not the locals at the back of the crowd.

"And here's your pay," I said, dropping both coins into Vantine's breast pocket.

There was sick horror in Vantine's eyes. I didn't much like myself, but I'd done what I'd needed to.

At least the pay was fair. The Sanhedrin had only paid thirty pieces of silver to finger a victim for crucifixion.

"Everybody's aboard, sir," Dole called over the clamor of men claiming bits of shipboard territory after days of freedom to move around. "Smetana was sleeping it off behind Gun One so I didn't see him."

Piet nodded to me. I ran two seconds of feedback through the tannoys as an attention signal, then announced, "Five minutes to liftoff."

I'd told Stephen he should take the right-hand couch since Guillermo was in the *Iola,* but he'd insisted I sit there instead. At least I could work the commo as well as the Molt could, and it wasn't as though the process of lifting to orbit required a third astrogator.

Piet's screen echoed the settings that Salomon had programmed. Salomon flipped to an alternate value, then flopped back to the original, all the time watching Piet.

"Either," Piet said with a smile. "But yes, the first, I think, given the *Iola*'s present orbit."

The *Oriflamme*'s displays were razor-sharp, though the lower third of my screen was offset a pixel from the remainder ever since we'd come through the Breach. The population of New Troy watched from buildings and the road.

I could have expanded any individual face to fill the entire screen. That probably wouldn't be a good idea.

Stephen knelt beside my couch. "Have they let Duquesne out of his cage yet?" he asked.

I shook my head. "I don't see any of that lot," I said. I slewed and expanded the slave pen in the field. The prisoners were still there behind razor ribbon. "Maybe the locals are afraid that he'll start shooting and we'll flatten the town."

"Maybe they just don't like the bastard," Stephen replied. He laced his fingers and forced them against the backs of his hands. His face was empty; that of a man you saw sprawled in a gutter. "Lightbody says the pair of women you released stole a boat and headed upriver."

He raised an eyebrow. I shrugged.

Piet leaned toward me. "We've made a preliminary examination of the database you found, Jeremy," he said.

I turned away from Stephen. "Was it valuable?" I asked. "I don't see why it was part of Duquesne's stash."

"Valuable, though perhaps not in market terms," Piet

said. "It's a courier chart. It has full navigational data for the Back Worlds and the longer route to the Solar System. The value to us is . . ."

He smiled like an angel. "Perhaps our lives."

"Shall I initiate, sir?" Salomon asked sharply.

Piet's attention returned to the business of planning lift-off. "One minute!" I warned over the PA system.

I swung the magnified view on my screen sideways a touch, focusing on the woman at the wicket beside the Commandatura.

"We couldn't bring her along, you know," Stephen said in a low voice. "Anyone female."

"She didn't ask, did she?" I said. I didn't realize how angry I was until I heard my tone. I started to blank the display, then instead expanded it further. The discontinuity fell just at the point of Alicia's chin.

"It wasn't a clever plan, Stephen," I said softly. "I didn't ask her about anything. She volunteered . . . She volunteered everything that she gave me."

Stephen put his hand on my arm. "Best I get to my hammock," he said as he rose.

Salomon engaged the AI. Our roaring thrusters drew a curtain of rainbow fire across the face of a woman I would never see again.

ABOVE QUINCY

Day 127

Men in hard suits were around us in the forward hold, though our cutter's optics were so grainy they suggested rather than showed the figures. Clanks against our hull were probably restraints closing; chances were the ramp had locked shut since I didn't feel the vibration of the closing mechanism anymore.

"All right, you lot," Lightbody ordered as he lifted himself from the pilot's couch. "Open her up! Ah—"

He remembered I was alone in the back of the cutter. "Ah—sir!"

Baer rose from the attitude controls. I'd already freed the undogging wheel by bracing my boots against thwarts and slamming a spoke with the shoulder of my hard suit. I spun the wheel fully open, then let Baer help me slide the hatch back over the dorsal hull.

The two sailors Piet gave me to crew the cutter were solid men, either of them capable of piloting the vessel alone in a pinch. Lightbody wasn't used to thinking of a landing party as two sailors and a gentleman, though.

The crew of the *Oriflamme* was at action stations. I'd been sent down to the settlement on Quincy to gather information. I could be spared if *Our Lady of Montreal* appeared while the cutter was on the surface.

I floated out of the cutter's bay. Maher, one of the sailors who'd locked us into the hold, grabbed me with one hand as he hinged up his visor with the other.

"Captain Ricimer's waiting on you forward, sir," he said. He aimed me toward the companionway, then shoved me off like a medicine ball. A sailor waiting there absorbed my momentum and redirected me up the tube.

Dole hugged me to him as I drifted into the forward compartment. He kicked off, carrying us both to the navigation consoles—skirting the 17-cm plasma cannon with a neat carom from the ceiling gunport, still for the moment closed.

I didn't know whether the men were obeying Piet's orders or if they'd simply decided on their own that Mister Moore in free fall was clumsy as a hog on ice. Maybe the process was demeaning, but it'd halved the time I would've taken to negotiate the distance on my own.

I gripped Piet's couch to stay in place. I'd expected to see Stephen, but I realized he would be with the assault party in the after hold.

Piet's screen and that of Salomon to his left were filled with navigational data in schematic and digital form. Guillermo's display showed the world we were orbiting. Quincy was ninety percent water, with strings of small volcanic islands and one modest continent— for the moment on the opposite hemisphere. Ivestown, the planet's sole settlement, was on the continent's north coast. Farms nearby provided garden truck and fruit for starships which stopped over to load reaction mass, but there was no large-scale agriculture and nothing of interest in Ivestown save the pair of brothels.

Piet turned the PA system on to echo my words. He lifted himself on his left arm to face me directly, since the hard suit prevented him from twisting his torso in normal fashion. We'd radioed from Ivestown before lifting off to return, but face-to-face communication was far better than depending on RF transmissions through Quincy's active ionosphere.

"The *Montreal* hasn't arrived yet," I explained. "Nobody down there is even expecting her."

I shook my head in renewed wonder. "It's like talking to a herd of sheep. There's eighteen, twenty humans in Ivestown, and about all they're interested in is scraping local algae off the rocks and eating it. It turns their teeth brown. I suppose there's a drug in it."

"They could be lying," Salomon said. "To keep us here instead of following the *Montreal*."

"No," I said. "No. Lightbody checked the field. He says there hasn't been a ship landed at Ivestown in weeks. Sure, the *Montreal* could land anywhere on the planet, but they wouldn't have. And—you'd have to see the people down there. They don't *care*."

I suppose all four of the colony's women worked in the brothels when a ship was in; maybe some of the men did too. I'd have found coring a watermelon a more satisfying alternative. Piet couldn't have asked a better proof of Fed colonies being garbage dumps rather than frontiers.

Salomon sighed and relaxed his grip on the arm of his couch. Because the navigator had unlatched his restraints to look at me, his armored body began to rise. "It might be weeks before the *Montreal* arrives," he said. "We might have to wait for months. *Months*."

Piet looked toward the screen before him. I don't know whether he was actually viewing the course equations displayed there or letting his mind expand through a range of possibilities as vast as the universes themselves.

"We've waited months already," Piet replied. His voice was soft, but the PA system's software corrected to boom the words at full audible level from the tannoys in all the compartments.

Salomon looked at me for support. I wanted desperately to be back in a gravity well. My hard suit's rigid presence constricted my mind. We hadn't stayed long enough on the ground for me to take the armor off. I said nothing.

"If we land . . ." Salomon said. The prospect of an indefinite stay in weightless conditions was horrifying to veteran spacers as well as to me, but Salomon still wasn't willing to complete the suggestion. He knew it was a bad one, knew that landing would jeopardize the whole expedition.

"If we land," Piet said with his usual quiet certainty, "then we have to hope that the *Montreal* sets down without first determining who we are. If instead she transits immediately, we won't be able—"

"The Feds are too sloppy to worry about a ship on the ground," Salomon said. His voice didn't have enough energy to be argumentative. "Especially on the Back Worlds."

"We've risked a great deal," Piet replied. "Many of our friends have died. Many others as well, and they're also human beings. We aren't going to cut corners now."

He tapped his armored fingertip twice on the audio pickup as a formal attention signal. "Gentlemen," he said, "you may stand down for the moment. Don't take off your hard suits. I regret this, but we have to be ready to open the gunports at a moment's notice."

I nodded within the tight confines of the helmet sealed to my torso armor by a lobstertail gorget. My eyes were closed. I'd like to have been able to pray for mercy.

"Men," Piet said. "Comrades, *friends*. With the Lord's help, we'll prevail. But it's up to us to endure."

The tannoys chirped as Piet switched off the PA system.

We would endure.

ABOVE QUINCY

Day 129

I unlatched the waste cassette—the shit pan—of Stephen's hard suit. You can change your own, but you're likely to slosh the contents when you reach beneath your fanny with arms encased in rigid armor.

This cassette leaked anyway. Stephen made a quick snatch with a rag. A few droplets of urine escaped despite that. Because we were in free fall, the drops would spread themselves across the first surface they touched, probably a bulkhead.

That wouldn't make much difference, because the *Oriflamme* already stank like a sewer from similar accidents. What bothered me worse was the way my body itched from constant contact with my suit's interior.

"If I ever have a chance to bathe again," I said softly, "all that's left of me is going to melt and run down the drain like the rest of the dirt."

The *Oriflamme*'s crew hung in various postures within the compartment. The only comfortable part of free fall was that any of the surfaces within the vessel could serve as a "floor." Piet lay on his couch, apparently drowsing. Dole was on lookout at the left console. Guillermo's usual position was empty. The Molt had gone into suspended animation and was bundled against the forward bulkhead in a cargo net.

The displays were set for blink comparison. Images of the stars surrounding the *Oriflamme* flashed against images taken at the same point in the previous orbit. The AI corrected for the vessel's frictional slippage and highlighted anomalies for human examination. In two days of waiting, we had the start of a catalog of comets circling Quincy's sun.

Kiley held open the clear bag so that I could add my cassette to the dozen already there. A detail of sailors would open the after hold and steam the day's accumulation, but there were limits to the cleaning you could do in free fall and vacuum.

Stephen slapped an empty cassette into the well of his suit. "You've never been on a slaving voyage, with Molts packed into the holds and all the air cycled through them before it gets to you," he said. "Though we didn't have to stay suited up that time, that's true."

I looked at him. "I didn't know that you'd been a slaver," I said.

Stephen turned his palms up in the equivalent of a shrug. "Back when we were trying to trade with Fed colonies," he said. "The only merchandise they wanted were Molt slaves. Piet wasn't in charge."

He smiled. "Neither was I, for that matter, but it didn't bother me a lot." There would have been as much humor in the *snick* of a rifle's breech opening. "And that was back when some things did bother me, you know."

"Hey?" said Dole. Piet, who I'd thought was dozing—and maybe he was—snapped upright and expanded by three orders of magnitude a portion of the starfield blinking on his display. Dole was still reaching for the keypad.

The magnified object was a globular starship. We had no way of judging size without scale, but I'd never heard of anything under 300 tonnes burden being built on a spherical design. Plasma wreathed the vessel. Her thrusters were firing to bring her into orbit around Quincy.

Piet wound the siren for two seconds. The impellers couldn't reach anything like full volume in that time, but the moan rising toward a howl was clearly different from all the normal sounds of the *Oriflamme* in free fall.

"General quarters," Piet ordered crisply. "Assault party, remain in the main hull for the moment."

He paused, his armored fingers dancing across his console with tiny clicks. "My friends," Piet added, "I believe this is the moment we've prepared and suffered for."

Stephen checked the satchel which held charged batteries to reload his flashgun. I bent and held him steady with both hands to get a close look at his waste cassette. It was latched properly.

When the *Oriflamme*'s gunports opened, we'd be in hard vacuum. That was the wrong time to have the pressure within somebody's suit blow his waste cassette across the compartment, leaving a two-by-ten-centimeter hole to void the rest of his air.

Lightbody unbound Guillermo and pumped his arms to break him out of his trance. The Molt was a doubly grotesque figure in the ceramic armor built for his inhuman limbs.

Salomon slid into his console as Dole propelled himself clear. The bosun could land the vessel manually and run the AI during normal operations, but he lacked the specialized training to match courses with a ship trying to run from us. With a competent navigator like Salomon backing Piet Ricimer at the controls, the Federation vessel didn't have a prayer of escaping either in the sidereal universe or through transit.

I'd hung a cutting bar from one of my hard suit's waist-level equipment studs. I unclipped it. There was no need to, but it gave me something to do with my hands. Catching our quarry was only the first part of the business.

"Prepare for power!" Salomon warned. Veteran sailors had already made sure their boots were anchored on the deck, "down" as soon as the thrusters fired.

A 1-g thrust simulated gravity. I was at an angle, because my right foot bounced from the deck. Stephen kept me from falling.

The Fed vessel's image filled the main screen. That was another jump in magnification, though I supposed we were closing with them in real terms. Some of her plating had been replaced, speckling the spherical hull with bright squares. Her lower hemisphere was crinkly with punishment from atmospheric friction and the bath of plasma exhaust during braking.

Everyone in our forward compartment stared at the

screen. The men amidships and in the stern cabin could only guess at what was happening, since the navigation staff was too busy to offer a commentary.

Our quarry's hatches would lower like sections of orange peel. There was an inlay of contrasting metal set beside one of them. I couldn't read the lettering, but I made out the figure of a woman with her hand outstretched.

"See the Virgin?" I said to Stephen. "I think she's the *Montreal*."

"Half the Feds' shipping is our lady of this or that," Stephen said. His voice was that of a machine again. "But if not this time, then another. And we'll be ready."

As Stephen spoke, his hands moved as delicately as butterfly wings across the stock and receiver of his flashgun. He'd folded the trigger guard forward so that he could use the weapon with gauntlets on.

"Unidentified vessel," crackled the tannoys. Piet had set them to repeat outside signals. This must have been from a communications laser since our thrusters and those of our quarry were snarling across the RF spectrum. "Sheer off at once. This is the Presidential vessel *Montreal*. If you endanger us you'll all be sent to some mud hole for the rest of your life!"

"Gentlemen," Piet ordered, "seal your suits."

He snapped his visor closed. I tried to obey. The cutting bar clacked against my helmet. I'd forgotten I was holding it. I couldn't feel it in my hand because of the gauntlets.

Our commo system switched to vacuum mode instead of depending on atmospheric transmission. Piet's voice, blurred almost beyond understanding, growled through the deckplates and the structure of my hard suit. "Run out the guns."

We dipped lower into orbit around Quincy, losing velocity from atmospheric friction as well as from our main motors. The *Oriflamme* began to vibrate fiercely. The *Montreal*'s image trailed a shroud of excited atoms.

The gunport in the starboard bulkhead swung inward, glowing with plasma from our own exhaust. The *Oriflamme*'s outrushing atmosphere buffeted us and carried small objects—a glove, a sheet of paper, even a knife—with it.

Ambient light vanished because there were no longer enough molecules of gas to scatter it. All illumination became direct, turning armored men into outlines lit by the gunport. When hydraulic rams advanced the muzzle of the Long Tom through the opening, we became a ship of ghosts and softly gleaming highlights.

The image of the *Montreal* on our main screen took on a slickness that no working starship could have in reality. The tornado of exhaust and roaring atmosphere degraded the data from our optical pickups. The screen's AI enhanced the image in keeping with an electronic ideal, substituting one falsehood for another.

Three gunports slid open along the midline of the *Montreal*'s hull.

Our hard suits didn't have individual laser commo units, though a few of the helmets could be hardwired into the navigational consoles. Radio was useless while the main engines were firing anyway. I touched my helmet to Stephen's and shouted, "Why don't we shoot?"

The muzzles of plasma cannon emerged from the *Montreal*'s gunports, setting up violent eddies in the flow of exhaust back over the globular hull. The guns looked very small, but the lack of scale could be deceiving me. Unlike us, the Federation crew wouldn't have been waiting in hard suits. A handful of gunners must have suited up hastily while the bulk of the personnel aboard prayed the gun compartments would remain sealed from the remainder of the vessel.

"If we disabled them now"—Stephen's voice rang through the clamor shaking our hull—"they'd crash and we'd have only a crater for our pains. Of course, they aren't under the same con—"

The *Montreal*'s guns recoiled into the hull behind streaks of plasma. The *Oriflamme* grunted, shoved by atmosphere heated from a near miss.

"—straints," Stephen concluded.

"Assault party to the aft hold," a voice buzzed. The order could have been a figment of my imagination. Dole and Stephen were moving, as well as other figures anonymous in their armor.

I'm going to die in this damned hard suit, and I can't even scratch. I started to laugh, glad no one could hear me.

Our four 15-cm cannon amidships were trained to starboard like the Long Tom. Wisps of our thrusters' plasma exhaust wreathed the weapons through the gap between the ports and the guntubes.

Stampfer sat at a flip-down console against the opposite bulkhead. The 15-cm magazines to either side of him were locked shut for safety. I wondered how long that precaution would be followed during the stress of combat. If a bolt hit an open magazine, the *Oriflamme*'s hull might survive. I doubted that any of the crew would, hard suits or no.

I glanced over the gunner's shoulder as we passed. *Our Lady of Montreal* was centered on the director screen, but several phantoms overlaid the main image. The console was calculating the effect of atmospheric turbulence, our exhaust, and the target's own exhaust. Because a plasma bolt is by definition a charged mass, contrasting charges could affect it more than they would a bullet or other kinetic-energy projectile.

I was halfway down the companionway when a shock jolted my grip loose from the ladder. I fell the rest of the way into the after hold, landing like a ton of old iron on Stephen's shoulders.

I managed to keep a grip on my cutting bar. I had only an instant to feel foolish before the next man fell on top of me.

Stephen helped me up. Armored men staggered into line like trolls. Stephen and I took our places in the front rank, facing the bulkhead that would pivot down into a boarding ramp.

The *Oriflamme* had dived deep enough into the atmosphere that the interior lighting appeared normal again. I took a chance and raised my visor. Stephen did the same. The air was hot and tasted burned because of traces of thruster exhaust.

"The *Montreal* doesn't mount heavy guns," Stephen said. "They won't be able to do us serious damage in the time they'll have before we land."

His face was quietly composed, and his eyes still looked human. There was nothing to do until the ramp opened, so Stephen's mind hadn't yet reentered the place that it went when he killed.

The man beside us bobbed his face forward to look through his open faceshield. It was Dole. There were twelve of us in the front rank this time, packed so tight that the bosun couldn't turn to face us he normally would while suited up. "Bastards did good to hit us the once," he shouted. "Don't worry about them getting home again, sir."

"Don't discount the Fed gunners," Stephen said calmly. "They may have somebody as good as Stampfer. It only takes one if they have director control."

"I'm not worried," I said. I stood in the body of a man about to charge through a haze of sun-hot plasma toward a ship weighing hundreds of tonnes and crewed by anything up to a thousand enemy personnel. I wasn't a part of that suicidal mission, I was just observing.

The siren sounded, warning that we were about to touch down. Stephen and I linked arms and braced one boot each against the ramp. I felt a sailor in the second rank clasp my shoulder. There were no individual gripping points within the hold, but if we locked ourselves together, I figured the whole assault party would be able to stay upright.

Our rate of descent was much higher than Piet's normal gentle landings because we had to remain parallel with *Our Lady of Montreal.* She was dropping like a brick, either from panic, general incompetence, or as a calculated attempt by the Fed captain to get an angle from which he could send a bolt into the thruster nozzles on our underside.

Braked momentum slammed down on me at 6 g's. I though we'd hit the surface, but Piet had instead opened the throttles at the last instant. The ground effect of our rebounding exhaust rocked the *Oriflamme* violently from side to side. *Then* our extended skids hit the surface.

Everybody in the hold fell down like pieces of a matchstick house. I was under at least two men. Somebody's gauntlet was across my visor. I supposed I should be thankful that he'd forced the visor shut instead of ramming his armored fingers directly into my eyes.

I'd thought we could remain standing no matter how hard we hit. Man proposes, God disposes . . .

The men on top of me got up. One of them was Stephen, identifiable because he carried both his flashgun and a rifle. Somebody else tried to step across my body. I pushed him back as I lurched to a squat. I found my cutting bar beside me and stood up with it. I clipped the weapon to an equipment stud again. I should have left it there until it was time to use the blade.

The hatch unsealed. Air charged by our exhaust swirled around the edges of the ramp in a radiant veil. As the lip lowered, I saw *Our Lady of Montreal* looming like a vast curved wall before us. She was at least fifty meters tall through her vertical axis, and no farther than that from us. The hatches that could open out from the great sphere's base were closed, but I saw unshuttered gun ports on the lower curve.

A 15-cm plasma cannon fired directly overhead. Its brilliance was so dazzling that it rocked me back against the men behind. My faceshield reacted instantly, saving my vision by filtering black everything except the ionized track itself. Even combed by the filter, the bolt was bright enough to turn the massive shock wave five milliseconds later into anticlimax.

A fireball shrouded *Our Lady of Montreal.* Her own vaporized hull metal had exploded into white flame.

The bubble of light lifted away on the gases expanding it. Our bolt had punched a hole a meter in diameter in the *Montreal*'s lower quarter. The edges of the gap glowed for a moment; then the *Oriflamme*'s second gun blew a similar blazing hole beside the first.

Stampfer was firing our battery with a two-second pause between bolts—time to dissipate the ionized haze which would lessen the effect of an instantly following round. The *Oriflamme* rocked at each discharge. The recoil of a few grams of ions accelerated to light speed was enough to shake even a starship's hundred tonnes.

The Long Tom fired. Its discharge was heavier than the midships guns' by an order of magnitude. The *Oriflamme*'s bow shifted a centimeter on the landing outriggers.

The lower quarter of the Federation vessel was a fiery cavity. The hatch had been blown completely away, but the mist of burning metal beyond was as palpable as marble.

The end of our ramp was still a meter and a half in the air. The blast of the main guns had deafened me. I couldn't even hear my own voice shouting, "God and Venus!" as I leaped to the ground.

I crashed down on my face. The plasma cannon firing from the *Montreal* hit the sailor behind me instead and blew him to vapor. Bits of his ceramic armor scattered like grenade fragments.

I got to my feet. Stephen aimed his flashgun up at a 45° angle. His laser bolt, so bright under most conditions, was lost in the greater brilliance of the plasma weapons moments before.

I stumbled toward the cavity Stampfer's guns had blasted for our entry. It roiled with ionized residues of the cannonfire and the ordinary conflagrations which the bolts had ignited in the compartments beyond. With my visor down, I was breathing from the suit's oxygen bottle.

An explosion above us almost knocked me down again. Stephen's bolt had punched into the cannon's 5-cm bore, damaging the nearly spherical array of lasers within the chambered round. The lasers were meant to implode a deuterium pellet at the shell's heart and direct the resulting plasma down a pinhole pathway aligned with the axis of the gun barrel.

Instead, the cannon's breech ruptured. The blast was more violent than the one which killed the man behind me, and I doubted whether Federation armor was as good as our Venerian ceramic.

The rocky soil beneath the *Montreal* was glazed by exhaust and our heavy cannon. The hatch had been wrenched away, but the lintel was square and a meter and a half above ground level. Stalactites of nickel-steel plating hung from the lower edge of the wound.

The white glare of the vessel's interior had dulled to a deep red. Fluid dribbling from the ruptured hydraulic lines burned with dark, smoky flames.

I gripped the lower lip of the opening and kicked myself upward. To my amazement, I wobbled into the hold despite thirty kilos of hard suit and weakness from the days we'd spent in free fall.

The vessel's cylindrical core held tanks of reaction mass and liquefied air behind plating as thick as that of the external hull. Shock waves had started a few of the seams, but the structure in general was still solid. Dual companionways to the higher decks were built into the core structure.

The horizontal deck was 1-cm steel. Blasts generated by our plasma bolts had hammered the surface downward as much as twenty centimeters between frames. The hold's internal bulkheads were flattened, and the hatches that should have closed the companionways had been blown askew.

Five Federation crewmen in the lower hold were in metal hard suits when our first 15-cm bolt penetrated the hull. The suits remained, crushed and disarticulated. From the top of a thigh guard stuck the remains of a femur burned to charcoal. That bone was the only sign of the people who'd been wearing the suits.

I looked behind me. Several men in armor were trying to clamber up with one hand hampered by weapons. I clasped the nearest man under the right shoulder and heaved. His face was down, so I don't know who he was. He skidded aboard, got to his feet, and clumped toward a companionway.

Half the assault party still straggled between the *Oriflamme* and the Federation vessel. We'd landed on an expanse of stony desert, well inland of Ivestown. I doubt the *Montreal*'s captain had chosen the site deliberately, but at least we weren't going to fry the colonists and their hundred or so Molt slaves as a byproduct of the fighting.

Stephen, his flashgun slung over the rifle on his left shoulder, heaved himself upward. I grabbed him and brought him the rest of the way. Other sailors were pairing, one to form a stirrup for the foot of the second. A plasma cannon, too light to be one of ours, fired. I saw the reflected flash but not the point of impact.

A bullet whanged down a companionway and ricocheted from the deck. I reached the helical stairs ahead of Stephen. He grabbed my shoulder to stop me, then stuck his flashgun up the vertical passage. I unclipped my cutting bar and switched it on.

Stephen fired. Sparks of metal clipped by the laser pulse spat down the shaft in reply. The bolt wasn't likely to have hit anybody, but it might clear the companionway for a few seconds. Stephen clapped me forward. His gauntlet cracked like gunfire on my backplate. I started up the steps.

The hatch to the next deck upward had either been open or blown open by gouts of plasma belching up the companionway every time our cannon hammered the hold. The compartment beyond, once an accommodation area, was a smoky inferno.

Plastic and fabrics of all sorts burned in the air the fire sucked from the companionway. The atmosphere of the sealed deck must have been exhausted within a few minutes of the moment our cannon flash-ignited everything flammable.

I could have charged into the blaze, protected by my hard suit, but there was nothing there for us. The fires would destroy all life and objects of value before they burned themselves out. If the *Montreal*'s decks were pierced by too many conduits and water lines, the blaze here was likely to involve the whole ship.

The hatch to the third level was closed. I passed it by and continued climbing. The gunports were higher on the hull. We had to silence the *Montreal*'s plasma cannon.

A bare-chested man with a short rifle stuck his head from the next hatchway, saw me three rungs below him, and ducked back. A Molt with a cutting bar lunged out instead. I slashed through his legs between the upper and

lower knee joints. He fell backward in a spray of brown
ichor. I crushed his weapon hand against the flooring, then
stepped over him into the cargo deck beyond.

The *Montreal*'s fourth deck was stacked with bales and
crated goods within woven-wire restraint cages. There were
no internal bulkheads. At the end of an aisle between ranks
of cargo were three Molts wearing oxygen masks and padded garments of asbestos or glass fiber. They were trying
to pivot a light plasma cannon away from the gunport so
that it could bear on me.

The man with the rifle leaned over a row of crates and
fired. His bullet hit me in the center of the chest and
splashed upward, staggering me. I recovered and charged
the Molts at a shambling run.

One of them swung at me with the kind of long forceps
the Feds use to load their solid-breech plasma cannon. My
bar screamed through the levers in a shower of sparks.

The alien scrambled away. I chopped the back of a
Molt's head, then reversed my stroke through the right
arm and into the chest of his fellow who was tugging on
the gun's tiller.

The surviving Molt flung the handles of his forceps at
me. They bounced off my helmet. I cut him in half. My
bar's vibration slowed momentarily, then spun up again
through a spray of body fluids.

The human stepped around a row of cargo and aimed
at me. The butt of Stephen's flashgun crushed his skull
from behind.

The cannon that'd exploded was ten meters farther along
the curve of the hull. The blast had crushed the stacks of
cargo outward in a wide circle. The feet of three Molts
and another human were carbonized onto the deck near
the gun's swivel, but nothing above the ankles remained
of the crewmen.

I couldn't see any other Feds in the jumble of cargo.
My whole body was on fire. I lifted my faceshield to take
an unconstricted breath.

Stephen slammed my visor back down. He reached past
me to tilt the plasma cannon toward the ceiling a meter
above our heads.

I turned away. The world went white with a blast that spreadeagled me on the deck. Stephen was still standing, I don't know how.

I pushed myself to a crouch, then stood in a fog of swirling metal vapors. The point-blank charge of plasma had blown a two-meter hole into the level above. Fires burned there and among the cargo around us.

Stephen restacked one crate on another beneath the hole. A Molt fell through from the deck above. A bubble of vaporized metal had seared the creature's thorax white.

I wasn't sure I could lift Stephen, so I hopped onto the crates and raised my right foot. Stephen made a step of his hands. His powerful thrust popped me through onto the deck above.

The large compartment was Molt accommodations. I guessed the aliens were crew rather than cargo. Though the facilities were spartan, there were hammock hooks and cages for the Molts' personal belongings.

The plasma bolt had blown out half the lights. I couldn't see more than twenty Molts huddled in space meant to quarter a hundred.

I reached for Stephen with my left hand. I had to jab the tip of my bar down like a cane to keep from overbalancing. Every heartbeat swelled me tighter against the oven of my armor.

Stephen crashed upward. I staggered toward the single hatch out of the compartment. My vision was so focused that I didn't know whether Stephen was behind or beside me. Molts had squeezed against the internal bulkhead when the deck burst in a fireball near the curve of the hull. They scattered to either side of my advance like chickens running from the axe.

I pushed at the hatch. It didn't move. I raised my bar to cut through. Stephen reached past me and pulled the handle open.

I lurched into a corridor ten meters long. It was full of Fed personnel, human and Molt. A four-barreled cannon on a wheeled carriage faced one companionway; a tripod-mounted laser whose separate power pack must weigh fifty kilos was aimed at the open hatch of the other.

An officer wearing gold-chased body armor turned and pointed his gun at me. The weapon had a thick barrel with only a tiny hole in the middle of it, and the stock fitted into a special rest on the breastplate.

I swung my bar at the Fed. He was too far away for me to reach before he fired. A starship hit and spun me around. I bounced onto the floor on my back. My faceshield was unlatched, but the helmet had rotated sideways 20° to cut off part of my vision.

Stephen stepped across my body with his flashgun raised. I threw my left arm across my eyes. Side-scatter from Stephen's bolt glared off the corridor's dingy white walls. A crate of shells for the cannon blew up like so many grenades. Stephen fell over me.

I twisted out from under his legs. The blast had knocked down the nearest Feds as well, though the crew of the laser five meters away at the opposite end of the corridor was trying to swing its weapon onto us. The cable to the power pack wasn't flexible enough for them to change front without repositioning all their equipment.

I jerked off my helmet and flung it at the Feds. The four Molts gripping the power pack's carrying handles continued stolidly to walk it around.

I could see again and I could breathe. The officer's projectile had hit the top of my breastplate at a flat angle. It shattered the plate and tore loose the clamps holding plastron, gorget, and helmet together.

Half my breastplate flopped from the waist latches. Ceramic continued to crumble away in bits from the broken edge, because the shock had completely shattered the plate's internal structure. Breath was a sharp pain. I didn't know whether the chest muscles were bruised or if cracked ribs were ripping my lungs every time I moved.

I walked toward the laser. I would have run, but my backplate clanked behind me like a ceramic cape and caught my heels.

A human sailor with a full mustache and sideburns that swept up to bright chestnut hair gaped at me. He was wearing padded protective gear like that of the gunners on the deck below. He dropped his side of the laser and sprang toward the companionway hatch.

His human officer shot him in the back with her double-barreled pistol. She aimed at me past the power supply. Her head jerked back, and she fired the pistol into the ceiling as her nerves spasmed.

Her body toppled forward. There was a bullet hole over her right eye, and her brains splashed the bulkhead behind her.

I hacked at a Molt. He staggered back, bleeding from the stump of an arm and the deep cut in his carapace.

The nearest Molt wrapped his hard-surfaced arms around me while the others scrambled toward the cross-corridor at the end of the main one. They kept the power pack between me and them. Stephen fired his rifle again, but not in my direction. I cut awkwardly at the Molt's back. My limbs were still in their jointed ceramic cylinders, and the damned backplate dragged at me like an anchor.

The Molt moaned through the breathing holes along his lateral lines. My bar wouldn't bite—the battery was drained. I screamed in frustration, pounding the Molt with the pommel. He slipped down under the impacts, but his arms wouldn't release. His skull was a mush of fluids and broken chitin, but he wouldn't let go.

Stephen grabbed the Molt's shoulder with his left gauntlet and flung the corpse away from me. I staggered against the jamb of the hatchway. I wanted to get rid of the backplate, but I couldn't turn the studs behind me. I stripped off my right gauntlet instead as Stephen closed the firing contacts of the Federation laser and hosed its throbbing light across the other gun crew.

Stephen's flashgun was a monopulse weapon. This tripod-mounted unit had two separate tubes. It sequenced its output through them in turn to avoid the downrange vapor attenuation that reduced continuous-beam lasers' effectiveness.

The Fed officer who'd shot me was loading another fat cartridge into the breech of his weapon. The beam glanced from his polished breastplate in dazzling highlights, then hit him in the neck and decapitated him.

I flung away my left gauntlet. My hands curled with

pleasure at being free. The backplate latches turned easily.

Two Molts were starting to rise. Their thoraces burst soggily as the beam vaporized soft parts within the chitin shell.

A man in Venerian armor with his chest burned out lay just within the companionway hatch. He was probably the fellow who'd gone on while I helped Stephen into the hold. He held a rifle, and a cutting bar was clipped to his armor.

Exploding ammunition had knocked the multibarrel cannon sideways in the corridor. Stephen concentrated his flux on the breechblocks. The laser's feedline was beginning to smoke. The unit should have been allowed to cool every few seconds between bursts. Stephen was deliberately destroying both the weapons that could endanger a man in a Venerian hard suit.

Shells in the four cannon barrels cooked off in quick succession. Three of the weakened breeches failed, flinging fragments of jagged tool steel across the corridor and shredding two of the Molts who'd been crippled by the initial blast. There had been another human gunner also, but she must have run down the end corridor.

I took the cutting bar from the dead Venerian's waist stud and started up the companionway. My armored boots clanged on the slotted metal treads. I hadn't had time to take off the leg pieces.

The important thing was that my face and chest were free. The weight didn't matter so much, but days of constriction had driven me almost mad.

Or beyond almost.

The companionway was full of smoke from the fire on the lower deck, but because the air wasn't circulating the conditions weren't as bad as I'd thought they would be. I wished I'd thought to detach the oxygen bottle from my suit; but I hadn't, and anyway the projectile that smashed the breastplate had likely damaged the regulator as well.

Shots and screams echoed up the tube. Some of what sounded like human agony probably came from machines. I wondered if other members of the assault party had climbed this high. Movement in hard suits was brutally exhausting, and other men hadn't had Stephen to help them forward.

The hatch onto the next deck was closed but not dogged tight. I could hear people raggedly singing a hymn on the other side. The leader was a female, and hers was the only voice that didn't sound terrified. I passed the hatch by and turned up the final angle of the companionway to the highest deck.

The hatch was sealed. I tugged at an arm of the central wheel. They'd locked it from the inside. I paused, thinking about the hatches I'd seen on the *Montreal*'s lower decks.

A bullet howled up the companionway. It or a bit of it dropped at my feet, a silvery gleam, before it rattled its way back down through the stair treads.

The locks were electrical, activated by a button in the center on the inner dogging wheel. The powerline ran through the upper hinge.

I set my bar's tip on the hatch side of the hinge and squeezed the trigger. Nothing happened. I was dizzy from smoke and fatigue. I'd forgotten that the dead man wouldn't have slung his bar with the power switch on.

I thumbed the slide and tried again. The blade screamed angrily and sank into the tough steel. Chips, yellow and blazing white, spewed from the cut. The severed power cable shorted through the hatch metal in a brief halo of blue sparks.

I tugged again on the wheel. This time it spun freely, three full turns to withdraw the bolts which clamped the hatch to its jamb. I grasped the vertical handhold, pulled the hatch toward me, and charged onto the bridge of *Our Lady of Montreal*.

I thought they'd be waiting for me, alerted by my bar's shriek and the inner wheel spinning as I undogged the hatch. I'd forgotten how much else was going on. There were six humans and maybe ten Molts in the domed circular chamber. They turned and stared at me as if they'd just watched the Red Death take off his mask.

I suppose they were right.

Nearest to me were a pair of humans in white tunics. I

thrust rather than slashing at the face of the woman who held a cutting bar. She staggered backward. The man tried to point his rifle but I grabbed it by the fore-end and twisted the muzzle upward. He shrieked and pulled away, but I held him by the weapon he didn't think to drop. My bar cut spine-deep in his neck, drowning his cry in his own blood.

The bridge instrumentation was a ring of waist-high, double-facing consoles. The three human officers in the center of the ring wore metal helmets and gleaming back-and-breast armor. One of them shouted an order.

Molts sitting at the outer positions lurched toward me from seats configured to their alien torsos. None of them had weapons, though one Molt picked up a portable communicator and threw it at my head.

I chopped a Molt's skull, then backhanded a deep gouge across the belly plates of another. I watched my body in amazement. The animal controlling me moved with the relentless fury of a storm against cliffs.

I still held the rifle like an oar in my left hand. I jolted a Molt back with the butt, then sawed through his ankles with a stroke that buried my bar momentarily in the pelvis of the creature who'd grabbed my forearm. I kicked the Molt free with an armored boot.

A bullet hit the back of the Molt toppling beside the cut-off feet. One of the officers was shooting at me with a handgun. His two fellows had ducked behind the ring of consoles. When he saw me turn toward him, he dropped flat also.

The screen of the nearest console showed a real-time image of the *Oriflamme*. Our five big plasma cannon had cooled enough to be reloaded and run out, but Stampfer hadn't fired again for fear of hitting those of us aboard the *Montreal*.

Additional men in ceramic armor trudged across the fused plain toward the Federation vessel. They looked pathetically small compared to the *Oriflamme,* much less the *Montreal.*

Molts threw themselves on me from right and left. I twisted my arm to saw the carapace of one with the back of my bar. The Molt's hard thorax jolted against me as a gun fired and an awl of red pain stabbed through my upper abdomen. The Fed soldier with his back to the other hatch had fired his shotgun.

I punched the Molt holding my right arm with the cutting bar's pommel. I broke the chitin, making the creature move back enough that I could draw the blade down through his right thigh.

Two of the Fed officers rose from behind the consoles again. My legs were mired in thrashing Molts whose muscles contracted as they died. I dropped the cutting bar and brought the butt of the rifle I'd grabbed around to my right shoulder.

The woman fired her pistol at me from three meters away and missed. The man who'd shot at me before gripped his pistol with both hands as he pointed it. I thrust the muzzle of my rifle in his direction and jerked the trigger.

My bullet blew apart the screen of the console a meter to the right of him. The woman behind that console gasped and doubled up, clutching her groin. Instead of shooting me, the man threw himself under cover again.

I couldn't move my legs. The soldier with the shotgun closed the breech over a fresh cartridge and raised his weapon again. My rifle had a tube under the barrel so it was probably a repeater, but I didn't know how to chamber a new round. I threw it at the soldier and missed. The Fed ducked for an instant anyway.

I squatted on the pile of spasming Molts, trying to find my cutting bar or some other weapon. The Fed soldier dropped his shotgun and raised his hands over his head.

Stephen and Piet Ricimer stepped past me. They still wore their hard suits, but their visors were raised. Stephen deliberately fired into the curving outer bulkhead to ricochet a bullet behind the ring of consoles. A Molt hiding there jumped up. A charge of buckshot from Piet's shotgun knocked the Molt back with a ragged hole in his plastron.

The officer with the handgun raised his head to see what was happening. The second bullet from Stephen's revolving-chamber rifle hit the man in the forehead and spun his helmet into the air in a splash of brains.

The Fed sprang fully upright, his arms flailing. Stephen shot him again, this time through the upper chest, but when the man turned and fell we could see his skull had already been opened like a soft-boiled egg.

The *Montreal*'s bridge was thick with gunsmoke and blood. I was beginning to lose color vision, and I didn't seem to be able to stand up even though the Molts had finally become shudderingly flaccid.

"I surrender!" a man screamed from within the ring of consoles. I remembered that there had been three officers there when I burst into the compartment. "In the name of Christ, have mercy!"

"Stand with your hands raised, then!" Piet ordered with his shotgun still butted on his shoulder. He stepped aside, putting his back to a bulkhead rather than the open hatchway.

Stephen knelt beside me. His rifle gestured the Fed soldier farther away from the shotgun the man had dropped. Somebody hammered on the sealed hatch. They'd pay hell trying to break in like that.

The third Fed officer rose from his hiding place. He peered from behind the helmet he'd taken off to hold in front of his face. There was a pistol holstered at his side, but I'm sure he'd forgotten it was there.

Stephen traded the rifle for his flashgun. He nodded toward the hatch. "Open it," he said to the captured soldier. Stephen was ready, just in case whoever was on the other side came in wearing metal rather than ceramic armor.

"Order your men to stop fighting," Piet said to the captured officer. The Fed was the youngest of the three on the bridge. He was pudgy, and his hair was so fine and blond that his pink scalp showed through it. "There's no need for more deaths."

"How bad are you hit?" Stephen asked, his eyes focused on the hatch the prisoner was undogging.

"I'm just tired," I said. "None of this is my blood."

Dole stamped through the hatchway with a cutting bar and a chrome-plated rifle. The gun's muzzle had been sheared off at an angle, but I supposed it would still shoot at the ranges we'd been fighting here.

The stink of opened bodies was making me dizzy. I had to get out of the stench, but I was too dizzy to stand.

"The hell it's not," Stephen said. "Dole, come here and give me a hand. We need to get him back to Rakoscy."

His gauntleted fingers tore the side of my tunic the rest of the way open. There were two puckered, purple holes on the side just below my rib cage. The Molt hadn't shielded me completely from the shotgun pellets after all.

"Surrender!" the Federation officer called into a microphone flexed to his side of a console. "Captain Alfegor is dead! Surrender! Surrender! They'll kill us all!"

Echoes of his voice rumbled up the companionways. I could still hear shots, though.

"Didn't know where you'd gone to," Stephen said quietly. He reached around my back and under my knees. Dole knelt to link arms with him. "Had a dozen of them charge around the back corridor just when I'd drained that damned laser. Could have been a problem if Piet hadn't come up the companionway about the same time."

"I know how you felt," I said; or I tried to, because about that time the stink of death swelled over the last of my consciousness in a thick purple fog.

NEW VENUS

Day 140

The planet was uncharted. Piet had located it at a good time. The last day of the run, we'd used personal oxygen bottles because a patch had cracked badly.

I didn't have enough energy to run out with the others as soon as the ramp lowered. I sat in the hold on a pallet of chips, far enough back that the heat still radiating from the glazed soil didn't bother me. The naming ceremony on the lakeside was over, and the crowd of relaxed sailors was breaking up.

At the base of the ramp, ten men under Salomon argued bitterly among themselves about the hoses we'd taken from *Our Lady of Montreal* to replace the set damaged when we fled Templeton. The Federation equipment was the correct diameter, but both ends of the hoses had male connectors—as did the fittings of our water tanks. We'd have to make couplers to use the hoses. That job could have been done during the long run from Quincy if any-body'd noticed the problem before.

I got up very carefully and walked down the ramp. I'd be in the way if I stayed in the hold. Salomon would have enough problems doing shop work without offloading the treasure first.

The chips had come cheap enough, I suppose. Three dead, only two wounded. The Feds hadn't been equipped to deal with our hard suits. Smetana had lost his leg— stupidly—by getting it caught in the mechanism of the *Montreal*'s cargo lift. My wound was pretty stupid too.

The men fell silent as I walked past them. "Good to see

you, Mister Moore," Salomon said formally. I gave him a deliberate nod.

The story'd gotten around. More than the story, the way it usually happens. The men seemed to think I was a hero. *I* thought—

The soldier's face dissolving in a red spray as I rammed my bar through her teeth and palate, then jerked the blade sideways.

I tried not to think at all, and it didn't help.

Piet, Stephen, and Guillermo were chatting at the lakeside. I joined them. Nearby, men had started laying out the temporary houses they'd live in while we were on New Venus.

"Feeling better, Jeremy?" Stephen asked to welcome my presence.

"I'm all right," I said. "Just tired. You know, the bruises I got from the back of my breastplate when the bullet hit me are worse than the little shot holes."

I waggled my left hand in the direction of where Rakoscy had removed the buckshot. I could move my arms well enough, but it still hurt to twist my torso.

"And if Rakoscy hadn't clamped off the vein those shots punctured," Piet said with a cold smile, "you wouldn't have felt any pain at all from your ribs. I hope the next time you'll remember you have nothing to prove. Nor did you on Quincy."

I shook my head. Shrugging was another thing I had to avoid. "It just happened," I said. "I wasn't trying . . ."

I wasn't human when it happened. I didn't want to say that. "The ground cover doesn't have a root structure to bind turf," I said. I pointed to the men surveying the ground beside the *Oriflamme.* "How are they going to make houses?"

"Oh," said Piet, "a frame of brush, then a spray glaze to seal and stabilize it. We won't be here but a week at the most."

He looked back at the *Oriflamme* and frowned. "The patch that failed could have killed us. It was my fault."

"Piet," Stephen said forcefully, "the only way we could've checked the substructure—which is what failed, not the patch—is to have removed the inner hull in sections. Which would've taken us three months, sitting on the ground beside the *Montreal* and wondering when the next Fed ship'd pass by and snap us up. I *still* don't believe that a fifty-millimeter Fed popgun cracked a frame member that way."

"Well, it was probably the strain of the Breach," Piet said. "I know, I know . . . But not only can't we afford mistakes, we can't afford bad luck."

"I'd say our luck had been fine," I said. "At least half the *Montreal*'s cargo was of current production chips, not pre-Collapse stock. There's enough wealth to . . ."

The value was incalculable. I would have shrugged. I turned my palms up instead.

"The value is roughly that of the gross domestic product of the Free State of Venus," Stephen said quietly.

I looked at him: the scarred gunman, the consummate killer. It was easy to forget that Stephen Gregg had once been in the service of his uncle, a shipping magnate. I suspected that he'd been good at those duties too.

Piet grinned, his normal bright self again. "I think I'll cast a plaque claiming the world for Governor Halys," he added. "Do it myself, I mean. We can weld it to one of those rocks."

He pointed. Three natives—Rabbits—who certainly hadn't been on the clump of boulders twenty meters away when Piet started speaking took off running in the opposite direction. The two males were nude except for body paint. The female wore a skirt of veins combed from the sword-shaped leaves of a common local plant. Her flaccid breasts flopped almost to her waist.

Piet and Stephen darted to the side so that they could watch the Rabbits past the boulders. Guillermo and I followed slowly. It hurt me to move, and I doubt the Molt saw any reason for haste.

Several of the crewmen noticed the fugitives as well. Kiley shouted and started to run, though he didn't have a prayer of catching them.

"Let them go!" Piet ordered. I was always surprised how loud his voice could be when it had to.

Brush grew down to the lakeshore a little north of where we'd landed. The Rabbits vanished into it.

"I thought I'd seen a village in that direction while we were making our approach," Piet said.

"There are no industrial sites on this world," Guillermo said. If he'd been human, his voice would have sounded surprised. "I examined infrared scans. Even overgrown, the lines of human constructions would show up."

Stephen looked at him. "You do that regularly?" he asked. "Check on IR while we're orbiting?"

"Yes," the Molt said simply.

Piet shrugged. "This world isn't in the chart Jeremy found for us," he said. "Even though the Federation cartographers had access to pre-Collapse data."

Stephen was the only one of us who was armed. He'd unslung his flashgun when the Rabbits appeared, though he'd kept the muzzle high. Instead of reslinging the weapon, he cradled it in his arms.

"During the Collapse," he said, "colonies pretty much destroyed themselves. It wasn't Terran attacks, certainly not here on the Back Worlds. Maybe their ancestors—"

He nodded in the direction the Rabbits had fled.

"—came from Templeton or the like as things were breaking down there. Trying to preserve civilization."

Piet sighed. "Yes," he said. "That could be. But you don't preserve civilization by running from chaos."

He glanced back at the ship. Dole headed a crew working on the section damaged by the *Montreal*'s plasma cannon, and Salomon's men had already stretched the hoses to the lake.

"I think we can be spared to visit the native village," he said, smiling again. "They don't appear dangerous."

Stephen shrugged. "If we go," he said, "we'll go armed."

He glanced at me, I guess for support. My mind was lost in the maze of how you preserve civilization by cutting apart the face of a woman you hadn't even seen five seconds before.

●　　●　　●

"The *Montreal* carried a couple autogyros," Stephen said as we broke out of the path through the brush. "You know, one of those would have made scouting around our landing sites a lot simpler."

The Rabbit village was in sight beneath trees that stood like miniature thunderheads. Up to a dozen separate trunks supported each broad canopy.

"Woof!" said Maher, the last of the six in our party. "'Bout time we got clear of that!" Not only was Maher overweight, he'd decided to wear crossed bandoliers of shotgun shells and to carry a cutting bar. His gear caught at every step along a track worn by naked savages.

"You were going to fly the autogyro, Stephen?" Piet asked mildly. "Or perhaps we should have brought along one of the Federation pilots to do our scouting for us."

The Rabbits lived in a dozen or so rounded domes of wattle-and-daub. There were no windows, and they'd have to crawl on hands and knees to get in through the low doors. I wondered whether they had fire.

Stephen laughed. "Well, they're supposed to be easy to fly," he said. "Not that we had room to stow another pair of socks, the way we're loaded with chips."

Rabbits began to congregate in front of the huts as we approached. There were more of them than I'd expected from the number of dwellings, perhaps two hundred. The adult males carried throwing sticks, shell-tipped spears, and what were probably planting dibbles, though they would serve as weapons.

"Open out," Piet ordered in an even voice. "*Don't* point a weapon."

We fell into line abreast as we continued to saunter at the pace Piet set toward the village. He and Maher carried shotguns. Loomis had a rifle, Stephen his flashgun, and even Guillermo wore a holstered pistol, though I doubt he'd have been much use with it.

I held a cutting bar in both hands like a baton. Even its modest weight strained my abdomen if it hung from one side or the other.

"Stephen," I said. "Will you teach me to shoot?"

"Yes," he said, the syllable pale with lack of affect.

"We won't need weapons now," Piet said briskly. "Wait here."

He strode ahead of the rest of us with his right hand raised palm-outward. "We are peaceful travelers in your land," he called in Trade English. "We offer you presents and our friendship."

Piet was still ten meters from the Rabbits when they threw themselves to the ground. The men lashed themselves with their own weapons; the women tore their skirts into tufts and tossed them in the air with handfuls of dirt. Small children ran screaming from one adult to another, demanding reassurance which wasn't to be found.

"Wait!" Piet boomed in horror as he sprang forward. "We aren't gods to be worshipped, we're men!"

He forcibly dragged upright a Rabbit who was drawing a barbed spearhead across his forearm. "Stop that! It's blasphemy!"

Stephen pushed his way against Piet's side, though if the Rabbits had turned on us, there wasn't a lot he could have done. I'd have been even more useless, but I stood to Piet's right and grabbed the polished throwing stick that a Rabbit was beating himself across the back with. I wasn't about to try lifting anybody in my present condition, but the Rabbit didn't fight me for the stick. It was a beautifully curved piece. The wood was dense and had a fine, dark grain.

"Stop!" Piet thundered again.

This time the Rabbits obeyed, though for the most part they huddled on the ground at our feet. The children's shrieks seemed louder now that the adults weren't drowning them out.

An old woman came from a hut, leaning on the arm of a young man. She wore a pectoral and tiara made from strings of colored shells.

The youth supporting her was nude except for a genital cup, like most other males. A middle-aged man walked a step behind and to the right of the woman. He wore a translucent vest of fish or reptile skin. I could see the impressions the scales had left after they were removed.

The ordinary villagers edged back. They crawled until they'd gotten a few meters away, then rose to a crouch. Except for the man in the vest, the villagers looked ill-nourished. That fellow wasn't fat, but he had a solid, husky build. He stepped ahead of the old woman, keeping enough to the side that he didn't block our view of her.

We shook ourselves straight again. I still held the throwing stick. I stuck my cutting bar under the front of my belt to have it out of the way.

The two sailors ostentatiously ported their guns. I'd been too busy to look, but I'd bet they'd been aiming into the crowd and now hoped Piet hadn't seen them. Piet probably *had* seen them, the way he seemed to see everything going on, but he didn't choose to comment. Could be he thought Loomis and Maher showed better judgment than the rest of us had.

The old woman stretched out both arms and began speaking in a cracked voice. Her words were in no language I'd ever heard before. She paused after each phrase, and the man in the vest thundered what seemed to be the same words. They didn't make any more sense the second time at ten times the volume.

Maher looked at me and frowned. I nodded the throwing stick as a shrug. I didn't know how long this was going to go on either. At least it wasn't an attack.

After ten minutes of stop-and-go harangue, the old woman started to cough. The youth tried to help her, but she swatted at him angrily. The man in the vest looked back in concern.

The woman got control of her paroxysm, though she swayed as she lifted the clicking pectoral off. She handed it to the youth, mumbled an order, and then removed the tiara as well. It had been fastened to her thinning hair with bone pins.

The youth walked to Piet, holding the objects at arm's length. The Rabbit was shivering. His knees bent farther with every step, so that when he'd reached Piet he was almost kneeling.

"We thank you in the name of our governor," Piet said as he took the gifts. "We accept the objects as offered by one ruler to another, not as the homage owed only to God."

He turned his head and hissed, "Loomis? The cloth."

Loomis hastily pulled a bolt of red fabric out of his pack. He'd forgotten—so had I—the gift we'd brought. The cloth came from the Commandatura on Trehinga, but it might well be Terran silk. Stephen had suggested it would be useful for trading to Rabbits and free Molts.

Piet held the bolt out to the youth. The youth turned his head away. The man in the vest snarled an order. The youth took the cloth. He stumbled back from Piet, crying bitterly.

Piet's mouth worked as though he'd been sucking a lemon. "Well," he said. He turned and nodded back the way we'd come. "Well, I think we've done all we can here."

That was true enough. Though I for one wasn't about to bet on what we *had* done.

NEW VENUS

Day 143

The moon was up, so I hadn't bothered to take a light when I went walking. The satellite was huge, looking almost the size of Earth from Luna, though it had no atmosphere and its specific gravity was only slightly above that of water.

The four crewmen's lodges were laid out as sides of a square. A bonfire leaped high in the middle and a fiddler played dance music. Repairs to the *Oriflamme*'s hull were complete, or as complete as possible. Liquor acquired on Trehinga and Templeton competed with slash the motor crewmen brewed from rations.

Being able to walk for the past three days had loosened up my chest muscles. I still got twinges if I turned too suddenly, and when I woke up in the morning my lower abdomen ached as though I'd been kicked the night before; but my body was healing fine.

I was returning to the *Oriflamme*. I'd continued to bunk aboard her. The minimal interior illumination hid rather than revealed the ground beneath the starship, but the moon was so bright that I noticed the hunching figure while I was still fifty meters away.

"Hey!" I shouted. I wasn't carrying a weapon. I ran toward the figure anyway. Adrenaline made me forget the shape my body was in as well as damping the pain that might have reminded me. "Hey!"

The figure sprang to its feet and sprinted away. When it was out of the *Oriflamme*'s shadow I could see that it was a Rabbit—a female, judging from the skirt.

193

Piet opened the forward hatch holding a powerful light in his left hand and a double-barreled shotgun by the pistol grip in his right. The light blazed onto the Rabbit and stayed there despite her attempts to dart and twist out of the beam. Furrows dribbling fresh blood striped her back.

The Rabbit finally vanished into the brush. None of the men celebrating at the shelters had taken notice of my shout or the Rabbit.

Running—jogging clumsily—actually felt good to me, though I didn't have any wind left. The short spurt to the ramp left me puffing and blowing.

I knelt beneath the ship where the Rabbit had hidden. She'd dropped or thrown away something as she fled. I doubted it was a bomb—fire was high technology for these savages—but I wasn't taking chances.

Piet flared his lens to wide beam. "Anything?" he asked as he hopped down beside me.

"This," I said, picking up the handle of a giant comb: a carding comb for stripping leaf fibers so they could be woven into cloth. The teeth were long triangles of shell mounted edgewise so that they wouldn't snap when drawn through tough leaves.

The teeth were smeared a finger's breadth deep with blood so fresh it still dripped. Piet switched off the handlight. I crawled carefully from beneath the *Oriflamme;* it'd be several minutes before I had my night vision back, and I didn't want to knock myself silly on a landing strut.

"Perhaps we should set guards," Piet said. "Of course, we'll be leaving tomorrow. If all goes as planned."

I flung the comb in the direction of the village a kilometer away. There were drops of blood on the glazed soil where the Rabbit had hidden for her ceremony. I sat down on the ramp. I felt sick. Part of it was probably the exertion.

Piet sat beside me. "You wouldn't have had to go as far as the village to find a woman for your desires," he said. "You could just have waited here."

There was nothing in his tone, and his face—softened by the moonlight—was as calm as that of a statue of

Justice. The fact that he'd spoken *those* words meant the incident had bothered him as much as it did me. Wine let the truth out of some men; but for others it was stress that made them say the things that would otherwise have been hidden forever in their hearts.

"I was just walking, Piet," I said quietly. "There's some of the men gone up to the Rabbit village, I believe; but I was just working the stitches out of my side."

He nodded curtly. "It doesn't matter," he said. "That sort of thing is between you and the Lord."

I got up and raised my face to the moon. "I haven't lied to anybody since I came aboard the *Porcelain,* Piet," I said. My voice shuddered with anger. *With all the things I'd done, before and especially after I met Piet Ricimer, to be accused of this—*

I thought about what I'd just said, and about the cloak of moral outrage I'd dressed myself in. I started to laugh. Some of my chest muscles thought I shouldn't have, but it was out of their control and mine.

Piet stood with a worried look on his face. Maybe he thought I'd snapped, gone mad in delayed reaction to . . . to too many things.

"No," I gasped, "I'm all right. I was just going to say, I haven't been lying to anybody except maybe myself. And I'm getting better about that, you see?"

We sat down again. "Jeremy," he said, "I'm sorry. I shouldn't have spoken."

I shrugged. I could do that again. "If you hadn't," I said, "you'd have gone the rest of your life thinking that's what I was doing out there tonight. When I was just going for a walk."

Fifty meters away in the temporary accommodations, the fiddler was taking a break. A chorus of sailors filled in *a cappella,* "A mighty fortress is our God, a bulwark never failing . . ."

They might as easily have swung into *The Harlot of Jerusalem.* I started to laugh again. This time my ribs forestalled me.

"I'm fine," I repeated. I was beginning to wonder, though, and it wasn't my body that caused me the concern.

"If President Pleyal establishes the rule he wants over all mankind," Piet said, "his fall will be a collapse worse than the Collapse. Because we don't have the margin for survival that men had risen to a thousand years ago. Folk like these—"

He waggled a finger northward.

"—mistaking men for gods, they'll be all that remains of humanity. We *have* to succeed, Jeremy."

"I'll be glad when we lift," I said. I looked at Piet, leaning back with his arms braced on the ramp. "Because you're wrong, you know. It's not gods they think we are. They're not worshipping, they're trying to placate demons."

I shuddered, closed my eyes, and opened them again on the vast, raddled face of the moon. "Which is why," I went on, "that quite apart from standards of hygiene, the women here are in no danger from me. I'm not interested in a woman who thinks she's being raped."

I clasped my hands together to keep them from shaking. "Particularly one who thinks she's being raped by a minion of Satan."

And if God was Peace, then she would surely be correct.

DUNEEN

Day 155

My rifle roared, lifting the muzzle in a blast of gray smoke. I now knew to hold the weapon tight against me. The first time I'd instinctively kept the buttplate a finger's breadth out from my shoulder. The rifle had recoiled separately and *fast*. Instead of pushing my torso back, it whacked me a hammerblow.

"Did I hit it?" I asked, peering toward the target—a meter-square frame of boards twenty meters away. The aiming point was a circle of black paint. My bullet holes spread around it in a shotgun pattern against the rough-sawn yellow wood.

"You hit it," Stephen said. "Reload and hit it again. Remember you want to be solid, not tense. You're using a tool."

I cocked the rifle, then thumbed the breech cam open and extracted the spent cartridge for reloading. "It'd be easier if all our guns were the same kind, wouldn't it?" I said. I nodded toward the revolving rifle in the crook of Stephen's left elbow.

"All machine work instead of craftwork?" Stephen said. "Where that thinking ends is another Collapse—a system of automatic factories so complex that a few hit-and-run attacks bring the whole thing down. Everybody starves or freezes."

I pulled a cartridge from my belt loop but held it in my hand instead of loading. "That's superstition," I said, more forcefully than I usually spoke to Stephen. This was important to me. "Civilization isn't going to fall because every gunsmith on Venus bores his rifle barrels to the same dimensions."

If man was ever really to advance, we had to design and build our own electronics instead of depending on the leavings of pre-Collapse civilization. That required something more structured than individual craftsmen like Piet's father casting thruster nozzles.

Stephen shrugged. I couldn't tell how much it mattered to him. "It isn't the individual aspect," he said. "It's the whole mind-set. On Earth they're setting up assembly lines again."

"But for now . . ." I said as I slid the loaded round into the chamber sized to it and not—quite—to that of any other rifle aboard the *Oriflamme*, "I'll learn how to use whatever comes to hand."

During the voyage from New Venus, Stephen had showed me how to load and strip each of our twenty-odd varieties of firearm. It gave us both something to concentrate on between the hideous bouts of transit. This was the first time I'd fired a rifle.

I thought of the officer on the *Montreal*'s bridge clutching the hole in her groin as she fell. The first time I'd practiced with a rifle.

One of the local herbivores blundered into the clearing. A peck of fronds was disappearing into its mouth. Spores, unexpectedly golden, showered the beast's forequarters and the air above it.

The creature saw us. The barrel-shaped body froze, but the jaws continued to masticate food in a fore-and-aft motion. My shots hadn't alerted the creature to our presence. The local animals didn't seem to have any hearing whatever.

"We have plenty of meat," Stephen said. "Let it go."

The creature turned 270° and crashed away through the vegetation. I could track its progress for some distance by the spores rising like a dust cloud.

I glanced down at my rifle. "I wasn't going to shoot it," I said.

I meant I wasn't going to try. The board target was considerably larger than the man-sized herbivore. The skill I'd demonstrated thus far wasn't overwhelmingly high.

"It gets easy to kill," Stephen said. His voice was slipping out of focus. "Don't let it. Don't ever let that happen."

"One more!" I said loudly. I closed the breech with a distinct *cluck*, seating the cartridge, and raised the butt to my shoulder again.

Concentrate on the foresight. The barrel wobbled around the target, let alone the bull's-eye. *Squeeze the trigger, don't jerk it.* My whole right hand tightened.

I tried to hold the rifle as I had the cutting bar as we sawed boards for the target, firmly but without the feeling of desperate control that the firearm brought out. I wasn't making something happen. I was easing the trigger back against the rough metal-to-metal contact points of a mechanism made by a journeyman rather than a master.

The muzzle blast surprised me the way Stephen said it was supposed to. Splinters flew from a hole a few centimeters left of the bull's-eye.

"Yeah," Stephen said. "You're beginning to get it. In another day or two, you'll be as good as half the crew."

He shook his head disgustedly. "They think they can shoot, but even when they practice, they plink at rocks or ration cartons. If they miss, they don't have a clue why. They'll make the same damned mistake the next time, like enough."

I extracted the empty case. Powder gases streamed through the open breech. "What does it take to get as good as you are, Stephen?" I asked, careful not to meet his eyes.

"Nothing you can learn," he said. He sat down on the trunk of a fallen tree with bark like diamond scales. "And it's not something you'd think was worth the price, I suspect."

I sat beside him. I couldn't hear the *Oriflamme*'s pumps anymore. They must have completed filling our water tanks. "Do you know how long Piet intends to lay over here?" I asked. "It seems a comfortable place, if you don't mind muggy."

I flapped the front of my tunic, sopping from the wet heat.

"The only thing that worries me is the Avoid notation in the database you found for us," Stephen said. He half cocked his rifle and began to rotate its five-shot cylinder with his fingertips, checking the cartridge heads. The pawl clicked lightly over the star gear. "There's nothing wrong with the air or the biosphere, so why avoid it?"

"There's a hundred charted worlds with that marker," I said. "Maybe Pleyal woke up on the wrong side of the bed the morning the list was handed him."

"Come on back and we'll clean your weapon," Stephen said as he rose. "Don't leave that to somebody else to—"

I was staring skyward. Stephen followed my eyes to the glare of bright exhaust. "God *damn* it," he said softly. "It's a starship landing, and it sure isn't from Venus."

We ran through the forest as the *Oriflamme*'s siren sounded.

The strange vessel drifted down like a dead leaf. Starships—the starships I'd seen landing—tended to do so in a controlled crash because the forces being balanced were so enormous. This ship must have a remarkably high power-to-weight ratio, even though its exhaust flames were the bright blue-white of oxy-hydrogen motors rather than the familiar flaring iridescence of plasma.

Dole was leading a party of twenty men from the main hatch into the forest. "Mister Gregg, do you want to take over?" the bosun shouted when he saw us. All the men were armed, but several of them hadn't waited to pull on their tunics when the alarm sounded.

"No, go ahead," Stephen ordered as he sprang up the steps to the cockpit airlock.

Dole's section would hide in the forest so that we weren't all bottled in the *Oriflamme* if shooting started. It would take anything from ten minutes to half an hour for the ship to lift. In the meanwhile, the *Oriflamme* was a target for anybody in orbit who wanted to bombard us.

To a degree that worked both ways. The *Oriflamme*'s gunports were open, though of course our guns couldn't sweep as wide a zone as could those of an orbiting vessel able to change its attitude. Stampfer was raising the 17-cm gun into firing position. The violent blasphemy he snarled during the process, only a meter from Piet's couch, showed how nervous the gunner was.

Stephen grabbed the flashgun slung from the same hook as his rolled hammock. I think if he'd had his favored weapon, he would have stayed with Dole outside. Stephen took a repeating rifle with him when we left the ship because the dog-sized local predators hunted in packs of three or more.

Piet glanced aside from his console. "They've announced they're friendly," he said. "And I presume they are or we'd know it by now, but . . ."

Because the strangers didn't use plasma motors, they could communicate by radio even while they were landing. That didn't seem a sufficient trade-off for the greater power of fusion over chemical energy, but it had its advantages.

Stephen donned his helmet as he stepped out the airlock again. Piet smiled and returned to his plot.

I followed Stephen. I still carried the slung rifle. I'd picked up my cutting bar also, as much for the way it focused me as for any good I'd be able to do with it against a starship.

The strange vessel was no bigger than a featherboat, though it was shorter and thicker than the *Nathan*, say, had been. It settled only twenty meters from the *Oriflamme*, bow to bow. Its combustion engines were loud by absolute standards, but they whispered in comparison to those of a normal starship. Plasma thrusters mixed low-frequency pulses with the *hiss* of ions recombining across and beyond the upper auditory band, creating a snarl more penetrating and unpleasant than I could have imagined before I heard it myself.

The ship's four stubby legs seemed to be integral rather than extended for landing. Portions of the scaly brown hull were charred from heat stress during reentry, but the material didn't look like the ablative coatings I was familiar with. It looked like tree bark.

The strange vessel had no visible gunports or hull openings of any kind. I walked toward it; either leading Stephen or following him, it was hard to say. A spot grew in the mid-hull. At first I thought a fire smoldered on the coating, but it was a knot opening as it spun slowly outward.

The hole froze when it reached man-size. The figure that stepped out of the ship was humanoid but certainly not human, though most of its body was covered with a hooded cape of translucent fabric. It had reptilian limbs and a face covered with patterned nodules like those of a lizard's skin. The jaw was undershot, the eyes pivoted individually, and the hands gripped a stocked weapon with a ten-liter pressure tank.

"I'd worry," Stephen murmured, "if they weren't armed." His voice was in the husky, dissociated mode in which I knew he didn't worry at all; only planned whom to kill first.

The second person out of the ship was a human, though he wore a flowing cape like that of the guard who preceded him. Tiny flowers filled the socket of his left eye like a miniature rock garden, and his right leg beneath the cape's hem was of dark wood with a golden grain. When the cape blew close to his body, I could see a handgun of some sort tucked against the front of his right shoulder.

"Hello, Gregg," the man said. It was hard to think of someone with flowers growing from his face as being human, and the fellow's rusty voice didn't help the impression. "I thought the Feds had killed you on Biruta."

Two more reptiles, armed as the first had been, got out of the strange ship. Their capes were a uniform dull gray, but the human's had underlayers which returned sunlight in shimmers across the whole optical spectrum.

"Hello, Cseka," Stephen said. "They tried, but we got away."

Cseka glanced beyond us. Piet stood in the cockpit hatch. "Ricimer too, eh?" Cseka said. "Well, I didn't get away. They caught me on Biruta and they made me a slave. How long's it been, anyway? Standard years, I mean."

"Five years, Captain," Piet said. "Would you come aboard the *Oriflamme*? Your friends, too, if they care to."

"Aye, we'll do that," Cseka said. He spoke a few throaty words to his guards and stumped forward. "These are the

Chay," he said, again in Trade English. "And I'm no longer a captain, Ricimer, I'm chief adviser to the Council of On Chay."

Cseka walked with a stiffness that the false leg didn't fully explain. I wondered what other injuries the cape concealed.

"And I'm the worst enemy Pleyal and his bastard Federation will ever have," Cseka added as he climbed the cockpit ladder. He spoke quietly, but his voice squealed like chalk on slate.

The Chay walked with quick, mincing steps, though there was nothing birdlike about their erect bodies. Their bulging eyes swept at least 240° even when they faced front, and they continually rotated their heads to cover the remaining arc.

"The mummy on Respite," I murmured to Stephen as we followed the guards back aboard the *Oriflamme*.

"I was thinking that," he said. "And now I really wonder how long ago he was buried."

Stephen was still distant from his surroundings. Perhaps it was mention of Biruta, where Pleyal's men had treacherously massacred Venerian traders. For reasons of state, there was still formal peace between the Free State of Venus and the North American Federation; but because of Biruta, there was open war beyond Pluto, and survivors like Piet and Stephen were the shock troops of that war.

Piet and Stephen and Captain, now Chief Adviser, Cseka.

The Long Tom was aligned with the bow port—and the Chay vessel—but not run forward to battery. Stampfer was still with the gun, but he'd sent his crew aft so that only he and the navigation officers waited for us in the bow compartment. Piet had dropped the table which hung on lines from the ceiling. Men watched through the hatch and from an arc outside the cockpit.

"Five years," Cseka said. "You lose track. Five years."

He took the tumbler of cloudy liquor Piet offered him: slash distilled from algae. This was a bottle we'd brought from Venus rather than what the motor crews brewed whenever we landed, but there wasn't a lot of difference.

"We have, ah, wines and such," Piet said. "Loot, of course."

Cseka drained his tumbler in three wracking gulps. Slash proved anywhere from fifty to eighty percent ethanol. "A taste of home, by God," he muttered. "The Chay, they can do anything with plants, but they can't make slash that's real slash."

"Perhaps they're too skillful," Stephen said. I don't know whether he was joking. "Slash doesn't permit subtlety."

"I was their slave for . . ." Cseka said. He frowned and refilled his tumbler. "Years. You can't measure it. Pleyal's slave, bossing gangs of Molt slaves all across the Back Worlds. The eye, that was from Biruta. They took my leg off on a place that hasn't any name. Pleyal doesn't waste medicines on slaves when amputation will do."

He swallowed another three fingers of slash. Cseka's eye was fixed on the bottle, but I can't guess what his mind saw.

"And then the Chay raided the plantation I was running on Rosary." Cseka gave us all a broad, mad grin. The tiny flowers wobbled in his eye socket as he turned his head. "I escaped with them. They might have killed me before they understood. That would have been all right, I'd still have been free of Pleyal."

The Chay had a sweetish odor like that of overripe fruit. I couldn't tell whether it was their breath or their bodies. They looked silently around the compartment. One of them reached toward the 17-cm cannon, but his long-fingered hand withdrew before it quite touched the gun. Stampfer, squat and glowering, relaxed minusculely.

"I've been guiding On Chay ever since," Cseka said. "Not leading—the Council leads. But I know the Feds, and I help the Chay fight them. The *bastards*."

"We came through the Breach," Piet said, "but we'll have to return the long way to Venus. We'll carry you back with us and give you a full share of—"

"No!" Cseka shouted. His hand closed on the neck of the bottle. I thumbed the power switch of my cutting bar and opened my left hand to grab the nearest Chay's weapon before he could—

Cseka relaxed and beamed his clownface grin at us again. "No, I'm where I belong," he said. He spoke now in a cracked lilt. "Killing Feds. Killing all the Feds, every one of the bastards, every one."

He poured more slash. Stephen almost hadn't moved, but "almost" was the amount he'd tucked the flashgun into his side to have a full stroke when he swept the butt across the heads of Cseka and the guard nearest him. Piet had reached across the back of his couch, where a double-barreled shotgun hung by its sling, and the lever from the plasma cannon's collimator was in Stampfer's hand.

"I want you to come back to On Chay with me," Cseka said, sipping this time instead of tossing the liquor off. "I told our scouts to look for ceramic-hulled ships, you know. To report to me at once and not to attack. And here you appear in *this* system."

He seemed to be oblivious of what had almost happened. Perhaps he didn't remember. The Chay hadn't moved, but their facial skin had shifted from green/brown to mauve.

"We appreciate the offer . . ." Piet said. "But—"

"No, it's not out of your way," Cseka said with a dismissive wave of his hand. "The fourth planet here."

"That's a gas giant," Salomon said sharply from his console.

"Yes, the second moon out," Cseka agreed. He was all sweet reason now. The sharpness was gone, but his voice still sing-songed. "It'll be worth your time. The Chay grow tubular fullerenes, *grow* them, any length you want. Kilo for kilo, they're worth more than new-run chips."

Piet's face grew blankly quiet. He wasn't looking at anyone. We all waited for him to speak. The *Oriflamme* wasn't a democracy.

He smiled dazzlingly. "Yes, all right," he said to Cseka. "We'll follow you, then?"

Cseka nodded, the flowers bobbing in his eye socket. "Yes, yes, that's what we'll do," he said. Suddenly, fiercely he added, "I knew there'd be ships from Venus sooner or later. Between us, we'll kill them all!"

He turned and slammed out through the open airlock
without further comment. The three guards exchanged
glances, only their eyes moving, before they strutted after
their human leader.

Stephen relaxed slightly. "Cseka was always a bit of a
hothead," he said in an emotionless voice.

Piet watched the castaway climb back aboard the vessel
in which he had arrived. "That was a different man, the
one we knew," he said.

"You trust him, then?" I said. I switched off the cutting
bar and hung it, so that I could work life back into the
hand with which I'd been gripping the weapon.

"No," said Piet. The port of the Chay vessel began to
rotate closed before the last of the guards hopped through.
"He's obviously insane. But he's different from the man
Stephen and I knew."

He pushed the button controlling the *Oriflamme*'s siren,
calling the men aboard for liftoff.

I dropped my rifle and ammo satchel on the deck. "I'm
going with them," I said. I jumped from the airlock instead
of using the steps. Over my shoulder I called, "We need
to know more about the Chay than we do now!"

Men piling aboard via the ramp looked in surprise as I
sprinted to the alien vessel. Nobody tried to call me back
from the bridge. Piet and Stephen weren't the sort to waste
their breath.

"Cseka!" I shouted. "Open up! Let me ride with you!"

The port continued to spin slowly closed. It had shrunk
to the size of my head. I stuck the blade of my unpowered
cutting bar into the opening.

The port stopped closing. I waited. The Chay vessel's
hull pulsed slowly as I stood beside it with my hand on
the grip of my bar.

After a minute or so, the knot rotated the other way
again. When the opening was large enough, I climbed
aboard.

ON CHAY

Day 156

The engines' firing level reduced gradually, as though someone was shutting down the fuel valves by micro-adjustments as we settled toward the moon's inhabited surface. Some *thing* was, but not a person, unless the Chay vessel herself had personality as well as life.

One of the reptiles chewed a banana-shaped fruit that dribbled purple juice down his jaw and the front of his cape. It seemed to have a narcotic effect. The Chay's eyes hadn't moved since he began eating; translucent lids slipped back and forth across them at intervals.

Cseka lay on his back, staring at the frameless screen that covered the cabin ceiling. Instead of a real-time scan, adjusted images swept over the display area at one- or two-second intervals.

None of the vessel's crew was anywhere near the controls aft. The ship was landing itself.

"Are those irrigated lands?" I asked, gesturing toward a swatch of blue-green on the surface swelling toward us. It could as easily have been a lake. I wasn't sure whether the patterns I saw in the colored area were real or an artifact of the unfamiliar optical apparatus.

"We live on mats of vegetation," Cseka said in a drugged voice. He didn't look at me when he spoke. "On Chay has too many earthquakes to live directly on the ground. The mats slide when the earth shakes, you see."

"Life couldn't arise on a planet—'moon'—so unstable," I said, speaking the thought I'd had ever since I connected the Chay with the mummy on Respite. "It must

207

have been colonized from somewhere else. Perhaps in the far past."

"Yeah, that's probably so," Cseka agreed without interest. "There's maybe a hundred Chay worlds. They all call themselves On Chay. I suppose the Chay had a Collapse too."

Translucent circles like strings of frog eggs clung to one another within the mat we were approaching. Elsewhere, larger circles differed in hue from the neighboring vegetation. The primary lowered in the sky above us, a turgid purple mass shot with blues and yellow.

The controls spoke in a guttural, blurry voice. The two sober Chay looked around. Cseka roused himself from his couch and growled toward the controls.

The engines fired at high output. We accelerated sideways, and I fell against a bulkhead. The resilient surface cushioned me, then formed into a grip for my furious hand.

"I'm to guide your friends down outside the city," Cseka grumbled. "I forget the way plasma thrusters tear up everything around."

The Chay vessel was smaller inside than I'd expected. The thick hull contained everything necessary for the starship's operation and the well-being of the crew, but it didn't leave much internal volume.

"The *Oriflamme* is already in orbit?" I asked.

Cseka looked at me as if he were trying to remember where I'd come from. I hadn't noticed anything odd when I ate rations prepared for Cseka—none of the food was meat, according to him, though I'd have sworn otherwise. Most likely, the castaway's problems had nothing to do with his present diet.

"You said we were guiding my friends down," I prodded. "So they were waiting for us?"

"Yeah, sure," Cseka said with an angry frown. "Look, we got here, didn't we? Our ships don't process course equations as fast as the Feds do, maybe, but they don't come down sideways because a cosmic ray punched the artificial intelligence at the wrong time."

We'd transited from above Duneen almost as soon as

we reached orbit. A human vessel—even the *Oriflamme*
with Piet running the boards—would have taken at least
half an hour to calibrate.

The next transit, from a point so removed that the system's sun was only a bright star when it rotated across the
ceiling screen, had taken what I think was the better part
of a day. I was used to transits in quick series, several to
several score insertions in sequence, followed by periods
of an hour or more to recalculate. Chay vessels used a
completely different system.

The advantage—it minimized the horrible sickness of
transiting through nonsidereal universes—was balanced by
the fact that the Chay didn't continue accelerating during
calibration. We were in free fall all the time we waited for
the brain built into the vessel's hull to prepare for the
next transit. Combustion rockets weren't as fuel-efficient
as plasma thrusters, and the navigational system obviously
didn't cope with small, sudden changes as well as humans'
silicon-based microprocessors did.

"They were met in orbit," Cseka murmured, settling
back onto his couch. "But they didn't want to land until
we'd arrived. You had."

The ceiling visuals were more like mural paintings than
the screens I was used to. The mat of vegetation covered
the bow third of the image. There were circular fields of
varying size within the general blue-green mass. Occasional bright, straight lines suggested metalwork. From
what Cseka had told me about Chay culture, I assumed
they were biologically formed as well.

I'd thought the castaway would be babblingly glad of
human company after his years among aliens. Instead,
Cseka remained in his own world throughout the voyage. He gave verbal orders to the controls when the ship
demanded them. My questions were answered in mono-
syllables or brief phrases, the way a busy leader snaps at
an importunate underling; responses only in the technical
sense, which in no way attempted to give me the understanding I'd requested.

Despite that, I'd learned a great deal about the Chay to
guide Piet when he dealt with the race. A day's discomfort

was nothing compared to what we'd been through already; and the risk—

I'd made that decision when I came aboard the *Porcelain.* So had we all.

The vessel was settling to the west of the mat. As we neared the ground I realized that resolution of the Chay optics was amazingly good, more like still photographs than the scanned images I was used to. The visuals were real, too, not data cleaned up by an enhancement program. The surface had all the warts and blemishes of a natural landscape.

The soil beneath us was russet, yellow, and gray. There were dips and outcrops, but no significant hills. Frequent cracks jagged across the surface, often streaming sulphurous gases. Vegetation outside the large mats was limited to clumps and rings. None of it was high enough to cast a shadow from the primary on the eastern horizon.

"Is it breathable?" I asked as I watched a fumarole just upwind of where we trembled in a near-hover. "The air."

"What?" Cseka said. He blinked, then frowned. "Of course it's breathable. A little high in carbon dioxide, that's all. These—"

He plucked the cowl of his cape. It stretched across his face as a veil.

"—filter it. I'll have some brought to your ship."

He spoke to the vessel's controls again. We resumed our descent at less than three meters a second.

"The Chay wear them also," I said. We would land in a shallow depression hundreds of meters in diameter, half a klick from the inhabited vegetation. Atmosphere vessels—platforms supported by three or more translucent gas bags—drifted from the city toward the spot.

"When they're out of their domes, yes," Cseka said.

I squatted against the bulkhead's lower curve, not that we were going to land hard enough to require my caution. If the Chay couldn't breathe the atmosphere of On Chay without artificial aids, there was no question at all that they were the relicts of a past civilization rather than autochthons.

The engines roared at higher output and on a distinctly

different note. I recalled how the nozzles had dilated as the Chay vessel landed on Duneen. The exhaust spread to reflect from the ground as a cushion against the lower hull.

"Do you have a filter for me?" I asked, pitching my voice to be heard over the engines. How quickly did CO_2 poisoning become dangerous? Could I run to the *Oriflamme* after she landed?

"Christ's blood," said Cseka. He wiped his good eye with the back of his hand, then waved toward the guard whose muscles had frozen while the last of the fruit was a centimeter from his mouth. "Take his!"

Cseka growled a few additional words to the Chay. The mobile guards unfastened their fellow's cape by running a finger down a hidden seam. They pulled the garment away from him as we landed lightly as thought.

One of them handed the cape to me. I wrapped it around my shoulders, avoiding the patch of sticky purple juice. The edges sealed when I pressed them together, though the fabric felt as slick as the surface of the *Oriflamme*'s hull.

The Chay's naked body was skeletally thin. The pebbly frontal skin was light gray-brown, while the sides and back were a darker shade of the same drab combination. The color variations of the face and arms were absent.

The creature wore a net garment similar to a bandeau across its midriff. A few small objects hung from the meshes. I couldn't guess what their human analogs might be.

One of the Chay spoke. It was the first time I'd heard one of their voices. The word or words seemed sharper than those of Cseka speaking the language, but obviously he managed to communicate.

The whorled patch of bulkhead spun slowly outward, opening to a dark sky and the coruscation of the *Oriflamme*'s thrusters descending. I smoothed the sides of my borrowed cape over my nose and mouth, then ducked through the hatchway as soon as it had opened enough to pass me.

The *Oriflamme* dropped in a wide circle of Chay vessels, ten or a dozen of them. These ships were constructs, three to six pods linked by tubes fat enough that a man or Chay could crawl between them.

The individual hulls were similar to the one that had carried me to On Chay. I had a vision of giant pea vines festooned with starships. I suppose that was pretty close to the truth.

The *Oriflamme* wobbled slightly like a man walking on stilts, though anyone who'd seen another starship land would be amazed at how skillfully Piet balanced the thrust of his eight engines. The Chay escort kept formation around him like fish schooling rather than individually-controlled machines. They dropped with less than a quarter of their jets lighted, further proof of how much less massive they were than human vessels.

I'd used my hand to block the glare of the *Oriflamme*'s thrusters. When Cseka got out behind me, he'd sealed the front of his cowl up over his eyes. I tried the same thing. The fabric blocked the high-energy—UV and blue—portion of the exhaust and dimmed the whole output to comfortable levels, without degrading the rest of my vision more than ten or twenty percent. That was about as good as our helmet visors.

The dirigibles I'd seen on our vessel's screen sailed nearer. The supporting gas bags were the size and shape of the starship hulls, though the walls were thin enough to be translucent. Eight to ten meters beneath each set of bags hung a platform, some of which were large enough to hold several score Chay.

The bigger dirigibles mounted a plasma cannon at the bow. The weapons were metal and of small bore, swivel guns like those *Our Lady of Montreal* had carried.

I nudged Cseka. "Where do they get the cannon?" I shouted over the *Oriflamme*'s hammering roar.

"Trade," he said. "For fullerenes. We've got embassies from most of the states of Earth here, but the shipments go through too many hands. That's why we want Venerians. To set up our own foundries."

About half the Chay riding the dirigibles wore plain gray capes like those of Cseka's guards. The remainder were clad in a variety of other metallic hues. Most of these were shades of silver, but cinnabar reds and blues as poisonous as that of copper sulfate were dazzlingly present. A few Chay gleamed with the same gold undertones as Cseka's cape.

A hundred meters up, the Chay vessels increased thrust and hovered while the *Oriflamme* dropped out of their circle. Moving in a single flock, the escorts pulsed sideways through the sky in the direction of the mat of vegetation.

The *Oriflamme* landed nearby in an explosion of dirt. Each of the thruster nozzles acted as a shaped charge blasting straight down. The soil was friable, without enough sand in the mixture to bind it into glass.

I hunched and covered my head with my arms. Cseka remembered to duck a moment later, but the two guards who'd followed us out of the ship continued gaping at the *Oriflamme* until the dirt cascaded over us. It was like being caught in a rugby scrum.

I fell over on my right side. One of the rocks that bounced off my forearm would have knocked me silly if it had hit my head instead. Pebbles settled while the wave of lighter dust traveled outward in an expanding doughnut. A dirigible nosed toward us through the cloud.

I shook the hem of my cape free of the dirt loading it and jogged toward the *Oriflamme*. Cseka shouted something, but I couldn't understand the words. Maybe he was calling to the Chay in their own language.

The forward airlock opened as I neared the *Oriflamme*. Stephen, identifiable even in a hard suit by his size and the slung flashgun, swung down the integral steps and stamped toward me across the glowing crater the plasma motors blew around the vessel.

He raised his visor when he was clear of the throbbing boundary. "I'll carry you," he said.

"I hoped you might," I said, but he didn't hear me because he had to lock his visor down again to draw a breath.

I stepped into his arms and, like Saint Christopher carrying our Lord, Stephen tramped back across the blasted soil and up the steps into the *Oriflamme*. The ground had cooled below the optical range, but radiant heat baked the sweat from my calves and left arm in the few seconds I was exposed.

Both valves of the airlock stood open until Stephen set me down. The forward compartment was closed off from the rest of the ship. Piet and half a dozen senior members of the complement waited for us in oxygen masks.

"This is a filter," I said, plucking the hood down from my eyes. I realized how strange I must look. "How high *is* the carbon dioxide?"

"Five and a half percent," Piet said. The outer door had closed, so he took his mask cautiously away. "I'm surprised the Chay breathe Duneen's atmosphere when their own is so different."

"They're as alien here as we are," I said. "From what I could drag out of Cseka—believe me, he's crazy. It's like his mind was dropped and all the pieces were put together blind."

I hawked to clear my throat. My cape's filter mechanism didn't seem to bind the ozone formed by plasma exhausted into an oxygen atmosphere. On the main screen, three dirigibles moved toward the *Oriflamme*. Cilia on the platforms' undersides rowed the air. They raised some dust from the ground, but less than turbines of similar thrust.

"There's a hundred or so Chay worlds," I resumed. "There's no overall direction—they're as likely to fight with each other as trade."

"How unlike humans," Piet said dryly.

"Some of them do trade with the Feds," I said. "And it sounds like the Feds have taken control of some Chay worlds. Most of the Chay, though—like this system, they're marked 'Avoid' on the pilotry chart because a Fed ship gets handed its head if it messes with the locals."

One of the dirigibles swung broadside to the *Oriflamme;* it hovered with its platform on a level with the cockpit hatch. The six supporting gas bags loomed above us. Their total volume was several times that of the starship. Low-ranking Chay stood near bales of gray capes like those they themselves wore, waiting for our hatch to open.

"I didn't see a single piece of metalwork, much less ceramic, on the ship," I said. I nodded toward the image of the armed dirigible. "They've got cannon—"

"Southern Cross work," said Stephen without bothering to look again at the weapon he'd already assessed. "And about as dangerous at one end as the other, I'd judge."

"They can do anything with plants," I said. "They can sequester lanthanides in fullerene tubes a meter long, Cseka swears."

"What good is that?" Stephen asked.

"On Earth, they're starting to use them to replace damaged nerves," I replied. "Cseka wants us to set up a cannon foundry here. In exchange, they'll provide either biological products or the plant stocks that make them. He's serious, but—"

"*Us,* to set up a foundry?" said Piet. "Or Venus?"

I nodded with my lips pursed. "Yeah, that's the thing. I think maybe he means us. We could convince him that we don't have the expertise ourselves, but—"

"Unless he remembers what my father does for a living," Piet said with a smile.

"We can't train this cack-handed lot to cast cannon!" I snapped. "Any more than I could teach them to build silicon AIs. Or breathe water! But I don't know how well Cseka is going to hear anything that doesn't agree with what he wants to hear."

Piet nodded. "Not a unique problem," he said. "Though I think we'd better meet with his leaders. Compressed fullerenes are what give our hulls—"

He tapped Stephen's breastplate affectionately.

"—and armor hardness that Terran metallurgists can't equal. If the Chay are so much better at creating fullerenes than we are with our sputtering techniques—"

Piet smiled.

"—then we owe it to Venus to learn what we can."

He fitted the mask back over his face. "Our hosts have waited long enough," he said. "I'll take a few men and some gifts to meet with them. And we'll see what we see."

Stephen frowned at "*I'll* take"; but as I'd noticed before, he didn't waste his breath in futile argument. "I'm one of the men," he said.

"And I'm another," I added.

• • •

"Yeah, those are food crops," Cseka agreed, peering over the edge of the platform at the brown and ocher vegetation twenty meters below. "The inside stems and the leaves both. You wouldn't know it was the same plant."

The platform didn't have a guardrail, but Piet seemed equally nonchalant as he leaned forward to view the fields. Chay agriculture was labor-intensive: at least a hundred gray-clad figures stooped over the sinuous crop, pruning and cultivating. The vines were as big around as my thighs, but the relatively small leaves looked more like fur than foliage.

Stephen and I stayed back a step from the edge. He grimaced every time Piet overhung the platform, and his free hand—the one not on the grip of his flashgun—was poised to snatch his friend back if a jolt sent him toppling.

However, the dirigible rode as solidly as a rock. The platform was suspended on hoselike tubes that stretched and compressed as the gas bags lifted or fell in the breeze. The deck undulated only slightly as cilia beneath stroked us forward.

We slid between two brown-tinged domes together covering nearly a hectare. "Workers' housing," Cseka volunteered, gesturing with his elbow toward the dome on our side of the platform. I could see the dim outlines of tiered buildings under the curving surface. Cseka had spoken more during the ride from the *Oriflamme*'s landing site a kilometer away than he did during the day's voyage from Duneen.

I carried a flashgun too, but just as a gift to the council. Our ceramic cassegrain lasers were far superior to the nearest Terran equivalents, though not many Venerians cared to use weapons so heavy and unpleasant for the shooter. I sometimes wondered whether Stephen carried a flashgun because each round was so effective, or if a part of him liked the punishment.

A clear dome far larger than those housing the Chay workers loomed before us. The structures inside looked like mushrooms with multiple caps one above another on a single central shaft. Those near the middle of the enclosure had eight or nine layers.

Our dirigible settled to the ground. Rather, settled onto a living surface of hair-fine leaves woven as tightly as carpeting. The arched opening in the dome was big enough for three or four people to walk abreast. The passage writhed like an intestine instead of going straight through to the interior.

"Come," said Cseka. "The council will be waiting for us."

He stepped from the platform to the carpet of vegetation. Stephen and Piet fell in to either side of the castaway, while the three of us carrying presents—Dole and Lightbody with me—followed closely behind. Chay on the dirigibles wheezed a fanfare on horns several meters long driven by four musicians squeezing bellows simultaneously.

There wasn't a door at either end of the tunnel, but its walls were lined with fine hairs that greatly increased the surface area. That and the winding course—the dome's wall was only three meters through even here where it was thickened, but the passage was a good twenty—served to filter the carbon dioxide down to levels the Chay found comfortable.

A crowd of Chay with their cowls thrown back lined both sides of the route inside the dome. At least half of them wore the colored garments I'd come to associate with higher ranks. As we six humans entered the enclosed area, the spectators began to stamp their feet in a slow rhythm. The flooring was as hard and dense-grained as a nutshell, and the dome reverberated.

We walked along a boulevard a hundred meters wide, thronged with stamping Chay. Musicians from the dirigibles followed us, wheezing on their horns. Additional spectators leaned from the upper stories of buildings.

"Do they have radio, do you suppose?" I said. I was speaking mostly to myself at first, but I added loudly enough to be heard by the men ahead of me, "Captain Cseka, do the Chay have radio?"

A party in silvery capes marched to meet us. They

played instruments a meter and a half long; bangles on either end clattered like the beads of an abacus when the musician plucked his one string. These strings, the bellows trumpets, and the stamping crowd each kept an individual rhythm. Only the cacophony aboard *Absalom 231* in the atmosphere of Decades approached the result.

Cseka turned his head. "Only to talk to human ships," he shouted. "We use beans that vibrate the same as others from the same pod instead."

He shrugged. "The range is only a few light-seconds and they aren't faster than light, nothing like that. But they work."

The string players reversed course to precede us down the boulevard. The towers were arranged in three rings of increasing height. At the center of the enclosure, a low building sat in a circular court several hundred meters across.

Near the entrance to the central structure was a cage, grown rather than woven in a lattice with about a hundred millimeters across openings. The two lines of string players parted around it. A man—a human being in the remnants of a Federation uniform—clutched the bars to hold his torso upright.

There were—three at least, maybe more—human corpses in the cage with the living man. One of them had been dead long enough that the flesh had sloughed to bare his ribs. The stench of death and rotting waste was a barrier so real that I stumbled three steps away.

Piet stopped and touched his hand to Cseka's arm. "What's this?" Piet asked, exaggerating his lip movements to be understood without bellowing.

"Sometimes we take Feds alive," Cseka said nonchalantly. "They're brought here for entertainment."

His right hand came out from beneath his cape with the handweapon I'd seen outlined there. Grip, receiver, and barrel were one piece of dark brown, black-grained wood. A lanyard growing from the butt quivered back in a springy coil which held the pistol out of the way when it wasn't in use.

Cseka fired. A snap of steam lifted the gun muzzle. The

prisoner screamed and arched convulsively. He skidded on his back, thrashing across a floor slippery with filth.

Cseka held his weapon up for us to see. "Darts," he said. "They're not fatal, not usually. But they drop a fellow quicker than bullets. And they—"

He aimed again toward the prisoner. The procession halted when we did, but the wracking music continued.

Piet put two fingers under the barrel of the dart gun and lifted it away. "Please don't," he said. "The things we have to do in war are terrible enough."

"Nothing could be enough!" Cseka shouted. He raised the pistol and brought it down in a slashing stroke at Piet's head. Stephen blocked the blow with his left forearm, catching Cseka's wrist numbingly. The pistol flew loose and slithered back under the cape.

Cseka began to giggle. "Nothing could be enough," he repeated. "Some day we'll have them all here, with your help."

He strode around the left side of the cage. We five Oriflammes scrambled to catch up, but the Chay in the procession resumed marching without missing a step.

The Chay hadn't reacted to the momentary human conflict. The Fed prisoner lay quiescent. His eyes were open, and his chest trembled like that of a dog panting.

"Our rifles throw fireballs a hundred meters," Cseka said, his voice raised only to be heard over the background noise. The maniacal rage switched itself off and on in an eyeblink. He tapped the barrel of Stephen's flashgun. "Within their range, they're better than this."

"Within their range," Stephen repeated. There was nothing in his tone to suggest he believed the Chay shoulder weapons—they certainly weren't rifled—were really as effective as his laser at any range.

The string players flared to either side of the central building. The structure was nearly cylindrical, as if a balloon had been inflated in a tube. The walls slanted slightly inward and the roof edge was a radiused curve instead of square.

We walked into the building. The single chamber held several score Chay in golden capes and at least a dozen humans. Like us, the humans wore the gray local garment, but their hats were of a number of Terran styles. I recognized a pair of Southerns, a large man in a kepi with United Europe military insignia, and a pair of women from the Independent Coastal Republic. Their state had been fighting for thirty years against Pleyal's federated *remainder* of North America.

There was an open aisle down the center of the room. Cseka led us toward the empty dais at the end. The music and stamping outside stopped, but the chamber sighed with the spectators' breathing. The walls were lighted from within, giving the effect of translucence which the black exterior belied.

We halted two paces from the dais, as close as any of the spectators stood. A human leaned close to me and said in Trade English, "You're from Venus, is it not so? You're bringing arms to trade?"

"We're passing through," I replied; in a whisper, though the questioner had spoken normally. I think he was a European. United Europe had no extra-solar colonies, but several of its states engaged in trade beyond Pluto.

He sniffed. "There's nothing they want but arms, cannon especially," he said. "Well, there's enough for all."

The wall behind the dais rotated open like the port in the Chay starship. Ten Chay carried through three others on a litter whose wooden surface gleamed like polished bronze.

The trio were completely naked and very old. They hunched like dogs sitting up. Their skins were nearly white. Their three tails twisted together and appeared to have fused into one flesh.

The silver-caped porters lowered the trio to the dais. The spectators shouted. The voices of the Chay were more or less in unison though of course unintelligible. The humans—the man next to me, at least—cried, "Hail, the all-powerful council!"

The trio's mouths opened as one. "Greetings to this worshipful assembly," boomed the front wall of the chamber while the two side walls were snarling something in the language of the Chay themselves. The Trade English words seemed synchronized with the lipless mouth of the center councilor.

The room stilled. The walls had been suffused with amber light. The floor level was now emerald green, and the hue was slipping upward as if by osmosis. The councilors focused their independently-rotating eyes on us.

"We have discussed you with Lord Cseka," said the center figure. His voice through the front wall was understandable despite the sidewalls' accompanying harsh gutturals. "Your enemies are our enemies. Together we will drive the Federation pirates out of existence except as our slaves and your slaves."

The trio paused. The councilors were as thin as mummies, pebbly skin sunken drumhead-tight over an armature of bone. Their ribs fluttered when they breathed.

Piet lifted his arms forward to call attention to himself without advancing into the cleared zone before the dais. "All-powerful council!" he said in a voice pitched to be heard in a larger arena than this one. "We bring you the greetings of Venus and our ruler, Governor Halys. We ourselves are but chance travelers, but permit us to offer a few trifles as a foretaste of the trade the future will bring between your people and ours."

He twisted his head back toward me. "Jere—" he murmured. I gave him the flashgun before he finished the request.

"A laser with a range of kilometers," Piet called. The weapon weighed nearly twenty kilos, as I well knew, but he balanced it on the palm of one hand so that he could deploy the charging parasol from the butt with the other.

"In good light, you can fire every three minutes at full power!" he added. We weren't providing spare batteries as a part of this gift. "Your enemies and ours of the Federation have no handweapons so effective."

A porter took the gift from Piet and set it on the dais beside the council. Lightbody held his load out. Piet shook his head curtly and gestured to Dole instead.

Dole handed forward a round bowl a meter in diameter. Piet raised it overhead and turned it so that all the assembly could see Governor Halys' gray pearl charge on a field of creamy translucence.

"As your folk with plants, so ours with ceramics," Piet said. "This is merely a symbol of—"

He flung the bowl down on the floor as hard as he could. It bounced back into his hands with the deep, throbbing note of a jade gong. The assembly, Chay and humans alike, gasped with surprise.

"—the skill with which our experts, experts whom I can encourage to journey here from Venus, cast plasma cannon!"

The sidewalls rumbled phrases in the local tongue, though the councilors weren't speaking. Chay spectators whispered among themselves. The human ambassadors eyed us with speculation and some disquiet.

"One last thing," Piet said as a porter took away the undamaged bowl. He was emphasizing that we were geese who would lay golden eggs, a prize for what we would bring rather than what we were. "Like the others, this is only a symbol of the trade that will start upon our return to Venus."

Piet took from Lightbody the navigational computer we'd stripped out of one of the Federation ships captured on Trehinga. I'd have reduced the simple unit to components for ease of storage, but Piet stopped me for reasons I now understood.

"In order to capture a vessel in transit," Piet said, "your AI must solve the same equations the other vessel's does. We of Venus will supply you with electronic artificial intelligences that will allow you to track Federation ships across the bubble universes instead of being limited to attacking those you find grounded or in orbit. There will be no safety for the enemies of On Chay and Venus!"

This time the Chay spectators stamped their feet as the translation boomed to them from the sidewalls. It was almost a minute after a porter took the—crude—AI that the chamber quieted again.

The walls replied in the councilors' three voices, "Men of Venus, our folk are already delivering to your vessel phials of drugs, fabrics, and the tubular fullerenes we know your folk especially prize. Trade for the future, yes . . . But we will propose to you other arrangements as well. Go now, and tomorrow we will meet with you again."

Piet bowed low. I knelt and tugged Dole and Lightbody down with me. The aisle through the assembly had closed, but the spectators squeezed aside again to let us pass. The Chay were stamping their enthusiasm.

I was in the lead of our party, walking with the steady arrogance that befitted a gentleman of Venus. I'd never before in my life wanted so badly to get out of anything as I did that drumming council chamber.

"I wonder if this balloon can go faster than it has so far?" Piet said, looking over the fittings of the dirigible carrying us back to the *Oriflamme*. We were traveling at about 20 kph, the speed of a man jogging.

He raised an eyebrow in question as he swept his glance over the airship's crew. The dozen Chay present on the return journey wore the gray of common laborers. They continued to ignore Piet and the rest of us.

"The big ones with guns," Dole said, answering the surface question. "They've got more legs on the bottom than these do." He thumped his bootheel on the platform.

"They might speak English anyway," I said.

"My thought as well," Piet agreed in a satisfied tone. This was no place to discuss our real intentions.

The primary was past mid-sky, flooding the land with soft blue light. On Chay was a warm world for all its distance from the sun. The planet it circled was nearly a star in its own right, and vulcanism spurred by the gas giant's gravity warmed the satellite significantly.

Another pair of small dirigibles passed ours on their way back to the city. Tents of thin sheeting had sprung up around the *Oriflamme* during our absence, and bales of unfamiliar material were stacked near the main hatch. The council had been as good as its word when it promised gifts.

"They really want to be our friends," I said. Even if the

Chay understood English, they weren't going to pick up my undertone of concern.

"On their terms," Stephen said, "they certainly do."

Men wearing Chay capes moved out of the way so that the dirigible could land beside the open forward airlock. The ground had cooled, so we didn't have to hop from the platform to the ship in reverse of the way we had disembarked.

The first thing I noticed when I stepped down was that the ground wasn't still. Microshocks made the surface tremble like the deck of a starship under way.

Dole must have thought the same thing. He nodded to the tents crewmen were building from fabric the Chay had brought and said, "Even if we get a big one and they come down, it's not going to hurt nobody."

I nodded agreement, then grinned. A seasoned spacer adapted to local conditions; the landsman I'd been six months ago would have been terrified. On Venus, ground shocks might rupture the overburden and let in the hell-brewed atmosphere.

"Guillermo?" Piet called to the Molt who'd been directing outside operations during our absence. "Turn things over to Dole and join us on the bridge, please."

The Chay crew paid us no attention. They backed the dirigible from the *Oriflamme* before turning its prow toward the city. Again I noticed the delicacy of the driving cilia. Mechanical propellors or turbines would have scattered the tents our crew had just constructed.

Salomon waited for us alone in the forward section, though as we entered a pair of sailors carried bedrolls toward the main hatch while discussing the potential of converting Chay foodstocks into brandy.

"I've run initial calculations for an empty world twenty days from here," the navigator said. "We'll have to refine them in orbit, of course."

"I don't know that it's come to that, exactly," Piet said cautiously. I'm sure he would have started the calculations himself if Salomon hadn't already done so.

"Cseka scares the hell out of me," I said. "The Chay scare me even worse. They—"

"They're friendly," Piet said.

"They're not *human,*" I said. "An earthquake may not hurt you, but it isn't your friend. There's nothing I saw in there today—"

I waved in the direction of the city.

"—that convinces me they won't decide to eat us because, because Stampfer's got red hair."

"I haven't had a chance to look over the goods they've brought us . . ." Stephen said. He took off his helmet and kneaded his scalp with his left hand. "But I don't think there's much doubt that trade—in techniques, at least, given the distance—could be valuable."

He gave us a humorless grin. "Of course, that's only if the Chay decide to let us go. Jeremy's right, there."

Guillermo had said nothing since he entered behind us. He was seated at his usual console. His digits were entering what even I recognized as a sequence to lift us to orbit.

Piet laughed briefly. "So you all think we should take off as soon as possible," he said. "Even though Chay knowledge could give Venus an advantage greater than all the chips the Federation brings back from the Reaches?"

"What we think, Piet," Stephen said, "is that you're in charge. We'll follow whatever course you determine."

"I'm not a tyrant!" Piet snapped. "I'm not President Pleyal, 'Do *this* because it's my whim!' "

I swallowed and said, "Somebody has to make decisions. Here it's you. Besides, you're better at it than the rest of us. Not that that matters."

I grinned at Stephen. His words hadn't been a threat, because the big gunman accepted that all the rest of us knew the commander's decision was the law of this expedition. As surely as I knew that Stephen would destroy anything or anyone who tried to block Piet's decision.

"Yes," said Piet. He sat down at his console and checked a status display. "Air and reaction mass will be at capacity within the hour. We'll check the gifts, see what's worth taking and what's not, but we'll leave the bales where they are for the time being. We don't want to give the impression that we're stowing them for departure."

He looked up at the rest of us and smiled brilliantly. "Primary set is in six hours. An hour after that, we'll inform the crew to begin loading operations. When they're complete—another hour?—we'll close the hatches and lift."

Piet rubbed his forehead. "I didn't," he added as if idly, "much care for the way our hosts treat their prisoners."

The *Oriflamme* shuddered as another shock rippled through the soil beneath us.

The primary was just below the horizon. The sun at zenith in the clear sky was only a blue-white star, though it cast a shadow if you looked carefully.

Three dirigibles rested outside the entrance to the domed city, their partially deflated gas bags sagging. The airships and their crews were armed, but the Chay all wore gray. None of their officers were present, and the guards themselves didn't bother to look at me as I walked into the dome.

Half a dozen Chay in orange and pastel blue capes preceded me by twenty meters. A group of gray-clad laborers followed at a similar distance, chattering among themselves. Like me, some of the laborers left their cowls up and the veils over their faces even after they entered the dome.

I hadn't done a more pointlessly risky thing since the night I went aboard the *Porcelain*. Though . . .

Boarding the *Porcelain* hadn't made me a man, perhaps, but it had made me a man I like better than the fellow who'd lived on Venus until then. I wasn't going to leave a human prisoner here to be tortured to death.

The hard floor of the dome was a contrast to the springy surface of the mat on which it rode. The cape hung low enough to cover my feet, but I was afraid somebody would notice that the sound of my boots differed from the clicking the locals made when they walked. I took deliberate, quick, mincing steps.

There were hundreds of pedestrians out, but the broad boulevard seemed deserted by comparison with what I'd seen in the afternoon. Though the dome was clear, it darkened the sky into a rich blue that concealed all the stars except the sun itself. The walls of overhanging apartments wicked soft light from within, but even the lower levels weren't bright enough to illuminate the street.

I could see the cage ahead of me. I gripped the cutting bar beneath my cape to keep it from swinging and calling attention to itself; and because I was afraid.

I could claim to be looking around; but the Chay would want to carry me back to the *Oriflamme,* and if they did that they'd see we were loading the ship to escape. To save the others, I'd have to insist on staying overnight in the city. What would the Chay do with me when the *Oriflamme* lifted?

Lord God of hosts, be with Your servant. Though I'd been no servant of His; a self-willed fool, and a greater fool now because I wouldn't leave an enemy of mine to die at the hands of enemies of his.

I'd slipped away from the *Oriflamme* without causing comment. I told Dole I was going for a walk to calm my nerves. I didn't want my shipmates to worry if they noticed I was gone.

It didn't seem likely they would notice, what with the work of preparing for departure. I was only in the way.

There were no guards around the Council Hall or the cage in front of it. Occasional Chay strode across the court, on their way from one boulevard to another, but they didn't linger. Even those in bright garb were hard to see. My gray cape would be a shadow among shadows.

A Chay in silvery fabric walked out of the Council Hall carrying a bundle. I paused beside a tower, close against the wall. If the fellow had been a moment slower, I'd have been crossing to the cage myself. The grip of my bar was slick with sweat.

The Chay thrust his bundle into the cage. He had to wiggle it to work it through the mesh. It fell with a slapping sound to the floor within. The Chay called something obviously derisory in his own language, then went back the way he'd come.

Feeding time at the zoo. The prisoner didn't move. I couldn't even be sure which of the still forms within the lattice was the living man.

There wouldn't be a better time. I walked to the cage, keeping my steps short. Out of the corner of my eye I saw a Chay laborer start across the courtyard. I continued forward, my heart in my throat. The Chay disappeared past or into a neighboring residential tower.

I took the cage in my left hand and shook it to test the structure. The bars were grown as a unit, not tied together where they crossed. They were finger-thick, hard and obviously tough; but my bar would go through them like light through a window.

"Ho! Federation dog!" I snarled. I pitched my voice low though loud enough for the prisoner to hear. I could still brazen out my presence if I had to. "Come close to me or it'll be the worse for you!"

"I don't think he can move, Jeremy," Piet said from behind me. "We'll have to carry him."

I turned, my mouth open and the tip of the bar sliding from beneath my cape. Piet was indistinguishable from a Chay in his gray cape, but his voice was unmistakable.

"Yeah, well," I said. I switched my bar on. "I'll drag him out, then."

The blade *zing*ed across the bars. I cut up, across and down, then bent to slash through the base of the opening. I wondered how the Chay had created the cage to begin with, since it didn't appear to have a door anywhere. I couldn't believe they'd simply grown it around their prisoners.

Piet caught the section as it started to fall. He held a cape to me as I hung my bar. I'd brought an extra garment myself, so Piet tossed his spare onto the cage floor to be rid of it.

My boot skidded on the slimy surface. I had to grab the frame to keep from falling. One of the prostrate figures moaned softly. I raised his torso, tugged the cape around him, and lifted him in a packstrap carry.

The cut section now hung from the hinge of tape Piet had wrapped around it. When I ducked out, he taped the other side so that our entry wasn't obvious.

The prisoner was a dead weight, though a modest one. It was like carrying an articulated skeleton, more awkward than heavy. Piet took the man's other arm and we strode back the way we'd come.

"Do Chay get drunk, do you suppose?" I said.

"Let's hope so," Piet said. "We're a couple of fools to do this."

The few remaining pedestrians scurried along with their heads down. "If the Chay have a curfew . . ." Piet said, speaking my thought.

"The dome wall isn't very thick except where the door is," I replied. "I can cut a way out if the gate's closed. We can."

The tunnel was open. A Chay in a violet garment entered as we neared it. We passed him in the other direction. He called out in his language. We ignored him. I walked on my toes to approximate the mincing Chay gait until we were around the first bend in the gateway.

The sunlight outside was as faint as my hope of salvation. I drew a great breath through my filter and said, "So far, so good."

The crews of the airships on guard didn't challenge us. Some of the Chay were eating beneath their veils. The mat of vegetation rolled underfoot, absorbing high-frequency ground shocks and smoothing them into gentle swells.

A tall figure strode toward us from the shadow of a translucent brown dome. "I'll carry him, if you like," Stephen offered in a low voice.

"He's not heavy," Piet said.

We walked on. Stephen fell into step behind us and a little to Piet's left, where he could watch our front as well as guarding the rear. This final part of the route was over an organic causeway crossing scores of circular fields only ten or twenty meters in diameter.

The ground rumbled. A line of dust lifted in the distance, kicked into motion by the quake. The causeway swayed gently. Beneath us, plants waved their zebra-striped foliage at us.

"I hadn't expected that the two of you would do this

together," Stephen said in a pale voice. We hadn't spoken during the trek, but we could see that now there were no Chay between us and the edge of the mat.

"We weren't, Stephen," Piet said. "Jeremy made a foolish decision quite independently of me."

"I jumped out of a year's growth when he spoke to me," I said.

My voice sounded almost normal. That surprised me. I'd just learned that Stephen thought I'd supplanted him in Piet Ricimer's friendship. I'd known there were a lot of ways this jaunt could get me killed, but that one hadn't occurred to me.

"Tsk," said Stephen. "I don't lose control of myself, Jeremy."

I stumbled, then stared at him past the sunken form of the man we carried. "Do you read minds?" I demanded.

"No," said Piet. "But he's very smart."

"And a good shot," Stephen said with a throaty chuckle.

I laughed too. "Well, nobody sane would be doing this," I said aloud.

Though the mat felt like a closely woven carpet to walk on, it was actually several meters thick. The edge was a sagging tangle of stems, interlaced and spiky. There were no steps nor ramp off the island of vegetation; the Chay never walked on bare soil. The ground beyond bounced the way tremors shake the chest of a sleeping dog.

Stephen hopped down ahead of us. "Drop him to me," he said, raising his arms. "I'll take him from here."

I looked at Piet. He nodded. "On three," he said. "One, two, *three*—"

Together we tossed the moaning prisoner past the border. Stephen caught him, pivoting to lessen the shock to the Fed's weakened frame. The landscape heaved violently. Stephen dropped to his knees, but he didn't let his charge touch the ground.

My cape tore half away on brambles as I clambered down, baring my legs to the knee. There was no longer need for concealment, only speed.

Stephen strode onward with the Fed held lengthways across his shoulders like a yoke. Small shocks were incessant now. I had to pause at each pulse to keep from falling when the ground shifted height and angle.

"I should have allowed more time," I muttered. The *Oriflamme* was still out of sight beyond the rim of the bowl in which we'd landed.

"You were there before I was," Piet reminded me.

"Don't worry," Stephen said. "They aren't going to leave without us."

Piet laughed. "I suppose not," he agreed.

"I'd thought . . ." I said. "Maybe I'd just put him out of his misery. But I couldn't do that."

Stephen gave an icy chuckle. "We've brought him this far," he said. "We may as well take him the rest of the way."

We reached the lip of the bowl. The center of the depression was only twenty meters or so lower than the rolling plain around it, but that was still enough to conceal a starship. Sight of the *Oriflamme* warmed my heart like the smile of a beautiful woman.

A squeal similar to that of steam escaping from a huge boiler sounded behind us. It was more penetrating than a siren and so loud that it would be dangerous to humans any closer than we were.

I turned. Three cannon-armed dirigibles lifted above the city.

"Here," said Stephen, swinging his burden to Piet as if the Fed were a bundle of old clothes. "I'll watch the rear."

He locked a separate visor down to protect his eyes. A full helmet would have been obvious even under his cowl. Stephen parted his cape and threw the wings back over his shoulders, clearing his flashgun and the satchel of reloads slung on his left side.

I seized the Fed's right arm. "Run," Piet said, and we started running.

The *Oriflamme* was three hundred yards ahead of us. The ground had been still for a moment. Now On Chay shook itself violently. I stumbled but caught myself. The prisoner's legs swung like a pendulum to trip Piet and send him sprawling.

As Piet picked himself up, I glanced over my shoulder. The Chay dirigibles were a hundred meters high. Stephen walked sedately twenty meters behind us, watching our pursuers over his shoulder. The alarm still screamed from the Chay city.

Piet and I ran on. We'd taken only three strides when the bolt from a plasma cannon lit the soil immediately behind us into the heart of a sun.

The shock wave flung us apart. I smashed into a waist-high bush that might have been the ancestor of the mat on which the city was built. It clawed my chest and my legs as I tore myself free.

The cannon that had fired was a bright white glow in the bow of the center dirigible. Stephen swung his own weapon to his shoulder. A meters-long oval of soil blazed between him and us where the slug of plasma struck.

Stephen fired. The bolt from his laser was a needle of light against retinas already shocked by the plasma discharge.

The underside of a gas bag supporting the right-hand dirigible ruptured in a veil of thin blue flames. The Chay used hydrogen to support their craft. The fire spread with the deliberation of a flower opening, licking the sides of the bags adjacent to the one the bolt had ignited. The craft sank out of sight. The crew was trying desperately to land before the conflagration devoured them as well as their vehicle.

Piet stumbled forward alone with the prisoner. I grabbed the Fed's free arm and shouted, "D'ye have a gun?"

"Only a bar!" Piet said. "I didn't *want* to hurt the Chay, just free this poor wretch."

A laser pulse plowed glassy sparkles across the ground ahead of us. The bastards were shooting at us with the flashgun we'd given them that morning!

Stephen fired. A microsecond following the *snap* of his bolt, our world erupted in another plasma discharge.

The shock threw Piet and me sprawling, but this time the cannoneers were aiming at Stephen. Dirt fused into shrapnel and blew outward in a fireball which kicked Stephen sideways with his cape afire.

Fifty meters from us, Salomon or Guillermo lit the *Oriflamme*'s thrusters momentarily to check the fuel feeds. Bright exhaust puffed across the encampment, blowing down tents and disturbing the piles of Chay goods we were abandoning. Grit sprayed the back of my neck.

We had no secrets now. Stampfer would be screaming curses as he tried to rerig the Long Tom for combat, but that would take minutes with the *Oriflamme* laden as heavily as she was now.

I started toward Stephen. His flashgun had ignited a bag of the left-hand dirigible an instant before its plasma cannon fired. Blue hydrogen flames, hotter than Hell's hinges for all their seeming delicacy, wrapped the mid-line gas bag and involved the sides of the bags adjacent to it.

I'd seen Stephen shoot before. If he hadn't hit the Chay gunner, even at five hundred meters, it was because he didn't choose to kill even at this juncture.

The dirigible's crew dumped their remaining lift to escape. The platform dipped out of sight, taking with it the white glare of the plasma cannon's stellite bore. Only the center vehicle was still aloft; its cannon would be too hot to reload for some minutes yet.

Stephen rolled to his feet before I could reach him. His fingers inserted a charged battery in the butt of his flashgun and snapped the chamber closed over it before he tore away the blazing remnants of his cape. The rocky soil still glowed from the second plasma discharge, and a nearby bush was a torch of crackling orange flames.

I turned again. Piet was beside me. The Fed had managed to lift his torso off the ground. We snatched him up again and bolted for the *Oriflamme*'s ramp, dragging the fellow's feet. Stephen staggered behind us like a drunk running.

Twenty men spilled out of the *Oriflamme*'s main hatch. Those with rifles banged at the dirigible. Given the range and light conditions, I doubt any of them were more effective than I would have been.

"Get aboard!" Piet screamed. Kiley and Loomis each took the prisoner in one hand and one of us in the other, as if they were loading sacks of grain. "Don't shoot at the Chay, they're—"

The sky behind us exploded. A sheet of fire flashed as bright for a moment as if the primary had risen. I looked back. Bits of the last dirigible cascaded in a red-orange shower while hydrogen flames lifted like a curtain rising.

A Chay plasma cannon would cool very slowly because of its closed breech and the high specific heat of the metal from which it was cast. The gunners had tried to reload theirs too soon, and the round cooked off before it was seated. The thermonuclear explosion shattered the platform, rupturing all six hydrogen cells simultaneously.

Parts of the fiery debris were the bodies of the dirigible's crew.

We tumbled together in the forward hold. The ramp began to rise. Dole was shouting out the names of crewmen present. I hoped nobody'd gone so far from the hatch that he was still outside.

The *Oriflamme* lifted before the hatch sealed. Reflected exhaust was a saturated aurora crowning the upper seam.

Men of the support party disappeared up the ladderway in obedience to the bosun's snarled orders. I lay on my back, too wrung out to move or even rise. Piet bent over the rescued prisoner, so Piet at least was all right. Rakoscy ripped away Stephen's smoldering trousers with a scalpel.

I rolled over, but my stomach heaved and I could barely lift my face from the deck. Molten rock had burned savage ulcers into Stephen's calves above the boot tops. Bloody serum oozed as Rakoscy started to clean the wounds. Stephen rested on one elbow, holding his flashgun muzzle high so that the hot barrel wouldn't crack from contact with the cooler deck.

"Christ's blood, I shouldn't have gone back to the city!" I said. Piet was there to free the prisoner also, but that didn't change my responsibility. "Now I've made the Chay enemies for all their soldiers we killed."

"Dole," Piet ordered, "send this man up to the forward cabin and get some fluids in him. We don't want him to die on us now."

"We didn't kill anybody, Jeremy," Stephen said. He

wasn't looking at me. He wasn't looking at anything, though his eyes were open.

"Ferris and Lightbody!" Dole snapped. "You heard the captain. And a bath wouldn't hurt him, neither."

I managed to sit upright. I didn't speak. Maybe Stephen hadn't seen the third dirigible explode, hadn't seen the Chay bodies trace blazing pinwheels toward the ground . . .

"As for what the plasma cannon did . . ." Stephen continued in an emotionless voice. "I'll take responsibility for my own actions, Jeremy, but not for what others choose to do."

"Here, I've got your flashgun, Stephen," Piet said, gently lifting the weapon from his friend's hand.

"I've got enough company in my dreams as it is," Stephen said as our thrusters hammered us toward orbit.

NEW ERYX

Day 177

The portable kiln chuckled heavily on the far side of the *Oriflamme,* spraying a smooth coat of glass onto the cracks in the hull. The run from On Chay hadn't been unusually stressful, but the *Oriflamme* was no longer the vessel that had lifted in maiden glory from Venus.

The constant drizzle didn't affect the kiln, but I already felt it was going to drive me mad in much less time than the week Piet said we'd need to refit. "Does it ever stop, do you think?" I muttered. "The rain, I mean."

"The globe was almost entirely overcast when we orbited," Piet said mildly. He smoothed the throat closure of a Chay cape. Because of the confusion of loading, we had fifty-odd of the garments aboard. They'd turned out to be waterproof. "There's no pilotry data, of course."

The world he'd named New Eryx—after the factorial hold of Stephen's family on Venus—was uncharted, at least as far as the Federation database went. Piet and Salomon had extrapolated the star's location by examining the listed gradients and found a planet that was technically habitable. Even if it was driving me insane.

"I've never gotten used to a bright sky," Stephen said. "Too much Venus in my blood, I suppose. I like the overcast, and I don't mind the rain."

Lacaille, the prisoner we'd rescued, came by with a file of sailors who carried the trunk of one of the squat trees growing here in the dim warmth. They didn't notice the three of us sitting on a similar log.

Lacaille had been first officer on a ship in the Earth/Back Worlds trade, a year and a half's voyage in either direction for Federation vessels. Now he was talking cheerfully with men who'd helped kill a hundred like him the day we boarded *Our Lady of Montreal.*

"I'm glad we rescued him," I said. "He's a . . ."

"Human being?" Piet suggested. There was a smile in his voice.

"Whatever," I said. Trees like the one the men with Lacaille carried had a starchy pith that could be eaten— or converted to alcohol. Lacaille said identical trees were common on at least a score of worlds throughout the region. New Eryx wasn't on Federation charts; but some-body'd been here, and a very long time ago.

"He's fitting in well," Stephen said. "Of course, we saved his life. You did."

I snorted. "I can't think of a better way to make a man hate you than to do him a major favor," I said. "Most men. And damned near all women."

Stephen stood and stretched powerfully. He'd slung a repeating carbine over his right shoulder with the muzzle down to keep rain out of the bore. The only animal life we'd seen on New Eryx—if it was either animate or alive—was an occasional streamer of gossamer light which drifted among the trees. It could as easily be phos-phorescent gas, a will-o'-the-wisp.

"Think I'll go for a walk," Stephen said without looking back at us. He moved stiffly. The burns on his legs were far from healed.

"Do you have a transponder?" Piet warned.

"I'll be able to home on the kiln," Stephen called, already out of sight. "Low frequencies travel forever."

"Because he seems so strong," Piet said very softly, "it's easy to overlook the degree to which Stephen is in pain. I wish there was something I could do for him."

He turned and gave me a wan smile. "Besides pray, of course. But I wouldn't want him to know that."

"I think," I said carefully, "that Stephen's the bravest man I'll ever know." *Because he gets up in the morning after every screaming night, and he doesn't put a gun in his mouth;* but I didn't say that to Piet.

I cleared my throat. "What'll happen with the Chay, do you think?" I said to change the subject.

"There's enough universe for all of us, Chay and Molts and humans," Piet said. "And others we don't know about yet. I wouldn't worry about what happened at On Chay, if that's what you mean. There'll be worse from both sides after we've been in contact longer, but eventually I think we'll all pull together like strands in a cable. Separate, but in concert."

"Optimist," I said. Christ! I sounded bitter.

Piet laughed and put his hand over mine to squeeze it. "Oh, I'm not a wide-eyed dreamer, Jeremy," he said. "We'll fight the Chay, men will, just as we fight each other. And the Chay fight each other, I shouldn't wonder."

His tone sobered as he continued, "The real danger isn't race or religion, you know. It's the attitude that some men, some people—Molts or Chay or men from Earth—have to be controlled from above for their own good. One day I believe the Lord will help us defeat that idea. And the lion will lie down with the lamb, and there will be peace among the nations."

He gave me a smile; half impish, half that of a man worn to the edge of his strength, uncertain whether he'll be able to take one step more.

"Until then," Piet said, "it's as well that the Lord has men like Stephen on His side. Despite what it costs Stephen, and despite what it costs men like you and me."

The kiln chuckled, and I began to laugh as well. Anyone who heard me would have thought I was mad.

UNCHARTED WORLD

Day 232

We touched the surface of the ice with a slight forward way on instead of Piet's normal vertical approach. For this landing, he'd programmed a ball switch on his console to control the dorsal pairs of attitude jets. He rolled the ball upward as his other hand chopped the thrusters.

The three bands of attitude jets fired a half-second pulse. Their balanced lift shifted enough weight off the skids to let inertia drag us forward. Steam from the thrusters' last spurting exhaust before shutdown hung as eight linked columns in the cold air behind us as the *Oriflamme* ground to a halt.

Salomon unlatched his restraints and turned to face Piet's couch. "Sir," he said, "that was brilliant!"

I swung my feet down to the deck. Men with duties during landing had strapped themselves to their workstations. The rest of us were in hammocks on Piet's orders. No matter how good the pilot, a landing on an ice field could turn into disaster.

The reaction-mass tanks were almost empty, though. Our choice had been to load a nitrogen/chlorine mixture from the moon of one of the system's gas giants, or to risk the ice. The gases would have given irregular results in the plasma motors as well as contaminating the next tank or two of water. Nobody had really doubted Piet's ability to bring us down safely.

"Thank you, Mister Salomon," Piet said as he rose from his console. "I'm rather pleased with it myself."

He glanced at the screen, then touched the ramp control.

"At least we don't have to wait for the soil to cool," he added.

The center screen was set for a 360° view of our surroundings. There was nothing in that panorama but ice desert picked out by rare outcrops of rock. Irregular fissures streaked the surface like the *Oriflamme*'s hull crazing magnified. The ice crevices weren't dangerously wide. Most of those I could see were filled with refrozen meltwater, clearer and more bluish than the ice surrounding.

"I'll take out a security detail," Stephen said. He clasped a cape of some heavy natural fabric around his throat and cradled his flashgun. I didn't have warm clothing of my own. Maybe two or three of the Chay capes together . . .

"Security from what, Mister Gregg?" Salomon asked in surprise.

"We don't know," Piet said. "We haven't been here before."

I picked up my cutting bar and snatched a pair of capes as I followed Stephen aft. Crew members weren't going to argue the right of a gentleman to appropriate anything that wasn't nailed down. Besides, this wasn't a world that even men who'd been cooped up for seven weeks were in a hurry to step out onto.

The ground beneath the *Oriflamme* collapsed with the roar of breaking ice. We canted to port so violently that I was flung against the bulkhead. Men shouted. Gear we'd unshipped after our safe landing flew about the cabin.

The vessel rocked to a halt. I'd gotten halfway to my feet and now fell down again. The bow was up 15° and the deck yawed to port by almost that much. I was afraid to move for fear the least shift of weight would send the *Oriflamme* down a further precipice.

Piet stood and cycled the inner and outer airlock doors simultaneously from his console. "Mister Salomon, Guillermo," he said formally. "Stay at your controls, please. I'm going to take a look at our situation from outside."

Stephen and I followed Piet through the cockpit hatch. Elsewhere in the ship, men were sorting themselves out. Their comments sounded more disgruntled than afraid.

I was terribly afraid. I'd left the capes somewhere in the cabin, but I held my cutting bar in both hands as I jumped the two meters from the bottom of the hatch ladder to the ground.

The wind was as cold as I'd expected, but the bright sunlight was a surprise. Unless programmed to do otherwise, the *Oriflamme*'s screens optimized light levels on exterior visuals to Earth daytime. This time the real illumination was at least that bright.

The *Oriflamme*'s bow slanted into the air; her stern was below the surface of the shattered ice.

"We're on a tunnel," Stephen said, squatting to peer critically at the ground. "We collapsed part of the roof. Do you suppose the sunlight melts rivers under the ice sheet?"

"Can we take off again?" I asked. The wind was an excuse to shiver.

"Oh, yes," Piet said confidently. "Though we'll all have blisters before we dig her nozzles clear . . ."

LORD'S MERCY

Day 233

The sweat that soaked my tunic froze at the folds of the garment. The mittens I'd borrowed were too large. We'd reeved a rope through the tarp's grommets to serve as handles. It cut off circulation in my fingers even though there were four of us lifting the hundred-kilo loads of ice and scree away from the excavation.

At least we weren't going to be crushed if we slipped. Stampfer headed a crew of ten men, off-loading the broadside guns using sheerlegs and a ramp. If a cannon started to roll, it was kitty bar the door.

We reached the crevice fifty meters from the *Oriflamme*. Maher and Loomis at the front of the makeshift pallet were staggering. Dragging the tarp would have been a lot easier, but the gritty ice would have worn through the fabric in only a trip or two.

"Stand clear," I ordered. The sailors in front dropped their corners. Lightbody and I tried to lift ours to dump the load down the crevice. I could barely *hold* the weight; Lightbody had to manage the job for both of us. Next load Maher and Loomis would have that duty, but the load after that—

"About time for watch change, isn't it, Mister Moore?" Maher asked in a husky whisper.

"One more trip," I muttered. I didn't have any idea how long we'd been working. Blood tacked the mittens to my blistered palms, and I'd never been so cold in my life.

"Yes, *sir!*" said Maher.

242

We started back to the excavation. I could barely see, but the route was clear of major obstacles.

In the pit, men worked with shovels, levers, and cutting bars to clear the thruster nozzles. The whole plain was patterned with tunnels chewed through the ice by a creature several meters in diameter. It had moved back and forth like a farmer plowing a square field, each swing paralleling without touching the one laid down previously in the opposite direction.

I suppose Piet was right to name the world Lord's Mercy. If we'd set down exactly parallel to the tunnel pattern, the *Oriflamme* might have flipped upside down when the roof collapsed. On the other hand, if we'd landed perpendicular to the tunnels, we might never have known they were there.

The *Oriflamme*'s siren moaned briefly: it was time to change watches after all. We were working two hours on, two hours off. I didn't dare think about how much longer the process would have to go on.

"I'll take it," I said. The men dropped their corners of the emptied tarp; I started to drag it alone toward the excavation.

"Dear *God* I'm tired," I muttered. I didn't know I was speaking aloud.

"You got a right to be, sir," Lightbody called appreciatively as he and the others slanted away toward the hatch.

The common spacers were each of them stronger than me and knew tricks that made their effort more productive besides. I was helping, though, despite being by birth a gentleman. A year ago I'd have found that unthinkable.

"We'll take that now, sir," said Kiley, at the head of the team from the starboard watch replacing mine. I gave him the tarp. Our replacements looked stolid and ready to work, though I knew how little rest you could get in two hours on a ship being stripped of heavy fittings.

I thought of Thomas Hawtry. Would he and his clique have been out working beside the sailors if they'd made it this far on the voyage?

Stephen limped up the ramp from the excavation. He

hadn't been directing the work: Salomon did that. Stephen was moving blocks that only one man at a time could reach, and nobody else on the *Oriflamme* could budge.

I laughed aloud.

"Eh?" Stephen called.

"Just thinking," I said. Oh, yes, Hawtry would have obeyed any order that Stephen Gregg was on hand to enforce.

Stephen sat down on a stack of crates, loot from *Our Lady of Montreal;* for the moment, surplus weight. I sat beside him. "Are you feeling all right?" he asked.

His flashgun was in a nest of the crates, wrapped in a Chay cape to keep blowing ice crystals from forming a rime on it. I'd set my cutting bar there too when Salomon put me on the transport detail. Stephen wore his bar slung. He'd used it in the excavation, so refrozen ice caked the blade.

"I feel like the ship landed straight on top of me," I said. I heard Dole snarling orders to the men in the excavation. "You look a stage worse than that."

"I'll be all right," Stephen said. His voice was colorless with fatigue. "I'll drink something and go back down in a bit. They need me there."

He glanced at the closed forward airlock. Piet hadn't moved from his console since he'd organized the procedures. He even relieved himself in a bucket. If the *Oriflamme* started to shift again, it would be Piet's hand on the controls—balancing risk to the ship and risk to the men outside, where even exhaust from the attitude jets could be lethal.

"They'll need you when the port watch comes back on," I said forcefully. "Until then you're off duty."

I was marginal use to the expedition as a laborer, but I could damned well keep Stephen from burning himself out. Having a real purpose brought me back from the slough of exhaustion where I'd been wallowing the past hour.

Stephen shook his head, but he didn't argue. After a moment, he removed a canteen from the scarf in which he'd wrapped it to his waist cummerbund-fashion. Body heat kept it warm. He offered it to me. I took a swig and coughed. Slash that strong wasn't going to freeze at the temperatures out here in any case.

Stephen drank deep. "There's algae all through this ice," he said, tapping his toe on the ground. "That's why it looks green."

He offered me the canteen; I waved it away. Kiley's men stepped briskly toward the crevice with their first tarpaulin of broken ice. They'd be moving slower by the end of their watch . . .

"There was a lot of rock in some of the loads we brought out," I said. "We're not down to the soil, are we?"

Stephen laughed. He was loosening up, either because of me or the slash. "Frass," he said. "Worm shit. The tunnel was packed solid for a meter or so like a plug. If we'd landed just a little more to the side, the skid would've been on top of it and we might—"

Three hundred meters from where we sat, ice broke upward as if it were being scored by an invisible plow. I jumped to my feet and shouted, "Earthqua—"

It wasn't an earthquake. The head of a huge worm broke surface. The gray body, flattened and unsegmented, continued to stream out of the opening until the creature's whole forty-meter length writhed over the plain.

The transport crewmen dropped their tarp to stare. Diggers climbed from the excavation, summoned by shouts and the sound the worm made breaking out. Stephen had unwrapped his flashgun, but the worm didn't threaten us. It was undulating slightly away from the *Oriflamme*.

"I doubt it even has eyes," I said. "Maybe it hit a dike of rock that it's going to cross on the surface."

"All right, all right," Dole hectored. "You've had your show, now let's get this bitch ready to lift, shall we?"

Something dark green and multilegged climbed out of the opening the worm had made. This creature was about three meters long. Its mandibles projected another meter. They curved outward and back like calipers so that their points met squarely when the jaws closed.

The predator took one jump toward the worm it had been

pursuing through the tunnel, then noticed the *Oriflamme* and the men outside her. The beast turned, hunched on three of its six pairs of legs, and leaped toward us.

"Back to the ship!" Dole bellowed. The men of his watch turned as ordered and ran for the excavation.

I unhooked my cutting bar. The main hatch couldn't be closed because of ice wedged into the hinge. There'd seemed no need to clean it while the excavation was still in process . . .

A second beast like the first hopped from the tunnel; a third member of the pack was directly behind the second. The worm wriggled into the distance, perhaps unaware that its pursuers had suddenly turned away.

The leading predator covered ten meters at each hop. Because its legs worked in alternate pairs, the creature no more than touched the ice before it surged forward in another flat arc.

Stephen's flashgun *whack*ed. The bright sunlight of Lord's Mercy dimmed the weapon's normally dazzling side-scatter.

The bolt hit the predator's first thoracic segment and shattered the plate in a spray of creamy fluid. The head, the size of a man's torso, flipped onto the creature's back. It was attached by only a tag of chitin. The enormous mandibles scissored open and loudly shut.

A fourth hard-shelled predator crawled from the tunnel. The three living members of the pack hopped toward us, ignoring the thrashing corpse of their fellow.

Either the creatures thought the *Oriflamme* was prey, or they were reacting to us individual humans as interlopers in their hunting territory. Either way, their intentions weren't in doubt.

Stephen clicked up the wand that supported his laser's solar charger, then spread the shimmering film. He hadn't brought spare batteries with him this time.

"I'll draw them away from the hatch," I said. I began walking out onto the ice field. I didn't trust the footing enough to run.

Stephen set his flashgun on the crates with the panel tilted toward the sun. He left it there and strode parallel to me, triggering his cutting bar briefly to spin the blades clear of ice. The predators angled toward us, one after another.

Ice powdered beneath the creatures every time they sprang. The bottoms of their feet were chitin as jagged as the throat of a broken bottle. It gave the beasts good purchase on any surface soft enough for it to bite.

A band of single-lensed eyes gleamed from a ridge curving along the top and front of each predator's headplate. Though the individual eyes didn't move, the array gave the creatures vision over three-quarters of the arc around them.

The nearest creature focused on me. Its mandibles swung a further 30° open, like a hammer rising from half to full cock. Its deliberately short hop put me exactly ten meters away for the final spring.

I threw myself forward, holding my bar vertical in front of me. The predator slammed me down, but I was inside the circuit of its mandibles instead of being pierced through both sides when the tips clashed together.

The knife-edged chitin was thicker than that of a Molt's carapace, but my bar's ceramic teeth could have sheared hardened steel. The blade screamed as I cut the left mandible away. The creature stood above me, ripping my thighs with its front pairs of walking legs.

I held my bar in both hands and cut into the predator's head. Side-hinged jawplates cracked and crumbled on the howling bar.

The creature sprang back. White fluid gushed from the wound in its head. The creature's abdomen was slender and hairy, like that of a robber fly. It twisted around under the thorax as the creature went into convulsions.

Stephen was holding the second predator's mandibles away from his chest with both hands. The beast shook him violently, trying to break his grip. Stephen had dropped his cutting bar. It lay beneath the creature's scrabbling back legs.

I rose and slashed at the base of the right mandible, again using both hands. My feet slid out from under me. I caught the target in the belly of my blade, but my long draw stroke cut into the joint at a flatter angle than I'd intended.

Weakened chitin cracked like a rifle shot. Stephen tossed the mandible away. A ribbon of pale muscle fluttered behind it.

Stephen still had to hold the remaining mandible to prevent it from impaling him. I stood and fell down again immediately. I was slipping on my own blood and fluids from the creatures I'd butchered.

The last predator poised ten meters from Stephen for the leap that would cut him in half. A laser bolt stabbed through its open jaws. The flux lit the creature's exploding head through translucent flesh and chitin.

Piet flung down the flashgun. The solar panel that had recharged it quivered like a parachute. He raised a cutting bar. "Handweapons only!" Piet shouted as he charged the wounded predator. Twenty men carrying tools from the excavation followed him, slipping on the ice.

Stephen let the creature throw him free. It poised to leap onto him again, predator to the last. Piet sawed three of its legs apart in a single swipe. In a few seconds, all the left-side legs were broken or sheared. Men hacked with clumsy enthusiasm into the creature's thorax.

I stood up, then fell over again. Hall and Maher ran to me. Stephen crawled on all fours behind them.

"Rakoscy!" Piet shouted. "Rakoscy, get over here!"

"Christ's blood, his legs've been through a fucking meat grinder!" Dole cried. "Bring that fucking tarp over here! We need to get him into the fucking ship!"

"Mister Moore," somebody said with desperate earnestness. "Please let go of your bar. Please. I'm going to take it out of your hand."

The last voice I heard was Stephen's, snarling in a terrible singsong, "He'll be all *right* and I'll *kill* any whoreson who says he won't!"

WEYSTON

Day 249

Piet lifted the cutter's bow so that we wouldn't stall even though the thruster feed was barely cracked open. The display held a 30° down angle to our axis of flight, paralleling the barren ground a thousand meters below.

"You know . . ." Stephen said, one leg braced against the sidewall and his left hand gripping the central bench on which the two of us sat. "You're going to feel really silly if you have to explain how you got yourself killed on a sandhill like this."

"Tsk, don't call it a sandhill," Piet said cheerfully. "The name honors your uncle, remember. Besides, it's not a stunt, I saw something when I brought the *Oriflamme* in."

"And why shouldn't the officers go on a picnic?" I said. My legs were straight out, but I was trying my best not to let them take any stress. Though the shins were healing well, they hurt as if they were being boiled in oil if I moved the wrong way.

Lightbody's lips moved slowly as he watched the screen from the jump seat and separate attitude controls behind Piet's couch. I think he was murmuring a prayer. From Lightbody, that would be normal behavior rather than a comment on the way the cutter wallowed through the air. I doubt it occurred to Lightbody to worry when Piet was the pilot.

"Found him!" Piet said./"Eleven o'clock!" Stephen said, pointing./"There it is!" I said.

Metallic wreckage was strewn along hundreds of meters of sandy waste, though the ship at the end of the trail looked healthy enough. It was a cheaply-constructed freighter of the sort the Feds built in the Back Worlds to handle local trade.

"They came in on automated approach," Piet guessed aloud. He boosted thrust and gimballed the nozzle nearly vertical. "Hit a tooth of rock, ripped their motors out, and there they sit since. Which may be fifty years."

The cutter dropped like an elevator whose brakes had failed. Piet made a tight one-eighty around the crash site, killing our momentum so that he didn't have to overfly for the horizontal approach normal with a single-engined cutter.

"Not very long," Stephen said. "Light alloys wouldn't be so bright if they'd been open to the atmosphere any length of time."

We crossed the trail of torn metal, then blew out a doughnut of dust as we touched down within twenty meters of the freighter's side hatch.

Piet turned his head and smiled slightly. "If I don't keep my hand in, Stephen," he said, "I won't be able to do it when I have to."

"You could fly a cutter blindfold on your deathbed, Captain," Lightbody said. "Begging your pardon."

Lightbody squeezed by to undog the hatch. I could have done that job if anybody's life had depended on it, but none of us still aboard the *Oriflamme* needed to prove things to our shipmates.

Weyston's air was thin and sulfurous, unpleasant without being dangerous. The system was charted but unoccupied. Federation cartographers hadn't even bothered to give the place a name, since there was nothing beyond the planet's presence to bring a vessel here.

We needed to reseal the *Oriflamme*'s hull; this was the suitable location closest to Lord's Mercy. We had sufficient reaction mass for some while yet—which was a good thing, because observation supported the note in the pilotry data that the planet had no free water whatever.

I stood deliberately as Lightbody swung himself onto the coaming of the dorsal hatch. "Give you a hand, sir?" he asked, reaching toward me.

"I'm not proud," I said. I clasped the spacer's shoulders and paused, steeling myself to flex my legs and jump.

"I've got him, Lightbody," Stephen said. He clasped me below the rib cage and lifted me like a mannequin onto the cutter's hull.

I laughed. "All right," I said, "you've convinced me I'm bloody useless and a burden to you all. Can we look over the wreck, now?"

Stephen handed Lightbody a rifle and his own flashgun as I slid down the curve of the hull to the ground. This flight was basically recreation, but there was no place on the Back Worlds where we were safe. By now, it didn't strike any of us as silly to go armed on a lifeless world.

There was movement inside the wreck.

"Hello the ship!" Piet called. No one responded. I powered my cutting bar.

A man in gray trousers and a blue tunic hopped from the hatch. Stephen presented his flashgun. "No!" the stranger shouted. "No, you can't shoot me!"

"We don't have any intention of shooting you, sir," Piet said. He crooked his left index finger to call the man closer. The fellow had a sickly look, but he was too plump to be ill fed. "Are there any other survivors?"

"No one, I'm the only one," the Fed said.

I walked around him at two arms' length. I wouldn't have trusted this fellow if he'd said there was a lot of sand hereabouts. He'd been relieving himself out the hatch; and almost out the hatch.

"Anybody aboard?" I called, waiting for my eyes to adapt to the dim interior. The power plant was dead, and with it the cabin lights.

The chamber stank. Blood and brains splashed the forward bulkhead above the simple control station.

I jerked my head back. Piet and Stephen were behind me. The castaway squatted beneath the muzzle of Lightbody's rifle.

"His name's McMaster," Stephen said, nodding toward the Fed. "He was the engineer. Doesn't seem as happy to be rescued as you'd think."

"Let's check the other side," I said, walking toward the freighter's bow. "Is there any cargo?"

The hatch from the cabin to the rear hold had warped in the crash, though there was probably access through the ship's ripped underside.

"Windmills," Stephen said. "They lost the starboard thrusters maybe a month ago on a run from Clapperton to Bumphrey. This was the nearest place to clear the feed line, but the AI wasn't up to the job of landing."

Piet said, "Two Molts and the human captain were killed in the crash. I don't think McMaster is completely . . ."

"Oh, he's crazy," Stephen said. "But he started out a snake or I miss my bet."

The graves were three shallow mounds in the lee of the wreck. I prodded with the blade of my cutting bar and struck mauve chitin ten centimeters below the surface. Stephen dragged the corpse of a Molt out by its arm. The creature's plastron was orange and had a spongy look.

"She hit the bulkhead during the crash," Piet said. "I don't think we need disturb the others."

Together we scooped tawny sand over the corpse again. I used my bar, the others their boots. "Decided where the next landfall is going to be?" Stephen asked.

"Clapperton," said Piet. "There's a sizable Fed colony there, but Lacaille and the pilotry data agree that only one of the major land masses is inhabited. We can fill with water and maybe hunt meat besides."

We had the Molt covered as well as it had been when we started. Stephen stepped back from the grave and surveyed the landscape. "What a hell of place to be buried," he said.

"It's only the body," Piet said in mild reproof.

We all felt it, though. This was a world with no life of its own, that would never have life of its own. Being buried here was like being dumped from the airlock between stars.

Stephen frowned. He stepped to the third mound and pulled something from the sand.

I squinted. "A screwdriver?" I said.

Stephen held it out to us. "That's what it was made for," he said softly.

The shaft was stained brown. Sand clung to the dried fluid. Not blood, but very possibly the copper-based ichor that filled a Molt's circulatory system.

Stephen wagged the tool delicately in the direction of the castaway on the other side of the wreck. "Didn't trust there'd be enough food to last till . . . whenever, do you think?" he said.

"The crash unhinged him," Piet said.

Stephen raised an eyebrow. Piet grimaced and said, "We can't leave a human being here!"

Stephen flung the screwdriver far out in the sand. "Then let's get back," he said mildly. "Only—let's not name this place for Uncle Ben, shall we? He won't know, but I do."

CLAPPERTON

Day 290

Air heavy with moisture and rotting vegetation rolled into the hold as the ramp lowered. Though we'd landed after sunrise so that the glare of our thrusters wouldn't alert distant Fed watchers, the thick canopy filtered light to a green as deep as that reaching the bottom of a pond. Treetops met even over the river by which we'd entered the forest.

We piled out of the vessel. Our exhaust had burned the leaf mold to charcoal traceries which disintegrated when a boot touched them. Black ash spurted to mix with steam and the gray smoke of tree bark so wet that it only smoldered from a bath of plasma.

There were twenty of us to start, though another crew would lay hoses to the river as soon as we were out of the way. Six of the men were armed. The rest of us carried tools and the net which, once we'd hung it properly, would camouflage the *Oriflamme*'s track. Piet had nosed us between a pair of giant trees and almost completely into the forest, but the starship's stern could be seen from an autogyro following the river at canopy height.

"Good *Christ!*" said Stampfer, pointing his rifle with both hands. "What d'ye call *that!*"

Piet had taken the *Oriflamme* straight over the bank at a point that the river kinked. Bobbing belly-up in the slight current at the bend was a creature twenty meters long. Its four short legs stuck up stiffly; the toes were webbed, but the forefeet bore cruel claws as well.

The smooth skin of the creature's back was speckled black over several shades of brown, but the originally white underside now blushed pink. We'd boiled the monster as we coasted over it.

Its head was broad and several meters long. The skull floated lower than the creature's distended belly, but I could see that the long, conical teeth would interlock when the jaws were closed.

"The big predators here live in the water," Lacaille said. He gestured with his three-hooked grapnel. He and I were one of the two teams who'd climb to anchor the top of the net. "That's good that that one's dead. It'll be a month before another big one moves into the territory."

The Federation officer chewed his lower lip. "I didn't know they got *that* big," he said. "They don't around North Island base."

"Let's go, you lazy scuts!" Dole ordered. "Quicker we get this hung, the likelier you are to get home and sling your neighbor off the top of your wife!"

Strictly speaking, the bosun was talking to the men dragging the net out of the hold. Everybody knew that the likely delay was in getting lift points twenty meters up the tree boles, though.

I waved acknowledgment and walked back to the left-hand tree of the pair at the *Oriflamme*'s stern. Stampfer started with us. Stephen called, "I'll keep an eye on this end," and waved the master gunner toward the center of the track.

"Are there many dangerous animals?" I asked Lacaille with a nod toward the predator floating in the shallows. The corpse had bloated noticeably since I'd first seen it.

Unlike McMaster, Lacaille had become a willing shipmate. He was a real ship's officer, not a noble who'd had authority but no skill. I think he was glad to serve with a company of spacers as good as Piet Ricimer's. There wasn't a better crew in the human universe.

"No big carnivores on land," Lacaille said. "There's dangerous animals, sure, and some of the plants are poison. The garrison burns back the jungle for a hundred meters around the base."

He shrugged. "A soldier got bitten on the foot and had his leg swell up till they cut it off. But it could've been a thorn instead of a sting. Liquor's killed twenty-odd that I know of."

We'd told both Federation officers that we'd drop them with their own people when we could. I don't think that affected either Lacaille's helpfulness or McMaster's surly silence. People's dispositions were more important than their attitudes.

The tree Lacaille and I were to climb had shaggy buttress roots that spread its diameter at the base to almost twenty meters. The three of us walked carefully to the far side of the bole where plasma hadn't scoured the hairy surface.

I'd insisted on being one of the climbers, because I needed to convince myself that my shins had healed properly. Maybe Lacaille had something similar in mind. The Chay had certainly handled him worse than the bug on Lord's Mercy had done me.

The *Oriflamme* didn't carry climbing irons, so Lacaille and I wore boots with sharpened hobnails. This tree's shaggy bark and the stilt roots of the giant on the other side of the *Oriflamme* ought to make it easy to get to the height required.

"Trade me for a moment," Stephen said. I didn't know what he meant till he handed me the flashgun and slipped the grapnel and coil from my belt. Stephen stepped back and swung the hooks on a short length of line.

The trunk started to branch just above where the top of the buttress roots faired into the main trunk. Leaves fanned toward the light seeping through the thin canopy over the watercourse. The lower limbs were stubby and not particularly thick, but they'd support a man's weight. Our exhaust had shriveled some of the foliage.

Stephen loosed the grapnel at the top of its arc. The triple hook wobbled upward, stabilized by the line it drew. It curved between the trunk and the upraised tip of a limb. As the line fell back, it caught on rough bark and looped twice around the branch. The hooks swung nervously beneath the limb with the last of their momentum. If the line started to slip under my weight, the points should lift and bite into the wood.

I returned Stephen's flashgun. I hadn't brought a weapon; my cutting bar would just have been in the way as I climbed. The weight of the cassegrain laser felt good. Among the forest sounds were a series of shrill screams that made me think of something huge, toothy, and far more active than the predator now bloating in the river.

Lacaille started up the line ahead of me. *Hey,* I thought, but I didn't say anything. He ought to be leading, because he still had a grapnel to toss to a higher branch.

I followed the Fed, walking up the top of a buttress root like a steep ramp. The 8-mm line was too thin for comfortable climbing. Lacaille and I wore gloves with the fingers cut off, but my palms hurt like blazes whenever I let my weight ride on the line. I used my hands only to steady myself. Fine for the first stage, but there were another ten meters to go.

Lacaille got out of my way by stepping to the next limb, 15° clockwise around the tree bole though only slightly higher. He tried to spin his grapnel the way Stephen had. The hooks snagged my branch.

"Hey!" I shouted—more sharply than I'd have done if I hadn't still been pissed at Lacaille taking the lead. Besides, I was breathing hard from the exertion, and my shins prickled as though crabs were dancing on them.

"Sir!" Lacaille said. "I'm sorry!"

He slacked his line. Weight pulled the hooks loose for Lacaille to haul back to his hand.

"Look," I said, "neither of us is"—I shrugged—"an expert. Just toss the damned thing over a branch a couple meters up. That's all I want to climb at a time on the straight trunk anyway."

I crossed my legs beneath the branch as I worked my own grapnel loose for the next stage. The line had cut a powdery russet groove in the bark. Sticky dust gummed both the line and my fingers.

Lacaille tossed his grapnel, this time with a straight overarm motion. More our speed. He set his hooks in a limb not far above him and scrambled up, panting loudly.

That was a three-meter gain, a perfectly respectable portion of the ten we needed.

I stuck the grapnel's shaft under my belt and shifted to the branch Lacaille had just vacated. My line dangled behind me like a long tail. I paused to brush sweat out of my eyes. I saw movement to the side.

Three creatures the size of bandy-legged goats peered down at me from a limb of an adjacent tree. Two were mottled gray; the third was slightly larger. It had a black torso and a scarlet ruff that it spread as I stared at it.

"Holy Jesus!" I shouted. I snatched at my grapnel, the closest thing to a weapon I was carrying.

The trio sprang up the trunk of their tree like giant squirrels. They vanished into the canopy in a handful of jumps. Divots ripped from the bark by their hooked claws pattered down behind them.

"Are you all right?" Stephen shouted. "What's happened?"

"We're all right!" I shouted back. I couldn't see the forest floor, so Stephen couldn't see us, much less the creatures that had startled me. "Local herbivores is all."

That was more than I knew for certain, but I didn't want Stephen to worry.

"There's something sticky here," Lacaille warned. "I think it's from the tree. Sap."

I peered upward to make certain that Lacaille was out of the way before I started to climb. This portion of the trunk was covered with a band of some mossy epiphyte. Tiny pink florets picked out the dark green foliage.

Something was pressed against the bark a few degrees to Lacaille's left and slightly above him. I doubted that he could see the thing from his angle. It eased toward him.

"Freeze, Lacaille!" I shouted.

"What?" he said. "What?" His voice rose an octave on the second syllable. He didn't move, though.

The thing was a dull golden color with blotches of brown. It could almost have been a trickle of sap like the one Lacaille had noticed, thirty million years short of hardening to amber.

Almost. It had been creeping sideways across the bark's

corrugations. The creature stopped when Lacaille obeyed my order to freeze.

I drew the grapnel from my belt, then paid the line out in four one-meter loops.

"What's happening, Moore?" Lacaille said. He had his voice under control. He was trying to look down at me without moving anything but his eyes.

"Not yet," I whispered. Lacaille couldn't hear me. I was speaking to calm myself.

I lofted the grapnel with an underhand toss. It sailed as intended through empty air past the creature.

The thing struck like a trap snapping. Its head clanged against the grapnel's slowly rotating hooks and flung them outward—with the creature attached.

"Watch out below!" I screamed. The snakelike thing streamed past me, dragged by the weight of steel where it had expected flesh. I let go of the line.

The creature was a good ten meters long, but nowhere thicker than my calf. Tiny hooked legs, hundreds of them, waggled from its underside.

I heard the ensemble crash into the ground. A cutting bar whined. The blades *whang*ed momentarily on metal, probably the grapnel's shaft.

"What was it?" Lacaille demanded. "Can I move now? What *was* it?"

"It was a snake," I said. "I think it was a snake."

I wiped my eyes again. "Stephen?" I called. "Tell them to hitch the hawser to Lacaille's line where it is, will you? We've gone as high in this tree as *I* want to go."

"Roger," Stephen said, his voice attenuated by distance and the way the foliage absorbed sound.

I looked at Lacaille. "Yeah, it's all right now," I said. "I hope to God it's all right."

I stepped away from the 2-cm hawser so that Dole and his crew could begin lifting the camouflage net. Lacaille knelt beside the creature a few meters out from the cone of roots. The snake had slid the last stage of its trip to Stephen's cutting bar.

Stephen looked from the creature to me. "Don't touch

the damned thing unless you want to get clawed by those feet," he said. "*I* think it's dead, but it has a difference of opinion."

I squatted beside Lacaille. The creature's skull was almost a meter long. Stephen had cut it crosswise, then severed the back half from the long body—which was still twitching, as Stephen had implied.

"I should've taken a bar with me," I said. "I was crazy not to."

"This worked pretty well," Stephen said. "I don't see how you could improve on the results."

He tilted up the front of the creature's skull on his bar. A bony tongue protruded a handbreadth from the circular mouth. The tongue's tip had broken off on the grapnel. The sides of the hollow shaft were barbed and slotted. The tongue was designed to rip deep through the flesh of the creatures it struck, then to suck them dry.

"Wonder if it injects digestive fluids?" Stephen mused aloud.

Lacaille stood, then doubled up and began to vomit.

"Get him back to the ship," Stephen suggested quietly. "Guillermo can find some slash if you can't."

"I can find something," I said. "Come on, Lacaille. I need a drink, and out here is no damned place for anybody who feels as queasy as I do right now."

"I'm all right," Lacaille muttered as he cautiously straightened. He wiped his mouth with the back of his hand before he turned to face me.

"Any one you walk away from, hey?" he said with an embarrassed smile. "I suppose I can walk."

He could. We could. Dole's men were raising one end of the net by the hawser Lacaille and I had drawn into the branches on Lacaille's grapnel line. We'd wired a pulley to the limb as well. It wasn't strictly necessary, but it made the lift a lot easier for the men below.

I was only half kidding about needing a drink. Since the snake stalked us, I'd trembled while we continued to work high in the tree. Seeing the creature close up made the fear worse.

We stepped over the rolled net. The bosun was arguing

precedence with Salomon, whose men were laying hoses
to the river. Both men paused and nodded to us. Piet,
examining the tree that would anchor the other end of
the camouflage, waved cheerfully.

"You saved my life," Lacaille said in a low voice.

"That fellow might have decided I looked juicier," I
said. "He wasn't anybody's friend."

We had to pick our way carefully across the burned
patch surrounding the *Oriflamme*. Dense roots withstood
the gush of plasma and lurked within the ash, ready to
turn an ankle or worse.

"Look," Lacaille said. He stopped and waited for me to
meet his eyes. "I won't fight my own people."

"Nobody asked you to," I said. "Christ's blood, d'ye
think we can't do our own fighting?"

Lacaille grimaced and shook his head in frustration.
"Look," he said. "McMaster? You should have left him
where he was."

"You're not the first to think that," I said slowly. I
glanced around. I didn't know where McMaster was. I
couldn't find him outside nor among the party shifting
gear in the hold ten meters from where Lacaille and I
stood. "Piet's . . . soft-hearted, though."

"Tonight," Lacaille said. "When shortwave propagation's good, McMaster's going to signal the North Island
base on the backup commo suite aft."

Salomon's men joined Dole's on the 2-cm hawser. It
would be easier to slide the hoses under the hem of the
camouflage net than to lift the roll, so the teams were
combining to do the jobs in sequence.

"He told you?" I asked without emphasis.

"McMaster *brags* about things that nobody would
admit!" Lacaille said. "Not just this, terrible things! He's
a terrible man."

Piet walked toward us, probably wondering what we
were discussing.

"Yeah, I can believe that," I said. It wasn't surprising
that a man who'd been swimming for years in the filthy
slough of President Pleyal's colonies would be unable to
recognize that Lacaille might have feelings of gratitude

toward those who'd saved his life. Far more surprising that Lacaille's personal decency *had* survived.

"Ah . . ." I added. "Don't say anything to Piet, though. All right?"

Lacaille nodded in relief. "You'll tell Mister Gregg?" he asked.

"Stephen's got enough on his conscience as it is," I said, putting on a bright smile to greet Piet. "I'll see that this one's handled."

We sat at trestle tables sawn from the local wood with cutting bars. The boards' surface was just as rough as you'd imagine. The afternoon's downpour had driven the ash into the clay substrate in a butter-slick amalgam. We'd spread cover sheets over us, but the rare chinks of evening sky we could see were clear.

"You know . . ." said Dole with a mouth full of tree-hopper, maybe one of the trio that'd startled me. It had peeked down at the commotion, this time where Stephen could see it. "That fellow out in the lake might not have steaked out so bad."

"Not for me, thanks," I said, thinking about the monster's teeth. At the other table they were eating a ragout of the local "snake." I didn't even look in that direction.

"Precooked, even," Piet said with a grin. He looked as relaxed as I'd seen him in a long while. We'd have known by now if a Fed on Clapperton's far side had chanced to notice us sliding into the forest. "Well, we had other things on our mind."

Winger, the chief motor mechanic, said, "I don't like the way the main engine nozzles are getting, sir. We've switched out the spares aboard, and they're getting pretty worn themself."

"Umm," Salomon said. "They wouldn't pass a bottomry inspection at Betaport, but I don't think we need to worry as yet."

An animal screamed in the near distance. It was probably harmless—and the "snake" couldn't have made a sound if it had wanted to—but my shoulders shrank together every time I heard the thing.

The local equivalent of insects swarmed around the hooded lights we'd spiked to tree boles to show us our dinner. The creatures were four-legged. They varied in size from midges to globs with bodies the size of a baseball and wingspans to match. They didn't attack us because of our unfamiliar biochemistry, but I frequently felt a crunch of chitin as I chewed my meat.

"The nearest place that'd stock thruster nozzles is Riel," Lacaille volunteered without looking up from his meal. "But the port gets a lot of traffic, and it's defended."

"Real defenses?" Dole asked, glancing over at Lacaille. "Or a couple guns and nobody manning them?"

"I'd sure rather have warehouse stock than cannibalize a ship," Winger said. "It's a bitch of a job unscrewing burned-in nozzles without cracking them."

The little receiver in my tunic pocket squawked, "Calling North Island Command! Calling North Island Command! This is—"

Everyone in hearing jumped up. The opposite bench tilted and thumped the ground. Lacaille's mouth opened in horror.

"What in the name of Christ is that?" Stephen asked softly. He wasn't looking at me. His eyes roved the forest, and the flashgun was cradled in his arms.

"It's all right!" I said. "Sit down, everybody. It's all right."

"Yes, sit down," Piet decided aloud. He bent to help raise the fallen bench, holding his carbine at the balance so that the muzzle pointed straight up. He'd jacked a round into the chamber, and it would take a moment to clear the weapon safely.

He sat again and looked at me. "*What* is all right?"

"—Venusian pirate ship full of treasure," my pocket crackled. I took the receiver out so that everyone could see it. "Plot this signal and home on it. I don't have the coordinates, but it's somewhere in the opposite hemisphere from the base. Calling—"

I switched the unit off. Dole said, "McMaster!" and stood up again.

"Don't!" I said.

Dole stepped over the bench, unhooking his cutting bar.

"Sit down, Mister Dole," Piet said, his voice ringing like a drop forge.

The bosun's face scrunched up, but he obeyed.

"And the rest of you," Piet said, waving to the men at the other table and the far end of ours. They'd noticed the commotion, though they couldn't tell what was going on.

"I fiddled the backup transmitter," I said in a voice that the immediate circle could hear. "No matter what the dial reads, it's transmitting a quarter-watt UHF. He could be heard farther away if he stood in the hatch and shouted."

Stephen made a sound. I thought he was choking. It was the start of a laugh. His guffaws bellowed out into the night, arousing screamers in the trees around us. After a moment, Stephen got the sound under control, but he still quivered with suppressed paroxysms.

"We still have to do something about the situation, though," Piet said softly.

"No," I said. From the corner of my eye, I noticed a shadow slip from the main hatch and vanish into the forest. "The situation has just taken care of itself."

A smile of sorts played with Piet's mouth. "Yes," he said. "I see what you mean. He doesn't want to be aboard the target his friends are going to blast."

He turned his head. "Mister Dole," he said crisply, "we'll have the net down at first light. The voyage isn't over, and we may need it another time. I expect to lift fifteen minutes after you start the task."

"Aye aye, *sir!*" the bosun said.

"I suppose it'll be weeks before another big gulper takes over this stretch of the river," Lacaille said.

"Maybe not so long," Stephen said. He got up and stretched the big muscles of his shoulders. "And anyway, I'm sure there are more snakes and suchlike folk than the one you and Jeremy met."

He chuckled again. The sound was as bleak as the ice of Lord's Mercy.

ABOVE RIEL

Day 311

Guillermo's screen showed the world we circled in a ninety-four-minute orbit. The central display was a frozen schematic of Corpus Christi, Riel's spaceport, based on pilotry data, Lacaille's recollections, and images recorded during the *Oriflamme*'s first pass overhead.

"There are fourteen vessels in port that probably have thruster nozzles of the correct size," Piet said, sitting on the edge of his couch. Thirty of us were crowded into the forward compartment, and his words echoed on the tannoys to the remainder of the crew. "Besides those, there's a number of smaller vessels on the ground and a very large freighter in orbit."

"Freighter or not . . ." Kiley murmured, "anything that weighs two kilotonnes gets *my* respect."

"Two of the ships are water buffalos without transit capability," Piet continued. "We'll have to carry our prize off to an uninhabited system to strip it, so they're out. Likewise, a number of the ships are probably unserviceable, though we don't know which ones for sure. Finally, there's a Federation warship in port, the *Yellowknife*."

There was a low murmur from the men. Somebody said, "*Shit,*" in a quiet but distinct voice.

"Yes," Piet said. "That complicates matters, but two of our nozzles have cracked. Maybe they just got knocked around when we tipped on Lord's Mercy, but it's equally possible that the other six are about to fail the same way. This will be risky, but we have no options."

"Hey, sir," Stampfer said. "We'll fucking handle it. You just tell us what to do."

That wasn't bravado. Stampfer and everybody else in the *Oriflamme*'s crew believed that Captain Ricimer would bring us all home somehow. Emotionally, I believed that myself. Intellectually, I knew that if I hadn't stumbled as I ran toward the *Montreal,* the Fed plasma bolt would have killed me instead of the man a step behind.

"For ease of drawing reaction mass," Piet said, "the port is in the bend of a river, the Sangre Christi. It's a swampy area and unhealthy, since Terran mosquitoes and mosquito-borne diseases have colonized the planet along with humans."

Men glanced at one another in puzzlement. Malaria didn't seem a serious risk compared to the others we'd be chancing on a raid like this.

A slight smile played across Piet's mouth. "As a result," he explained, "the governor and officers of the garrison and ships in port stay in houses on the bluffs overlooking the river."

His index finger swept an arc across the display. "That should slow down any response to our actions."

Piet sobered. "I'll take the cutter down at twilight, that's at midnight ship's time, with fourteen men aboard," he said. "A party of six will secure the Commandatura and port control—they're together."

"I'll take care of that," Stephen said.

Piet's grin flickered again. "Yes," he said. "I hoped you would."

He looked at me. "There are four gunpits with laser arrays. The fire control system and the town's general communications both need to be disabled. You can handle that, Jeremy?"

"Sure," I said. The task was a little more complicated than it might have sounded to a layman. You have to identify the critical parts in order to cut off their power, blow them up, whatever. But I shouldn't have any difficulty.

"Or Guillermo could," Stephen said, scratching the side of his neck and looking at nothing in particular.

"*I'll* do it!" I said.

"I'll need Guillermo for the other phase of the operation," Piet said. "I don't expect any trouble about landing a cutter without authorization, but I personally can't go around asking which of the ships ready to lift have thruster nozzles in good condition. Guillermo can speak to Molt laborers and identify a suitable prize without arousing suspicion."

He glanced down at the navigator in the couch to his left. "Mister Salomon, you'll command the *Oriflamme* in my absence. We'll rendezvous, the *Oriflamme* and my prize, at St. Lawrence. I don't believe there's any reason to proceed there in company."

Salomon nodded. Men were tugging their beards, rubbing palms together—a score of individual tricks for dealing with tension. I kept clearing my throat, trying not to make a noise that would disturb the others.

"All right," said Piet. "Stephen, you and I will get together and decide on personnel. When we've done that, then we'll go over tactics. I'd like the rest of you to vacate the compartment for a time, please, so that we can organize the raid."

His eyes met mine. "Not the people already told off for the mission, of course."

Crewmen drifted toward the passageway aft. Dole and Stampfer waited grimly. They obviously weren't about to leave unless they got a direct personal order to do so. I doubted Piet would push the point. You want your most aggressive men on a project like this.·

I shoved off carefully and caught the stanchion to which Stephen was anchored. "Didn't want me along?" I said very softly.

Stephen shrugged. He didn't look at me. "I don't much want Piet risking his neck by leading this one," he said in a similar voice. "But there wasn't a prayer he'd listen if I said that."

He gave me a broad smile. "I'm responsible for you, Jeremy," he said in a bantering tone. "I brought you aboard."

"Then remember I'm a member of this crew," I said. "And a gentleman of Venus!"

The compartment had cleared except for the officers and two petty officers. "Stephen?" Piet called. "Jeremy?"

"Oh, I won't forget that, Jeremy," Stephen said. He directed himself with an index finger toward the consoles at the bow. "Nor, I think, will our enemies, hey?"

RIEL

Day 312

Our outer hull pinged as it slowly cooled. The pilot's screen was coarse-grained and only hinted at our surroundings. Besides, with fourteen men packed onto a cutter, there were too many heads and torsos in the way for me to see more than an occasional corner.

"Hell," said Winger. "With all the chips we're carrying, it'd be easier to buy the engine hardware."

"This'll be easy enough," Stephen replied in his chilling singsong. "It always has been in the past. Dead easy."

No one spoke for a moment. Our harsh breathing sounded like static on a radio tuned to open air.

"All right," Piet said decisively. "Commandatura team and Guillermo first, we others wait five minutes. I don't want anyone to notice just how full this cutter is."

Dole and Lightbody undogged the hatch, though the bosun would go with Piet to capture the ship that Guillermo picked. Fourteen men weren't many to operate a starship of a hundred tonnes or more, so Piet had picked the most efficient members of the *Oriflamme*'s crew.

Stephen was the first out, jumping lightly to the ground. Under ordinary circumstances, Stephen seemed a little clumsy. Now, and at previous times like this, he moved with a dancer's grace.

"Hand me the crate," he ordered bleakly. Lightbody and I, seated on the hatch coaming, swung the chest of weapons into Stephen's waiting hands. He didn't appear to notice weight that had made the pair of us grunt.

I hadn't missed anything for being unable to see the vision screen. Piet had brought us down at the north end of the field, some distance from the river. The cutter was tucked in between a freighter that was either deadlined or abandoned—several of her hull plates were missing—and a water buffalo, a tanker that hauled air and reaction mass to orbiting vessels too large or ill-found to land normally.

Neither of our neighbors was lighted. There was no likelihood of anybody noticing that the cutter's sheen was that of hard-used ceramic, not metal.

We hopped down from the hatch. Guillermo was the last out. A Molt who disembarked from a Fed vessel ahead of humans would be whipped to death for his presumption.

Guillermo skulked away from us, heading toward a large freighter in the second row back from the river. A gang of Molt laborers was carrying cargo aboard from high-wheeled hand trucks.

"Take it easy, stay together, and ignore the other people out on the streets tonight," Stephen said. His eyes passed over us, but they didn't appear to light anywhere. "If we do our jobs, there won't be a bit of excitement. That's the way we want it."

A dead man wouldn't have spoken with less emotion.

We set off toward the Commandatura, three short blocks beyond the inland side of the field. Kiley and Lightbody carried the packing crate. We wore a mix of garments picked up on Federation planets, exactly like the crews of ships in Back Worlds' trade. None of the men or Molts on errands about nearby vessels gave us more than a passing glance.

The port was fenced off from the town of Corpus Christi. The pivoting gate was open, and the Molts in the guard shack were eating some stringy form of rations. Nearby was a gunpit. The multitube laser there was also crewed by Molts.

The street cutting the chord of the riverbend was paved. We sprinted to avoid a truck whose howling turbogenerator powered hub-center electric motors in all six wheels.

A Molt drove the vehicle, but he was obviously under the direction of the man on the seat beside him. The human waved a bottle out his side window and jeered us.

"Wait a little, buddy," Kiley said. He was breathing hard because of the load of weapons. "Just you wait . . ."

The street leading directly to the Commandatura was paved also and lighted. Stephen, walking with the stiff-legged gait of a big dog on unfamiliar territory, led us down one of the parallel alleys instead.

Buildings in this part of Corpus Christi were wooden and raised a meter above the ground on stilts. Individual structures had porches, but they weren't connected into a continuous boardwalk between adjacent buildings. We walked in the street itself, one more group among the sailors and garrison personnel.

If the town had a sewer system, it'd backed up during some recent high water. Enough light came from the signs and screened windows of the taverns for us to avoid large chunks of rubbish. Vehicular traffic disposed of most of the waste by grinding it into the mud in a fetid, gooey mass. The air was hot and still, and insects whined.

A flung chair tore through the screen of a building we'd passed. Inside, a shot thumped. My right hand reached for the cutting bar that I didn't have.

"Keep moving!" Stephen ordered without raising his voice.

"Yellowknife! Yellowknife!" men shouted in unison above a rumble of generalized rage. Crewmen from the warship were fighting with port personnel, nothing for us to worry about.

My right hand clenched and unclenched in sweaty desperation. Bells rang. A van tore past, towing a trailer with barred sides and top. We walked on.

The Commandatura was a two-story masonry building with an arching facade that added another half story. It stood on a low mound, but floodwater had risen a meter up the stonework at some point in the past. A double staircase led to the lighted front door on the second story. CONSTABULARY was painted in large letters on the wall above the street-level entrance on the side.

There were twenty steps from the street to the Commandatura's front door. Originally there'd been a park in front of the building, but it was full of rubbish now. The governor and folk of quality wouldn't spend enough time here to make the effort of beautifying it worthwhile.

The door was unlocked. Stephen entered. I gestured Kiley and Lightbody in ahead of me, then helped them snatch open the lid of the crate of weapons. The feel of my cutting bar was like a drink of water in a desert.

No one was at the counter on the left side of the anteroom. The plaque on the door to the right read COMMUNICATIONS. A hallway ran past that room toward the back of the building. The door beside the commo room was steel with the stenciled legend KEEP LOCKED AT ALL TIMES. Other doors were wooden panels, some of them ajar.

Stephen signaled Kiley and Maher to watch the hall, then tapped his own chest before pointing to the commo room. Lightbody gripped the door handle and rotated it minusculely to be sure that it wasn't locked.

He nodded. The rest of us poised. Stephen lunged in behind the opening door.

No one was inside the windowless room. The atmosphere was stifling and at least 10° C above the muggy heat outside. The air-conditioning vents in the floor and ceiling were silent; banks of electronics clicked and muttered among themselves.

"I've got it," I whispered, stepping to the box that controlled the building's own alarm system.

"Just because you can breathe the muck here," Loomis said in genuine indignation, "that's no cause to let your air-handling system go like this. What kind of people are these?"

On Venus, as surely as in interstellar space, a breakdown in the air system meant the end of life. Loomis' father supervised a public works crew in Betaport, but I think we all felt a degree of the same outrage.

"Lightbody, watch Jeremy's back," Stephen said. "The rest of you come along. There's somebody supposed to be on duty, and they may not have gone far."

The job centered me so completely that I wasn't conscious of setting the cutting bar down to open my tool kit. After I disconnected the alarms, I went to work on the port's defenses.

A vehicle clanging its alarm bell pulled up beside the building. My hand moved for the cutting bar as I looked at Lightbody in the hallway.

He nodded and stepped out of my angle of vision. I heard the front door open, then close. Lightbody was back. "It's all right, sir," he whispered. "It's the Black Maria bringing a load of drunks to the lockup down below."

I went back to work. A fire director in the southern gunpit controlled the four laser batteries. I couldn't touch the director itself, but its data came from the port radar and optical sensors. I switched them off, then used the tip of my bar to cut the power cable to their console. Sparks snapped angrily between strands of wire and the chassis, but the tool's ceramic blades insulated me.

I heard steps in the hallway. "It's Kiley," Lightbody said.

"There's four guys in the lounge," Kiley said as he joined Lightbody in the hall. "We're tying them up. Mister Gregg didn't want you to worry, sir."

I nodded. I'd found the circuitry powering Corpus Christi's landline telephones. I could shut the system down, but I wasn't sure I wanted to. If the phones went out, people all over the community would run around looking for the cause of the problem. Some of them would come here.

The steel door clanked. Somebody had rested his hand against the other side as he worked the lock. I moved to the commo room doorway with my cutting bar; Kiley and Lightbody flattened themselves on either side of the steel door.

The panel swung inward. A Fed in a gray tunic and CONSTABULARY brassards on both arms stepped through. He had a cut on his forehead and an angry look on his face.

"Hey!" he snarled. "If you fuckers can't get the air-conditioning fixed, we're going to have somebody croak in the cells down there!"

He glared at us momentarily. Concrete steps led down behind him to a room full of echoing metal and alcoholic vomit. I grabbed his throat in my left hand and jerked him forward. Lightbody clubbed the Fed behind the ear as Kiley pulled the door closed.

I let the Fed fall as a dead weight. I drew a deep breath. Lightbody took the man's wrist and pulled him into the commo room.

"I think he's still alive, sir," Lightbody said. He poised the buttplate of his carbine over the man's temple. "Do you want me to . . ."

"Yes, tie him," I said. I was pretty sure that wouldn't have been Lightbody's first suggestion, Lightbody shrugged and undid the Fed's belt for the purpose.

"Here's the others coming," Kiley murmured.

"Come on," I heard Stephen's muffled voice say. "We'll head back to the cutter."

I went to the console and dumped the phones after all. The more confusion, the better . . .

"Wouldn't it be better to go to the new ship?" Loomis asked.

"Only if we knew which it was," Stephen replied in a tone so emotionless that I shivered.

I opened the unit's front access plate. There were three circuit cards behind it. I pulled them.

Stephen stuck his head into the commo room. "Trouble?" he said, glancing at the unconscious Fed.

"No sir, not so's you'd mention it," Lightbody said.

The unlocked stairwell door swung open. Stephen turned. Loomis tried to point his shotgun but the steel panel banged closed again, knocking the gun barrel up.

"Grubbies!" shrieked a voice attenuated by the armored door.

"Outside!" I shouted as I zipped my kit closed over a jumbled handful of tools.

Stephen pushed the door open and fired his flashgun down the stairs one-handed. Metal in the cells below vaporized, then burned in a white flash. Stephen clanged the door shut again.

We bolted out the front of the Commandatura, carrying our weapons openly. Lightbody jumped aside to let me lead.

The van towing the cage was pulled up to the side door. Nobody was inside the vehicle, but the diesel engine was running. A Fed ran out the constabulary door. Kiley fired, knocking the man's legs out from under him with a charge of buckshot in the thighs.

The constabulary door banged against its jamb and bounced a few centimeters open. Stephen's laser spiked at a nearly reciprocal angle to that of his first bolt. Men screamed as more burning metal sprayed.

I'd never seen controls laid out like those of the van. The steering wheel was in the center of the front compartment. There were hand controls to either side of the wheel, but no foot pedals.

"I'll drive, sir!" Loomis cried, handing me his shotgun. I slid across the bench seat as the others piled in.

Loomis twisted the left handgrip and let a return spring slide it to the dash panel, then pulled the right grip out to its stop. The diesel lugged momentarily before it roared, chirping the tires. We pulled away from the Commandatura. The door of the trailer for prisoners wasn't latched. It swung open and shut, ringing loudly each time.

Loomis turned us and headed up the paved street directly toward the gate. The trailer oscillated from side to side. It swiped a stand of pickled produce, hurling brine and glass shards across the front of the nearest building, then swung the other way and hit a cursing pedestrian who'd managed to dodge the careening van.

A siren sounded from the spaceport. It can't have had anything to do with us, there wasn't time. Stephen reached past Loomis from the other side and flicked a dash control. Our bell began to clang.

Three Molts were swinging a gate of heavy steel tubing across the port entrance. Their officer, a human wearing a gray tunic, saw our van coming. He waved his rifle to halt us.

The four Molts who crewed the port-defense laser were watching the commotion among the ships on the field. The siren came from the *Yellowknife*. All the Fed warship's external lights were on, flooding her surroundings with white glare.

Loomis steered for the narrowing gap between the gate and its concrete post. The Molts continued to trudge forward. The officer threw his rifle to his shoulder and aimed. Stephen's flashgun stabbed. The Fed's chest exploded.

Our left fender scraped the gatepost. My door screeched back in an accordion pleat. The right-side wheels rode over the bottom bar of the gate. The second and third bars bent down but the sturdy framework as a whole didn't flatten.

The van tilted sideways to 45°, then flipped over onto its roof in sparks and shrieking.

I was in the backseat, tangled with Tuching and Kiley. Lightbody had wound up in front. Stephen was kicking open the door on his side and Loomis lay halfway through the shattered windshield. The van's wheels spun above us till Lightbody had the presence of mind to rotate a handgrip and disengage the transmission.

One of the Molts lay pinned between the pavement and the twisted gate. He moaned in gasping sobs that pulsed across his entire body.

The gatepost had stripped off the sliding door in back before we went over. I crawled out. The gunpit crew were running to their multitube laser.

The leading Molt wore a white sash-of-office. Stephen shot him. The bolt hit the right edge of the alien's carapace, spinning the corpse sideways in a blast of steam to trip another member of the gun crew. Stephen bent and snatched the carbine which Lightbody had thrust through the window as he started to wriggle from the van.

I still held Loomis' shotgun. I raised it, aiming for the Molt climbing into the seat on the left side of the gun carriage.

My target was ten meters away. Stephen had taught me that a shotgun wasn't an area weapon: it had to be aimed to be effective. The Molt's mauve plastron wobbled, but not too much, over the trough between the side-by-side barrels. The charge of shot would kick the gunner out of his seat, his chest shattered in a splash of brown ichor. All I had to do was pull the trigger.

I couldn't pull the trigger. I couldn't kill anything *this way,* in the dispassion that distance brought. Not even though the laser's six-tube circular array depressed and traversed toward me at the Molt's direction.

Stephen shot the gunner in the head. The Molt went into spastic motion as if he was trying to swim but his limbs belonged to four different individuals.

Another Molt jumped into the right-hand seat. Stephen worked the bolt of his rifle without taking the butt from his shoulder and blew the back off the second gunner's triangular skull also. The last member of the crew disentangled himself from his dead leader, stood, and immediately fell flailing.

"Come on!" Stephen shouted. He set the carbine on the pavement beside him and braced his hands against the van's quarterpanel. "We'll tilt this back on its wheels!"

I handed the shotgun to Lightbody and ran toward the gunpit. Loomis pulled himself the rest of the way through the windshield and rested on all fours in front of the van. His palms left bloody prints on the concrete, but if he could move, he was in better condition than I'd feared.

A 300-tonne freighter midway in the second row fluffed her thrusters. The plume of bright plasma wobbled toward the town as it cooled, borne on the evening breeze from the river. The engine test would go unremarked by Feds in the port area in the present confusion, but for us it identified the vessel Piet and his men had captured.

The dead Molts had fallen from the gun's turntable. I sat in the left seat and checked the control layout: heel-and-toe pedals for elevation and traverse, a keyboard for the square 20-cm display tilted up from between my knees.

The laser hummed in readiness beside me. The tubes were pumped by a fusion bottle at the back of the pit. One such unit could have driven all four guns, but the Fed planners had gone to the extra expense of running each laser array off a dedicated power source.

If there'd been a common power plant, I could probably have shut it down from the Commandatura. At the time that would have seemed like a good idea, but I'd have regretted it now.

Gunports fell open along the *Yellowknife*'s centerline, black rectangles against the gleaming metal hull. The muzzle of a plasma cannon slid out. The gunners began to slew their weapon to bear on the captured freighter.

Loomis knelt with his hands pressed to his face. Stephen and the other three crew members rocked the van sideways, then pulled it back and gathered their strength for a final push. Either they'd unhitched the trailer, or the crash had broken its tongue.

My targeting screen set a square green frame over the bow of the *Yellowknife*. I keyed a 1 mil/second clockwise traverse into the turntable control. A hydraulic motor whined beneath me.

The van rolled onto its right side in a crunch of glass, then up on its wheels again as my friends shouted their triumph. The motor was still snorting. The diesel must have been a two-stroke or it would have seized by now for being run upside down.

The manual firing switch was a red handle mounted on the gun carriage itself, rather than part of the keyboard. I threw it home against a strong spring, then locked it in place with the sliding bolt.

Flux hundreds of times more concentrated than that of Stephen's flashgun pulsed from the six barrels in turn as the array slowly rotated its fury along the *Yellowknife*'s hull. I jumped from the gun carriage and ran to the van as Stephen tossed Loomis into the back. He piled in beside Lightbody in the driver's seat.

Metal curled from the *Yellowknife* in dazzling white streamers. The pulses hammering the hull would make her interior ring like a bell.

The laser array was a defense against the organic vessels of the Chay. No hostile human ship would dare land with its thrusters exposed to the port's fire, but the *Yellowknife* was too solidly constructed for the flux to penetrate her broadside.

The line of blazing metal slid a handbreadth beneath the open gunports instead of through them. I'd aimed too hastily or the Fed gunners hadn't properly bore-sighted their weapon.

We accelerated toward the captured freighter. A wheel was badly out of alignment. The studded tire screamed against its fender, throwing sparks out behind us. Another ship lit its thrusters to the north edge of the field.

The *Yellowknife* fired a plasma cannon. The intense rainbow flash shadowed my bones through the flesh of my hand. The laser array erupted in white fire. The fusion plant continued to discharge in a blue corona from the fused power cable.

Part of the slug of charged particles missed the gun mechanism and blew out the walls of a building across the street. The wooden roof collapsed on the wreckage and began to burn.

A cutter—*our* cutter—lifted from the edge of the field. It sailed toward the *Yellowknife* at the speed of a man running. Loomis screamed in terror as he realized the vessel was in an arc only five meters high at the point it would intersect our track.

Stephen grabbed the steering wheel with his left hand and spun it clockwise. The van skidded in a right-hand turn. The rubbing tire blew and we fishtailed.

The cutter passed ahead of us in the iridescent glare of its thruster. Its skids touched the concrete and bounced the vessel up again. A human figure leaped from the dorsal hatch, tumbling like a rag doll.

Riflemen in the *Yellowknife*'s open hatch shot vainly at the oncoming cutter. The siren continued to scream. A plasma cannon fired, but the weapon didn't bear on anything: the bolt punished the sky with a flood of ravening ions.

Stephen thrust his flashgun into the backseat. I grabbed it. He opened his door and hung out, gripping the frame with his huge left hand as Lightbody fought to brake the van.

Stephen straightened, jerking Piet off the pavement and into the van with us by the belt of his trousers. A wisp of exhaust had singed Piet's tunic as he bailed out.

The cutter slanted into the bow of the *Yellowknife*. The light ceramic hull shattered like the shell of an egg flung to the ground, but the Federation warship rocked back on its landing skids from the impact. Steam gushed from gunports and a started seam, enveloping the *Yellowknife*'s stern.

"A feedline broke!" Tuching, an engine crewman, shouted.

Lightbody steered toward the captured freighter again. He had to struggle with the shredded tire and Piet squirming to sit up on Stephen's lap beside him.

The wreckage of the cutter fell back from the *Yellow-knife*. The warship's bow was dished in and blackened; smoky flames shot from an open gunport.

A green-white flash lifted the *Yellowknife*'s stern centimeters off the ground. The *CRACK!* of the explosion was lightning-sharp and as loud as the end of the world. The van spun a three-sixty, either from the shock wave or because Lightbody twitched convulsively in surprise.

We straightened and wobbled the last hundred meters to the freighter waiting for us with the main hatch open. "*Not* a feedline," Piet said in rich satisfaction. "An injector came adrift and they tried to run their auxiliary power plant without cooling. They'll play hell getting *that* ship in shape to chase us!"

I suppose Guillermo was at the controls of the captured vessel, for she started to lift while Piet and the rest of us were still in the entry hold.

If the three remaining laser batteries had human crews, they might have shot us out of the sky. Molts didn't assume in a crisis that anything moving was an enemy.

Therefore we survived.

ST. LAWRENCE

Day 319

We watched the double line of prisoners dragging the thruster nozzle on a sledge from the captured freighter, the *17 Abraxis,* to the gully where Salomon had landed the *Oriflamme.* The Molts—there were thirty-one of them—chanted a tuneless, rhythmic phrase.

Two of the freighter's human crew had been wounded during the capture. The remaining ten were silent, but they at least gave the impression of putting their weight against the ropes. Lightbody and Loomis, watching with shotguns, wouldn't have killed a captured Fed for slacking; but at least in Lightbody's case, that's because Piet had given strict orders about how to treat the prisoners.

Lightbody's perfect universe would contain no living idolators; Jeude's death had made him even less tolerant than he was at the start of the voyage. The Fed captives were wise not to try his forbearance.

"Rakoscy says the communications officer is going to pull through," Piet remarked. "I was worried about that."

"That Fed worried me about other things than him taking a bullet through the chest," I said. I wasn't angry—or frightened, *now.* Neither had I forgotten driving across the spaceport under fire because the commo officer of *17 Abraxis* had gotten off an alarm message before Dole shot him out of his console.

The gully contained vegetation and a little standing water, and the defilade location saved the *Oriflamme* from exhaust battering when Piet brought our prize in close by. Though the air was only warm, the sun was a huge red curtain on the eastern sky. That sight wouldn't change until the stellar corona engulfed St. Lawrence: the planet had stopped rotating on its axis millions of years before.

"He was doing his job," Stephen said mildly. "Pretty good at it, too. There aren't so many men like that around that I'd want to lose one more."

"Fortunately," Piet added with a smile, "the staff of the *Yellowknife* hadn't plotted the vessels on the ground at Corpus Christi, so they didn't have any idea which ship was under attack."

We were in the permanent shade of four stone pillars, the fossilized thighbones of a creature that must in life have weighed twenty tonnes if not twice that. The bones had weathered out of the softer matrix rock, but they too were beginning to crumble away from the top.

I turned my head to gaze at the tower of black stone. "Hard to imagine anything so big roaming this place," I said. Vegetation now grew only in low points like the arroyo, and we hadn't found any animal larger than a fingernail.

"A *long* time ago," Stephen said with emphasis. "Who knows? Maybe they developed space travel and emigrated ten million years back."

"Put your backs in it, you cocksucking whoresons," came the faint fury of Winger's voice from the underside of *17 Abraxis,* "or as Christ is my witness, you'll still be here when your fucking beards are down to your knees!"

Piet frowned at the blasphemy (obscenity didn't bother him), but the men were far enough away that he must have decided he could overlook it. The job of removing thruster nozzles—without dockyard tools—after they'd been torqued into place by use was just as difficult as Winger had grumbled it would be when we were on Clapperton.

"They've got seven," Stephen said quietly. "This last one and we're out of here."

"If we don't take spares," I said, deliberately turning my head toward the *Oriflamme* to avoid Piet's eyes.

He glared at me anyway. "The prisoners can get back to Riel on four out of twelve thrusters," he said. "They *can't* get back on two. We aren't going to leave forty-three men here on the chance that somebody will come by before they all starve."

Twelve humans and thirty-one Molts. All of them "men" to Piet, and you'd best remember it when you spoke in his hearing.

"You could manage on two, Piet," Stephen said with a grin. "I'll bet you could take her home on one, though I guess we'd have to gut the hull to get her out of the gravity well to begin with."

I knew Stephen was joking to take the sting out of Piet's rebuke to me. I'd promised Winger that I'd try to get him a spare nozzle, though.

Piet chuckled and squeezed my hand. "All things are possible with the Lord, Stephen," he said, "but I wouldn't care to put him to *that* test. And, Jeremy—"

He sobered.

"—I appreciate what you've tried to do. I know the motor crew is concerned about the wear we'll get from tungsten, and they have a right to be. But if these nozzles don't last us, we'll find further replacements along the way. We won't leave men to die."

I nodded. I looked up at the femur of a creature more ancient than mankind and just possibly more ancient than Earth. Black stone, waiting for the sun to devour it.

A tiny, intense spark shone in the sky where the thigh pointed. I jumped to my feet.

"There's a—"

"*Incoming* vessel!" Piet bellowed as he rose from a seated position to a dead run in a single fluid motion. "Don't shoot! Don't shoot! If she crashes, it could be anywhere!"

Stephen and I followed at our best speed, but Piet was aboard the *Oriflamme* while we were still meters from the cockpit steps.

"This is close enough," Stephen ordered, dropping into a squat a hundred meters from the strange vessel's starboard side. "This swale doesn't look like much, but it'll deflect their exhaust if they try to fry us. Can't imagine anything else we need to worry about, but don't get cocky."

Piet and the rest of us knelt beside him. Stephen, commander of his county's militia before he ever set foot on a starship, was giving the orders for the moment.

Dole's ten men were still jogging to where they'd have an angle on the stranger's bow. Fifty-tonne freighters built like this one on the Back Worlds weren't likely to have hatches both port and starboard, but we weren't taking the risk.

Stampfer was half a kilometer behind us, aligning the 4-cm plasma weapon *17 Abraxis* carried for use against Chay raiders. The *Oriflamme*'s guns were useless while she was in the gully. Salomon, Winger, and the bulk of the crew weren't going to be ready her to lift for an hour or more despite desperate measures.

"You'd think," I said, "that they'd have signaled they were coming in."

Stephen shrugged. "Maybe they don't have commo," he said. "The Feds'd leave the air tanks off to save money if they could get away with it."

"Southerns, sir," Lightbody said unexpectedly.

Stephen and I looked at him; Piet grinned and continued to watch the strange vessel. "This one's Southern Cross construction, sir," Lightbody amplified. "Not Fed. The pairs of thrusters are too far apart for Feds."

The vessel's hatch clanged twice as those inside jerked it sideways by hand rather than hydraulic pressure. Six figures got out. They jumped as far as they could to clear the patch of thruster-heated ground.

One of the newcomers was a woman; common enough for a Terran crew, though I heard Lightbody growl. None of the strangers was armed, and their assorted clothing was entirely civilian.

Piet got up and strode to meet them.

"Guide a little left, Piet," Stephen said as he trotted to Piet's right side. Stephen's left index finger indicated a 30° angle. I moved over to give Piet room but he ignored the direction.

"Piet," Stephen said calmly, "Stampfer will have that plasma cannon trained on the open hatchway. I trust Stampfer, but I don't much trust junk he crabbed out of a Federation freighter. I'd really rather you didn't take the chance of something unlikely happening."

From the tone of Stephen's voice, he could have been asking where to place a piece of furniture.

Piet clicked his tongue, but he bore to the left as directed. "Where would you be without me to fuss over, Stephen?" he murmured.

Possible answers to that falsely light question rang through my head like hammerblows.

"Sirs?" the leader of the newcomers asked. "Are you from the North American Federation?"

He spoke Trade English with a distinct Southern accent. A good dozen additional people, including a few more women, climbed from the vessel behind him. They moved with greater circumspection than the initial party.

The ten of us spread slightly as we bore down on the strangers. We weren't being deliberately threatening, but a group of grim, armed men must have looked as dangerous as an avalanche.

"We are not," Piet said in a proud, ringing voice. "We are citizens of the Free State of Venus."

"Oh, thank God!" cried the woman at the leader's side. She knelt and kissed a crucifix folded in both her hands.

I grabbed Lightbody by the front collar and jerked him around to face me. "No!" I shouted.

I held the spacer till the light eased back into his eyes and he began to breathe normally again. "Sorry, sir," he muttered, bobbing his head in contrition.

Everyone was staring at us. I flushed and lowered the cutting bar in my right hand. Lightbody hadn't done anything overt.

I think Piet understood. I know Stephen did, because he gave me a slow smile and said, "If you ever change sides, friend, I'm not going to let you get in arm's length alive. Hey?"

In context, that was high praise.

The newcomer's leader embraced Piet. "Sir," he said, "I am Nicolas Rodrigo and these are my people, twenty of us."

I eyed the group quickly. If there were only twenty, then they were all in plain sight by now. There were no Molts in the group, surprisingly.

"Until forty days ago, we maintained the colony on Santos," Rodrigo said. "Then two Federation warships, the *Yellowknife* and *Keys to the Kingdom,* arrived under a beast named Prothero. He—"

The woman had risen again. At Prothero's name, she spat. Our eyes meshed, then slid sideways. Quite an attractive little thing in a plump, dark-haired fashion. Young; 18 or 20 at the outside, as compared with Rodrigo's 35 or so.

"—told us that the Southern Cross had been placed under President Pleyal's protection, and that he was taking control of Santos on behalf of the Federation. He—"

"What do you have aboard your ship?" Stephen interjected abruptly.

"What?" Rodrigo said. "Nothing, only food. Ah—we took back the *Hercules,* this ship, on Corpus Christi. There was confusion when a freighter crashed into the *Yellowknife.*"

Kiley chuckled. "I wonder if them poor bastards'll *ever* figure out quite what happened," he said.

"Come along back to our ships, then," Piet said. "We'll be more comfortable there, and I don't want my men I've left there to be concerned."

The bosun's party was moving toward us, slowed by their weight of weapons and, for a few of them, armor. "Mister Dole?" Piet called. "Set five of your men to secure the ship, if you will."

Stampfer must have realized the situation was peaceful; he tilted the muzzle of the light cannon up like an exclamation point above the hasty barricade of crates across the hold of *17 Abraxis.* Maybe the gesture helped the others relax.

Me, I was still trembling in reaction to a few minutes before, when I stopped Lightbody from blowing a pretty woman's head off.

"Prothero put his own men on Santos as overseers," Rodrigo explained, drinking a thimble glass of slash cut three to one with water. "The plantations are worked by Molts, of course. We don't—we didn't export, we just supplied convoys in the Back Worlds trade stopping over."

The Southerns mixed freely with the *Oriflamme*'s crew. A joint party had gone back to the *Hercules,* for supplies including Santos wine. The Federation prisoners watched sullenly as they resumed hauling heavy thruster nozzles.

Piet, Stephen, Lacaille, and I sat with the Southern leaders at a trestle table on the shaded side of the gully. Rodrigo's wife, Carmen, was at his side across the table, occasionally eyeing me as she raised the glass to her lips. She wasn't actually drinking.

"I know Prothero," Lacaille said. "I don't know anybody who likes or trusts him, but he's . . . Able enough. In his way."

The Southerns watched the Fed castaway sidelong, uncertain about his status. I guess we all were uncertain, Lacaille himself included.

"The *Hercules* was on Santos when the Federation ships arrived," Rodrigo continued. "Captain Cinpeda commanded."

A short, dark Southern nodded. He'd drunk his slash neat. His eyes never left the carafe I'd deliberately slid out of his reach.

"Prothero filled the *Hercules* with food and put his own crew aboard," Rodrigo said. "It was no more than piracy. But how could we fight with no warships of our own?"

Stephen's lips smiled; his eyes did not. Ships don't fight: men do. And Rodrigo wasn't that sort of man.

"Prothero took us with him on the *Yellowknife*," Rodrigo said. "The *Keys to the Kingdom* was his flagship, but she needed repairs. He left her on Santos while he went ahead to Riel."

"She's a great, cranky tub of eight hundred tonnes, the *Keys,*" Lacaille said. "I'm not surprised she broke down. Her water pumps again?"

Cinpeda nodded to Lacaille with respect.

"They can't be depopulating all the Southern colonies," I said. "Can they?"

"I think," Carmen Rodrigo said with her eyes lowered, "that the decision was Commander Prothero's. I believe his intentions toward me were . . . not proper. Though he already has a mistress!"

"Prothero's always operated as though the Middle Ways were his own kingdom," Lacaille said. "I doubt he was acting completely on orders."

"We took our chance when the emergency siren sounded," Rodrigo said. "We thought it was a Chay raid. The prize crew had left the *Hercules,* so we went aboard and lifted as soon as the computer gave us a course."

"To home," Carmen said. "We're going back to Rio. Better Pleyal a continent away than Prothero in the next cabin."

There was an edge in her tone that I thought I understood. Carmen Rodrigo might or might not be a virtuous wife; I had my doubts. But she certainly intended to make any decisions of that sort on her own.

"Why *this* course, to St. Lawrence?" Piet asked suddenly. "It's a week's transit in the wrong direction if you intend to return to the Solar System."

"Reaction mass," Cinpeda grunted. "I wonder, master, could you . . ."

He extended his tiny glass. I filled it from the carafe.

"Ah, thank you, thank you indeed, master," the Southern captain said. He shuddered as he tossed the shot down, but his eyes gained a focus that had been missing a moment before.

"Reaction mass," Cinpeda repeated. "Prothero's crew, they'd refilled the air tanks when they landed on Riel, but they hadn't hooked up to the water yet. Food we had, air we had, but there wasn't water for ten days under power."

"There *is* water here, isn't there?" Rodrigo asked in sudden concern as he gazed around him. The planet must have looked like a desert from orbit, and the slight greenery of this arroyo wasn't much more inviting.

"We've bored a well," Piet said. "You can draw from it, now that we've topped off."

"If you were trying to escape," Stephen asked, "why did you land by us—and without signaling?"

"Fucking collimator's out," Cinpeda said with a scowl. "On the laser communicator. Fucking thing drifts. And the VHF transmitter, it's been wonky since they installed it."

He looked as though he was going to ask for another drink. I shook my head minutely.

"We thought you'd done the same thing we did," Rodrigo said, answering the first part of the question. "Come here to get away from Prothero. We knew other ships escaped when we did."

"Didn't even notice this one before we landed," Cinpeda said with a nod toward the *Oriflamme*. "What is it—don't you reflect radar?"

I shrugged. Ceramic hulls did reflect radar, but not as strongly as a similar expanse of metal. The *Oriflamme* was an outcrop in the gully to a radar operator unless the fellow was actively looking for a Venerian ship here.

"And there was no reason to come to *this* place," Carmen added, "except to avoid being on Riel. So we thought you might be from the Southern Cross too, until we saw your guns."

"Does your vessel carry guns?" Stephen said. There was no challenge in his tone, only the certainty of a man who *will* be answered.

"A small cannon," Rodrigo said. "For the Chay, and perhaps not much use against them. We can't defend ourselves against you, sirs."

Piet stood up with a nod. "Nor do you need to," he said. "We have our own needs and can be of little help to you, but we certainly won't hinder."

"How long will you remain on this planet?" Carmen asked without looking—pointedly without looking—at me.

"No longer than it takes to mount two more thruster nozzles, madam," Piet said with a wry grin. "Which is some hours longer than I wish it would be, now that you've arrived."

"Are we so terrible?" Carmen said in surprise.

"The people who may follow you are," I explained gently. "The Feds know how much reaction mass they left on your ship, and they've got the same pilotry data as you do to pick the possible landfalls."

"But we'll deal with them, if it comes to that," Stephen said, hefting his flashgun. His eyes had no life and no color, and his voice was as dry as the wind.

No Federation force would be half so terrible as we ourselves were.

"Piet?" I said as I stood up. "The *Abraxis* has a first-rate commo suite. If you'll let Guillermo help me, I can swap it into the *Hercules* in less time than it takes Winger to fit the nozzles."

"That leaves the *Abraxis* without . . ." Piet said. He smiled. "Ah. One ship or the other."

"And the choice to the men with the guns," Stephen said. He was smiling also, though his expression and Piet's had little in common. "As usual."

"Yes," Piet said. "Go ahead."

"Guillermo!" I shouted as I ran for the forward hatch and my tool kit. "We've got a job!"

The *Oriflamme*'s siren shut off as Guillermo and I clambered aboard the *17 Abraxis*. Piet had held the switch down for thirty seconds to call the crew aboard. Men were scattered from here to the *Hercules*. Hell, some had probably wandered off in the other direction for reasons best known to themselves.

When the alarm sounded, Fed prisoners returning the sledge to the *17 Abraxis* slacked the drag ropes to see what was happening. The Molts continued to pace forward. Maher, one of the pair on guard this watch, punched a Fed between the shoulder blades with his rifle butt.

The prisoner yelped. He turned. Maher prodded his face with the gun muzzle. The Feds resumed the duties they'd been set.

"We don't want to screw up the navigational equipment when we lift this," I said to Guillermo as I tapped the freighter's communications module. "Do you know if any of the hardware or software is common?"

"No, Jeremy," the Molt said. "I could build it from parts, of course, since one of my ancestors did that a thousand years ago."

Guillermo's thorax clicked his race's equivalent of laughter. His three-fingered hands played across the navigation console. "What we can do, though, is to bring up the AI and keep it running while we separate the communications module and attempt to run *it*."

"Right," I said. Molts were supposed to operate by rote memory while humans displayed true, innovative intelligence. That's what made us superior to them. You bet.

I bent to check the join between the module and the main console. The speaker snapped, "Presidential—

I jumped upright, grabbing my cutting bar with both hands to unhook it. The only reason I carried the weapon was I hadn't thought to remove it after we returned from the *Hercules*.

"—Vessel *Keys to the Kingdom* calling ships on St. Lawrence! Do not attempt to lift. You will be boarded by Federation personnel. Any attempt at resistance will cause you both to be destroyed by gunfire. Respond at once! Over."

The commo screen was blanked by a nacreous overlay: the caller could, but chose not to, broadcast video.

"Stay in the image!" I said to Guillermo. Venerian ships didn't have Molt crew members.

The voice had said, " . . . you both . . ." The Feds had made the same mistake as Captain Cinpeda: they'd seen the metal-hulled vessels, but they'd missed the *Oriflamme* in her gully.

My fingers clicked over the module's keyboard. It was an excellent unit, far superior to the normal run of commo gear we produced on Venus. I careted a box in the upper left corner of the pearly field for the *Oriflamme*.

Piet looked at me, opening his mouth. I ignored him and said, "Freighter *David* out of Clapperton to Presidential Vessel, we're laid up here replacing a feedline and our consort's commo is screwed up. What the hell's got into you, over?"

Guillermo stood with his plastron bowed outward. He scratched the grooves between belly plates with a finger from either hand. I'd never seen him do anything of the sort before. The activity looked slightly disgusting—and innocent, like a man picking his nose.

"Who are you?" demanded the voice from the module. "Who is this speaking? Over!"

Piet nodded approvingly. At least *he* thought we looked like the sort of folks you'd find on the bridge of a Federation merchantman . . .

"This is Captain Jeremy Moore!" I said, tapping my chest with the point of my thumb. "Who are you, boyo? Some bleeding Molt, or just so pig-faced ugly that you're afraid to let us see you? Over!"

Through the open hatch I saw men staggering aboard the *Oriflamme.* Sailors' lives involved both danger and hard work, but their normal activities didn't prepare them to run half a klick when the alarm sounded.

The sledge sat beside the *17 Abraxis,* ready to receive the eighth and final thruster nozzle. It had taken an hour, minimum, to transport each previous nozzle, and another hour to fit the tungsten forging into place beneath the *Oriflamme.*

Guillermo balanced on one leg and stuck the other in the air. He poked at his crotch. I noticed that he'd dropped his sash onto my cutting bar on the deck, out of the module's camera angle.

The pearl-tinged static dissolved into the face of a man who'd been handsome some twenty years and twenty kilograms ago. At the moment he was mad enough to chew hull plates, exactly what I'd intended. Angry people lose perspective and miss details.

"I'll tell you who I am!" he shouted. "I'm Commodore Richard Prothero, officer commanding the Middle Ways, and I'm going to have your guts for garters, *boyo!* My landing party will be down in twenty minutes. If there's so much as a burp from you, I'll blast a crater so deep it goes right on out the other side of the planet! Do you understand, civilian? Out!"

Prothero's three quarters of the screen blanked—completely, to the black of dead air rather than a carrier wave's pearly luminescence. Piet nodded again and crooked his index finger to Guillermo and me.

I didn't imagine that Prothero could intercept the laser link I'd formed between us and the *Oriflamme,* but we needn't take unnecessary risks. The necessary ones were bad enough.

"You'll need more than your helmet," Stephen said in a voice as if waking from a dream. "Put the rest of your armor on, Jeremy."

"When we lift, I'll put my suit on," I said. I wondered what I sounded like. Nothing human, I supposed. Very little of me was human when I slipped into this state.

"The Federation warship orbiting St. Lawrence is an eight-hundred-tonner mounting twenty carriage guns." Piet's voice rang calmly through the tannoy in the ceiling of the forward hold. "We'll be lifting on seven engines, so we won't be as handy as I'd like. In order to return home, we must engage and destroy this enemy. With the Lord's help, my friends, we *will* destroy them and destroy every enemy of Venus!"

Twelve of us waited in the hold. Kiley, Loomis, and Lightbody carried flashguns, but Stephen alone held his with the ease of a man drawing on an old glove.

We'd had time to rig for action, but it would be tight working the big guns with everybody in hard suits. They were probably cheering Piet in the main hull. None of us did. For myself, I didn't feel much of anything, not even fear.

"They must've landed on Riel just after we left," Maher said. "The *Keys* must. Pity they weren't another month putting their pumps to rights."

"We'll lift as soon as the enemy ship is below the horizon," Piet continued, "and our marksmen have dealt with the Federation cutters. The enemy is in a hundred-and-six-minute orbit, so we'll have sufficient time to reach altitude before joining battle."

Even on seven thrusters? Well, I'd take Piet's word for it. Aloud I said, "Lacaille says that the *Keys* is falling apart. You've seen the sort, older than your gramps and Fed-maintained as well. We'll give her the last push, is all."

"Too right, sir!" Kiley said, nodding enthusiastically. He knew I was just cheering them up before we fought a ship with enough guns, men and tonnage to make six of us. All the sailors knew that—and appreciated it, maybe more than they appreciated me standing beside them now. They expected courage of a gentleman, but not empathy.

Two exhaust flares winked in the sky. I lowered my visor. For the moment, the riflemen and I were present to protect the flashgunners from Feds who managed to get out of the landing vessels. I'd wear my suit when it was that or breathe vacuum; but I wouldn't put on that jointed ceramic coffin before I had to.

"I'll take the right-hand one," Stephen said in a husky, horrid whisper. He clicked his faceshield down. "Wait for me to shoot. If anyone jumps the gun—if you survive the battle, my friend, you won't survive it long. On my oath as a gentleman."

"Almighty God," said Piet. "May Thy hand strengthen ours in Thy service today. Amen."

Lacaille was suited up aboard the *Oriflamme*. He'd repeated that he wouldn't fight his own people; but he'd asked not to be left on the ground, either.

We owed him that much. The prisoners locked for the moment in the hold of the *17 Abraxis* would identify him quickly enough to survivors of the Federation landing party. Besides, Lacaille was one of us now—whatever he said, wherever he was born.

"Easy, gentlemen," Stephen said as he lifted his flashgun to his shoulder.

The Fed boats leveled out from their descent and cruised toward the *17 Abraxis* a hundred meters in the air. They were bigger than our cutter, almost the size of featherboats. They didn't act like they saw us. Small-craft optics are crude, and the Feds weren't expecting to find anything in the shadow of the arroyo.

The nearer vessel slowed to a crawl while five meters in the air. It began to settle beside the freighter. Its plasma exhaust flared in an oval pattern that swept stones as big as my fist from the ground.

Stephen fired. His bolt struck the side of the boat's thruster nozzle, close to the white-hot lip. The exhaust already sublimed tungsten from the nozzle's throat and left a black smear on the ground where the metal redeposited.

The laser pulse heated the point it hit to a fractionally greater degree than the metal casing around it. The nozzle lost cohesion. The side blew toward us in a bubble of green vapor as intense as the plasma that drove it. The *crash!* of metal exploding was more dazzling than the flash.

The vessel rolled clockwise on its axis and nosed in almost upside down. The dorsal hatch flew off. Members of the landing party flew out in a confusion of weapons and white tunics.

The second craft was thirty meters in the air and a hundred meters beyond the first. Our three remaining flashgunners fired in near unison. Two of the bolts glanced from the cutter's hull, leaving deep scars in the metal and puffs of aluminum vapor in the air. The third man aimed better but to even less effect: his flux stabbed toward the nozzle but was smothered in the cloud of ionized exhaust.

The boat rotated toward us. A port in its blunt bow gaped open. The riflemen beside me volleyed at the little vessel, flecking the hull when they hit.

Stephen clacked the battery compartment closed and raised his reloaded flashgun. The muzzle of a twin-tube laser thrust from the Feds' gunport. Even pumped by the thruster, it couldn't seriously damage the *Oriflamme*'s hull; but it could kill all of us in the hold, hard suits or no.

The vessel slid toward us in a shallow dive. Stephen fired.

The thruster nozzle was only a corona beneath the craft's oncoming bow. A cataclysmic green flash lifted the vessel in what would have been a fatal loop if the pilot hadn't been incredibly good or incredibly lucky. The cutter screamed overhead and skidded along the ground on its belly for two hundred meters beyond the arroyo, strewing fragments of hull behind it.

The *Oriflamme*'s engines roared. The deck vibrated fiercely, but it would be a moment before thrust rose beyond equilibrium with our mass and we started to lift. Men started for the companionway to the main deck, cheering and clapping one another's shoulders with their gauntleted hands.

My hard suit waited for me in a corner of the hold. I began to put it on, trying not to get rattled as I performed the unfamiliar, unpleasant task of locking myself into armor. Because Stephen and Lightbody helped me, I was suited up within a minute or two of when the hatch sealed out the buffeting of the atmosphere the *Oriflamme* was fast leaving.

ABOVE ST. LAWRENCE

Day 319

Oriflamme's guns were run out to starboard. Stampfer was amidships with the fire director, but the Long Tom's six-man crew stood close about their massive gun.

Gaiters did a halfhearted job of sealing the gun tube to the inner bulkhead. The pleated barriers kept the cabin air pressure high enough to scatter light and even carry sound, but we were breathing bottled air behind lowered faceshields.

The *Keys to the Kingdom* hung on Guillermo's display. It wasn't a real-time image. We viewed one frozen aspect of the spherical vessel, and even portions of that had the glossiness of an electronic construct rather than the rough, tarnished surfaces of physical reality.

There was nothing for scale in the image, but "800 tonnes" meant something to me now as it had not at the start of this voyage. It meant the *Keys* was significantly larger than *Our Lady of Montreal;* and unlike the *Montreal*, she was first and foremost a warship.

God knew, so was the *Oriflamme*, and we of her crew were men of war.

The *Keys'* bridge, indicated by sensor and antenna concentrations, was in the usual place at the top deck. The generally globular design was flattened on the underside so that the thrusters could be grouped in the same plane.

Ramps on the deck above the thrusters served for loading and unloading the vessel on the ground. Because the *Keys* was so large, she was also configured to load in orbit through large rectangular hatches at her horizontal centerline. Her gun decks, indicated by a line of ports that were still closed when our optics drew the image on display, were above and below the central deck.

About twenty guns, Lacaille had said. They'd be smaller than ours and less efficient; but . . . twenty guns.

The usual digital information filled Salomon's screen. I glanced at Piet's display and found, to my surprise, that I understood its analogue data to a degree.

The gray central ball was St. Lawrence. The bead on the slightly elliptical green line circling the planet was the *Keys to the Kingdom* in orbit, while we were the indigo-to-blue line arcing up the surface. The difference in color indicated relative velocities: the *Keys,* in her higher orbit, moved slower than we did as we circled toward the Feds from below under power.

The image on Guillermo's display suddenly shifted into motion, as though a paused recording had been switched back on. We'd come out of the planet's shadow; our sensors were getting direct images of the *Keys to the Kingdom* again.

Our approach was from the *Keys'* underside. Her twenty-four thruster nozzles were arranged four/six/four/six/four. A faint glow still illuminated their heavy-metal casings.

I put my helmet against Stephen's and said, "Don't they see us?"

Plasma flooded from the *Keys'* thrusters. The cloud expanded to hundreds of times the volume of the starship from which it sprang. A moment later, attitude jets spurted lesser quantities of gas which swiftly dissipated. The sphere shuddered and began to rotate so that its main engines weren't exposed to our fire.

"Now they see us!" Stephen replied. Even thinned by conduction through his helmet and mine, his voice was starkly gleeful.

The bubble of exhaust separated from the *Keys to the Kingdom.* It drifted away, cooling and still expanding until it was only a faint shimmer across the starscape. The Fed commander was putting his ship in a posture of defense, because he'd realized that he couldn't escape us.

Even on seven thrusters, the *Oriflamme* had a much higher power-to-mass ratio than the huge *Keys* did. We could literally run circles around the Feds in the sidereal universe. If they attempted to transit, we would jump with them: two AIs with identical parameters would *always* pick the same "best" solution.

And that would be the end of the *Keys to the Kingdom*. Piet would bring us up beneath the Feds at point-blank range—and Stampfer would blow the *Keys'* thrusters out, leaving the vessel to drift powerless in interstellar space.

The need to protect our thrusters was behind Piet's decision to disable the Fed landing boats before we lifted. The *Oriflamme*'s hull could take a considerable battering from heavy guns and still be repaired. Laser bolts or light plasma cannon could destroy our main engines, however. We couldn't risk being encircled by three hostile vessels, even if two of them were small by comparison with the *Oriflamme*.

Piet shut off our engines. I grasped a stanchion with my left gauntlet as I started to drift up from the deck. The bead that was the *Oriflamme* drove silently across the main display on a course that would intersect the *Keys to the Kingdom* in two minutes, or at most three. The arc marking our past course was now turquoise.

The carriage of the 17-cm gun crawled slowly sideways, making the deck tremble. The fire director was keeping the muzzle pointed at the target Stampfer had chosen.

"All weapons bear on the enemy, sir!" the master gunner announced over the radio intercom. Motors in the gun training apparatus crackled across Stampfer's voice, but so long as the main engines were shut down the whole crew could hear him over the helmet radios.

"Thank you, Mister Stampfer," Piet said in a tone that was so calm he sounded bored. "I trust your aim, but I think we'll close further so that the charges will dissipate less."

Static roared on the intercom. My hair stood on end from a jolt of static, and the hull beside me rocked to a white-hot hammerblow.

There was enough atmosphere at this altitude to light the tracks of the *Keys'* plasma bolts across our optical screen. The Feds had salvoed ten guns. Only one round had hit squarely. It was powerful enough to shatter our tough outer hull and craze the inner one in a meter-diameter circle between the gunport and the navigation consoles.

The *Oriflamme* rocked with the impact of ions moving at light speed. Attitude jets snorted, returning us to our former alignment. The Long Tom's gear motors tracked and tracked back, holding a calculated point of impact.

The *Keys to the Kingdom* filled Guillermo's screen. Our green bead and the chartreuse bead of the Federation vessel were on the verge of contact on the analogue display.

"Fire as you bear, Mist—" Piet's voice ordered before static and the ringing *CRASH!* of five heavy guns recoiling blotted out all other sound.

Two of the directed thermonuclear explosions struck the *Keys'* upper gun deck, two struck the mid-line deck, and the last ripped a collop out of the lower gun deck in a grazing blow. Eight cargo hatches blew out along the centerline. Our plasma charges expanded the deck's atmosphere explosively, pistoning the Fed vessel open from the inside.

Bolts that hit the *Keys'* gun decks ripped huge, glowing ulcers in the hull plating. White-hot metal blew inward, mixed with the residual atmosphere, and burned in secondary pulses. The initial impacts wracked the *Keys'* internal subdivisions. These follow-up blasts penetrated deep into the vessel, spreading pain and panic among those who'd thought themselves out of immediate danger.

Attitude jets puffed, rotating the *Oriflamme* on her axis so that our spine rather than our starboard was presented to our enemy. We'd taken one hit and were likely to take others. Piet was adjusting our aspect so that the Feds couldn't concentrate on the weakened portion of our hull.

The Long Tom had recoiled two meters on its carriage. Efflux from the plasma bolt had blown the gaiters inward so that a rectangle of hard vacuum surrounded the barrel.

A crewman spun the locking mechanism and swung the breechblock open.

The thermonuclear explosion had heated the gun's ceramic bore to a throbbing white glow. In the absence of an atmosphere, cooling had to be by radiation rather than convection, but even so an open tube would return to safe temperature much sooner than closed-breech weapons of the sort the Feds used. A few wisps of plasma twinkled within the bore like forlorn will-o'-the-wisps.

I caught a momentary glimpse of a sunlit object through the gunport: the *Keys to the Kingdom*. In astronomical terms, we and our enemies were almost touching, but the human reality was that kilometers separated our vessels. The Fed warship was a glint, not a shape.

A four-man damage-control team covered the crazed portion of our hull with a flexible patch. The men moved smoothly, despite weightlessness and their hard suits. Glue kept the patch in place, though positive internal air pressure would be a more important factor when we really needed it. The refractory fabric didn't provide structural strength, but it would block the influx of friction-heated atmosphere during a fast reentry.

Our thrusters roared for twenty seconds to kick us into a diverging orbit. The Federation vessel rotated slowly on Guillermo's screen. All the *Keys'* mid-line cargo hatches were gone.

Additional gunports swung to bear on us. I expected the Feds to fire, but for now they held their peace. Prothero realized that we could reload faster than his gunners dared to. If the Feds fired their ready guns now, they would have no response if we closed to point-blank range and raked them again.

A figure anonymous in his hard suit came from the midships compartment and pushed by me with as little concern as if I'd been the stanchion I held. I thought it was someone bringing Piet a message that couldn't be trusted to the intercom. Instead the man stooped to view the bore of the Long Tom.

The ceramic was yellow-orange at the breech end. Its color faded through red to a gray at the muzzle which only wriggled slightly to indicate it was still radiating heat.

I saw the man's face as he rose: Stampfer, personally checking the condition of his guns rather than trusting the assessment to men he had trained.

"Sir," he said over the intercom, "the broadside guns are ready any time you want them. The big boy here forward, he'll be another three minutes, I'm sorry but there it fucking is."

"Thank you, Mister Stampfer," Piet said. I watched his hands engage a preset program on his console. He still sounded like he was checking the dinner menu. "We'll hit them with four, I think. Load your guns."

Stampfer swooped through the internal hatch in a single movement, touching nothing in the crowded forward compartment. Our attitude jets burped; I locked my left leg to keep from swinging around the stanchion. The main thrusters fired another short, hammering pulse. The curve our course had drawn across that of the *Keys to the Kingdom* began to reconverge.

Stampfer was a lucky man to have a job to do. The cutting bar trembled vainly in my gauntleted hand.

The Federation vessel grew on Guillermo's screen. Black rectangles where the hatches were missing crossed her mid-line like a belt. Apart from that, her appearance was identical to that of the ship we'd first engaged: the damage we'd done, like the guns that had fired on us, was turned away.

We were already closer than we'd been when the *Keys* loosed her opening broadside. This time she held her fire.

"Come on," somebody muttered over the intercom. "Come on, *come—*"

Guillermo's left hand depressed a switch, cutting off general access to the net. His six digits moved together, reconnecting certain channels—Stampfer, Winger, Dole; the navigation consoles. I could have done that . . .

"It would make our job easier if Commodore Prothero was stupid as well as the brute I'm told he is," Piet announced calmly, "but we'll work with the material the Lord has given us. Mister Stampfer, we'll roll at two degrees per second. Fire when you bear."

*Thump of the jets, the torque of my armored body trying
to retain its attitude as my grip on the stanchion forces it
instead to the ship's rotation . . .*

Chaos. The 15-cm guns firing amidships and—so sudden it seemed to be a part of the broadside—the smashing
impacts of two, maybe three Federation bolts.

Residual air within the *Oriflamme*'s hull fluoresced a
momentary pink. The normal interior lights went out; the
constant tremble of pumps and drive motors through the
ship's fabric stilled.

The navigation consoles were still lighted. Salomon
lifted himself in his couch to look back. Piet did not.
His armored fingers touched switches in a precise series,
looking for the pattern that would restore control.

The *Oriflamme*'s axial rotation continued, modified by
the recoil of our broadside guns and the hits the Feds
had scored. What size guns did the *Keys* mount: 10-cm?
Perhaps bigger; that last impact rang through our hull as if
the *Oriflamme* had been dropped ten meters to the ground.

The attitude jets fired, then fired again in a different
sequence. Piet damped first the planned component of
our rotation, then brought the plasma-induced yaw under
control.

Red emergency lights came on. Because there wasn't
enough atmosphere to diffuse their illumination normally,
they merely marked points on the inner hull.

A man bowled forward from amidships: Stampfer again.
He snatched a spherical shell from Long Tom's ready
magazine and settled it into the weapon's breech, using
his fingertips rather than the alignment tool shaped like a
long-handled cookie-cutter.

The *Keys to the Kingdom* was turning slowly on at
least two axes. Our broadside had struck in a concentrated
pattern on the huge vessel's lower gun deck and the deck
immediately below that. Three of the bolts had burned a
single glowing crater that could have passed a featherboat
sideways. The fourth was a close satellite to the merged
trio. Vapor spurted from it, indicating that we'd holed
either an air or a water tank.

A crewman swung the Long Tom's breech shut and
turned the locking wheel. Bracing themselves against the
steps cut into the deck for the purpose, the men ran their
weapon out. Emergency power wasn't sufficient to operate the hydraulics, but Stampfer's crew knew its job.

The master gunner himself crouched beside the individual gunsight set into the Long Tom's trunnion. He had to
edge sideways as his men shifted the gun to battery. The
fire director must have gone out. At least one of the Fed
bolts hit us amidships. We might have lost a gun or even
all the broadside guns.

A team ran cable sternward from a manhole in the deck
behind me. The auxiliary power unit was amidships, in the
bulkhead between our fore and aft cargo holds. These men
were tapping one of the main thrusters for power.

"Steady, Captain!" Stampfer's voice demanded. He
sounded like he was trying to pull a planet out of its
orbit. Up to now, he'd been speaking on a net limited
to his gunners. "Stead—"

The Long Tom flashed its horrid rainbow glare as it
recoiled into the compartment. There was no air to com-
press, but the massive cannon drove back with a crushing
psychic ambience.

The 17-cm bolt pierced the blurred crater the triplet of
broadside guns had melted in the Federation vessel's hull.
Because the *Keys* was slowly rotating, the angle of the
impact was different. More important, this bolt released
all its energy within the spherical hull instead of on the
exterior plating.

Silvery vapor geysered from the *Keys'* lower gun deck:
metal heated to gas. It slammed outward at a velocity
that chemical explosives couldn't have imparted. In the
shock wave tumbled shredded bulkheads, dismounted cannon, and the bodies of personnel stationed on the deck our
guns had ravaged.

Our internal lights came on; I felt vibration through the
stanchion I held as the great pumps begin to tremble again.
Stampfer moved amidships, toward his broadside guns.
The Long Tom's bore was a cylinder of hellish white,
breech to muzzle.

"Holy Jesus preserve us," Salomon said. I looked around. The digital information on his screen meant nothing to me, but I could understand the third track rising from the planetary surface on Piet's display.

Guillermo split his optical screen, setting the *Keys'* image to the right. On the left half was the *Hercules,* rising to higher orbit to join the battle.

The freighter's hatch was open. The 5-cm plasma cannon we'd left the Southerns was mounted on a swivel in the center of the hatchway. Our optics and the software enhancing them were so good that I could make out at least a dozen armored figures within the freighter's hold.

The Southern refugees didn't have hard suits. The *Hercules* was crewed by survivors from the *Keys'* landing party, and perhaps by prisoners released from *17 Abraxis* as well.

The two Federation ships were the jaws of a nutcracker, and the *Oriflamme* was their nut. One hit, even by the swivel gun, on our thrusters and we would no longer be able to maneuver with the *Keys to the Kingdom.* One hit . . .

"Piet," Stephen said, "bring us in tight to the *Keys.* I'll take a party aboard and we'll clear her."

"Prothero's holding his fire," Piet replied. I didn't know whether Guillermo had included me in the command channel, or if the whole crew was hearing the debate. "He'll salvo into our hold if we come within boarding distance. That's what he wants!"

I couldn't command, I couldn't even talk. I trembled in my hard suit. There was a red haze over my vision and I wanted to kill someone, I wanted to kill more than I'd ever before in my life wanted anything . . .

"Jesus *Christ* will you bring us close?" Stephen shouted. "Will you have those whoresons peck us to death and no answer? Bring us close, damn you, bring us close!"

It wasn't anger in his tone. It was white fluorescent rage, and I knew because the same need surged through me, ruling me, *would I never swing my arm and see faces dissolve in blood again?*

"We—" Piet shouted.

The *Hercules* was on an intersecting but not parallel path to the paired orbits of the *Keys* and the *Oriflamme*. Cinpeda had told us—and would tell anybody at gunpoint—that the reticle of the *Hercules'* laser communicator wasn't aligned properly. The Federation crew had to make a close approach to the *Keys* in order to coordinate their attack on us.

I knew that. Until the *Keys to the Kingdom* fired all her loaded guns into the *Hercules,* it didn't occur to me that Commodore Prothero knew nothing of the sort.

The freighter burst into a ball of opalescent vapor. Her own thrusters ruptured, adding their ionized fury to the directed jolts of the Federation cannon. The *Hercules'* light-alloy hull couldn't contain or even slow the cataclysm.

"All personnel except those with immediate gunnery or engineering tasks, assemble in the holds," Piet ordered in a voice as thin as a child's. "Starboard watch to the forward hold, port watch aft. Over."

I followed Stephen toward the compartment bulkhead. Because we hadn't yet loaded the *17 Abraxis'* cutter to replace the one we'd lost on Riel, there was room in both holds for boarding parties.

I noticed that the Long Tom's crew was headed aft with us. They'd apparently interpreted "immediate tasks" to mean tasks more immediate than the six to eight minutes the 17-cm gun would take to cool for the next shot.

The midships compartment looked like the remains of a lobster dinner. Fragments of flesh and ceramic armor floated in the air. Much of the blood had spread across the bulkheads in viscous blotches. Sufficient droplets, wobbling as they tried to remain spherical, still floated in the compartment to paint the suits of us coming from the bow.

The bolt had entered through Number Two gunport at a severe angle, taking an oval bite from the coaming. The main charge had struck Number Three gun, vaporizing the left side of the carriage, much of the gun tube behind the second reinforce, and parts of—

Three men, maybe five. It was hard to say. There were so many body parts drifting in the compartment, rebounding from the bulkheads in slow curves, that my first reaction was that everyone amidships was dead.

Rakoscy was working on an armless man in a transparent cocoon meant as emergency shelter if the ship lost its atmosphere. The bubble was a tight fit for two men wearing most of their hard suits. Another crewman, anonymous in his armor, stood over the cocoon to illuminate Rakoscy's work with a handlight. There wasn't room for an aide within the distended fabric.

It didn't look to me as if the victim had a prayer. I don't suppose Rakoscy could afford to let himself think that way, though.

The forward hold was crowded. Stephen pushed to the front. A Fed bolt had struck near the cross-bulkhead. It hadn't penetrated, but the upper aft corner of the hatch was fractured in a conchoidal pattern. I wondered if Winger would be able to bring the APU back on line . . .

Dole, his helmet marked with three fluorescent bars, stood beside the hatch controls. Lightbody and Maher were at the arms locker beside the bosun. They gave us room as they recognized Stephen, Stephen and me.

"I'll take the line, Mister Dole," Stephen announced, reaching for the magnetic grapnel in the bosun's left hand. "Gentlemen to the front."

"Yessir," Dole said, giving up the grapnel. "If you'd really rather."

Lightbody hooked the line onto one of Stephen's equipment studs. The grapnel had permanent magnets on its gripping surface, but unless something went wrong, its electromagnets would be powered through the line itself.

There was also a suction device to grip nonferrous surfaces. From the way the *Keys to the Kingdom* had resisted our plasma bolts, there was no doubt that her hull was steel, and thick steel besides.

"I'm next," I said to Lightbody. There was movement in the hold, men entering and shifting position. My eyes were focused on the back of Stephen's helmet, and I wasn't seeing even that.

"Sir, will you take a rifle?" a voice said.

The intercom worked with only the usual amount of static. Neither we nor the Feds were burning thrusters. Occasionally an attitude jet fired. For the most part, being weightless in a windowless hold had the feeling of being motionless.

Someone jogged my left hand. Maher was looking at me, offering a falling-block rifle. The side lever was deliberately oversized so that it was easier for a man wearing gauntlets to work.

"What?" I said. I shook my head. I wasn't sure he could see me behind the reflection from my faceplate. "No, no. I have to get closer to do any good."

I blinked, trying to remember things. "You can give me another bar," I said. "Hang it on my suit opposite the line."

I felt clicks against my hard suit. The suit wasn't trapping me this time. My mind was in a much straiter prison than that of my ceramic armor.

"Prepare to board," a voice ordered. Salomon or Guillermo, I couldn't tell which; not Piet.

Dole turned the control wheel and stepped out of my range of sight as he moved to take his own place on the boarding line. Six of our attitude jets fired together in a ten-second pulse, braking the *Oriflamme*'s momentum with perfect delicacy.

The hatch unlocked and began to lower. The fractured corner in front of me flaked off in a slow-motion snowstorm. Shards glittered as their complex surfaces caught the sunlight.

The *Keys to the Kingdom* hung twenty meters away, filling the sky.

The *Oriflamme* wasn't aligned on quite the same horizontal axis as the Federation vessel. I was staring straight into the *Keys'* upper gun deck, but men at the rear of our aft hold would enter through the Feds' centerline if they boarded directly.

The hatch cammed itself down with gear-driven certainty. Stephen gathered himself to jump. One of our plasma bolts had ripped the *Keys'* hull open between two gunports. The compartment beyond was dark, save for the glint of armored shadows.

Fed gunners thrust main battery guns from the ports to either side of the large hole. The muzzles glowed red; their breeches must be yellow-white. The Fed gunners had taken the desperate chance of reloading their weapons while the barrels still shimmered with the heat of previous discharges; taken the chance and succeeded.

The bore of the gun trained on me looked large enough to swallow a man whole, as the plasma it gouted would surely do.

White light with overtones of green and purple blazed through every opening in the *Keys'* gun deck. The shell in the gun aimed at me had cooked off before it could be triggered in proper sequence. The deuterium pellet fused into helium and a gush of misdirected energy, blowing the cannon's stellite breech across its crew and the Fed personnel nearby.

The second cannon fired normally. The bolt hit the forward edge of our hatch. Dense ceramic shattered in fragments ranging in size from dust motes to glassy spearpoints a meter long. One of the latter gutted the man to my right.

I felt the shock through my boots; a film of grit and ions slapped my armor. Stephen leaped. I leaped behind him.

If the Fed gunners had waited another second or two, their plasma bolt would have loosed its devastation in the packed hold instead of shattering the ramp as it lowered. The slug of ions would have killed a dozen of us, maybe more. That wouldn't have slowed the survivors, nor the men still climbing into the hold to join the boarding party.

Stephen sailed forward, his body as rigid as a statue. I twisted slowly around the line clockwise. In one sense it didn't matter, since the *Keys* wasn't under way. We'd be operating without any formal up or down. I couldn't judge where I was going to land, though.

A group of Feds wrestled a multibarreled weapon on the *Keys'* open cargo deck to bear. The human leader was in metal armor. His five Molt crewmen wore transparent helmets and suits of shiny fabric stiffened at intervals by metal rings.

A jet of plasma from one of our midships ports struck the gun carriage. The bolt was small by the standards of the broadside guns firing moments before, but it and the Feds' own munitions blew the weapon and crew apart.

I'd forgotten about the swivel gun Stampfer took from *17 Abraxis*. Stampfer hadn't forgotten.

Stephen bent as he approached the *Keys to the Kingdom*. He held the grapnel forward in his left hand. His arm compressed, taking the shock.

My left boot struck flat on the hull; my right speared through the crater our guns had torn. Swaths of rust and recrystallized steel vapor overlaid the *Keys'* plating. The light was too flat to wake colors, but reflection gave the surfaces different textures.

I hooked my right foreleg into the hole and unlatched myself from the line. A crewman in metal armor loomed from the darkness within the Fed vessel and fired a shotgun into my chest.

My breastplate survived the shock. The crashing impact blew me back out of the hole. My leg lost its grip, and my flailing arms touched nothing.

Piet Ricimer caught my right wrist in his left hand. He fired his carbine into the hole. The Fed shotgunner was pirouetting from his weapon's recoil. His breastplate sparked as the rifle bullet dimpled it. The Fed continued to spin slowly, but the shotgun drifted out of his hands and a smoky trail of blood froze in the vacuum around him.

I grabbed the rim of the opening and jerked myself aboard the *Keys to the Kingdom* again. Icicles of refrozen steel broke off in my grip.

The Fed constructors had used light alloys for most of the internal subdivisions. Our fire and the exploding cannon had blown them to tatters, leaving the gun deck open except for throughshafts and a pair of parallel hull-metal bulkheads that supported the upper decks when the vessel was on the ground.

Scores of bodies drifted in light that flickered through the hull openings. Most of the corpses were Molts. Their flexible suits were no protection against plasma or against the fragments of bulkhead, weapons, and bodies which the blasts turned into shrapnel.

Figures moved twenty meters from us, near a companionway shaft. A bolt from Stephen's flashgun sent one corpse toward the far hull, shedding limbs.

That corpse was a Molt. Riflefire winked, puncturing two other Molts whom the laser had lighted. A last Molt and an armored human vanished back into the shaft.

Men sailed toward the companionway from behind me. I headed for the freight elevator near the *Keys'* vertical axis. My initial jump was too high. I had to dab along the deck's scarred ceiling to redirect myself. There were no points for gracefulness today.

The circular shaft was of hull metal, but the outer doors were alloy. Blasts had bowed them into the shaft, springing the juncture between the leaves wide enough that I could probably have crawled through it as is.

I thrust my bar into the opening to cut outward and down. The blade almost bound, but I jerked it back across to complete the cut, doubling the size of the gap.

It was the first *action* I'd taken since I'd run from the *17 Abraxis* to the *Oriflamme.*

I didn't know where the elevator cage was. If it was below me, the bulged doors would keep it from rising. If not—I'd take my chances on being able to carve through the cage floor before it crushed me into those same jagged doors.

I was thinking very clearly. I wasn't sane, but that's a different question; and the situation wasn't sane either.

The dim ambience of the elevator shaft helped me when my eyes adapted to it. Actually, the light may not have been that dim. Although my faceshield filtered the quick succession of plasma bolts, they'd leached the visual purple from my retinas.

I rose three decks, using my left gauntlet on one of the elevator cables to control my speed and guide me. The sills and paired shaft doors told me where I was. I was pretty sure that the bridge was a deck or two higher yet, but this was as far as the cargo elevator went.

Holding the upper rim of the shaft opening, I cut an ellipse from the panel's inner sheathing. The pieces drifted away from the bar's last contact, tumbling across the shaft. There was no gravity to make them fall.

I should have brought a light . . . but I didn't have a hand for it, and I couldn't hold it in my teeth with the helmet on. The present illumination was good enough, because I knew what I was looking for.

The shaft doors were locked closed by pins under spring pressure. Electromagnets raised the pins when the cage and safeties were in the proper position. If the power was off—as it seemed to be now—the doors could be unlocked as I did, by pulling the mechanism out from the back.

I could have cut through the doors, but that would have warned the Feds on the other side that I was coming.

I wedged the side of a boot into the door seam, then forced the fingers of my left gauntlet in and levered the valves in opposite directions. Faces looked up in terror as I sailed into what had been a circular lounge giving access to individual suites against the hull.

This deck had atmosphere before it flooded past me and down the elevator shaft. Most of the personnel I saw as the light faded to the flatness of direct illumination wore suits, but their helmets were open. Hands groped to slam faceshields closed instead of swinging weapons toward me.

A team of twenty Molts was hauling a carriage gun across the lounge on four drag ropes. The 10-cm cannon was no less massive for being weightless. It slid on with the certainty of a falling boulder when the crewmen dropped their harness.

I let the impetus of my leap from the shaft take me into the crowd of aliens trying to close their helmets. I swung my cutting bar with no aim but to hit *something,* anything.

Ripping the Molts' fabric suits was good enough for my purposes. The limbs and gouts of fluid sweeping past me on the last of the deck's atmosphere were a bonus.

A rifle fired, its yellow powderflash huge for expanding in near vacuum. I was through the Molts within my immediate reach. I pushed off from the plasma cannon traveling relentlessly past me.

I couldn't have executed so complex a weightless maneuver if I'd practiced for weeks. Chance or murderer's luck took me on a vector to the Fed trying to lever another shell into his rifle's chamber as my bar jerked and sparked through the neck of his armor.

I spun and pushed myself toward the next large concentration of the enemy, the group fronting the companionway hatches. Some of the humans were screaming behind their faceshields. God knows I gave them reason to scream.

I grabbed a woman with my left gauntlet. She pounded the side of her riflebutt on my helmet, then tried to short-grip the weapon to shoot me. Her mass anchored my sweeping right-hand cut through her fellows.

The stiffeners in Molt suits were under tension. When my blade sheared a ring, the severed ends sprang apart and dragged the rip in the fabric wider. A bad design for combat . . .

I cut the line of a backpack laser and a corona of high-amperage blue sparks shorted through the metal armor of the man holding it. The Fed's body should have been insulated from the outer shell, but his liner had worn or frayed. The suit stiffened as his flesh burned, raising the internal pressure to several times normal.

I was shaking the woman in my left hand, but I didn't have time to finish her until I'd taken care of the laser and by then she was limp within her articulated armor. She'd lost her rifle; a bullet hole starred her faceshield.

Someone aiming at me, someone shooting at random; her own bullet, triggered at the wrong instant. I held her close as I scanned for living targets.

The 10-cm cannon continued its course into the partition bulkhead surrounding the lounge. This deck was given over to suites for powerful passengers and the *Keys'* command staff. Nonetheless, the hull was pierced with gunports and a few plasma cannon were placed here for emergencies. I'd interrupted a crew shifting an unfired weapon across the lounge to a compartment from which it bore on the *Oriflamme*.

The cannon's stellite muzzle hit the flimsy bulkhead at a skew angle and ground another meter forward, driven by the inertia of tonnes of metal in the gun and its carriage. The wall split at the point of impact and buckled inward across all four edges.

The door popped open like the cork from an over-charged bottle. The suite had still been under normal air pressure. Two Molts and a female servant spurted into the lounge. The servant tried to scream and she shouldn't have, though it didn't make more than a minute's difference since neither she nor the Molts had breathing apparatus.

The suite's main occupant was a plump woman of fifty, wearing a glittering array of jewelry and light-scattering fabrics cut too tight for her build. A transparent emergency bubble protected her. She stared transfixed at the cloud of lung tissue protruding from her servant's mouth.

Feds edged toward me around the right-hand curve of the lounge. There were half a dozen armored humans and as many Molts in the group. I flung away the corpse to drive me toward them.

The Feds hadn't identified me in the carnage and tricky illumination, but they noticed the movement. Muzzle flashes and the sparks of ricocheting projectiles brightened the lounge. The corpse spun as several rounds hit her, and the bullet that punched through my left shoulderguard flipped me ass over teacup.

My left shoulder was cold. Some of that would be the sealant oozing from between the armor's laminae to close the hole. I tried to wriggle my fingers. I couldn't tell if they moved.

My figure somersaulted five meters from the Feds. The Molts were less awkward in their flexible pressure suits, but only a few of them carried firearms. The humans aimed for another volley, and I couldn't do a *damned* thing but spin since I wasn't touching anything I could push off from.

I hurled my cutting bar at the Fed in a parcel-gilt hard suit pointing a rifle at me. A flashgun pulse flickered through his faceshield and ruptured his skull within. The bolt might have reflected harmlessly if it had struck his metal armor.

I unhooked the spare bar from my waist. Feds turned, flailing and throwing equipment in order to get behind the central shaft again.

Piet floated in the companionway hatch. His knees clasped the coaming to steady him against his carbine's recoil. He stripped a fresh clip into the magazine. Stephen's reloaded flashgun exploded a Molt who came on with a cutting bar when his human officers fled.

I tried to brake myself against the ceiling with my left hand. The arm moved, but not properly. My field of view spread into a line of infinite length and no height or width.

Consuming fire shrank to no more than normal pain. Stephen caught my elbow and pulled me to his side. He'd wedged a boot into the plumbing beneath an ornamental wall fountain.

Piet had backed within the companionway. I heard him on the intercom, calling, "Oriflammes to Deck Eight! Oriflammes to Deck Eight! We hold the stairhead, but they'll regroup in a moment!"

Each deck of the *Keys to the Kingdom* was a Faraday cage. The metal construction acted as a barrier impenetrable to radio propagation. If any Venerians happened to be in the companionway shaft—also a metal enclosure—they could hear Piet's summons. Perhaps they'd even be able to answer it; though not, I thought, in time to make a difference.

"Christ's blood, Jeremy," Stephen said in a tone of laughing wonder. "Did you do all this yourself?"

My vision had wobbled in and out of focus since I tried to use my left arm. Until Stephen spoke, I hadn't really looked at anything. The lounge was—

The lounge was very like what I'd passed through in the *Oriflamme*'s midships compartment a lifetime ago.

The bodies floating here were whole, or nearly whole. The head, arm, and torso-with-legs of a Molt had floated back together in a monstrous juxtaposition.

There may have been twenty corpses. It was impossible to be sure. I didn't remember killing that many.

"I suppose," I said.

There was so much blood. I dragged the back of my right gauntlet across my visor. *Again,* I suppose. I didn't remember doing that before either, though I must have. The ceramic dragged fresh furrows across the brown-red haze that dimmed my sight. I needed a wiping rag.

"Well, it's time to do some more," Stephen said. He aimed his flashgun toward a barricade of mattresses floating around the right-hand curve of the central column.

"That's mine," I said and launched myself toward the Feds.

They were coming from both directions this time. Three Molts wearing breastplates and carrying rifles swept out from the left. The flashgun lit the walls behind me as I slid blade-first toward the bedding from nearby suites.

Out of the corner of my eye I caught Piet's figure diving across the lounge. To get an angle from which to shoot, I supposed, but I had enough to occupy me.

The Feds had stacked three mattresses like a layer cake on end. The spun-cellulose filling wouldn't stop a bullet, but we couldn't see through it and it *would* absorb the bolt of a monopulse laser like Stephen's without any fuss or bother.

I ripped the mattresses and the pair of Molts pushing them with a deliberately shallow stroke. The bedding didn't affect my cutting blade, but it would've bound my arm if I'd let it.

The Molts sprang away. One of them was trying to hold the segments of his plastron together; the other didn't have arms below the second joint.

Two human officers in hard suits, and a gunner wearing quilted asbestos with an air helmet, followed the Molts. They'd been poised for attack over or around their barricade. I came through the middle of it with a backhand stroke and a cloud of severed fiber.

The gunner shot at me and missed, though the muzzle blast punched the side of my helmet. I stabbed him where his collarbone met the breastbone, then cut toward the officer on my right. She got her rifle up to block me. My edge showered sparks from where the barrel mated with the receiver.

The second officer put the muzzle of his rifle to my head. Everything was white light because Piet fired the carriage gun wedged into the bulkhead nearby.

This deck was sealed except for the shafts in the center. If the 10-cm cannon had been fired perpendicularly into the hull at this range, it would have blown a hole in the plating; but the *Keys'* hull was thick, and the gun's muzzle was caught at an acute angle to the curve.

The slug of ions glanced around the inner surface of the hull: expanding, dissipating, and vaporizing everything in its immediate path into a dense, silvery shock wave. None of the internal bulkheads survived. Those closest to the muzzle became a gaseous secondary projectile which flattened partitions farther away.

The cannon wasn't clamped into deck mountings. It recoiled freely against the thrust of ions accelerated to light speed, tumbling muzzle over cascabel to meet the shock wave plasma-driven in the opposite direction.

The barrel finally came to rest not far from where Piet had fired the gun. Bits of the carriage still tumbled in complex trajectories. Dents from the tonnes of stellite pocked the hull plating.

Stephen had dodged back into the armored companionway. He lost his flashgun and the satchels of spare batteries he'd worn, but otherwise he was uninjured.

Piet survived because he was as far as possible from the ricocheting course of the plasma slug. The shock wave tumbled him, but the *Oriflamme*'s gunners had taken a worse battering and survived—most of them—when a similar bolt pierced our hull.

And I survived. I was out of the direct line of the plasma and swathed in mattresses besides. Everything went white; then I was drifting free on a deck from which all the internal lighting had been scoured. A Venerian focused a miniflood on me. Piet Ricimer caught me by the ankle and pulled me with him back to the companionway. I hadn't even lost my cutting bar.

I can't imagine the Lord wanted me to survive after what I'd done, but I survived.

Maybe some Feds in full hard suits were still alive. Bulkheads, furniture, weapons, and bodies—all the matter that had existed on Deck Eight was still there in the form of tumbled debris that could conceal a regiment. If there were any survivors, they were too stunned to call attention to themselves.

There were six of us now. Stephen led the way up the helical stairs, holding a cutting bar of Federation manufacture. Strip lights in the shaft still functioned. The sharp shadows they threw without a scattering atmosphere acted as disruptive camouflage.

A fireball burped into the shaft from a lower deck, then vanished as suddenly. Fighting was still going on below.

The companionway opened into a circular room on the bridge deck. There were four shafts in all. A bullet ricocheted up one, hit the domed ceiling, and fell back down another as a shimmer of silver.

Two inward-opening hatches on opposite sides of the antechamber gave onto the bridge proper. Against the bulkhead were lockers and, at the cardinal points between the hatches, communications consoles with meter-square displays.

A sailor pulled open a locker. Emergency stores spilled out: first-aid kits, emergency bubbles, flares.

Dole tried a hatch. It was locked from the other side. The left half of the bosun's armor was dull black, as though the surfaces had been sprayed with soot.

"Jeremy, can you get us through—" Stephen said, bobbing his helmet toward the hatch.

"Yes," I said, kneeling. The bulkhead was of hull metal, not duraluminum, but it couldn't be solid and still contain the necessary conduits.

"Wait," said Piet. He stepped to a console and toggled it live. The screen brightened with a two-level panorama of the circular bridge. Inside—

Four heavily-armed figures sexless in plated armor; five human sailors without weapons, armor, or breathing apparatus; three Molts, also unprotected and seated at navigation consoles; and a startlingly beautiful blonde woman in a sweep of fabric patterned like snakeskin, with jeweled combs in her hair.

Piet pressed his faceplate to the console's input microphone. "Commodore Prothero!" he said, shouting to be heard through the jury-rigged vocal pathway. "We're sealing this deck. Put down your weapons and surrender. There's no need for more people to die."

With time I could have linked the console to our intercom channel. There wasn't time; and besides, I couldn't see very well. I tried to wipe my visor again, but neither of my hands moved.

Dole and two other spacers were closing the companionway shafts. The hatches were supposed to rotate out of the deck, but long disuse had warped them into their housings. The bosun cursed and hammered the lip of a panel with his bootheel to free it.

Prothero would be the squat figure in gilded armor. Impervious to laser flux, but Stephen didn't have his flashgun any more. Prothero and his three henchmen spoke among themselves.

They must have been using external speakers instead of radio. We couldn't hear them through the bulkhead, but the blonde screamed and one of the unprotected spacers launched himself at Prothero when he heard the plan.

Prothero clubbed the man aside with a steel forearm. "Get us through!" Piet shouted.

I drew the tip of my bar down the bulkhead, cutting a centimeter deep. The sparkling metal roostertail was heated yellow but unable to oxidize in a vacuum.

Two more Fed spacers grappled with their officers. One of Prothero's henchmen blew them clear of his fellows with shotgun blasts, and Prothero himself pulled open the hatch beside me.

I rose, thrusting. Prothero fired a weapon with a needle bore and a detachable magazine for cartridges the size of bananas. The flechette struck the blade of my cutting bar.

Bar and projectile disintegrated in a white-hot osmium/ceramic spray.

I smashed the bar's grip into Prothero's faceshield. Red and saffron muzzle flashes shocked the corners of my vision. I could hear the shots as muffled drumbeats while the atmosphere flooded from the bridge to the open antechamber.

I couldn't hold Prothero with my left hand, but I wrapped my legs around his waist and I kept hitting him, even after the faceshield collapsed and the mist of blood dissipated and nothing was moving but my gauntlet, pumping up and down like the blade of a metronome. They say after that I tried to inflate an emergency bubble around one of the Fed spacers. I couldn't manage that, because my left arm didn't work and anyway, it was too late.

I don't remember that. I don't remember anything but the red mist.

LIMBO

A Place Out of Time

I lay at the edge of existence, and the demons wheeled above my soul.

"The controls weren't damaged," said the first demon. "Guillermo's interviewing the surviving Molts for a support crew. When he's done, I'll set her down on St. Lawrence."

"Rakoscy's on his way over. Stampfer's setting up an infirmary for him on Deck Two," said the second demon. "They're dumping cargo into space to make room." Then he said, "So much blood."

"What we did was necessary!" said the first demon in a voice like trumpets. "If we're to stop tyrants like Pleyal and butchers like his Commodore Prothero, then there was no choice. When the *Oriflamme* gets home, she'll bring freedom a step closer for the whole universe."

"We're not home yet," said the second demon, though he didn't sound as if he cared.

"We'll get back," said the first demon. "It's a long run, another ninety days or more. But there's nothing between here and Betaport to fear, save the will of God."

"I figured we'd seal the prisoners on Deck Six once we've swept it for weapons," the second demon said. "I suppose I ought to go take charge, but I'm so tired."

"Dole has it under control," said the first demon. I felt his shadow pass over me. "I wish Rakoscy would get here. I'm afraid to take his suit off myself."

"There's enough treasure on the *Oriflamme*," said the second demon, "to run the Federation government for a decade. Governor Halys will never give it up . . . but when she doesn't, there'll be all-out war between Venus and the Federation."

"It will be as the Lord wills," said the first demon.

My mind drifted from limbo to absolute blackness. Sinking into the embracing dark, I knew that I'd been listening to Piet and Stephen on the bridge of the ship we'd captured. They were no more demons than I was; and no less.

The black turned red as blood.

BETAPORT, VENUS

122 Days After Landing

"Ah, Cedric," said Councilor Duneen. "Let me introduce you to Jeremy Moore. Moore of Rhadicund. Jeremy, this is Factor Read, a businessman who understands the value of a strong navy."

I shook hands with a man younger than me. His eyes never stopped moving. They flicked over the withered arm strapped to my side, then back to my face without even a pause. Read's grip was firm.

"Jeremy will be marrying my sister Melinda this fall, as you may have heard," Duneen continued. "I've found him a townhouse near ours in the capital."

"The Moore who . . ." Read said, nodding toward the *Oriflamme* in her storage berth. Though he was shouting, I had to watch his lips to be sure of the words. None of the heavy machinery was operating today, but the big dock rang with laughter and hawkers' calls.

"Yes, as it happens," I said. I've seen snakes with more warmth in their eyes than Read had, but if reports were true he was the richest man in the Ishtar Highlands. The sort of fellow I'd need to cultivate in my new position as aide to Councilor Duneen, but for now . . .

"Councilor," I said, "Factor Read? Pardon me if you would, because I see some shipmates."

Duneen clapped me on the shoulder. "You can do anything you like here, my boy. You're the stars here today!"

It was the politic thing for the Councilor to say, since he didn't want a row in front of Read and Read's entourage. I had the feeling that he meant it, though.

There were as many folk around Piet and Stephen as there were with Read and Duneen, but some of those pressing for contact with the General Commander were magnates themselves. Mere money couldn't earn the sort of fawning adulation Piet had now.

Though he had the money as well, of course. The lowliest member of the *Oriflamme*'s crew had enough wealth to amaze, for example, a Betaport ship-chandler in a comfortable way of business.

Folk made way for me. Some of them recognized me—"*Factor Moore*," with a nod; broad, smiling, "*Jeremy, good to see you again!*"—and some did not, only knew what they saw on my face, but they all made way.

I came up behind a man named Brush. He controlled his niece's estate until she married; an event he was determined should not be before its time. A court toady, not as young as he wished he was, who pitched schemes to the unwary. "You know, Gregg," he said to Stephen, "a friend of mine has a business opportunity that might be the sort of thing that you want now that, you know, you're back."

Stephen looked past Brush to me, then back to the courtier. "Well, Brush," he said in a bantering voice. "It's like this. I'm young, I'm rich, I'm well born. I can do absolutely anything that I want to do. So that means—"

He smiled. Brush stepped back, then bounced forward from my chest like a steel ball shuttling between electro-magnets.

"—that the thing I've been doing *is* what I really want."

Brush vanished into the crowd. I touched Stephen's arm. I've never heard anything more stark than his words of a moment before.

Piet waved himself clear with both hands and a broad grin, turning to us. He was dressed in a suit of crimson silk slashed with a natural fiber from Mantichore. It looked like copper or shimmering gold depending on the angle of the light.

Piet touched the miniature oriflamme on my collar. "Well enough for now," he said with a grin, "but Duneen will be wearing your colors before long, Jeremy."

"The Councilor could do worse," Stephen said in the light tone that made strangers think he was joking. "Jeremy has a way of finding routes through unfamiliar systems."

I've heard Stephen's jokes, and they're not the sort of thing that others smile at.

There was a stir at the entrance to the storage dock. Governor Halys was entering with over a hundred courtiers and attendants. Her spot in the assemblage was marked by six members of the Governor's Guard in black hard suits, though the governor herself was hidden.

"Won't be long now," Piet said. For a moment we three were in a reverie, walled off by memories from the voices clamoring around us, at us.

"Hard to believe the ship made it home," said Stephen. "Or that we did either, of course."

I followed his eyes to the *Oriflamme* and for the first time saw her as she'd become on our voyage. Her bow and stern were twisted onto slightly different axes. I remembered Winger complaining about thruster alignment.

We hadn't replaced the forward ramp. The hull was daubed with a dozen muddy colors, remnants of refurbishing with the materials available on as many worlds. We'd had to recoat completely on St. Lawrence after the battle, but the russet sand hadn't bonded well to some of the earlier patches. On Tres Palmas we'd taken much of the stern down to the frames and tried again.

The *Oriflamme* leaked. Air through the hull, water from two of the reaction-mass tanks. All the living spaces were damp during the last three weeks of the voyage. Winger was afraid to run the nozzles from *17 Abraxis* on more than eighty percent thrust, but they were better than the replacements we found on Fowler, so we switched them back again for the last leg.

I think Piet must have had the same revelation. "To God, all things are possible," he said. "But some aren't—"

He squeezed us by opposite shoulders.

"—as probable as others, I agree."

The Governor's entourage paused while Councilor Duneen and other high dignitaries joined it. When the court

resumed its progress, attendants began herding a group
of bizarrely-dressed, worried-looking sailors aboard the
Oriflamme. Money hadn't given them either taste or con-
fidence in a setting like this one.

"I think it's unfair that a mob of *scruffs* should be given
places and *I* be refused!" said a slender, perfectly-dressed
woman, as straight as a rifle barrel and as gray.

I moved and Stephen grabbed me because he knew what
I knew, and what the other sixty-odd survivors knew; and
what nobody else in the universe would ever know.

"They were good enough to accompany me through
the Breach, madame," Piet said. "They will accompany
me now."

He didn't shout, but he spoke in a tone that cut this
clamor as it had that of so many battles. Everyone for
twenty meters heard, and the woman melted away from
his eyes.

Piet laughed. "Stephen, Jeremy," he said. "I need to
take my place, I suppose. See you soon."

He arrowed through the mob, heading for the Governor's Guard.

Stephen said, "Piet believes that God is aiding us to
do His will. I don't know what God's will is. But I don't
suppose what I know matters."

He looked at me and added, "I thought we might see
your fiancée here, Jeremy."

I shrugged with adrenaline nervousness and smiled.
"No," I said, "no. I asked Melinda not to come. I don't
want to connect her—in my mind. With this. I'd as soon
the Councilor weren't here, but he had to be, of course."

I smiled again. The lip muscles didn't work any better
the second time. I gripped Stephen's shoulder. "Stephen,
listen," I said. "It happened, it can't ever *not* have happened now. But it's over. We can go on!"

"I'm glad it's over for you, Jeremy," Stephen said.
He plucked gently at my sleeve, filling the fabric he'd
crumpled when he kept me from breaking a woman's
neck with my one good hand. "I was afraid for a time
that you were one of those it wouldn't be over for."

He smiled. "I'm responsible for you, you know."

I blinked so that I wouldn't cry. "Let's get aboard," I said loudly, turning toward the ship.

The crowd cheered as it parted to let us board the *Oriflamme*. There in a few minutes we would watch the governor's investiture of a potter's whelp from Bahama District as Factor Ricimer of Porcelain.